T0160850

A MEASURE OF
MERCY

Margaret Hatcher House

Clovercroft Publishing

A Measure of Mercy

Published by Clovercroft Publishing, Franklin, Tennessee

This book is published in association with The Benchmark Group
benchmarkgroup1@aol.com

Edited by Lee Titus Elliott

Cover Design by Debbie Manning Sheppard

Interior Design by Suzanne Lawing

Printed in the United States of America

978-1-948484-40-4

INTRODUCTION

Riverbend Plantation
Hart County, Georgia
May 1865

The Sinclair Plantation, carved from the Cherokee wilderness of northeast Georgia, stretched along the west bank of the Savannah River. Hundreds of rich fertile acres covered in may pop and honeysuckle vines lay fallow between the river and thick virgin woodlands. The singsong hum of field hands echoing across the fields were no longer heard.

A stately manor house nestled atop the grassy rise faced the big bend in the river from which the plantation drew the name. Looming above the fields and sparkling waterway, the brilliant façade of whitewashed boards, tall columns, wide verandas, and manicured grounds once gave proof of the family wealth. The boards were now faded, blistering in the hot Georgia sun, the grounds ragged and weedy. Yards once alive with the lively chatter of house servants scurrying here and there were quiet. The beauty of the once prosperous home was gone and the functioning plantation silent as death.

Annihilation of the productive plantation began March of 1863. The March winds brought the last bite of winter to the plantation, and news of Lincoln's Proclamation of Emancipation blew in, with the cold traveling swiftly through the slave quar-

ters. *At first only one or two young males would be unaccounted for at morning meals, but the number grew as the weather warmed and life of Riverbend changed. Operation of the plantation grew sluggish, and the graceful elegance of Riverbend began to disappear. An eerie silence slowly impregnated the fields and yards. Watching his beloved plantation reduced to beggary and the genteel life he valued slipping away was taxing on the master of Riverbend, and he suffered a stroke February 1864, leaving him bedridden and mentally impaired. The master's condition opened the flood gates for the remaining slaves. They began wandering away from the idle plantation a few at a time, until the slave cabins were empty. McMullan Sinclair, master of Riverbend, breathed his last April 1, 1865, leaving Riverbend, the Sinclair Plantation, in need of strong, caring hands.*

CHAPTER 1

Riverbend Plantation
Late Afternoon May 5, 1865

The sun inched down the western sky; shadows flirted across the land. Inky hues fell across empty pastures, fallow fields, and toppled fence rows. A quiet stillness hovered over the land, giving a ghostly mien of abandonment.

However, a unique remnant of seven souls called the plantation home. Four orphans and three former house servants remained. The Hatcher siblings were fostered to McMullen Sinclair, after their mother, Martha, died in childbirth, October 2, 1862, and their father, William, a hired substitute in the Confederate Army for the Sinclair heir was killed August 28, 1862, in the second battle of Manassas.

Santee, the personal servant of the late master; Keowee, former housekeeper; and Lovie, the couple's only child, refused to leave the orphans and the only home they knew. The seven persevered during the months of the master's illness and death, as well as the departure of the slaves. Alone on the secluded plantation, without the protection of the owner, in a land torn apart by war, they lived in a vulnerable and fearful state. Although conditions were unstable and their welfare insecure, they cared for the few animals left on the plantation, plowed, seeded, and worked patches of corn, wheat, and vegetables. Everyone but baby Lemuel worked long hard days. The relationship of the seven that began October 3, 1862, grew to a bond as tightly forged as any blood family. The warming kitchen, the brick room adjacent to the back of the manor house to keep food from the outer kitchen warm until it was served to the Sinclair family, was a haven for the seven during the master's illness and remained so after his death. The room was a place to cook, to eat their meals, to plan their day, and to gather at day's end. The kitchen was warm in the winter, with the ovens and the large fireplace, and cool in the summer, with large windows opened, allowing coolness of the shady oasis of trees surrounding the three outer walls to penetrate the room.

Whether sitting around the table in the late afternoon coolness or sitting in front of a roaring fire, while relating the day's deeds, mishaps, or dreams of a better time to come—it was all a time of pleasant, comforting kinship. In the evenings, they would linger, talking, laughing, and weaving dreams, until the dwindling sunlight forced their amusing chatter to cease and the family to seek their beds.

May 5, 1865, Late Afternoon
East Bank of the Savannah River

Twelve horsemen clad in dusty Union blue rode northwestward along the east bank of the Savannah River. Colonel Morgan Anderson, of the U. S. Cavalry, led this band of handed-picked seasoned soldiers, as he had for the past four years. Using the variable terrain to shield their passage, the troops traveled at a steady pace from the low country of South Carolina. The group began traveling in the early months of 1865, as the war seemed to be coming to an end. Their orders were to finagle out information regarding Confederate President Davis's retreat from Richmond, Virginia, through South Carolina. After General Lee's surrender, orders came to return to Washington. Colonel Morgan Anderson turned his men southwestward toward the Savannah River. Approaching the east bank of the river, he changed directions. This time, his men rode northwestward toward the peaceful, fragrant woods of the piedmont and the completion of a promise made.

Within twenty or so miles of the small town of Hartwell, Georgia, the troops approached a feeder creek to the river, and Colonel Morgan Anderson ordered the men to make camp on the upper side of the creek. The troops, deserving a day or two out of the saddle, found the spot ideal for a few days of rest. There was an ample supply of game and fish. The area seemed to have been chosen for the amenities it offered, but the colonel chose the spot because the Georgia plantation he planned to visit later that night was only a few miles south across the river.

With sentries posted, Colonel Morgan Anderson was the first to take advantage of the river. He washed away the trail dust that covered him from head to toe. Returning to camp, he located Captain Zackery Haygood, the next in command and his best friend for the last twenty years. He outlined his plans for the night, but before he could finish, Captain Zackery Haygood interrupted.

"Hold it a minute", Captain Haygood bellowed. "Are you crazy?

Morgan Anderson replied, "I imagine the answer to that question will depend on who you asked. However, I would say no more than usual."

Captain Haygood then pleaded: "Don't entertain thoughts of riding alone in hostile territory at a time when only thoughts of revenge will be on the minds of most Southerners. Take two or three of the men along."

"Zack," Colonel Morgan Anderson said, "I have given much thought to making this visit. The roads will be deserted late at night, and should I meet another rider, one Union soldier will not be as threatening as several. If I had not promised my stepmother I would check on Mac at the end of the war, I would not go near the Sinclair Plantation. Surely the people of Hart County have received word the war is over."

"At least let me ride with you," Captain Zackery Haygood said. "I would like to meet a Southern gent who is not aiming a rifle at me, with intent to kill. If you think he might shoot first and ask questions later if two blue coats show up on his front porch after midnight, I could hide in the bushes until we are made welcome."

"Zack" Colonel Morgan Anderson said. "I will be all right. You are needed here with the men. Besides, plantations do not have porches, you numskull; they have verandas."

Colonel Anderson held fast to his agenda, promising to be back in camp in time to wake Captain Haygood for the morning meal. With those words, he unrolled his bedroll beneath a large tree, lay down, turned on his side away from the men, and closed his eyes for a few hours of sleep before crossing the river come night.

May 5, 1865, Evening
Riverbend Plantation

Sam, the oldest of the Hatcher siblings, was the last to leave the warming kitchen, trudging up the back stairs with a bucket of well water in one hand and a kettle of steaming hot water in the other. No one went to bed dirty. Not on Keowee's clean linens.

Sam sought the chamber on the front northern corner. The chamber with the best view of the river and the cedar grove, where the plantation road met the gravel drive leading to the front of the house. A soft thud broke the silence of the bedchamber, as a well-placed foot kicked the heavy chamber door shut.

The kettle and the bucket were quickly emptied into the bathing tub, giving enough water for a thorough cleaning but not enough for a good soak. A swift flick of the left wrist sent a floppy hat sailing across the room, and work-roughened hands unbuttoned and removed a dirty, sweat-stained shirt. Nimble fingers slid over rows of tightly wrapped binding, finding and untying knots. Without a moment's hesitation, Sam pulled the cloth loose and released her firm breast. The willowy figure shed the last of her disguise, as she stepped from a pair of young men's trousers, gracefully toeing them onto the other articles of the charade she wore by day. At last, she stepped into the tub for a much-needed bath.

Sam often found herself not only physically exhausted at day's end but emotionally drained, as well. Fear that their vulnerability would be discovered plagued her days as well as her nights. However, fear was not new to her. She remembered well another time and the fear that engulfed a girl of fifteen left alone with three young brothers upon the death of both parents, not knowing what would become of them, as they were carried far from their home to the house of a stranger. Memories filled her mind.

Neither the largeness nor the magnificence of this plantation stirred my emotions, as we arrived at this strange and unfamiliar place. The one-horse wagon, driven by Reverend Henry, carried us four and the body of our mother. Although no one came to welcome or invite us to enter, Reverend Henry unloaded and ushered us up the front steps and through the big double doors. Depositing us on a bench in the hallway, he rushed into the door across the hall. After several minutes of loud, booming voices, a bellow that shook the rafters brought a tall, majestic black woman, calmly walking from the back of the house, smiling and nodding to us as she passed. Knocking lightly on the door where the loud voices could still be heard, the woman entered.

"My first time to see Keowee, the woman that would come to mean so much to the boys and me," Sam whispered and smiled, as her thoughts continued. Keowee returned to the hall, knelt in front of us. Looking up into our faces, she said, "I be Keowee, Mr. Sinclair's housekeeper. You younguns are to come with me. I be gonna take care of y'all." With baby Lemuel tucked in her arms, she walked back down the hall as calmly as she had come but with the three of us following close on her heels. After sending for a wet nurse for Lemuel, she sent for Santee. Keowee met a tall, elegant man who looked more Indian than African at the back door and told him, "The master wants you to have a box made and a hole dug for Miss Martha, the mother of these children." As Santee turned to obey the master's orders, Keowee issued her own order, "Dig that grave in the family cemetery."

The memories ebbed, and Sam reminded herself, "Today, there is more to concern me than the time when the boys and I were brought to Riverbend. I have the responsibility of not only the boys but also Keowee, Santee, and Lovie.

Her mind filled with the concerns of today, after that reminder. Without a white adult male in residence, we are at the mercy of anyone whose aim is to create mischief or do harm. Keowee expressed concern about protecting my virtue and suggested I dress in clothes discarded by the errant Sinclair heir. I agreed to bind my cussed breast and appear outside my bedchamber dressed as a lad.

The room was void of sunlight, as she finished her bath and put her memories and concerns to rest. Emerging from the tepid water in the dim light, she groped for a towel. She made fast work of toweling. She yanked a nightgown from the back of the modesty screen, pulling it over her head and down over her hips. She was thankful for the warmth it provided, even though the hem reached only to the middle of her long legs. Promising to tidy up in the morning, she walked around the modesty screen into the twilight of the night.

Brushing the tangled from her hair, her ears attuned to every sound around her, she heard only the noise of her brothers, Floyd and David, making ready for bed. While the others took their night's rest, she would sit in the window seat, as was her habit, and watch the night, sleeping very little. Her sleeping in snatches began the night her mother was beaten and died. She had not been able to recapture the pleasure of a full night of peaceful slumber ever since, even during the years before Mr. Mac's death.

Finally, the house was quiet, except for the occasional creaking of the age-old dwelling. Kneeling on the window seat, her elbows propped on the windowsill, she gazed out from her lofty perch at the view before her and watched the fleeting twilight become a veil of darkness, allowing the once-elegant Sinclair home to disappear in a blanket of darkness.

A soothing balm seemed to float across the land, as inky shadows darkened along crumbling fencerows and the night covered fields and pastures with sheets of ebony. Marveling at the canopy spreading over the deteriorating plantation, she drew comfort from the camouflage the night brought. Her dubious thoughts of living unprotected on this remote plantation were eased. With a sigh, mixed with serenity and sorrow, she whispered a prayer of thanksgiving for the measure of mercy the night gave, covering for a few hours the remnants of a dying South.

On the far side of the river, a white moon peeped over the treetops of the east river bank, creeping up till it hung in the sky like a majestic ball. As if by magic, a sheen of silvery light seeped onto the adumbrative stage, nibbling at the edge of its dark mask and adding a silvery magic to the darkened arena. Mesmerized by the mythical panorama, she yielded to the beauty of the night. Slipping off her knees, she stretched her long legs across the cushioned seat and braced her back against the side of the window alcove.

Relaxing in the magic of the moment and inspired by the enchantment of the evening, her starry-eyed mind conjured up images of handsome knights on magnificent steeds, charging to the rescue of damsels in distress.

Moonbeams slithered through the leaves of the old oak trees, casting rays of light on the darkened ground, and Sam's head slowly drifted backward, coming to rest against the alcove. She was hearing only the creaks and groans of the old clapboard house, signaling the peaceful slumber of her family. Her mind wove fantasies that young ladies are known to dream, and, in the silence of the bewitching night, her tired body surrendered to the restful surroundings. Samantha Lloyd Hatcher, the unofficial head of the diverse family occupying Riverbend Plantation, drifted off to sleep.

May 5, 1865, Late in the Night
The Camp of the Union Cavalry

Unaware of the unprovoked attack by Union Cavalry on the nearby town of Hartwell, Georgia, early in the morning of May 5, Colonel Morgan Anderson left camp. He rode up the east bank of the Savannah River to the shoals around Geneviève

Island and crossed in the shallow water to the west bank. He made his way south along the west bank, until he neared the ferry. Taking to the trees that lined the river bank, he climbed the hill that rose behind the ferry buildings. He emerged onto the road that the old stagecoach had traveled from Lexington, Georgia, to Anderson, South Carolina, before the war.

His knowledge of the area came from the many visits that he and his family made to the Sinclair home before the war. As he rode, pleasant childhood memories flowed freely, bringing to mind not only the road he traveled but visions of the river plantation, a picturesque haven carved from the wilderness of northeast Georgia. His mind's eye filled with fields white with cotton and spirited horses frolicking in lush green pastures. For a while, he savored the memories of years ago, but a whispered reminder, images of another time and of a South that no longer existed, brought him back to the road he traveled and his mission.

As he rode south, following the road down the hill toward Cedar Creek, his attention was again on the road he traveled, recalling that the road that ran up from Cedar Creek passed Cokesbury Church brought to mind the distance he needed to travel before reaching the turnoff to the plantation. Wanting to make the plantation road before a night traveler could spot his blue uniform, he urged Zeus, his gray stallion, into a trot.

The shield of darkness he traveled under since leaving his men was quickly becoming nonexistent. A round moon encroached upon the black night, gradually turning the darkness into a silvery gray. The heavenly light made his passage a little more precarious than he wanted, enticing him to move to the side of the road, where the trees offered a shadowy screen.

As Colonel Morgan Anderson crossed Cedar Creek and started up the long hill toward his destination, the sudden quiet of the night noises made him aware that something was amiss. As the crest of the hill rose ahead of him, his sharp eyes scanned the road that leveled out before him and the field to his right. The shadowy overlay had not concealed his identity, and before he could seek the safety of the forest, shots exploded, and shouts broke the silence: "There's one of them murdering blue bellies."

As he pulled the reins to the left, a burning pain hit his right thigh, and the piercing fire of a rifle ball dug into his right shoulder, inflecting a breath-stealing jolt. The force of the rifle ball would have unseated him if not for the sharp swerve to the left by his mount at the moment of impact, counteracting the backward force by swinging him instead to the left across the neck of the powerful steed, as it veered into the mass of woodland trees. Zeus moved cautiously without further command from his master, as bullets whizzed by both man and beast, cutting twigs above their heads and knocking bark from the trees at their sides. The horse moved deeper and deeper into the dark forest.

Moments passed like hours. Blood flowed from his wounds, making him wonder if he would be able to stay in the saddle and reach Riverbend safely. Shouts of the attackers began to grow faint, and he hoped that it meant Zeus was putting distance between him and his foe and not that his consciousness was waning. He knew not if the rebs were still in pursuit, but he was confident their mounts would prove to be no match for the maneuverability of Zeus. How long he would sit in the saddle he did not know.

The great horse slowed to a gentle walk, and the only sound audible to Colonel Morgan Anderson's ears was the soft clop of Zeus's hooves on the carpet of dead leaves covering the ground. He had eluded his attackers, whether Confederate soldiers unaware of the armistice or a group of ruffians bent on killing. It mattered not. All that mattered was finding his way to Riverbend.

May 5, 1865, Late in the Night
Riverbend Plantation

When Sam was awakened by mournful cries of pain, Sam's sleep-glazed eyes scanned the moonlit room for the source of the cries. Her first thought was to call her Papa, but as her eyes wandered over the room, she hesitated. Her sleep-clouded eyes adjusted to the dimness of the gray light, and cobwebs of sleep eased from her groggy brain. She recognized the large chamber, sorrowfully she realized she was not in the small bedroom of her childhood home.

"There is no need to call Papa," she moaned. Remembering she no longer had that security, she painfully added, "He cannot hear me."

Slowly, fragments and images of a torturous dream flowed together, echoing in her now-lucid mind. The agony of those days pierced her heart, and tears gushed from her eyes, as she bent double with the pain, pain almost too heavy to bear. Reliving those two days either in her dreams or in her thoughts always threatened to shatter the lock she fought to keep on her emotions.

Tonight there was no witness to her tears, so she leaned back against the alcove, allowing the tears to wash the grief momentarily from her soul. She cried alone in her borrowed room, without the love or comfort of either a mother or a father.

Drained of tears, she blew her nose and dried her face, forcing her memories back to the depth of her being, vowing never to forget or to forgive the ones responsible for her loss.

The cussed Yankees.

Hoping to regain the serenity of an earlier time, she turned back to the window and clambered up onto bended knees for a last look at the night before seeking her bed. Her eyes were drawn to the far north edge of the yard, and, in the edge of the silvery moonlight, a huge, gray horse stood paused.

She stared in awe, intrigued by the sight of such a magnificent animal, not knowing, at first, if the animal was real or a figment of her imagination. However, as she gazed upon the beauty of the valuable animal, reality prevailed.

As if it knew it had gained her attention, the animal slowly stepped forward, moving nearer, and she was stunned to see the outline of a body slumped over the neck of the great horse. The person lay still as death, and, with a slow and easy gait, the horse moved gracefully toward the front entrance of the house.

It was several moments before the jolt of what she was seeing receded, and she began to realize the significance of a visitor arriving at Riverbend at this hour. Her curiosity flourished, fueled by the intrigue of a horse of such value walking up to the front door, not to mention the rider's apparent condition. With her curiosity peaking, she ran out of the room, down the front stairs, and out onto the veranda, without another thought, not even a thought of caution. She did manage, however, to remain in the shadows of the veranda.

The horse's gait remained slow as it walked to the house, coming to a stop in front of the walkway to the veranda. The man astride the horse moved slightly, either attempting to dismount or reacting to the halting of his mount.

Sam called a warning, "Stay on your horse, soldier; we do not welcome strangers in the middle of the night." She was surprised at the strength she heard in her voice, since she had become weak in the knees the moment she had spied the cussed Union-blue trouser leg.

"I have a gun and will not hesitate to shoot," Sam informed the soldier, telling a little white lie.

"Cussed Yankees have come at last," she mumbled under her breath, trying to regain a little of the courage she lost the moment she became aware a cussed Yankee varmint was at the door.

"I mean you no harm," a weak raspy voice offered. The strange-sounding voice grated on her already-frayed nerves, but, anxious to get a closer look at her cussed Yankee enemy, she moved slowly toward the edge of the veranda, thinking, *My curiosity might be the death of me yet.* To her disappointment, she saw only a bloody coat sleeve and a bloody trouser leg.

She studied the motionless horse and soldier before her, deciding he was either unconscious or dead, and, spurred on by that same curiosity, she moved to see more of this Yankee. Slowly she descended the few steps to the walkway. Inching toward the pebble drive and the Yankee, she nervously ran her tongue over her lips, but there was not enough spittle to make the effort worthwhile.

Her eyes glued to the horse and rider, she watched for the slightest hint of movement from the soldier. The heartbeat pounding in her ears was deafening, and she forgot about swallowing, even forgot about breathing. She concentrated on putting one foot in front of the other. Finally, she stood next to the horse, staring at the soldier's bloody trouser leg. The moonlight gave her plenty of light to look the Yankee over, but, again, all she was able to see of her hated enemy was the soldier's right shoulder, arm, and leg. Blood dripped from the fingers of his hand hanging limp over the horse's right flank.

His trouser leg was also bloody, telling Sam a Reb shot him more than once.

"There is so much blood," she whispered squeamishly. "He will surely die from the loss of all that blood, if he is not already dead," she reasoned, thoughtfully adding, "If he dies or is dead, I will be able to keep his horse."

Before she completed the sentence, she was shaking her head in reproach, as *Thou shall not covet* popped into her head.

Ashamed to have entertained such a thought, she stepped back several paces, shaking her head in reproach. Mentally chiding herself for coveting the soldier's horse, she was startled out of her remorseful rebuke by the soldier's voice.

"I need to reach Riverbend. The home of Mac Sinclair. Can you point . . . " His words were weak and waning, but Sam heard Mac Sinclair's name loud and clear.

"Mercy me," she gasped. "Why on earth would a Yankee soldier be seeking Mr. Mac?" The Yankee's words put her mind in a tailspin.

"Goodness gracious," she said, "I have got to get a hold of myself. My mind is racing faster than a hound dog chasing a rabbit." And she thought, *I cannot let him know he has reached Riverbend until I know why he is here. We have no protection against a Yankee raid.*

"You will not find Mr. Sinclair at Riverbend, except in his grave," she heard herself croak.

Moving a few feet toward the horse's head, she mumbled under her breath, as her anger and hatred of Yankees raised their ugly heads, "Mr. Sinclair is in his grave, just as you will be if someone does not stop that blood or our boys in gray find you. Either way, it will not matter; you will get what you deserve."

Blood was still dripping from his hand, and Sam knew that

if he was to live, he needed help.

Sam's Christian beliefs began to battle with her hatred and anger.

"I seem to have two options," she reasoned. "Send him on his way or tend to his wounds."

She weighed these options calmly, considering she was standing barefoot in the moonlight, in a nightgown, staring at a cussed Yankee soldier, her hated enemy. A wounded, hated enemy, at that.

"He will surely die if his wounds are not tended to," she stated to the night, "and if the home guard discovers I aided a Yankee soldier, they will likely burn the house to the ground. So the house and cabins are out. Neither can I let the family know he is here. The fewer people that know there is a Yankee soldier hidden on Riverbend land, the safer we will be." She determined she would have to tend to his wounds alone.

"What am I planning to do?" she shrieked. She was shocked by her intention to find a place to tend to this Yankee and to keep his presence a secret.

"I am an idiot!" she scolded. "I cannot be considering helping a Yankee soldier. I hate Yankees! Do I have to remind myself a soldier like him killed Papa? It might have been him."

"Shush! Be quiet. I do not need reminding," she pleaded, placing her hands over her ears. *I will turn around and go back in the house and wash my hands of the whole affair,* crept into her weary brain.

"Just as Pilate washed his hands of Jesus?" she asked.

"Mercy, I am crazy!" she confessed. "I must be. I am not only talking to myself; I am arguing with myself." Giggles were beginning to well up from deep down in her chest; then they bubbled up and slipped from her lips.

"Send him on his way, or tend to his wounds," she repeated.

Can I help a Yankee? Even after I swore to kill the first Yankee I saw?

However, her tender heart and Christian beliefs would not allow her to turn her back on someone who needed help. Even a Yankee.

The battle between her hatred of Yankees and her Christian faith was over, and she considered the grievous consequences that could come from her decision.

However, she put these concerns and her argument with herself behind her and pondered where she could hide him, while she tended to his wounds. The granite cave came to mind. Immediately and without a moment's hesitation, she took the horse's reins in hand. Cautioning the soldier to hold on, she slowly led the horse and the rider toward the river and the granite cave.

The white moon that had shined a magical light on her mystical stage earlier was now just a source of light for the path across the hard, ragged ground between the house and the river. Her thoughts were no longer filled with romantic images of heroes and beautiful damsels but with uneasy thoughts of what the presence of a wounded Yankee soldier could contribute to the vulnerable situation of the ones living on Riverbend.

"Do you argue with yourself often?" a shaky voice asked, interrupting her thoughts. "I was sure I would bleed to death before you settled your disagreement." The voice was weak, but, to her ears, it held a bold, strange inflection in the utterance of his words.

"I was not aware I had an audience as I spoke my thoughts!" She was throwing that snide remark to his question across her shoulder. A quiet giggle passed her lips, as a memory of her brothers' teasing. *They are right; I do talk to myself.*

Sam led the horse down the rocky draw and into the river, wading out into the water a few feet, until the sandy bottom turned to smooth rock, a granite ledge hidden below water level. Turning downstream, while leading the horse, she walked on the ledge toward the big bend.

She and Floyd had found the cave while swimming the past summer and had stocked it with supplies. The ledge was the key. It hugged the bank around the big bend to a granite bolder that was the downriver side of the bend. The bolder reached up to the top of the riverbank and was embedded a great distance back into the bank. The cave was in the upper part of the bolder. Bushes growing on the bank and in the crevices of the pieces of granite scattered up and down the bank concealed the cave opening.

The overhanging trees blocked some of the moonlight from the river, as the river began curving to the right, forming the big bend. A few more feet around the bend, and the ledge would disappear, and she would need to start angling up the steep incline of the bank opposite the bolder and to guide the horse through the brush and around the granite that littered the space between the water and the entrance of the cave.

"What will I do if the passage proves to be too difficult for you, big boy?" she whispered to the horse. She mulled this possibility over in her mind, as she approached the end of the ledge.

There is no need to fret about that; after all, the horse brought its master this far; surely a few rocks and saplings will not prove to be a problem.

She moved her hand up the reins until she touched the horse's neck; tightening her grip, she stood with her shoulder against the steed's left flank and tackled the tricky walk up the bank with determination and courage, as she did with every problem she faced. Moving as one, she maneuvered the horse up the dirt bank, through the brush, and around pieces of granite, to the cave entrance, with ease.

Inside, the cave was dark as pitch. No light from the moon penetrated the opening. Wasting no time, she found candles and flint. Soon, they were encircled in the dim light of the candle glow. Taking up the reins again, she led the horse to a straw-mattress pallet near the rear of the big room.

"You can dismount now, while I light a lantern." Her words brought no movement from the soldier. Sliding her hand around the animal's neck, she encountered the Yankee's left hand, limp against the horse's foreleg.

"Unconscious," she reasoned, and she led the horse around until the soldier's uninjured side was next to the straw mattress. She slipped his boots from the stirrups; with that task complete, she faced the soldier and jerked on the soldier's left arm, hoping to rouse him enough to slide him from the horse onto the mattress.

"Oh me, I jerked too hard," she gasped, as the soldier's lifeless body slid from the saddle, slamming his full weight against her, knocking her hard onto her heinie. His body proved to be too heavy for her to hold, causing her torso to follow her rump to the granite floor.

"Sprawled on my back with a ton of male flesh crushing the air from my lungs is not my idea of being a good Samaritan," puffed from her lips, with her panting breath.

The soldier lay on his stomach, sprawled across her, his injured shoulder lodged under her chin. Trying to free herself from beneath the load of bones and muscles, she twisted and pushed with all her strength.

"Hold it just a minute," a whispered plea came from the ton of flesh, as Colonel Morgan Anderson woke to the movement of a soft body beneath him. "Stop your wiggling. Give me a few minutes to catch my breath, and I will try moving myself."

"While you are catching your breath, you are mashing mine right out of me," she gasped.

"You weigh a ton. There is a pallet just to your left," she informed the soldier. "When you are ready I will push, and, maybe together, we can get you off me and onto the straw mattress."

"Do you promise it to be as soft as you?" Colonel Morgan Anderson asked.

"You cussed jackass," Sam said. "I cannot tend your wounds while you use me for a mattress. You have had plenty of time to catch your breath. Now move!"

With a groan, or it may have been a snicker (she was not sure which), the soldier used the little strength he possessed and rolled to his left, while Sam pushed, rolling him off her and onto his back. Scrambling to her feet as the load lifted, her eyes fell on a giant of a man lying half on and half off the pallet.

"Mercy, he is a big man," she countered, as she took his measure.

"He did not look that large, sprawled across his mount." she conceded.

Kneeling beside the soldier's legs, she slid her hands and arms under his legs, lifting them up onto the mattress. Turning, she looked for the first time at the face of her enemy and gasped in awe.

"Mercy me, I have never seen a more handsome masculine face," she sighed. Black eyebrows and lashes were very prominent against his pale face, but, despite the paleness of his skin, the strength of the man was evident. A strong jawline, a noble nose, and chiseled features all spoke of strength and created a much-too-handsome face by far. *Why could he not be wearing gray instead of Union blue?* her romantic heart pleaded.

She quickly assembled the supplies she would need. Lighting a lantern for more light, she knelt on folded quilts beside the Yankee's right side and began her task of unbuttoning and cutting away the bloody parts of his coat and shirt. Her fingers trembled, as the seriousness of her task loomed before her.

Working steadily for what seemed like a lifetime, Sam finally applied the last bandage. Needing to rest her knees and stretch the muscles in her back, she rose to her feet, wondering, *Have I done everything that needed to be done?*

Quickly rehearsing every detail of her care, she decided there was nothing else she could do, except to keep his fever down and to pray.

"His fate is now in God's hands," she whispered. Bowing her head, she asked God to bless every aspect of her efforts and to touch the soldier with his healing powers.

"Maybe somewhere, someone is praying for you," she whispered, as she looked down on the unconscious soldier.

"Truth be known," she said, "that someone is why I did this. That special someone who would feel the terrible pain of loss, should you die. I know well that pain."

A cup of spring water in hand, she walked toward the mouth of the cave to rinse out her mouth. As she walked to the entrance of the cave, her thoughts traveled to a place in Virginia, called Manassas, *I wonder if Papa had someone to tend him in his last hours or if he died alone?*

Lost in her thoughts of her papa, she was aware of movement in the cave, until something wet brushed against her arm. She jumped at the unexpected touch.

"Sweet Jesus!" she shrieked, turning to find the horse

claiming her attention. "Scare me to death will you? Well, I had forgotten about you for the moment. You waited patiently while I cared for your master, and now it is you turn." She reached for the reins and led it away from the entrance and removed the saddle.

Wanting to see if the man was still breathing, she knelt beside the pallet, but she could not detect the slightest movement of his chest. Afraid he was dead, she leaned over, her face nearly touching his lips, waiting! Moment after moment passed before a wisp of a breath caressed her cheek. Releasing the breath she was holding, she felt like crying with joy. He was still alive. She remained just a whisper away from his lips, until several more warm wisps of breaths fluttered across her cheek. *His breathing is shallow and weak, but maybe this giant of a man is strong enough to survive.*

For that, she was thankful, since she had no way of making him fall into a deep sleep while she probed his wounds. She covered him with a clean quilt, tucking the ends tightly under him, so as to conserve his body heat and keep the cool dampness of the cave away. Satisfied she had done all she could, she turned her thoughts to her house and her bed.

She was sure it had to be near dawn, but she had no way of knowing. She needed to return to her room before she could be missed. She tethered the horse just a foot or two from the entrance of the cave, in a spot where it would be hidden from anyone moving on the water. Returning to the cave one last time to check on her soldier, she was pleased to see that the outer bandages showed no sign of new blood and that he was still breathing.

After disposing of her bloody gown and taking a bath in the river, she retraced her steps of the night, heading up the river and through the field, but as she walked across the drive, she glanced to the spot where she first saw the horse. Noticing an object lying to the side of the drive, near the grove of cedar trees, she turned toward the grove, but before she reached the trees, she recognized the object. A blue cavalry hat.

"So this is where he lost his hat," she said to herself. "I wondered where he had lost it since he had arrived bareheaded." Retrieving the cussed Yankee thing, she hurried back down the drive, up the steps to the veranda, through the front door, up the front stairs, and into her room, praying that no member of her family was up before dawn and had witnessed her nude passage.

CHAPTER 2

Colonel Morgan Anderson awoke to total darkness. There was not even the glow of a candle, and, in the dark silence that engulfed him, questions began to fill his mind. *Where am I? Whose plantation or home did I stumble onto, and where is that hellion that greeted me? Why has she left me in this awful darkness. Has she left me here to die?* The last question was the most disturbing.

Finding no answers to the where, who, and why running through his mind, he used his left hand to throw off the cover that encased his body and reached across to his right shoulder, where the rifle ball had hit. Finding a thick bandage, he slid his hand lower to his thigh and discovered a slit in his trouser leg and another bandage. *Well, the little hellion bandaged my wounds. I hope that is a good sign. I surely hope she had sense enough to remove the lead first or at least got someone to do the digging. I am sure that rifle ball needed some coaxing before it relinquished the bed in my shoulder.* Exhausted from his investigation of his wounds, he drifted back to sleep.

Too soon, old red crowed proudly, announcing the new day. Sam sat motionless on the edge of her bed, her hair braided, her trousers on, and a roll of cloth binding in her hand. Tired of worrying about the binding of her breast, Sam flung the roll onto the bed, refusing to try again. Sighing with disgust and with her shoulders slumped, she rammed her hands into the sleeves of her work shirt, and pulled the shirt over her head.

Since opening her eyes from her short nap, images of the handsome Yankee drifted in and out of her thoughts. However, a lot of the past night was a little hazy, her memory a bit fuzzy from lack of sleep. Her mind was clear enough to remember her act of treason and the importance of keeping that she was hiding a Yankee soldier on Riverbend land from her family.

Colonel Morgan Anderson woke again sometime later and was again disturbed by the darkness that seemed to engulf him. "Where am I?" he yelled, but he heard only the faint echo of his own words in response. Then, parts of a strange conversation of sorts flickered through his mind—bits and pieces of a rambling argument the little hellion had had with herself about aiding a Yankee soldier and not letting anyone know.

Chuckling, he assured himself, "She has hid me for her family's protection."

Continuing to reflect on other bits of the night's conversation, he remembered, *She hates Yankees.*

"It's a miracle she did not finish me off and throw my carcass down a well. She doesn't have to like me, just so she patched me up so I can rejoin my men."

Changing his avenue of thought, he remembered the girl telling him Mac was dead. *My visit was for naught if the rumors I heard in New Orleans about Robert Sinclair's hasty trip to Europe were true. However, it is puzzling, since he was exempt from the army by sending a substitute.*

Before sleep could claim him again, the memory of a young lady kneeling by his side and the image of her in his mind had a halo of light around her head. With that recollection, he knew there had been light in this place. She had brought the light with her.

Sneering suspiciously, he continued to reflect on the night. *An angel of mercy. A southern angel with her soft drawl. A voice so sweet honey drips from her every word. Well, maybe not all of her words.*

Chuckling, he also recalled her burst of temper, but her tender compassion overshadowed her little temper spats. A measure of mercy for her sworn enemy. He grinned, *She must be some girl. No, this Southern angel is a very caution, yet a very strong-willed young woman.* As sleep once again began to claim him, he amended some of his last thoughts: *A very pretty, strong-willed young Southern lady.* She had to be pretty, because the young woman in his dreams was very pretty.

***

A soft rap on Sam's door pushed the problem of hiding a Yankee from her mind. "Come in," Sam called softly.

A pretty young woman with creamy brown skin opened the chamber door and entered the room.

"Morning Sam," she offered cheerfully, as she closed the door behind her. Lovie was the only child of Keowee and Santee and was a year older than Sam. The two had become fast friends during the years since Sam's arrival at Riverbend, and they were as close as sisters.

"Morning, Lovie. I am certainly glad you came upstairs this morning. Would you be a dear and help me with this binding?" Sam asked, pleadingly. "I cannot get it tight enough to flatten these cussed breasts."

"Cussed," Lovie giggled. "Not so. You are blessed with bosoms most young ladies would give their last dollar for. If they had a dollar."

"Not if they had to bind them every day. Will you please help me?" Sam begged, pulling off her shirt and holding one end of the cloth binding to her chest, as Lovie walked behind the modesty screen. Bringing Sam's dirty clothes from behind the modesty screen, Lovie got her first good look at Sam's face and caught her breath in empathy. Seeing the dark circles under Sam's eyes, she dropped the clothes to the floor and warned, "Mama gonna be a mite upset when she spies them eyes of yours, and she gonna give you one more tongue-lashing."

"What is wrong with my eyes?" Sam inquired.

Handing Lovie the roll of cloth binding, Sam urged, "Pull tight," as she turned round, encasing her breast in rows of cloth binding. As the end of the roll appeared, Lovie handed it to Sam.

"Hold this," Lovie said, "while I get the narrow strips and lace them over the binding to hold it in place."

"I want the knots tied in front, Lovie. It makes them easier to undo at night."

"Okay," Lovie agreed.

Crisscrossing the narrow strips around Sam's ribs and crossing them for the last time on Sam's back, Lovie brought the ties to the front, handing them to Sam. Lovie advised, "Here, tie them like you want."

"Thanks, Lovie," Sam said, "and what is wrong with my eyes? You never answered me."

"It's them dark circles under your eyes," Lovie replied. "Mama's gonna know you didn't sleep again last night, and she gonna give you one more tongue-lashing."

"I slept a little."

"Not in that bed you didn't, lessen you done made it, and I doubt that!" Lovie remarked sassily.

"I slept most of the night in the window seat," Sam said.

"Uh-uh," Lovie said, "that's what's gonna make her real mad. You sleeping while sitting at that window and not lying down in your bed."

Turning, Lovie gathered up Sam's dirty clothes from the floor and added, "I will take these on down."

"I am done here," Sam answered, as she grabbed her hat. "I will wake the boys, dress Lemuel, and be right down to help with breakfast."

"I already rousted the boys," Lovie said. "Woke them as I came up. They are probably at the table by now, knowing the appetites of them two. You can get Lemuel."

Sam made her way next door to her youngest brother, two-years-and-seven-months-old Lemuel. Getting him dressed in the morning was an enjoyable time of the day for her.

"You are a happy little bugger," she laughed, as she put on his socks and shoes.

"Thank God you are not old enough to realize the pain of losing Mama and Papa," she whispered.

"But you have not lacked for love and attention, have you, big boy?" She was talking and cooing to her brother, as she readied him for the day.

"Morning everyone," Sam greeted, as she entered the kitchen and placed Lemuel in his high chair. Turning to offer her help with serving the meal gave Keowee her first look of the morning at Sam's face, and, with that first glimpse, Lovie's prediction came true. Keowee's disapproval was unmistakable. It was evident in the tone of her voice, as she confronted Sam.

"Child, what are you trying to do to yourself? Don't you know you can't continue to go without sleep? What kept you awake last night?"

The tone of Keowee's voice left no doubt in Sam's mind that

she was upset with her, and while she gathered up plates and utensils to put on the table, she tried to ease Keowee's concern with a bold, "I slept."

"'Em dark circles under your eyes tells me you didn't sleep at all, and there be no need to make excuses."

"I told you she'd be upset, didn't I?" Lovie whispered, as she eased by Sam with a platter of food.

Not wanting Sam to offer her usual excuses and flimsy explanations, Keowee told her sternly, "Young lady, you will trot right back up 'em stairs after you've had your breakfast and spend the day in bed. If you don't sleep at night, you'll sleep during the day. Yes siree, you'll not go to the field this day."

"I am fine, Keowee," Sam said. "I am perfectly able to go to the field today. I slept enough last night." She did not want more of Keowee's prying questions.

"Is your bed mussed?" Keowee asked. "It's not, is it? 'Cause you didn't sleep in your bed. Did you?"

"I fell asleep stretched out on the window seat and slept for a while," Sam responded. "I don't know for how long, and, after that, I stretched out on the bed and slept until time to dress for the day." She hoped that wasn't a complete lie. After all, she did both things; she just failed to say what happened in between her naps.

"I knowed it," Keowee said. "I knowed it. That window gonna be the death of you yet. If you don't get your rest, you gonna wind up sick. Child, you needs to turn back 'em covers on that bed, stretch out on that soft bed, and let sleep claim you. You'll stay out of that field today."

Recognizing Keowee's tone of voice that bespoke no argument, Sam offered no retort to her mandate.

Bowing her head in a show of submission, she moved to

her chair, and as she gained her seat, she whispered, "Thank you, heavenly Father."

Elated at being ordered to stay in her room for the day, she almost giggled. She would be able to visit the cave several times during the day, without anyone knowing.

Santee, Floyd, and David finished their meal first, made their good-byes, and quit the room for the field. Sam felt God was answering her prayer when she heard Keowee remind Lovie she would join her in the wash house just as soon as she cleared the table. Sam's head shot up, and, in a sober voice, she volunteered, "I can clear the table, Keowee. I feel bad, as it is not doing my share of the work today. Please let me help you that much."

Keowee nodded her consent, and, with Lemuel in her arms, she left the kitchen. Sam was up before the door closed behind Keowee, scraping plates into the slop bucket, stacking the dishes in the wash pan. Faster than two shakes of a dog's tail, she covered and stored the leftover food in the pie safe, to be used at the noon meal, and she washed, rinsed, and dried the dishes. After filling a jar with broth from Keowee's stockpot, she bypassed the back stairs and walked out the front door and on her way to the cave and her soldier, giving no thought to her manner of dress, until she reached the riverbank and spied the water.

"Gracious me," she said to herself, "I am not dressed to wade in the water. Wet pants and shoes would be a dead give-away that I was up to something."

"There is only one thing to do—and that is to strip," she sighed. "Shoes will have to be first."

She perched on the stump, unlacing and removing shoes and socks. Untying the rope at her waist as she stood allowed her trousers to fall to the ground. The shirttail was long enough to reach midway of her thighs, but, from there down, she was bare. She was sure there was no one around to witness her state of undress; however, to be absolutely sure, she looked over her shoulder toward the house, as she stepped from her trousers.

Sam first untied the horse and led it inside the cave. Her mind was on seeing to her soldier, so she left the horse to find the pool of spring water in the rear of the big room. Locating a candle, she hurried to check the soldier. A crumpled quilt told Sam her patient had awakened and had stirred in her absence, giving her hope the soldier might have a good chance of surviving. She checked his bandages, and, seeing no fresh blood, she confirmed she had stopped the bleeding. Sighing deeply, she thought, *Maybe during my clumsy doctoring, I did something right.*

Slowly she straightened the quilt over his body, tucking the ends under his chin, and she noticed the darkening shadow of a beard on the soldier's handsome face. As she smiled, the thought flashed through her head, *The shadow does not hamper his good looks; the shadow adds a certain charm.*

There was no reason to hurry back to her room, so she sat on the folded quilts beside the soldier and gazed contentedly upon the face of her enemy. As she admired the soldier's features, she knew it was a face she would never forget, and she knew she would never see another face that would compare to it. For the moment, basking in the pleasure of admiring his handsome face, the Yankee blue uniform he wore was slipping from her mind. Without a thought to her allegiance, she was content to sit, her eyes resting on the soldier's face.

Sam's eyes began to feel heavy, as she sat admiring the handsome soldier and recalling Keowee's warning of what lack of sleep might do. She decided she should get back to her room and try to sleep, as ordered, never once aware of her fascination with her Yankee or at least not admitting that to herself.

She brought her admiring of the soldier to an end, returned the horse to the secure place on the riverbank, and left the cave for her bedchamber and a nap.

After she woke from her nap, Sam's first thought was to return to the cave. Making haste, she waded along the granite ledge, stopping only to untie the horse and lead it inside the cave.

Hurriedly lighting a candle, she laid wood in the pit, lit a fire, and placed a kettle of water and a pot of broth on the wire rack to heat, before checking on her soldier. He was resting easy at the moment, but she could tell he had stirred again from the condition of his covers. She checked his wounds and thought best not to change the bandages. Sitting Indian-style on quilts, she was content to sit and watch him sleep, marveling over his handsome face, even with the shadowy growth of a black beard. *I wonder if I gently rubbed my hand across his cheek and chin if he would awake and catch me in my foolishness. I really would like to know how his face feels with the beginning of that growth.* Mulling over that gamble, she sighed and continued thinking on the matter. *Would it be soft to the touch, or would it be scratchy?*

"Gracious me," she gulped, becoming aware of the path her thoughts were taking. *I hope he can't read my thoughts. I should not be thinking things like that. It's my cussed curiosity! If I am not careful, that curiosity will get me in serious trouble. I better get busy and get my mind off that cussed Yankee.* "An idle mind is the devil's workshop," she mentally recited.

However, she continued to sit, her thoughts running on the same path, until she glanced from his face to his blue uniform. That ended her fantasizing. *Do I have to keep reminding myself a soldier like him killed Papa? It might have been him*, she added, reprimanding herself for her senseless and shameful behavior and thoughts.

Turning her thoughts to more practical things, she remembered the broth and debated whether to wake him to eat or to let him continue to sleep. She concluded that he could only get nourishment when she was there to prepare it and that he could sleep when she was gone. But she continued to sit by his side, admiring the handsome soldier, after affirming her hatred of Yankees.

Her mind began to wander again in the same direction, and she snorted, "Heaven help me and my cussed curiosity."

Making herself stand and walk to the fire pit, she moved the kettle and the pot to the side of the rack; she dipped broth into a large bowl and carried it back to the place where the Yankee was sleeping. Sitting on the quilts, she placed the bowl on the granite floor, and, without a conscious thought, she placed her right hand on the Yankee's left cheek and gently slid her palm and fingers down his cheek and across his chin, thinking, *My goodness; that feels marvelous.*

"If you are through playing with my face, I would like a taste of whatever that is that smells like food," came from the awake soldier.

Gracious me! Caught in her foolishness and wondering if he had actually read her thoughts, she stammered in embarrassment, until she was able to turn on him.

"You jackanapes, I was not playing with your face. I was merely trying to awaken you gently, hoping to get you to eat this broth before leaving."

Sounds of soft chuckles teased her ears, as she picked up the bowl of broth, bringing it between them, and began spooning the liquid into his mouth. A smile continued to play across his face between each spoonful, causing her to wonder again if he really did know what she had been thinking. He finished the bowl with no trouble, gave her a great, big smile, closed his eyes, and was once again sound asleep.

Sitting for a while, she stared at the pieces of the Yankee-blue uniform coat that remained on the soldier. She reminded herself again of the danger that Yankees could be to the security of her family and that he or a soldier wearing the same uniform had killed her papa. She hoped that reflecting again on the insecurity of her family and her father's death by Yankees would stop her foolish woolgathering.

Using hot water from the kettle, she washed the bowl and the pot, stored the remaining broth, and returned to the pallet to check her soldier's bandages one last time before leaving the cave. After tucking the quilt around him, she lingered again and gazed at his handsome face, but before her thoughts could stray, she admitted to herself: *I cannot help myself. He is the handsomest young man I have seen. Even more handsome than the portrait of the Sinclair heir, Robert.* She stood and walked the horse out of the cave.

While she was tethering the animal, a thought came; *If there are soldiers traveling with this cussed Yankee, will they become aware he is not with them and come here looking for him? One thing is sure: they would not find him. No one but Floyd and me know of this cave, and Floyd knows nothing of the cussed Yankee being in the cave.*

Confident the family would be spared injury if Yankees came looking and found nothing, she removed her trousers and waded along the ledge back up the river, satisfied her soldier was mending nicely and her family should be safe.

I missed an opportunity to ask him who shot him and where he was when he was shot, she thought. With the water lapping around her legs, she reminded herself, *I also wanted to know why he was on his way to visit Mr. Mac.*

I cannot for the life of me imagine why a Yankee would have a reason to visit Riverbend. My thoughts running on that question maybe would keep my mind busy and off that cussed handsome face.

Sliding into her bed, Sam wondered if she would be able to close her eyes with her mind full of who, where, and why, plus the handsome face that kept slipping in and out of her mind's eye. She was unable to stop her brain from racing, and she tossed and turned for what seemed like hours, unable to fall asleep. Unsure of the time and not having a clock handy, Sam hoped there was time before the noon meal to return to the cave for a quick visit.

"That will be easily confirmed," she beamed, deciding to check the position of the sun. She eased out the chamber door and down the front stairs, leaving her shoes on the bottom step of the staircase. Slipping from the house, stopping a short distance from the veranda, she looked to the sky. "Judging from the location of the sun, I will have plenty of time before I will be called to the warming kitchen for the noon meal," she cheerfully estimated.

Stepping into the water, she was again conscious of her lack of clothing and prayed her family would never know how easy it was becoming for her to remove her trousers in broad daylight.

The sounds she heard as she entered the cave sent her rushing across the underground room. Her condemnations for parading around half-naked were completely forgotten, as her mind filled with only one thing. Her soldier.

She knew, from the sounds of his moans and his thrashing, that he was feverish, before she knelt at his side. Placing her hand on his forehead, she felt the heat confirming her suspicions.

"He is hot as blazes!" she exclaimed. Lighting a candle, she made a fire in the pit near the entrance, placed the wire rack over the blaze, and put on a kettle of water to boil. Gathering the vinegar and a soft cloth, she returned to her soldier.

Sitting on the cushion of folded quilts, she eased the covers from his right side and was happy to discover no signs of fresh blood at either wound. Satisfied with the condition of his wounds, she began to sponge him with the vinegar.

Getting the tea into him was easier than she had expected. With his restlessness, she had dreaded the task, but he seemed to trust her every move, and she wondered if she would be as trusting if their places were reversed.

Waiting for the tea to work its magic, she again sponged his feverish body. The experience of feeling the soft, black curls covering the soldier's bare chest was unsettling to her emotion, and, for that reason alone, she would be glad for the tea to reduce his fever so she could dispense with the sponging. She desperately wanted him to become lucid so she could question him as to how he had received his wounds and why he had been looking for Riverbend.

In time, she felt his hand lifting hers, placing it on his forehead. The soldier's forehead was clammy but cool, and, in seconds, he was sleeping soundly. A deep healing sleep. The tea had finally worked. She watched the easy rise and fall of his chest, basking in the quiet sound of his normal breathing.

The fire from the pit was warming the room nicely, coaxing her to think kindly of a nap, but before she could get too comfortable, she decided she had better nap in her own bed, in case someone came to call her to the noon meal.

She returned the vinegar to the shelf and washed the tea-cup. She jerked off her trousers and rolled them up, putting them under her arm. Stiffening her spine, she pointed her chin to the sky and walked from the cave, with her shirttail flapping in the wind.

CHAPTER 3

Returning from the last visit of the morning to the cave, Sam expected the house to be quiet, thinking all would be busy finishing their morning chores. However, entering the front door, she was startled to hear a din of loud voices coming from the warming kitchen. Drawn to the commotion, she ran toward the back of the house, through the downstairs hallway.

She forgot, for a moment, that she was supposed to be upstairs. Hastening to retrace her steps, she ran back up the hallway, bypassed the shoes she had left earlier on the front stairs, and ran up the stairs. She took two steps at a time, not slowing her pace, as she turned down the hallway of the upstairs. Only as she reached the back stairs did she slow her steps. Hoping to hear a word or two that would explain the cause of the loud talking, she walked quietly and calmly down the back stairs. Her ears were attuned to the uproar coming from the warming kitchen, but she was unable to comprehend a word of what was being discussed. Her patience came to an end, as she reached the bottom step, and she burst through the door. Her eyes quickly searched out each member of her family, as she entered the room. To her relief, all were there and appeared to be well. However, they were so absorbed in their excited chatter they did not notice her entrance.

Flustered by everyone talking at once, filling the room with the sound of jumbled words, she had the strangest urge to yell, "Who's listening?"

Instead, she screamed as loud as she could, "Stop this infernal noise!"

All tongues stopped at once, and all eyes turned in her direction. The room was silent as a tomb, as they all looked at her in amazement. No doubt, she had gained their full attention, but she could not help smiling at the look of shock on their faces. None of them had ever heard her holler quite so loudly.

Looking straight at her brothers, with that be-quiet-or-else look, she spoke, "Santee, what has happened that has all of you so disturbed?"

"Yankee cavalry raided Hartwell yesterday morning. *** The town's all shot to pieces, and Doctor Webb be dead. Shot by them Yankees. They also shot Doctor Webb's sister, Miss Annie. Sheriff Holland said she be pretty bad off."

No one made a sound, while Santee relayed the news to Sam, and no one made a sound after Santee finished talking. All waited to see Sam's reaction to the news. However, no one in the room would ever know the anxiety and the distress Santee's words caused. His words pierced Sam's heart, and the thought, *Is my soldier one of the raiders?* flashed through her mind.

Her family sat silent, not knowing how the news of the raid would affect Sam. They remembered she was fearful for weeks, after hearing the news of Yankee soldiers occupying Anderson, South Carolina. They remembered she was afraid Yankees would find their way across the river to Riverbend.

However, they all witnessed her face turn as white as one of Keowee's freshly washed sheets, and they all witnessed the stiffening of her stance, as she found her voice and uttered in a soft whisper, "Why?"

"No one knows why," Santee answered.

"Sheriff Holland says it couldn't be the war, 'cause the war done be over and has been since early April. General Lee done surrendered. He did say the troops came from the direction of Anderson and the talk among the folks seems to be they be looking for President Davis. The president ain't nowhere around here, and there be no reason for 'em Yankees to shoot up the town and kill that good doctor. He says the buildings are all full of lead, and there ain't no windows what had glass that ain't busted. He says the raid lasted about an hour. Afterward, they rode out of town on the Athens road."

"Where did they cross the river?" Sam asked.

"They didn't use the ferry," Floyd chimed in, "'cause the Sherriff said there were too many soldiers to fit on a ferry. They had to have ridden across."

"Most likely, they crossed at the shoals above Geneviève Island," Sam suggested, thinking that was a little too close to Riverbend.

"If so," Sam went on, "they were just a few miles north of us. The bastards! Yankees are not fit to tote guts to a bear—shooting and killing after the war has ended. I hope the same fate visits them before they reach Athens."

I pray there won't be no more killing," Keowee said softly.

Sam reined in her emotions for now, turning her attention to Santee's recounting of the raid. There was something she wanted clarified regarding the troops of cavalry leaving Hartwell.

"Santee, did you say the soldiers rode out of Hartwell on the Athens road?"

"Yessum."

"All of them? Could there have been any stragglers?"

"Not according to Sheriff Holland. Old Mr. Gaines asked him that same question. He told him he and a few men what had horses followed at a safe distance plum out of the county and none turned to the right nor the left."

"Where did you see Sheriff Holland?"

"Me and the boys went up to Bull Snort after finishing with that corn patch we's been hoeing out. Checking for some news from Mr. Roberts, but there was no letter. Sheriff Holland came by and was telling the men about the raid, and we's been hung around, listening."

"I'm glad you did." The news weighed heavily on Sam's heart, as she shared the noon meal with her family, and before the meal ended, she left the table without a word, escaping to her room. She hurried up the back stairs, with Santee's account of the terrifying attack echoing in her head. Breathless from her hurried steps, Sam slumped back against her closed chamber door, sliding to the floor. Needing the solitude of the room to soothe her frayed nerves, she had abruptly sought its refuge.

She was desperately hoping to shut out the horrid agonies of the war, if only for a little while. Propped against the chamber door, trying to calm her nerves, she reminded herself, *Until now, Hart County had been spared the trod of Yankee boots and the fire from enemy guns.*

Stretched on the cool floor, she planned to rest for a spell, but as soon as her body began to feel the coolness of the floor, something appalling flickered across her mind, or, rather, someone.

It was someone who had completely slipped from her mind in the confusion of her battle with her emotions, and her racing thoughts of Yankee raids and Riverbend's vulnerability. The recollection brought a weight of stone to her chest.

"Mercy me!" she gasped, sobbing.

"I am harboring a Yankee soldier. Hopefully not one of the soldiers that attacked Hartwell. Oh, I hope not. However, a soldier in Union blue, nevertheless. What shall I do?" Hoping to regain some of the comforting peace that she had experienced moments ago, she began to talk again to God and then to herself.

"For my peace of mind, I need to know when and where this Yankee soldier received his wounds and how he came to be in Hart County. If for no other reason than to satisfy myself that my soldier is not one of the raiders."

Troubled that she was hiding a cussed Yankee soldier who could be one of the raiders, she wanted him awake long enough so she could ask him who shot him and where he was when he was shot.

"I have no way of finding that out except to ask him. If he is one of the raiders, where did he stay until he was shot, and why did he wait until night to visit Riverbend? If he was shot near here, did some men come upon him on the road, thinking he was one of the raiders or not really caring? And did they then shoot him? I wonder if he wounded or killed some of his attackers."

Thinking on that question for a few moments, she remembered that the flap on his holster was still snapped when she had removed the belt and the holster. She exclaimed, "No, there was no exchange of gun fire! I am going to die from curiosity if he does not stay awake long enough for me to ask him how and when he was shot and where he came from."

"It really does not matter who shot him, when he was shot, or how he came to be in Hart County, looking for Mr. Mac. I am still harboring a cussed Yankee soldier." She was mentally scolding herself for giving him shelter and aid.

She added, "No one will ever know he has been here."

"I will keep him hidden until he is able to leave the cave," she promised, once again speaking to herself and the empty room.

Unable to settle down for a nap, she was up and out of the house and on her way to the cave, knowing only that she was anxious to see her soldier. She did not take time to remove her trousers until she reached the riverbank. Undressing to wade along the ledge was becoming a routine task she did with ease, and, in minutes, she was in the water.

I will not linger this time, gazing at the soldier's handsome face, she promised. After she heard of the Yankee Cavalry raid on Hartwell, her hiding the handsome Yankee soldier did not seem the romantic interlude it had earlier.

She could feel his eyes on her, as she moved toward the pallet. *It is a good thing I remembered to put on my trousers before entering the cave, or he would be witnessing my unlady-like fashion.* She chuckled to herself at that revelation, as she knelt beside him to check his wounds. There was no fresh blood, and the bandages were still clean, so she did not see the need to replace them. His eyes continued to watch her every move, as she checked his wounds and bandages.

"Who are you, and where am I? Whose plantation or home did I stumble onto?"

"Names are not important, nor is our location," she replied, hoping to quash his inquires with her reply, but she desperately wanted to know his name, where he came from, and why he was on his way to Riverbend.

"You will be strong enough in a few days to leave here, and all you need to know is we do not want any more Yankee soldiers coming to our home."

"You need not fear me or my men. The war is over, and we

have never intentionally harmed a woman or a child."

"So you say, and, yes, we have heard that the war is over. Your fever seems to be rising, and before it can get any higher, I need to give you a cup of sage tea. It will be night soon, and fevers usually get higher with the setting of the sun." She stood and returned to the fire and mixed the tea.

His eyes continued to follow her every move, and she knew he was trying to get a good look at her face. However, the candlelight kept her features in silhouette. Even when she was checking his wounds, her fat braids had shielded her face, as she bent down.

Needing to raise the soldier's head up so he could drink the tea, she stretched her arm under his shoulders, allowing him to rest against her. The width of his shoulders and the muscles she felt laced across his upper back attested to the strength and the power of the man before he had been taken down by a Reb's rifle ball.

Where he was when he was shot, who shot him, and why he was on his way to see Mr. Mac were questions she desperately wanted answered. So she appealed to him to satisfy her curiosity.

"Would you answer a question or two for me? Will you tell me where you were when you were shot, who shot you, and why you were on your way to the Sinclair plantation?"

"Those are three questions. Although you refused to answer my two questions, I will be polite and answer two of your questions, since you were kind enough to tend to my wounds. I will tell you when and where I became injured, but why I was traveling to the Sinclair plantation is none of your concern."

If you only knew how much your traveling to Riverbend concerns me! she wanted to scream.

"I do not know who shot me, whether rebel soldiers, the home guard, or the locals. The shots came out of the dark. I was on my way to the Sinclair plantation a little before midnight. When I reached the top of the hill above Cedar Creek, shots rang out. How I managed to get to you is a mystery."

She mulled over in her mind his account of his wounding and his refusal to shed any light on why he sought the Sinclair home. *His explanation of how and where he received his wounds is logical. If true, it halfway proves my thoughts of what could have happened, and it proves he did not leave the troops of cavalry on the Athens road to come here, but his refusal to explain his interest in finding the Sinclair plantation reinforces my determination to keep the knowledge of this cave's location a secret.*

The Yankee's fever began rising, as she had predicted, so she gave him another cup of sage tea and finished feeding him the broth. She washed the bowl and the spoon and tended the fire. The tea worked its magic, and the soldier fell into a healing sleep. Tucking the covers snugly around him, she left the cave.

"Pish-posh, I forgot to ask him where he traveled from," she scolded herself angrily. "Why can I not keep a level head around that cussed Yankee?"

CHAPTER 4

The sun was further down the western sky, as Sam walked from the river in the shadowy afternoon of the dying day. She pictured the Yankee in her mind, as he had watched her every move with his feverish eyes. Knowing he was trying to catch a glimpse of her face in the dim candlelight pleased her, for some unknown reason. She was basking in that pleasure, until her musing was interrupted by the sound and sight of two men on horseback, galloping fast from the back of the house and through the cedar grove and onto the plantation road. As she watched the men ride through the cedar grove, she spotted a cloud of dust in the distance. The cloud of dust could mean only one thing. More riders were leaving Riverbend land ahead of the two men she had just seen.

She ran to the house, not taking time to hide that she was downstairs and was entering the warming kitchen without slowing her steps. Just inside the door, she collided with Lovie, causing them both to teeter on the brink of tumbling to the floor.

"What's the matter with you?" Lovie blurted out, as she steadied herself. In Sam's uneasy state, Lovie's words did not even register. Sam was interested only in answers to reasons why she saw two men on horseback riding fast away from the house.

Anxious to know the answers, she looked at Keowee with her intention to know on her face, but before she could pose her questions, David spied her.

"Sam," he called, bringing her attention to him.

"You missed all the excitement," he announced, aglow with the biggest news of his eleven years, but he did not get the chance to relate his story.

Sam turned from David and looked at Keowee. "What excitement?" Sam demanded.

Before Keowee could answer her, Sam's thoughts turned to Floyd, and her eyes searched the room for his face.

"Where is Floyd?" she asked.

"Calm yourself. He be with Santee," Keowee assured her. "They be setting traps. We 's running low on meat, and Santee plans to get us a good-sized boar soes we can have us some fresh meat and hopeful enough to make up a batch of sausages."

Hearing Floyd was with Santee relieved Sam's mind regarding Floyd and brought her back to the two horsemen.

"What excitement Keowee?" Sam asked. "What was David raving about? What has happened? Does it have anything to do with the two men I saw riding away from Riverbend?"

"They had guns," David offered, as he came to stand beside Sam.

"Mercy! Who had guns? Yankees?" Sam asked.

"No, child, no" Keowee said. "Don't get all atwitter; no Yankees been here, although them wild men was a-hunting one."

"Who? What wild men?"

"Lordy, child, I done told you to calm yourself. Just a bunch of ruffians; if they had names, I don't know 'em. They ain't never been to Riverbend afore. The first bunch, that is. They be what's looking for a Yankee soldier. They say they done shot him last night up on the stagecoach road near Cedar Cheek. They say he's one of 'em what done killed poor Doctor Webb yesterday."

Determined not to be ignored, David yanked on Sam's shirtsleeve. "They were mean-looking and loud-talking until one of them spotted the sheriff coming across the back pasture, and they all took off faster than an old jackrabbit."

"Quiet, David; I want to know about the Yankee. Keowee, finish what you were saying, and tell me who the two men were that I saw riding around the house and what they wanted. Explain again who the other riders ahead of them were. I saw a cloud of dust on out a ways from here on the plantation road."

"Child, we was doing some mighty big talking, but I didn't realize it was loud enough to disturb you. Now Sheriff Holland and the other gentleman—I don't rightly remember his name—but they both visited Riverbend lots before the war. Mr. Mac sure did put a lot of stock in them two men. Yes siree; he sure did. Sheriff Holland was checking on us since all that trouble in Hartwell and he'd be chasing 'em ruffians. Says them ruffians be worrying folks all over this part of the county, bragging about they done killed one 'em Yankees what shot up Hartwell. He'd done told 'em to git on home."

Hearing about the gang of ruffians claiming they killed a Yankee near Cedar Creek confirmed Sam's soldier's explanation of where and how he had been shot.

"Keowee, was Sheriff Holland also looking for this Yankee?" Sam asked.

"I should say not," Keowee replied. "He was following that wild bunch to be sure they did as he told 'em to do. To git on home and stop bothering the folks. He was just making sure they did as he told 'em to do."

"Did you have a good rest? Did you sleep any?" Keowee asked, aiming to take Sam's mind off the visitors.

"Do you feel like helping me and Lovie get supper on the table?" Keowee asked. "Our two fellows gonna be here right shortly and they gonna be hungry as two old bears."

With her questions answered, Sam settled in to help getting the evening meal on the table. Her hands were not the only things that were busy. Her mind was filled with not only her leaving the midday meal but also the way in which she had left her family.

Everyone at the evening meal was troubled by the news and events of the day, and even though the raid on Hartwell intensified the vulnerability of Riverbend, Sam found some relief in learning her soldier was more than likely not one of the raiders. Still, Sam wrestled not only with the events of today and the vulnerability of Riverbend but also with her rude actions at midday. Leaving the table halfway through the noon meal bothered her terribly, causing her to ponder making an apology. *I need to apologize to everyone for leaving the table so abruptly.* Accepting her neglectful actions, Sam spoke to the table as a whole.

"Everyone, I am ashamed and sorry for leaving the table so abruptly during the noon meal. Not only did I not excuse myself; I also left too soon after learning the unsettling news of the raid on Hartwell. I should have stayed with you while we dealt with that horribleness together. Please accept my apology, even though the words do not even begin to justify my actions."

The family understood Sam's rapid flight from the warming kitchen and was more than happy to accept her apology. In their own way, they were all dealing with the news of the raid.

Like Sam, Keowee was distressed especially by the news of the raid. The vulnerability of their situation on the secluded plantation bore on her mind, too, and she knew this was behind Sam's reaction to the news of the raid.

After she returned from her late-night visit to the cave, the house was quiet, as Sam meandered up the darkened front stairs, with shoes in hand and her rolled-up trousers tucked under her arm. A short distance from the stop of the stairs, she entered her bedchamber and closed the door. Crossing to the window of her choice, she knelt on the window seat, scanning the moonlit grounds. *What a difference war and time have made* filled her mind. She sighed, as images of yesterday filled her mind. *Riverbend was something to behold in the months following our arrival,* she acknowledged, as memories of her first months on the Sinclair plantation began to emerge. *When we arrived. cotton was still being picked and brought in from the fields. All that month, the plantation was astir with workers—from sunup to sundown.*

Sights and sounds of the busy plantation of old filtered through her memory, and she chuckled and continued thinking, *Oh my, the noise of the place. Quiet came only as the sun slid down toward the western horizon. All work stopped for the night meal, and a peaceful night of sleep, disturbed only by the occasional lowing of a cow or the neighing of a horse..*

"Bewildering as it was, it did not quell the pain in my heart following Papa's death at Manassas and Mama's death at the hands of an unknown," she confessed, as her memories came full circle and her mind filled anew with the losses she had suffered. Turning from the window, she walked to the bed, turned back the covers, as Keowee had advised, crawled in, pulled the light cotton sheet up to her chin, and laid her head on the pillow and cried herself to sleep.

Sometime before dawn, Sam awakened to the semidark room, not knowing the time but feeling rested for the first time in days. Rising from the bed, she smiled as Keowee's comparison of her sleeping in the bed to sleeping in the window seat flashed through her mind.

"I do not know if my rejuvenation can be contributed to bed rest altogether," she speculated. "Or if, perhaps, my emotions were twisted in knots so tight I exploded into oblivion—maybe a little of both." Giggling, she left the room.

The raid on Hartwell, her wounded soldier, and the strange men riding in and out of Riverbend having left her mind for the moment, she was at peace with the world.

Without a care about leaving the house again dressed only in her nightgown and barefooted, she walked boldly down the front stairs and out the front door. The majestic white moon of the night chose that moment to hide behind a cloud. Her eyes adjusting to the dark, she made her way along the path to the river. It was not long before the moon slipped from behind the black cloud, but it played hide-and-seek with the cloud all along the path to the river.

As she stepped into the river, the chilly waters lapped around her legs, causing her to shudder and to suck in her breath for a few moments, shivering till she adjusted to the cool water of the night. Moonbeams danced on the water for a while, as she made her way downstream, and she reminded herself, *I do not have another gown to sacrifice for this Yankee. My gowns were numbered to two when I began this task, and, thanks to the Yankee's blood ruining one, I now have only one— the one I am wearing—so I will pay close attention to where I put my feet in this dark river.*

The overhanging trees blocked the moonlight from the river, as the river began to curve to the right. A few more feet around the bend, and the ledge would disappear. She made sure with each step that her foot touched solid granite before she shifted her weight. Slowly but surely, she came to the end of the ledge.

As she entered the cave, her mind was once again filled with the attack on the town of Hartwell and her betrayal for hiding and tending this wounded Yankee soldier. She was determined to stay only long enough to heat and to feed him some broth. She found flint and candle, and, with one flick, a dim, creamy light spread around her.

The soldier's head was turned in her direction, and his eyes were open, watching her. She faced the Yankee and was not surprised to hear him ask again, "Where am I, and who are you?"

She smiled, knowing he was more lucid now than when he had been on her other visits. She went about stoking the embers of the fire and placed a few sticks of firewood in the pit. She was sure he was trying to get a glimpse of her features, and, for some unknown reason, she did not want the soldier to know her face, even though she was sure she would never see him again after he left the sanctuary of the cave. While the broth was heating, she responded to his inquiry, "We have had this conversation before. Evidently, you do not remember, but, to repeat my last answers, there is no need for names nor concern for our location. For you will soon be well enough to be on your way."

"Do you remember telling me where and how you were shot?" she asked, as she replaced the old bandages with new ones. He did not respond to her reminding him of their earlier conversation, nor did he respond to her answers to his questions. However, she could feel his eyes searching for the least glint of her features that would help him form an image of the person who had tended to his wounds and who would soon be sending him back to where he came from. Fortunately, her hair was not braided and hung loose against her cheek, obscuring her profile from his vision. She had not been bothered before with such determined perusal, and she now attributed his additional curiosity to his improving health.

"The war is over, you know, or so we have been told," she mentioned, hoping to divert his interest away from her."

"Yes, I know," he said. "The armistice was signed on April 9."

"I am curious to know where you were traveling from when you were shot," she said.

"I was traveling from the Low Country of South Carolina," he replied.

These last words were said with difficulty, attesting to his weakened condition.

A smile touched Sam's lips, as she turned to see to the broth. Her smile was not due to his failed ploy to get her to tell him her name and their location but to the delight she had experienced in hearing the deep timbre of his voice, even though the hated Yankee accent was present. She grimaced in disgust at herself for her smiling, wanting to dispute the joy that brought about the smile. While she fed him the broth, her face remained in the shadows of the candlelight. However, the candlelight encircled her bowed head, as she bent to spoon the broth into the Yankee's mouth, giving the appearance of a halo and bringing credence to Colonel Morgan Anderson's earlier, semiconscious image of an angel.

Pleased with his improving health and knowing he would soon drift back into a healing slumber, she bid him good day and left the cave.

While she left the river, pink fingers of dawn rose over the eastern tree line, her walk back across the grounds to the house was slower than her passage to the cave, and the gleeful exuberance she had felt earlier was gone, replaced by a melancholy spirit of loss.

The morning started like any other workday. Santee, the boys, and Sam were working in a field near the house. Keowee and Lovie were weeding the vegetable garden at the back of the house. But, by midmorning, the outdoor work came to a halt, as black thunderclouds gathered in the sky. Santee and the boys skedaddled to the smithy, as the first big drops of rain hit. Sam rushed to the warming kitchen, where there was always some task she could do.

The rain lasted for several hours, giving the ground a good drink of water but leaving the land too wet to continue hoeing or plowing. The wet ground did not mean they would sit idle. Sam helped with the house chores, and Santee sharpened tools in the smithy. Floyd and David dug for worms and headed to the river. Catfish were known to bite a hook after a good rain. The idea of having fried fish for supper made everyone's mouth water for the taste of Keowee's fried catfish.

It was agreed during the meal that since all the indoor chores were done, they would take advantage of the wet ground and treat themselves to either a nap or an activity they enjoyed. Planning to visit the cave sometime during nap time, Sam eyed a slice of buttered bread smeared with honey. Thinking it would be something her soldier would enjoy, she wrapped it separately from the other bread.

"I think I will take this for an afternoon snack," she commented, not saying whose snack and hoping again she had not lied.

While Santee and Keowee napped, Sam selected books from the Sinclair library to occupy Floyd's and David's time. It was not likely the two would close their eyes for a nap, and she used every opportunity she could to keep the boys reading and learning, as did their parents before their deaths. Lemuel, on the other hand, was always ready for a nap. His days were long, too long for a little fellow.

Sam rested for a while, propped in the window seat, with a book she had brought up from the library to read before the arrival of the Yankee. After several minutes of her inattentive response to the book, she laid it aside, opting for a short visit to the cave.

The Yankee was resting peacefully, with no sign of fever. Standing for a while, she watched his restful breathing and was thankful she had tended to the Yankee soldier's wounds, even if her Christian duty made her a traitor to her papa and the Confederacy. She knew that her traitorous deed would be a secret burden she would carry for the remainder of her life and that she would carry the image of the handsome Yankee's face forever in her mind. Tears clouded her eyes, as she placed the wrapped slice of bread on her soldier's chest and slipped from the cave. She had stayed only a few minutes; as hard as it had been, she was able to deal with her curiosity and not to linger. As she opened the front door, a whiff of frying cat-fish assailed her wet nose, making her smile in anticipation of the meal to come, with gravy and maybe mashed potatoes, if any could be found in the potato hill Keowee fixed last fall. She grinned as she remembered Keowee working Floyd and David all one afternoon, making them bring buckets after buckets full of dry river sand to pour over layer after layer of potatoes she had arranged in the empty stall.

Once again, Sam climbed the stairs to the second floor, as her family would be expecting her to enter the warming kitchen from the back stairs. Sam turned her attention to placing plates, forks, and knives by each plate, along with the glasses for the milk.

Fried fish, mashed potatoes, creamed gravy, and green beans canned from last year's garden finally covered the table, and, as always, they were all standing behind their chair, anxiously awaiting Keowee's signal to be seated.

The fish was cooked just right, and the meal was everything Sam had expected, but her mind was not on the delicious food. She was lost in her own little world of her confused thoughts, when Santee's words, "Yankee cavalry," penetrated her thoughts.

"What did you say?" Sam asked, interrupting Santee. "Please repeat your last sentence. I did not quite hear all you said."

Santee, along with everyone else at the table, looked at Sam with disbelief, unable to understand why she had not heard every word Santee was saying.

"I said me and Floyd ran into a few Yankees today, while checking our traps; now if you will just let me get on with my tale, you will know all that I know, Missy."

"I am sorry I interrupted, but I thought I heard you say Yankee cavalry," Sam said.

"Well, Missy," Santee replied, in his soft, kind voice, "they shor nuff was dressed in that blue uniform we have heard so much about, and they shor nuff was all riding fine horses. Finest I seen in a coon's age."

"Were they on Riverbend land?" Sam asked, her voice quivering as she posed the question, and, again, all eyes were on her. She was usually the strong one, trying never to allow the others to witness any sign of fear. Her temper could explode, yes, but never her fear. However, Yankee soldiers coming to Riverbend was a horror they all wished never to see.

"I reckon so," Santee replied. "They been scouting this area for a few hours, before me and Floyd ran into 'em up on Cedar Creek, and I reckon they could have been over some of our woods and fields. I don't think they been as far as the house, or they would have made 'emselves known to you. A big, red-haired man did all the talking, and he was not bashful about asking questions."

"Biggest man I ever saw," Floyd offered, his attention never leaving the plate of fried fish sitting in front of him. Nothing ever interfered with his meals. It did not matter what Keowee put on the table, just as long as he got his share.

"Did they threaten you or harm you?" Sam asked, her words hardly more than a whisper.

"Either of you? In any way?"

"No, Missy," Santee answered hurriedly, wanting to relieve Sam of her unease. "Just stopped us and wanted to know if we seen a lone Yankee officer in these parts. Said he left camp night before last to visit a plantation on this side of the river."

"Are they some of the Yankees that raided Hartwell and killed Doctor Webb?" Sam asked, before Santee could tell her more.

"Do they know the war is over?" Sam asked.

"They ain't part of the troops that raided Hartwell," Santee said. "This group has been camped over on the east bank of the river for the last two nights. They left their camp around noon today, after their officer failed to return, and they crossed the river in search of the missing man. They said the officer crossed the river before midnight, night before last, but did not return to camp the next day, like he planned. Thinking he was having a pleasant visit at the plantation he was to visit, they were not concerned, but when he failed to return this morning, that changed. They started a search, and, yes, they know the war be over 'cause that was the first thing they told us. They also told us part of 'em would be camped up on Cedar Creek till they find their missing officer."

Chuckling, Santee looked at his wife and said, "I didn't exactly get to tell my big tale, did I? But I sure got to answer a heap of questions." Shaking his head and laughing, he returned to his supper.

All was quiet in the warming kitchen after Santee finished his account of his and Floyd's afternoon, except for the clinking of forks against plates. The missing officer occupied the thoughts of the usually talkative group. They were all strangely quiet, lost in their own thoughts.

"Where you reckon he be?" Keowee asked, breaking the hushed silence hanging over the room, putting into words the question all, except one, were thinking about.

"I bet he be the same soldier them ruffians been hunting," Keowee went on, "bragging all over the county they done shot him."

"Reckon he be dead?" she asked Santee with a more solemn tone, adding sorrowfully before he could answer, "If he be dead, we's be seeing the buzzards circling soon enough."

"If he is dead, I hope he ain't on Sinclair land," Santee said, worrying with the spoon in his empty cup. "'Cause I done told them soldier boys we's not seen no Yankee anywhere around here."

"You have not, have you?" Sam asked, hoping she was the only one of her family who knew the location of the missing Yankee soldier.

Santee's words had reminded both Sam and Keowee of the dangerous position of their family—danger not only from Yankee soldiers camped at the edge of Riverbend land but from any man or men unscrupulous enough to take advantage of their unprotected state since the death of Mr. Mac.

Alone in her room, Sam sat in her favorite window, wondering what the night would bring and knowing she dared not leave the house till all were asleep. Waiting for the others to fall asleep seemed unending, longer than any of the nights before. Sam became more fidgety by the minute. Her mind filled with the truth of her deed. *Now troops of Union cavalry are poking around, looking for their missing officer. Hiding this Yankee from the local people and my family was one thing, but to add Yankee cavalry to that list is more than I want to deal with.* Her fear of the Union army made the Yankees camped at the edge of Sinclair land frightening enough, but that they were searching for her soldier put her in a worse dither than she had been in since Mr. Mac died.

It is too much of a coincidence for both Yankees and ruffians to be looking for just any old Yankee soldier. They have to be searching for my soldier. The knowledge that it was time for him to leave made her feel odd, bringing tears to her eyes. *I am turning into a complete watering pot. I just do not understand myself these days; it must be all that has happened in the last two days, and my fear of Yankees.*

She should have found those tears more perplexing and looked for the reason for the tears, but she refused to acknowledge to herself or to let herself think that the soldier's departure could affect her emotions in any way, except relief. She blindly contributed becoming teary-eyed to her fear of being so near a Yankee camp, and she closed her mind to any other possibilities, convinced that everyone concerned would be better off, herself included, when she put her soldier on his horse, led horse and soldier up the river to the Yankee camp, and disappeared back to Riverbend.

The silver moon once again lit her way across the grounds to the bank of the river and around to the granite bolder. The cave was dark as Hades, but she was conscious of the soldier's presence the minute she entered the cave. Her delight of being near him did not ignite her curiosity as to why she had this elation.

She rushed across the smooth granite floor, her wet feet padding toward the straw mattress that held her soldier, her thoughts only of her soldier. *These two days I have focused solely on keeping my soldier's presence a secret, and not once have I given any thought to a plan for my soldier's leaving.* As this thought registered clearly in her mind, the two words, "my soldier," were a powerful blow. The two words echoed in her mind and froze her in her tracks. She stopped so suddenly she almost pitched forward onto her face. She had not been conscious of developing a possessiveness toward the Yankee soldier, nor did she think of him as her soldier.

Why did I just refer to that cussed Yankee as "my soldier"? she pondered. *I really must be on the brink of insanity, or I am acting like a silly goose.*

I hate Yankees. They killed Papa, she reminded herself sorrowfully. Embarrassed now by what she thought to be silly, girlish behavior, she felt her tears of shame turn to anger. For the first time since making the decision to tend to the Yankee's wounds, she balled her hands up into fists, wanting to strike the cussed Yankee. To punish him.

"It is one thing to be charitable out of Christian duty, but to claim a cussed Yankee as my own—never!" she expounded through her tears.

"Have I used those two words before?" she sadly whispered, shaking her head in denial, as she finished asking the question. And she answered, "Surely not. I know I would not have called him that," but a thought, *at least not consciously,* flashed through her mind.

"Well, he certainly is not my anything," she huffed. "Except my enemy!"

Satisfied that the two words, "my soldier," were just a one-time error in identification, she stomped angrily toward the sleeping soldier. She pounced on the Yankee, swinging with all her might at his face with both of her fist, but hands came out of the dark, gripping both of her wrists with the power to break the bones. Not only were her blows halted; she was also pulled across the soldier's body and beneath him, as he turned onto his stomach as quickly as a flash of lightning. His chest pinned her to the floor under him and while his hands held her hands above her head, he demanded to know, in a voice ringing with authority, "What the devil are you trying to do, lady? Are you trying to kill me after tending to my wounds and saving my life? If you wanted me dead, all you had to do was let me bleed to death." As Colonel Morgan Anderson realized that he had his angel right where he wanted her and and as he did not really care what her intention was at the moment, his voice mellowed, and he whispered, "Sweetie, you really do not want to kill me."

Releasing her hands, his fingers found a home in the soft, silky curls of Sam's hair, as his lips covered her lips and Sam experienced her first kiss.

His lips were soft and moist against Sam's mouth and very pleasing, filling her with wonder and joy she had never imagined existed. Her hands slowly uncurled, sliding up the rough texture of what was left of his blue Yankee jacket. Suddenly, the movement of his lips stopped, and the weight of the soldier's body became heavy against her chest. She lay motionless, in a breathless haze, unable to think clearly for a moment, but as her senses returned and her mind began to work, she recalled the Yankee grabbing her wrists, pulling her beneath him. Her hands again became fists, hammering his shoulders with all her might, fueled by her anger. Her attack was useless. He lay atop her, unmoving, feeling nothing.

His limited strength was exhausted from fending off her fisticuffs and kissing her.

With an effort that came from panic, she pushed him away and stood. Furious that her attempt to punish him had failed, she staggered into the night air, mad as a wet hen.

"I did not hurt him in the least bit. I just exhausted him!" she spat.

Stopping suddenly, she yelled, "He kissed me! The cussed Yankee kissed me!"

"My first kiss, and it came from a cussed Yankee soldier," she muttered disgustedly through gritted teeth. "What is even more disgusting is I must have let him. I did nothing to stop him."

She was shaken as the memory of that kiss brought a whispering memory of her soldier's lips caressing her lips. The euphoric feeling of the soft pressure of his lips moving on hers was as real, for a moment, as if he were still kissing her. She sighed as the memory brought a confusing truth, and she shamefully admitted, *I enjoyed his kiss and the way it made me feel.* As the feel of his lips on hers filled her being, tears clouded her eyes and, with the tears, there came a hint of sorrow and a feeling of loss. But anger soon followed. She welcomed the anger and savored her ire. *That cussed Yankee took liberties after I tended to his wounds and saved his life.*

Aiming all her fury at the soldier occupying the cave she had used to keep him safe, she called him every bad name she could think off, ranting and raving until her anger cooled. She could deal with her anger, and she hardened her heart, refusing to surrender to the soft, quiet, mysterious pleasure the memory of his kiss had brought.

"The South is defeated," she sobbed. "Doomed to be ruled by Yankees for some time, but I will rid my life and this plantation of one cussed Yankee this night."

With the bitterness of the South's defeat and the death of her papa in her heart and mind, she took swift, long strides that carried her back into the cave and to the Yankee's pallet. Moving, as if in a trance, she saddled the horse, readying it for travel. The nubbin of the last candle spit and sputtered, threatening to flicker out, as it cast a dim light across the room, erasing only a smidgen of the darkness.

Locating a pair of old, discarded boots, she slipped them on her feet. *I will need the protection of these this night, for the path will be strewn with snags and briars; it is not a smooth and easy way, but the most direct.*

With the toe of her boot, she poked the sleeping soldier in his ribs, awakening him from his exhausted, deep sleep. Before he could complain, she reached down and pulled on his uninjured arm, issuing an order to rise and mount his horse.

"Yankee, it is time for you to leave. I'm taking you to some Yankees camped near here."

Resisting her tug on his arm and thinking of the camp on the east bank of the river, he offered what he thought was the perfect solution, "You don't have to take me. Just send word to Captain Haygood, and he will fetch me."

"No," she yelled, as she continued to urge him up. "I will not bring another son of a Yankee snake to my home and put my family at a greater risk. I do not trust you blue bellies, and I am questioning where I put my brains when I decided to help you."

Angry tears welled up in her eyes, as she harshly told him, "You have overstayed your welcome, Yankee. Now get on your horse."

He rolled to his knees and grabbed the stirrup of Zeus's saddle with his left hand, pulling his body up. He was determined to make her realize that there was no danger to her or her family from him or his men, but standing for the first time since taking the rebel's bullets made him dizzy. He fell against his horse, grabbing the saddle horn with a death grip. Her words were jumbled in his groggy brain, but somehow he knew that she needed for him to mount Zeus and that she was taking him to his men. All the rest of her accusations, accented with pain and tears, were lost in his foggy mind. With her help, he mounted his horse and gave into the black void that was lingering on the edge of his consciousness. He never heard her order: "Hold on, Yankee, and keep your mouth shut, for the night has ears, and they might not be too friendly."

She led him up the riverbank to the place where Cedar Creek emptied into the Savannah River and waded across. The water came almost to her waist, but she gave no thought to a wet gown this night. Her mind was busy with plans to skirt around the Yankee camp and to approach it from the opposite direction from Riverbend.

The dense woods were more than dark, but the hefty pine trees grew in a pattern of sorts, making it easy for her to forge a path, and the dry pine needles cushioned the sound of her footfalls and the horse's hooves. She smelled the smoke of the Yankee campfires, as she neared the camp, and she proceeded with caution, afraid she would step on a sentry before she saw him. The sound of shuffling feet a short distance in front of her alerted her to the posted guard. Stopping a short pace in front of the man, she placed the reins she was holding around the saddle horn and eased back along the horse's side, brushing against the soldier's leg, as she retreated to the rear of the horse. Satisfied the horse was headed straight toward the sentry, she gave a strong whack to the horse's rump.

"Wounded Yankee coming in!" Sam yelled through clasped hands, as she disappeared back into the cover of the dark forest.

"Captain, it's the colonel," the sentry yelled, as he led the horse carrying Colonel Morgan Anderson into the camp.

Moving to the center of the camp, he continued to holler, "Captain Haygood."

"It's the colonel, Captain, and he's wounded."

The camp erupted with men scrambling from their bedrolls, as Captain Haygood stumbled barefoot from his bedroll.

"What the blazes is going on?" hollered Haygood.

However, in the dying light of the campfire, Haygood spied the familiar horse and hurried to his friend, issuing orders as he ran.

"Get him down off that horse and onto my bedroll," he hollered, turning his attention to the sentry with questions: "Who brought him in? And where the devil is the Reb?"

"Corporal, did you kill the Reb?"

"No sir. I saw no one, Captain. The colonel came out of the darkness. There was no one with him. I heard someone yell, "Wounded Yankee coming in," and the colonel appeared out of the darkness right in front of me."

Eager to see to his friend, he sent the corporal back to his post and returned to the site of his bedroll.

Squatting beside his motionless friend, Haygood looked Morgan over very carefully, scrutinizing every inch of him, from his two-day growth of beard to the ripped and cut uniform coat and shirt, from the clean bandages on his right shoulder to the slit in his right trouser leg and another bandage. He noticed especially the cleanness of the bandages and his friend that was not covered in Union blue. He was satisfied someone took very good care of his friend. *If Morgan would only wake up and answer some questions, I would rest easy.*

"Morgan, can you hear me? It's Haygood. Where have you been, and what happened to you? We have looked this area over and could not find hide nor hair of you."

"Angel, *Angel*," Morgan mumbled, hearing Haygood's voice. *"Angel where are you? Angggg . . . "*

"Captain, he is out of his head," Sergeant Bishop whispered worriedly.

"He's calling for an angel," the sergeant continued.

"No, he is not feverish, Sergeant," Captain Haygood said. "Just exhausted. Someone patched him up real good. It probably was an angel, an earthly angel." A smile creased Haygood's gloomy face for the first time in two days.

"A Southern earthly angel, and, from the looks of what's left of his bloody uniform and the bandages, he was hurt bad. No doubt, he bled a lot, and that Southern angel has been taking good care of him. After a good night's sleep, he will answer all our questions."

Sam hurried back through the woods and was running by the time she stepped into the water of the creek. She had a hard time suppressing her giggles, as she pictured Yankees trying to follow her in that dark thicket. They were, after all, interlopers, and they did not know the lay of those woods as she did. There were bound to be some sore noggins, bruised shins, and a few other banged-up unmentionable parts in the morning if they had tried to follow her.

Wet, dirty, and weary Sam stopped at the veranda steps and, in the moonlight, looked down at her soggy nightgown soaked with creek water and splattered with the same filth that covered her arms and legs.

"I sure need a bath," she said to herself, "but I am too tired to heat water and tote it up to my room. Besides, I am also a wee bit too dirty to enter the warming kitchen."

Running her fingers through hair stiff with the evidence of her night's travels, she knew there was only one place to get herself clean enough to sleep on Keowee's clean linens, and she headed straight to the well house and the large tub Santee and the boys used for bathing. The water placed in the tub earlier that evening after the last bather would not be hot, but it would be considerably warmer than water fresh from the well. There would also be soap and towels, because Keowee always kept a good supply on the shelf above the tub.

Holding her breath, she eased first one foot and then the other into the cool water and slowly immersed her body, goose bumps and all. Her body became acclimated to the cool water, and she pulled her nightgown over her head, lathering it well with soap, before dunking it several times into the water, rinsing away the dirt and the soapsuds. Her hair was next to get a good scrubbing, and, finally, she washed the dirt and the creek water from her body. Standing, she pulled the plug from the tub, allowing the dirty water to drain, and she poured buckets of clean water over her head and rinsed away soap and dirty water from her body.

Stepping from the tub onto the wooden platform surrounding the tub, she wrapped herself in a large sheet of toweling.

Wanting to leave the tub as it was found, she drew buckets and buckets of water from the well and filled the tub and rinse buckets. Taking her wet, but clean, gown, she hurried back to the house and her room for a few hours of sleep.

CHAPTER 5

As dawn broke the eastern sky, old red crowed his welcome to the Sabbath.

Sam opened her eyes to the dim light of the approaching morn; stretching lazily, she found a stiff back and sore muscles and complained, "Delivering that cussed Yankee to his men caused me to use muscles I am not accustom to using, and the trek to the Yankee camp must have been a longer walk than I had expected, because I am still tired."

Thankful the day was Sunday and there would be no work done in the fields, she rolled over onto her side, planning to sleep a little longer. The house was quiet, except for the faint sounds of Santee's snoring filtering up the back stairs. A comforting smile spread across her lips, as she listened to the familiar sound, but before the sun could completely push away the night, Sam's bare feet hit the floor with a thud that echoed across the silent room. The bed could hold her no longer.

"There is no rest for me here," she declared, scurrying across the cool floor. My body is too stiff and sore for me to go back to sleep." Ready to quit the bedchamber in lieu of the comfort of the warming kitchen in the early morning hours, she slipped from the room.

The pitter-patter of Sam's feet, the occasional squeak of a

disturbed board, and Santee's soft snores were the only noises in the quiet house at that time of the morning. However, slight the sound of her tread, it was magnified in the stillness of the morning, making her long for the thick carpet that once graced the hall floors.

As she hurried by the nursery, she detected no sound of Lemuel stirring or any sounds from across the hall, where Floyd and David slept, an indication she hoped that they were still fast asleep and would remain so for several more hours.

She needed no candle to light the back stairs, as she made her way to the large brick room adjacent to the back of the manor house. In years past, when the plantation was prosperous and alive with people, the warming kitchen could not have been her private, early-morning refuge. Females of all ages would have been slowly filling the room, ready to prepare the food from the outer kitchen for serving to the Sinclair family. Now it was the keeping room for the unique family calling Riverbend home. A room of peace and comfort.

Faint odors of the fried catfish the family shared last evening lingered in the cool air of the kitchen and attacked Sam's senses as she entered, making her mouth water for Keowee's breakfast that was soon to come.

She had eaten very little of the evening meal that she had waited all afternoon to enjoy.

News of Yankee cavalry camped a short distance from Riverbend's borders had stolen her appetite. Sam occupied herself with lighting the fire for the morning, trying to keep busy in the grey light of the coming day and not to think of her empty stomach or her Yankee soldier.

Coals from the previous night fire smoldered in the back of the chimney, and she pulled the hot embers to the front of the fireplace, laying on pine knots and wood from the wood box.

The flames would soon lick upward, she knew, and the blaze would give forth both warmth and light. Taking a shawl she found hanging on the back of the staircase door, she wrapped it snug around her shoulders, and she pulled a chair close to the hearth, waiting for the warmth to fill the room.

Sam smiled, as she watched the flames dance across the logs. The peaceful calm of the room was a balm to her tired body and the gloomy feeling of loss. In time, she relaxed, and her eyes closed. Asleep at last.

The creaking of the outer door and the swishing of feet being wiped on the moss-covered, whistling path woke Sam, telling her that her time of solitude was over.

Keowee, her ally, her friend, and the woman she and the boys considered their substitute mother since October 1862, would soon be coming through the door from the outside.

Santee, Keowee, and Lovie were the nearest thing to a family Sam and the boys had. The black couple had put the four under their protective care from day one, and, in her bossy, unopposed way, Keowee had run interference for the four, even with Mr. Mac. *We showed up on the front steps of this plantation, uninvited, in an old, one-horse wagon, weary, dusty, and hungry. Keowee was a measure of mercy from the beginning.* Sam smiled, as she again recalled her first meeting with Keowee, and the smile grew wider, as the familiar figure nudged through the back door.

"Aha, caught you dillydallying again," Keowee mocked, as she spied Sam awake but still lounging in front of the fire. Placing the contents of her apron on the table, she announced her good fortune, "I visited the hens early this day before any uninvited guest could help themselves to our eggs. On second thought, maybe Santee be right. There ain't nothing stealing our eggs. Them hens just have off days now and again, I guess."

So did Keowee confess, sneaking a glance at Sam, as she busied herself with preparing to start the morning meal. One look told Keowee the night was long and without much sleep for Sam. Dark circles were etched under Sam's eyes, revealing that more than a few hours had passed without sleep.

Sam giggled at Keowee's excitement at finding an abundance of eggs, but she knew she would gladly share her bounty. They were blessed with being able to grow enough food to feed their small group, and they always stood ready to give to the less fortunate, should any come by. The bond that had developed between the three former slaves and the Hatcher siblings over the years was strong. The thought of being ripped from this kindred attachment, should the day come, was terrifying.

Sam wrestled with that possibility off and on after Mr. Mac's death, but, this morning, her mind was filled with thoughts of the kindness of this dear woman.

"Keowee, do you remember the day the boys and I came to Riverbend and how you took charge of us, issuing orders right and left for our care, even before Mr. Mac said we could stay?"

Keowee was unprepared for what she thought might follow that question, as Keowee jerked her head around toward Sam, her face mirroring her uneasiness at the question. She had hoped that the who and why concerning that time in Sam's life had been buried with Mr. Mac and that Sam's curiosity would find other roads to tread. However, knowing Sam and her inquisitive nature, Keowee knew the questions would never be completely quieted until Sam had her answers. She would keep asking, until, one day, the truth would be unraveled. She just hoped that Sam would have a strong protector when that day came and she finally found the answers to all her questions.

Unfettered by Keowee's stare and her uneasy countenance

Sam continued, "You took us under your wing right away, and I have wondered at times what you would have done if Mr. Mac had refused to allow us to stay. After all, he did not seem overjoyed with our arrival. It was more like he tolerated us, but that is neither here nor there. I was just remembering your kindness on that October day in 1862, and the loving care you have given these nearly three years. Thank you, dear Keowee, for that delicious buttered bread with blackberry jam on that day and for all that has followed."

It would be some time before Keowee would need Sam's help with the morning meal. Leaning back with her feet up, she savored the comfort of the fire, as its warmth flowed through her stiff body, soothing her sore muscles.

Unbeknown to Sam, Keowee dealt with fears of her own—that the unjust deeds put in play by the cunning exploits born within the halls of Riverbend years earlier and again amidst the revelry of war would grow, manifesting more evil and pain on the children of Martha Hatcher.

Sundays were peaceful and restful days for the seven. After a good morning meal, the table would be cleared, the dishes would be washed, and the household would have their weekly Sunday worship time.

Sam started the Bible reading and prayer time soon after the siblings arrived at Riverbend. Although Cokesbury Church was up on the stage coach road, not far from the plantation, an invitation from Mr. Sinclair for the children to accompany him was never issued. Sam and the boys formed the habit of gathering in her bedchamber every Sunday after the morning meal for their Bible reading and prayer. When Mr. Mac became ill, Santee, Keowee, and Lovie moved into the main house to be able to care for the master round the clock, joining the siblings in their Sunday worship. The warming kitchen became the meeting place for the seven to worship and remained so after Mr. Mac's death. Sam thought it not wise to attend the local church, since they were trying to remain as inconspicuous as possible. She thought it best not to fan the gossip mill by making an appearance and explaining their existence at Riverbend. Keowee and Santee agreed. So, every Sunday, they had their Sunday worship in the kitchen and not in Sam's bedchamber.

Mealtime was a time of togetherness; talking and laughing and Sunday meals were no different. Events of the past week were usually the main topic of conversation. However, on this particular Sunday, as the family finished their meal and the spiels of jokes and laughter were winding down, they all agreed they hoped they had seen the last of ruffians, sheriffs, and Yankee cavalry. They also agreed they had seen enough of all three this last week to last a lifetime. After the midday meal, the table was cleared, leftover food was stored for later use, and the seven wandered off in different directions.

Needing to wait for the night and everyone to be sound asleep was crucial, and Sam knew the waiting would make the day long. Yes, the wait would be long.

Colonel Morgan Anderson slept late into the afternoon of the first day back with his men and awoke groggy and grouchy. Shards of sunlight shining through the leafy canopy above his head were the first thing he noticed, and he knew he was no longer in hiding. Turning his head, he looked straight into a familiar face, but it was not the face he had wished to see.

"How did I get here and what have you done with angel? Where is she, Haygood? You best not have harmed her."

"Well, it is good to see you, too. Just because the big bear has awakened in a grouchy mood, you do not have to growl at me. I am not hard of hearing, and another thing or two I would like to point out: I am not the bloody one who shot you, and I am not the one who has been missing."

"Haygood. I will not ask you again. Where is she?"

"Who?"

"My angel! The young lady who took the rifle ball out of my shoulder and the lead out of my leg and who kept me hidden. You had to have seen her. She would have been the one who brought me to this camp. It is the only way I could have gotten here—unless you came and fetched me."

"Morgan, there was no one with you, much less an angel."

"Then how did I get here? Someone had to have brought me, and my angel was the only one who knew about me. Someone had to have seen her. Who was on guard duty?"

"Corporal Brown was standing guard, and he saw no one."

"What the! On guard duty when I was brought into camp, and he saw no one with me?"

"He saw Zeus, and then you lying across the neck of the horse. The horse walked right out of the darkness, almost stepping on him. Recognizing Zeus probably saved you from another bullet. For all we know, your horse brought you to camp."

"Pray tell me: what was Brown doing? Was he sleeping? A person does not just walk in and out of a Union army camp unnoticed. Especially not an angel. Bring Brown to me. I want to question him, and he'd better be able to tell me more than you have."

"Morgan, Brown saw no one. He heard a shout, "Wounded Yankee coming in," just as Zeus came out of the darkness. But he saw no one, not even a female."

Pushing himself up with his left hand and resting on his left forearm, Morgan barked, "Bring the corporal to me—now!"

"Morgan."

"Now! Haygood."

"Washington is going to have us listed as deserters before we leave the South," Haygood mumbled, as he left Morgan in search of Corporal Brown.

"You wanted to see me, Colonel?"

"Yes, if you are the one who failed to detain the lady who brought me into camp."

"Colonel, there was no lady or anyone with you. Zeus came out of the darkness of the forest, walking right to me. There was no one leading the animal or walking beside the horse. No lady would have dared to be in these woods alone that late at night. I did hear a muffled shout, "Wounded Yankee coming in," just a second or two before I saw Zeus. Until then, I heard no twigs breaking, no footsteps or nothing. It was as if Zeus was a ghost. He just appeared out of the darkness. There was not even the sound of anyone retreating."

"Go over it again and tell me everything, no matter how unimportant you might think it to be, and then explain why you did not apprehend the person shouting to you, 'A wounded Yankee approaching.'"

"Begging your pardon, sir, but I have told you everything."

"Why did you not investigate where the voice came from? Why did you not, Corporal? Were you afraid?"

"No sir, I was not afraid. My first priority was to you, sir, getting you inside the camp and to Captain Haygood. We spent the biggest part of the day searching for you, sir. I could tell you were hurt, sir, but I could not tell how bad."

"Morgan," Captain Haygood said, "you are being unreasonable. It is dark as hades in this patch of woods after the sun goes down, and it was midnight or later when you were brought to camp. Unless you are familiar with this area, you would not be able to successfully maneuver without some source of light, and Corporal Brown saw no light. Whoever brought you in must really have known their way around these woods. Are you sure the lady that tended to you brought you to camp? She could have gotten a servant or a family member to bring you."

"Corporal, what direction did Zeus come from?"

"North, sir."

"Haygood, are we still camped on the east side of the river?"

"Yes, and no."

"What kind of a fool answer is that? You are not making any sense."

"Dismissed, Corporal," Captain Haygood ordered, before responding to Morgan's statement.

Turning toward the captain, Corporal Brown replied, "Yes sir." Saluting both officers, he returned to his bedroll.

"All right, Haygood, explain."

"Jameson, Whitfield, Adams, Seawright, and Madison are in the camp on the east bank of the river. I brought the other five with me to search for you. We left the base camp yesterday morning, after you failed to return. We searched the rest of the day and made camp here, near the creek, just before sundown. The black man we met and talked to late in the afternoon called the creek 'Cedar Creek.'"

"Where did you meet this black man?"

"A short distance south of where we are now. The other side of the creek."

"What farm or plantation was the black man from?"

"He did not say, and I only questioned him about seeing a lone Yankee soldier. He and a boy with him denied knowing anything about any Yankee. He told me his name, but it has slipped my mind. It was an unusual name. He was tall and looked more Indian than African. He and the boy were checking their traps."

"His name was Santee."

"Yes. Yes, that was his name. How did you know that?"

"You were on Riverbend land. Did you mention my name to him?"

"No."

"You can rest assured he knew nothing about me. If he had, he would have taken you to me. Riverbend is the plantation I was planning to visit. After I was shot, I escaped from my attackers in a forest of dense woods much like these and became disoriented. God only knows where I ended up. Haygood, I need to find my angel. She saved my life."

"Who attacked you? Soldiers, home guards, or citizens?"

"I have no idea. The shots came out of the night, as one of the attackers shouted, 'There is one of them murdering blue bellies.'"

"Several of the people we talked to yesterday said the town of Hartwell was raided by Yankee cavalry early in the morning three days ago. That would have been the morning of the day we arrived across the river. The town was bound to be up in arms about a raid and the killing of the town's doctor. Might be why you were shot. Not a friendly place to be right now. We got to hightail it back across the river. We do not want to be the cause of the war starting up again, and I hate to be an I-told-you-so. But!"

"I do not want to hear it. I want to find my angel. Send out a patrol. Have them look for her."

"Look for whom? What does she look like? What is her name? We have talked to everyone up the river from where we camped and down the river to where we met this Santee. No one knew anything about you. If you can give the men a description or a last name, even a first name, they might be able to locate her, but you say she kept you hidden. If she told none of her family or servants about you while she was tending to your wounds, more than likely she will not admit to having nursed you."

"I cannot give the men a description. I had only glimpses of a shadowy figure. I have only the memory of the sound of her voice. Most of the time, I was unconscious or burning with fever. She is a spitfire of a young lady. I can tell you that she also hates Yankees but that her compassion for her wounded enemy overshadowed her Southern hatred for this Yankee by far."

Morgan's voice softened, as he gave the only description he had of his angel, and he turned away from Haygood, lost in his thoughts. Haygood heard the chuckles escaping from down deep in Morgan's chest, as he finished speaking of his angel lady, and the look on Morgan's face intrigued him.

I have got to meet this angel lady somehow, and I have a feeling it will not be too far in the future. I want to see for myself what is so special about a female that Morgan Anderson cannot even describe but yet she can have this effect on him.

"You can come back later after things quiet down and look for your angel. You sure she is of this world?" Haygood asked, smiling.

"Yes. I was wounded, but I still could tell the difference between a real live woman and a spirit."

The memory came to Colonel Morgan Anderson, *Of the tender care of her callused hands, the melodious sound of her voice, and her clean sweet fragrance.*

"Yes, I could tell the difference," Morgan repeated.

As he continued to ponder his angel and her care of him, he wondered, *Who cares for her? Does she have someone who loves her and would see to her needs and protection? Is she all alone in this war-torn land?* All these questions brought a longing for him to be the one to see that she was safe and cared for. It had been a long time since he had cared for a woman's welfare.

Leaving his friend's side, Haygood gave orders to break camp, moving Morgan to the camp across the river.

***

Sam was sitting in the window seat, as she did most evenings, watching the night spread its blanket of darkness over the shambles of the Sinclair plantation. Her ears were attuned to every sound around, waiting patiently for the silence of peaceful slumber of her family. At last, she was rewarded with hearing only the groans and creaks of the ageing house. The time to make her last trip to the cave was here. She was still reluctant to examine her feelings of sadness and loss, as she walked the ledge, up the bank, and into the cave. The cave was black as pitch and empty. If nothing else conveyed to her the cause of her feeling of loss and of the knots in her stomach, entering the empty cave slapped it right in her face.

"He's gone forever," she whispered, as she slumped to the floor. While she sat Indian-style on the granite floor, her face in her hands, tears flowed down her cheeks.

Oblivious to the passing of time, as seconds ticked into minutes and as minutes gave way to more minutes, she wept.

Her tears stopped as quickly as they had begun. Stubborn to the last, she brushed the last teardrops from her face with the back of her hand. "Gracious, I am in need of a lot of sleep if I can cry because the cussed Yankee is gone and I am alone. I rarely cry."

I am not myself!" she blurted out.

After she found flint to light the candle she had brought from the house, there was soon enough light to tidy the room. She gathered up the jar that held the broth, which needed to be returned to the house, and she turned her attention to the pallet, where the soldier had lain. Folding the quilts and returning them to the shelf, she stripped the pillow and straw mattress of sheet and pillowcase. As she lifted the sheet, something fell to the floor, making a tinkling sound as it hit the granite. After putting the sheet and the jar in the pillowcase for easy carrying, she brought the candle nearer the pallet, placing it on the floor. With better light to search for the fallen object, she sank to her knees and scanned the area. Something sparkled in the candlelight just to her right, appearing to be some kind of metal. The moment she picked the object up, she knew what it was. The gold chain and pendant her soldier wore around his neck. She saw it every time she bandaged his shoulder or bathed his chest. Puzzled as to how the piece of jewelry came to be here and not around his neck, she held the chain up, examining the chain and the clasp carefully. "The clasp is still fastened, and the chain is not broken," she spoke aloud to the empty cave. "He had to have purposely taken the chain off, slipping it over his head."

"But why?" she whispered, staring at the chain and pendant in disbelief. She stood for a long time, while holding the chain and the pendant, pondering the why, as she rubbed her thumb over the face of the pendant. She decided, *He left this for me, leaving something to remember him by.*

Elated with that thought and with having something personal of her soldier that she could keep close to her, something no one else would be able to see, Sam bent her head and slipped the chain over her head and around her neck, letting the pendant fall to rest between her breasts. With tears burning her eyes, but a smile on her lips, for the first time tonight, she picked up the bundle of dirty sheets, the jar, and the Yankee scabbard with firearm intact and made her way to the house.

Hoping for several hours of sleep before old red crowed his announcement of the first day of the week, she dressed in her only nightgown and stretched out in the comfortable bed of her borrowed room, but sleep would not come. Her brain refused to shut down, and thoughts of the Yankee soldier plagued her. *Maybe I should not have moved him. I could have hidden him a few more days, but I was so angry. Me and my cussed temper, she fumed. What if it was too soon to move him after he lost so much blood? His coat and shirt were soaked with his blood before I started my probing, and he bled like a stuck hog, until I got that rifle ball out of his shoulder. Mercy, he might have been dead when I sent him into that Yankee camp.*

"Please, Heavenly Father, let him still be alive," she prayed. "Do not let him die. Please do not let anything bad happen to him because of my temper." She tried to console herself that, from all appearances, he was a strong and healthy young man before he was shot. *He was so big and hardy it was all I could do to push him off me. His chest was solid muscles and so wonderfully intriguing.* She sighed, remembering her surprise at finding his chest covered in soft, black curls, admitting the curls were not all that fascinated her. *The breath of his chest, the firm, powerful muscle I felt under all those curls as I washed away the blood and later sponged him with vinegar increased my interest.* She sighed again, remembering, at the time, how she wondered how it would feel to lay her cheek against that hard-muscled chest covered in soft, black curls.

"Why could he not have been wearing a gray uniform?" she whispered.

"Picturing him in a gray uniform does not help. It is not him without that cussed Yankee blue," she grimaced. She admitted, for the first time, she might have felt a strong emotional attraction to the soldier, and that was why her emotions were turned upside down when she was near him, but because he wore a blue uniform, she determined to rebuff the sensuous feelings she felt. Even now, she still tried to blame her constant thoughts of him and the sinking knot that hit the pit of her stomach each time she remembered the cave was empty on her lack of sleep and rest.

"Surely I will stop thinking about him in a day or two after I have had a few full nights of sleep. It is just that he is the first young man I have seen since I began to think about what it would be like to have a sweetheart, and he was a very handsome man, even if he was wearing that cussed blue uniform. I will never see another man as handsome."

More disturbing than the image of the tall, dark, handsome soldier in blue was the thought, *Will I truly ever forget his face and will I ever stop wondering how he fares?*

This man, despised in her mind because he wore a blue Yankee uniform, captivated her thoughts and stirred her emotions from the first moment she looked into his face. His handsome features and the strength his face revealed drew her eyes again and again to feast on his noble face. With each uncontrolled glance, her eyes lingered a little longer, and her heart beat a little faster, but she would not admit to herself that there was something about this soldier in blue that endeared him to her, although his face haunted her thoughts and her dreams and would continue to do so. Her stubborn Southern pride would keep her from being honest with her heart, denying, with all her might, that this Yankee had not touched her heart and refusing to think of her amorous feelings as anything other than silly outrageous behavior. She swore she would not allow herself to think of him in any manner, except as her enemy.

"It really does not manner how I remember him. I will never ever see him again," she told herself.

***

The next morning, Morgan ordered a litter to be constructed for Zeus to pull, after Haygood convinced him he was still too weak to travel any distance on horseback. Morgan agreed to travel on the litter, until they encountered a train heading for Washington or until he was strong enough to sit on a horse. The ride went a slow pace with the litter, but they were able to make close to twenty miles that first day.

During the first day, the boredom of the slow pace and having to view where they had been instead of where they were going, drove Morgan batty. By the end of that first day, Morgan ordered the litter demolished and dared Haygood to interfere, making it clear that, by morning, he would be in the saddle.

Haygood was surprised Morgan did not call an end to the litter after a few hours of traveling on his back, and he hid his amusement by busying himself with seeing that the camp was ready for the night.

Traveling on the litter was boring and harrying, but there was something else bothering Morgan. He felt as if he were leaving something behind, but just what it could be he was not sure exactly. It was not the chain and the pendant that he had left for his angel so she would have something that would remind her of him. That was not what was bugging him. Haygood pointed out that his sidearm and scabbard were missing, but that was not bothering him, either. He was sure she removed them so she could tend to his wounds. *Surely she was not afraid I would use the gun on her or her family. No, she was not afraid of me, afraid only that someone would find out she was hiding a Yankee. I hope she kept my gun to protect herself after I left. I don't know why I have this feeling. There is nothing else missing, except my hat, and I have several more. I was somewhere and with someone, but where and with whom I do not know. It will drive me crazy if I do not stop thinking about it and her.* His thoughts of where and who turned abruptly to his thoughts of the feel of soft, sweet lips motionless beneath his and the feel of a woman's firm breast pushed against his chest.

"I kissed her," he whispered, and smiled.

***

The morning came, like always. Old Red crowed his welcome to the day, and the household began to stir. Sam had slept the whole night in her bed; at least, she had stayed in the bed all night after her visit to the cave. Sleep had not come easy, and the state of the bed covers testified to her restlessness before falling asleep. She was tempted several times during the night to go to the window and to watch the night, except for the way she had been feeling of late, that she was afraid Keowee's predictions might be coming to pass. She knew she had not been getting full nights of rest and sleep for some time. She had gotten even less than usual during the two days the Yankee occupied the cave. But she was determined to turn over a new leaf, now that the soldier was gone, and she made herself stay in the bed.

"I do not feel too rested. My back feels like I slept all night, lying across a log," she complained.

Keowee and Lovie were already busy with cooking breakfast, and Sam greeted them both with her usual, "Good morning," as she sat Lemuel in his high chair.

Turning to her usual task of setting the table, she began to put plates, forks, knives, and spoons in front of each chair.

Cups and glasses were next to grace the table.

Keowee smiled, as she looked Sam over. "You look better this morning, a little more rested. 'Em dark circles are fading from under your eyes. You must be sleeping more."

Sam just smiled back at Keowee and nodded her head, thinking there was no need telling Keowee how long it took her to fall asleep while twisting and turning half the night and how stiff and achy she felt this morning. She thought, *Maybe it is better to sleep half the night lying in bed than sitting in the window seat with my head propped against the alcove, sleeping in snatches.* During breakfast, Sam forgot about sleeping, as she and Santee discussed what needed to be done and the best place to start doing it. After enjoying a good, hardy meal, Santee, the boys, and Sam left for the field, and Keowee and Lovie turned to the care of the house, to Lemuel, and to preparing food for the midday meal.

***

Despite Haygood's half-measured objection, Morgan was in the saddle the second morning after leaving the camp on the east bank of the Savannah River. They bypassed Anderson, South Carolina, Morgan and Haygood agreeing on that little detour, as the commanding officer of the troops occupying the town was not one of their favorite people.

On the first day of Morgan being back in the saddle, the pace of their journey more than doubled. Morgan set the pace, as always, when leading his men. Haygood, as well as the other men, wondered, *Why the rush?* At the end of each day, Morgan was the most haggard of the group and fell into his bedroll before the sentries were posted or the night's food was prepared. His unusual fast pace, at this time, seemed strange, even for Morgan.

Haygood began to wonder whether there was something Morgan was trying to outrun. *I have never known him to be afraid of anything or anyone. Could it be that little Southern angel has sneaked into the back door of Morgan's heart and that he is beginning to realize there was more to his wanting to find her than just to thank her for saving his life?* After chewing these thoughts over for a while, he was no longer guessing. He was sure he was on the right track.

Near the Virginia line, Morgan had all he could stand of Haygood's constant grinning, and he turned to him. "What in blue blazes do you find so funny on this dreary trek?" Morgan inquired.

"Nothing much," Haygood replied. "I just find it amusing watching you try to outrun whatever it is that you are trying to outrun." He tried hard to contain the laughter that was churning to escape. But, losing the battle, he roared with his merriment.

Already aggravated with Haygood's constant grinning and now to have him accuse him of running from someone, Morgan was fit to be tied. "Explain yourself, Zack, and it had better be a good explanation, or we are going to come to blows. It's been a long time since I whipped your ass, and don't let this insignia on my collar have any bearing on this."

"Morgan," was all Haygood managed at the time, as he was still enveloped in laughter, which seemed to make Morgan that much madder. Finally, Haygood took a deep breath and turned in his saddle to face Morgan. "I can't help it if my grinning face rubs you the wrong way, and you know that if I wanted to swing a few fists your way, nothing about you would stop me. I'm just not in the mood to knock your block off. I figure you are beating yourself up enough, so I'm just going to sit back and watch you make a fool of yourself, until you are ready to come to terms with whatever is driving you."

***

The days of May were spent with Santee plowing, Sam and the boys hoeing grass and weeds from patches of corn and occasionally helping with the weeding of the kitchen garden.

Surprisingly to the occupants of Riverbend, the month passed quietly, without incident, and the few patches of corn they were growing, along with their kitchen garden, kept everyone busy. The grass and weeds, for some reason, always grew at a faster rate than the plants and required long, back-breaking days of hoeing.

There was, however, one day that was different from the others: Sam's nineteenth birthday on May 16. There was no sugar to be found in the house, and there had not been any sugar for some time, but Santee and the boys located several combs of honey in a hollow tree. The find came just in time for Keowee to use some of the honey to sweeten the batter of a birthday cake for Sam, and the midday meal of May 16 turned into a party.

"Happy Birthday" was sung loudly, and Sam was presented with gifts from everyone.

Keowee gave her a beautiful green dress just the shade of her eyes. It did not matter that the dress was made from several, old, discarded dresses of the late Mrs. Sinclair. The material was gorgeous, and the fit was perfect.

Where she would wear the dress she did not know, but having something made just for her was special. Santee was not to be outdone. He gave her a pair of slippers made from several old pairs found lying around in the attic. The attic proved to be a treasure trove of useful items. The satin and the lace Lovie found to refurbish the skeleton of a discarded fan came from the attic also. Floyd and David presented her with items they had carved with Santee's help. David's present was a heart carved from a block of cedar to use to freshen the items in her vanity drawer, and Floyd gave her a statue of a horse he had carved from a block of oak. The only thing that could have made the day more perfect would have been the presence of her parents to share in her happiness.

June 1865
Washington, D.C.

The night was dark, without light from moon or stars, as Colonel Morgan Anderson walked from his horse to the bank of the Potomac River. *A perfect night for a little cloak-and-dagger,* he thought, as a cool summer breeze rolled off the water and brushed his face with a refreshing whisper. The message delivered thirty minutes earlier to his residence was brief but to the point: only instructions to follow the road south to the river. He was to wait at the water's edge for a craft to ferry him out to a waiting ship.

Offshore, a small-lantern glow flashed one quick burst of light, and Morgan hurried to the water's edge and to the rowboat that was materializing out of the darkness. He hoped the craft would carry him to the answer for this unexpected request. *This puzzle better have an explanation,* he thought, as he climbed into the boat.

Conversation was nil, as the men rowed against the wind that hindered the speed of the craft, but soon the bulk of a ship appeared. Anchored midstream, with her lights dimmed, she was completely undetectable from shore, and the quietness of the night was broken only by the slapping of the water resounding off the sides of the vessel, as Morgan climbed on deck. A squad of armed navy seamen halted his movements as he boarded, and a thorough search of his person was made before he was escorted down an inner corridor and shown a door for him to enter. A gravelly mountain drawl greeted him as the door closed behind him.

"Colonel, good of you to come on such short notice," the stocky man sitting behind the large oak desk offered, never raising his eyes, as he continued his intense study of the papers he held. Minutes crept by, seemingly stretching into hours, and as Morgan reflected on the conundrum of this situation, several things struck him as unusual, to say the least. Being addressed as "Colonel" rather than "Morgan," especially since he was no longer in the ranks, could be considered odd. A meeting onboard a ship in the middle of the night was rather theatrical, but his thoughts returned to the simplicity of the note and to the overtone of the message, which he interpreted to imply urgency. Yet he stood in limbo, with the door closed behind him and no invitation to proceed.

There was apparently no one else in attendance. Without further acknowledgement of his presence, his annoyance at the prospect that whatever he was here to discuss could easily be discussed at a more reasonable time and under less mysterious circumstances gave rise not only to his temper but also to numerous objections he intended to voice at the first opportunity.

However, amidst the grumbling of all his theorizing, he knew what he knew of the man sitting before him. The man's dislike for dramatics and his record for ethical behavior began to emerge and to weigh against the hostile surmising Morgan had posed in his mind's eye. Slowly, as if by design, the questionable cloak of suspicion fueled by temper was replaced with growing concern for whatever could have incited this man to take these actions. Finally, when the expressionless eyes of the tailor from Tennessee, shifted to his, a rather subdued civilian, namely, Morgan, acknowledged his host.

"Mr. President."

The night was well-spent before a haggard Colonel Morgan Anderson made his way back across the few hundred feet of riverbank to his horse, concealed in the tree line. His retirement from the military service was certainly short-lived, and, once again, he would have to put his somewhat personal life on hold. He did not particularly like that idea, and the thought of going south at this time pricked a nerve, but it raised his spirit. His family's connections with the South made him the ideal candidate for this mission, and his and Haygood's years of known carousing added just the right touch to the pseudonym he was to use.

However, this reassignment coming at this time would definitely add chaos to his life, beginning with his telling Haygood they were again in service to their country.

Morgan and Haygood's friendship began early in childhood, and their comradeship grew, as their boyish pranks and scrapes turned to more sophisticated adult adventures. Nothing or no one was able to break the bond.

As if on cue, Haygood emerged from the trees, as Morgan approached, Haygood's body as fleet as if he'd spent the night in the comfort of his own bed. His swift movements concealed the effect of the many hours of vigil. His long strides were quick and sure for a man of his stature, and, in a flash, he was abreast of Morgan, matching step for step. In the half light of dawn, the two men walked side by side, leading their horses without speaking a word, but, in a short distance, they mounted their horses, turning toward Anderson Place.

Haygood knew better than to press Morgan for details of the meeting. Morgan would talk when he was ready and only when he was good and ready. He had decided hours ago that the summons was authentic or that Morgan would have been ashore quicker than spit and madder than blue blazes. Whatever was discussed had really touched Morgan, for Haygood had not seen him this quiet and glum for some time.

Tonight reminded him of the years he and Morgan had spent serving their country.

They had carried out every mission to the best of their abilities, and they had been in a lots of close scrapes. Haygood was thankful they were no longer in the army. He had had his fill of special assignments, of dodging bullets, and of killing men he did not know. He vowed at the war's end that if he ever had to kill another man, he wanted to be sure the SOB deserved to die.

CHAPTER 6

Riverbend Plantation

The month of June brought warmer weather to Riverbend, and, late afternoon, the rain helped the crops and garden to grow, but it also made the pesky grass and weeds to sprout and grow. The last day of June brought a pest that could not be removed with a hoe or a plow, so Sam tried a more deadly means.

It was one of those days when they were blessed with a midmorning rain shower.

Black clouds appeared, and Sam, Santee, and the boys were chased from the field by the hard downpour. The clouds hung over the fields for several hours, giving the ground a good soaking and making the land too wet to be worked. The household took advantage of the soggy ground, lingering longer than usual around the table, after the noon meal, enjoying their break from the outdoor chores and the cool, rain-washed air.

Not long after the rain stopped, Floyd and David excused themselves and made their way to the river with cane poles and a jar of worms. After the boys quit the room, Santee thought of a few things that needed his attention and headed for the barn. The womenfolk were left with the task of clearing the table. Sam's hands were deep in hot, soapy water, as Lovie and Keowee scraped and stacked dishes next to the wash pan, when the boys ran in the back door, out of breath, and with a look of terror on their faces.

Sam forgot about dirty dishes and hurried to her brothers. Floyd calmed down first, enough to squeak out through gulps of air, "There's a fat Yankee soldier walking up to the steps of the front veranda."

Sam did not wait for another word; she grabbed her hat and pulled it down over her pinned-up braids. She ran out of the kitchen and flew up the back stairs, with only one thing in mind: retrieving the Yankee sidearm hidden in her room.

The sound of hammering came, as she neared the top of the stairs. She was in and out of her room as fast as lightning and down the front stairs, pulling open the front doors, with gun in hand. Sure enough, a pudgy blue belly, with the barrel of a Yankee revolver in his hand, was using the handle of the gun as a hammer, attaching something to one of the front doors.

Sam's abrupt opening of the doors, swinging them inward, caused the Yank to lurch backward across the veranda, wobbling on one foot and then the other, with arms and hands flopping in the air. Teetering backward down the steps, he lost his grip on his gun, and it fell to the ground, landing to the side of the second step, as he stumbled onto the pebble walk. He recovered his balance after his feet touched the drive, and his eyes went instantly to the doorway and to Sam and the Colt .44-caliber Army Model she was aiming straight at his heart. He felt for his gun and found his holster empty. Afraid to make any hasty moves, he slowly lowered his eyes, searching the ground. He looked between him and the house, spotting his gun lying on the ground next to the steps, several feet away. Finding his voice, he tried with all the authority he could muster to inform the young man (Sam being in her male attire) that he would be within his rights to shoot him or any Southerner who pointed a gun at him or interfered with his business.

As Sam walked to the edge of the veranda, she laughed, having seen his gun tumble to the ground. By this time, Santee and Keowee were coming through the door to Sam's aid. Stepping onto the veranda, they stopped dead in their tracks.

They were terrified at the scene before them. It was their worst nightmare: Sam with a gun in her hands and aiming it at a Yankee soldier.

Santee's first thought was to step in front of Sam to shield her from the soldier's bullets, should the soldier decide to shoot, but he noticed the Yankee's empty hand. His eyes immediately went to the soldier's holster and found it also empty. He changed his mind and walked behind Sam, coming to stand at her left.

Searching the ground around the soldier and between him and the veranda, he spied the Yankee's gun next to the steps and wondered how in the world Sam had managed that. However, he did not dare ask. He felt a little weak in the knees, as he realized that if he had stepped in front of Sam, he might have given the soldier a chance to retrieve his gun, and he might have shot them all. He decided very quickly that the best thing to do was try to calm the situation with words.

"Sir, Mr. Soldier, Sam here means you no harm; she—I mean Sam—just didn't know who or what was happening. We's just heard a lot of banging, and Sam thought that some-body was trying to break down the door, maybe to do us harm. Sam wouldn't shoot anyone without cause, especially when that person was unarmed and meaning us no harm. Uh, uh, just what is your business, sir?"

Even with Santee explaining that Sam would be hard-pressed to shoot anybody, she still did not lower the pistol she held so firmly in her hands.

"I am here on government business, darkie, and I have the U.S. Army's permission to shoot to kill any Southerner, black or white, that interferes in that business. I am serving notice that this place will be sold in thirty days for back taxes, if the taxes being owed are not paid. The eviction notice I was nailing to the door is not to be removed. Removal of that notice is a federal crime, and the person or persons removing said notice will be prosecuted. I also serve you notice that if I do not return to my headquarters in Athens by evening, a squad of soldiers will be here to investigate my detainment."

Gritting her teeth, Sam had stood silent as long as she could.

"There could be nothing to investigate when your squad of Yankees arrive," she sneered. "No one but the three of us have seen you on Riverbend land, blue belly, and there is a convenient fast-moving deep river just a few steps away."

Her anger evident by the way she emphatically grated out each word.

"Riverbend is not being sold for back taxes. You are a liar. Some Yankee carpetbagger wants this plantation and doesn't want to pay its worth."

"Child," Keowee pleaded, "please, the soldier is only doing what he's been told to do. Santee and me knows you means this man no harm. You are just scared. We's all scared, but since we knows the soldier means us no harm, let's offer him a cool drink of water and send him on his way, unharmed. Please, Sam, listen to me, and calm down. He's not here to do any harm to us."

"All right, Keowee," Sam said. "I'll do as you ask, provided Santee picks up the Yankee's gun and takes it to the river and throws it into the water."

"No way fellow," the Yankee soldier said, "I would be a dead man before I reached the Athens road. I cannot ride these roads unarmed. I would be a target for any Southerner I meet." The Yankee soldier was still not sure he would ever be able to make it off this plantation alive.

Sam laughed at his plea and thought, *That is just what I'm hoping will happen to you.*

"Sam," Santee's calm voice advised. "Let the soldier keep his gun. You don't want his blood on your hands, if he be killed after he leaves here because he could not defend himself. It would be your fault if you refuse to let him keep his gun. Let him put the gun in his saddlebag until he be off Riverbend land. We's can watch him through the cedar grove and on a ways to make sure he don't turn back."

Sam finally agreed to let the Yankee have his gun and leave peacefully. However, she still was not trusting the Yankee and said, "Santee, step down the left outer edge of the steps and retrieve the cussed Yankee's gun there beside the steps."

Santee didn't hesitate to do as Sam had asked.

Never taking her eyes from the Yankee, she listened for the sound of Santee's feet on the pebble walk and knew when he turned toward the Yankee.

"Wait a minute, Santee. You, blue belly, get on your horse," she ordered.

The soldier walked backward to his horse, watching Sam closely, even as he reached for the saddle horn and placed his foot in the stirrup and swung up into the saddle.

"Santee," Sam ordered, "place the cussed gun in that cussed Yankee saddlebag."

As Santee placed the pistol in the saddlebag and fastened the snap, Sam roared, "Git, you Yankee trash! And don't you show your face around here again."

The soldier lost no time leaving the three behind, and they watched his departure until he was out of sight. When Sam was sure the Yankee was gone for good, she turned to the door for her first look at the piece of paper the Yankee had nailed to the door. Without thinking, she reached out with her left hand, intending to snatch the cussed thing off the door, but Santee caught her wrist before her fingers touched the notice.

"Missy, you don't want to do that. You could get us all in a lot of trouble."

As Santee finished cautioning Sam, Keowee reached for Sam's other hand, raising it into plain sight.

"Child, where in this world gone mad did you get this gun?"

"I found it."

Santee's eyes going again to the gun in Sam's hand and his ears hearing her answer to Keowee's question, he didn't readily accept Sam's answer and inquired further.

"Just where did you find that gun? Was it just lying on the ground?"

Not surprised that neither Santee nor Keowee would accept her explanation about where she had found it, she began to weave a more in-depth tale, sticking as close to the truth as she dared.

"Yes, I found it on Sinclair land, and I did not tell you two at the time because I was sure it was a Yankee gun. It was during the time everyone was talking about or looking for that missing Yankee soldier. I was afraid it might have belonged to that soldier, so I hid it in my room, thinking that the fewer people that knew about it, the better."

Santee and Keowee looked at each other, bewildered, not

knowing what to make of Sam's last explanation, but Santee finally suggested, "Sam, maybe you should throw this gun in the river, as you had suggested doing with the soldier's gun, because there is no guarantee that Yankee won't bring a bunch of Yankees back here to get this gun. If you don't give it up, they'll search the house till they find it. That gun could have got us all killed today. Us Southerners were the losers in that war, and it's my understanding from what I hears. We are not allowed to have a gun."

"Well, when I found this gun, I kept it for our protection, and no Yankee, not even a squad of Yankees, is going to take it from me. I will keep it where they will never think of looking. They might have won the war, but they will not outsmart me." With those words, she left the black couple staring at her in disbelief and marched up the front stairs to her bedchamber.

Closing the chamber door, she walked straight to the bedside steps. Lifting the top of the second step, she removed the chamber pot, pried loose the plank the chamber pot sat on, exposing a cubbyhole beneath. She placed the gun into the cubbyhole, replaced the plank, returned the chamber pot, and closed the step. Brushing her hands in a show of satisfaction, she turned and left the room, heading for the river with the Yankee scabbard in hand.

July 1865
Washington, D.C.

The railroad ran on schedule, from Washington through Virginia and into North Carolina, almost to the South Carolina state line. The easiest and fastest route to New Orleans would have been by sea, but Colonel Morgan Anderson wanted to spend some time in Georgia. He planned to visit Riverbend on their way to New Orleans, and again after the assignment was completed. He was determined to find his angel.

Their trip was comfortable and pleasant enough, except for the lack of conversation. Haygood had reacted like a cyclone upon hearing Morgan's announcement of their reenlistment and this assignment. He had smashed everything in sight and had called Morgan numerous, unflattering adjectives, but, since his initial explosion, his silence was deafening.

"Say Red, you cannot stay mad," Morgan prodded, as they left the train car. I know my invitation to accompany me on this trek has left you speechless with happiness, but, surely with your gift for words, you can conjure up something appropriate to express your esteem."

"If not just think of all the fun we are going to have galloping across South Carolina on horseback," he teased.

"Groooooooooowl," Haygood roared, capturing the attention of everyone and everything within a the radius of a mile.

"Horses!" Haygood complained, growling again, as they unloaded their mounts from the freight car.

"One more thing I dislike about the army."

Deep, gut-wrenching laugher vibrated from Morgan, as he set the pace for their afternoon ride, thankful to have his friend back to normal. Well, maybe not normal, but as close to normal as possible for Haygood.

During the three and a half days of hard riding, with only needed stops for man and beast during the day and only a few hours each night for sleep, the pair rode across the Savannah River in the sultry heat of July.

Riverbend Plantation
Twelve Days after the Eviction Notice

After another sleepless night, Sam, once again, was first to enter the warming kitchen. The coolness of the night still filled the room, and she busied herself with starting the fire for the morning cooking. Night still enveloped the land, and as the flames soared and the logs crackled, she walked to the windows, facing east, her mind hundreds and hundreds of miles away. She stood staring, but not seeing or hearing.

Sometime later, Keowee entered the room, aiming to make the fire and to ready the kitchen for cooking the morning meal, and she found Sam standing at the east windows and a fire blazing. *That child gonna worry herself to death,* Keowee thought, as she observed Sam's slumped shoulders and was sure her mind was not there in the warming kitchen, but far away.

"Honey child, why's you up so early? You not still letting that old notice keep you from sleeping, are you?" Startled by Keowee's voice, Sam turned quickly, but she smiled, as she saw the sweet and loving black woman.

"You do not understand my concern over not having a place to live do you, Keowee?"

"No. Never had that worry. Just fearing who might be owning me next."

Understanding Keowee's fears, Sam lowered her eyes to the floor in empathy and noticed the first rays of the morning sunshine splattering against the stone floor, as they streamed through the windows. The kitchen was quiet, except for the noise of the blazing fire and Keowee's puttering around the kitchen. Sam moved to sit in front of the fireplace and once again was occupied with her thoughts, as she sat staring at the changing forms of the flames dancing over the logs. *I had questions two years and nine months ago, and I never received any answers to my questions.* The thought added to her anxiety and turned her anxious feelings into raging irritability. She stood, stomping her foot.

"Those cussed Yankees!" she swore and called through clenched teeth.

"What is taking that man so long to get home from Europe? The war ended over two months ago. Is he walking across the ocean?"

She turned to the older woman at the work table, her irritable mood deflating a little for the moment, as her eyes fell on Keowee.

"Keowee, tell me, 'What kind of man is Robert Sinclair?'" Sam pleaded. "Will he return in time to claim his inheritance?"

Across the room, Keowee watched Sam with sympathy, knowing that if they put their faith in Robert Sinclair, there would be little hope for any of them. *Even if the young master did come home, he had never been interested in running this plantation. Even when his pappy was alive and there was money to be made. He certainly ain't about to change now. Mr. Robert Sinclair cares only for himself. He would have no interest in saving Riverbend or honoring the agreement Mr. Mac made to care for these children, but there's no need in adding that to Sam's other worries.*

"Lord Jesus, help this old black woman this morning," Keowee whispered. "Help me to know what to tell this sweet baby."

Keowee spoke after a spell, choosing her words carefully, hoping to direct Sam's attention away from the the pending eviction and to encourage her to pray for a miracle.

"Pay no attention to that piece of paper and them rumors coming from 'em freed black folk that Santee's always talking about. They don't know nothing. They can't even do a good job of being free. Most of 'em be sick, starving, or both, and they're liable to say anything. Right now we's got a good roof over our heads and enough food to fill our bellies. Let's count our blessings and ask the good Lord to send us a miracle."

The last was said with a smile, as she took a clean rag from her pocket and stretched out her hand.

"Blow you nose, honey, and wipe 'em tears. Let's get the morning meal cooking."

Braving a smile at Keowee through tear-blurred eyes, Sam took a few steps to retrieve the rag from Keowee's out-stretched hand. Thankful for the comfort this woman was to her and yearning for a few more moments of solace, she threw her arms around Keowee, leaning her head against her shoulder. As many times before, strong arms encircled Sam's shoulders.

The morning was uneventful, with each member of the hodgepodge of a family going about his or her task with no mention of the impending eviction. The notice of the impending sale had been nailed to the front door twelve days before, and the expected outcome was the topic of conversation during most meals ever since. Everyone but Sam seemed to have come to terms with the notice. However, Sam was not so easily soothed, although she agreed with the others that the number of workers needed to make Riverbend a produc-tive plantation guaranteed that the former slaves would not be uprooted from their home. Sam knew that she and her brothers' future was not as secure.

Even though there was no mention of the impending evic-tion during this morning meal, Sam's mind was full of what would happen to the boys and her if the plantation was sold. She recalled the grin on the face of the Yankee soldier, as he gladly described the job he was sent to do. She repeated the same accusation she flung at the Yankee that day.

"Some Yankee carpetbagger has his eye on this plantation and wants it for nothing."

That speculation kept rattling around in her head during the morning hours, until she was fit to be tied.

***

The sun was midway up the eastern sky, shining brightly on the barren fields, as two riders emerged from the tree-lined road that gave access to the Sinclair plantation and stopped. The men sat for several minutes, staring at the devastation that stretched out before them. One of the men, in particular, was greatly moved by what he viewed. Nothing remained of the flourishing meadows and the productive fields that registered in his memory, and he wondered what he would find when he reached the house. He knew that most of the inhabitants of this area, with the exception of the town of Hartwell, never saw the first Union soldier. Nevertheless, the area was greatly affected by the war. As his eyes beheld the fields covered with weeds and bramble, it amazed him how a few years of neglect could change a place so drastically.

Sam's inner rage reached a boiling point by midmorning, and she needed to vent it somewhere, and she decided to do what she had wanted to do from the start. Only the pleading of her adopted family held her back.

"Just the sight of that blue uniform frightened them to within an inch of immortality," she fumed.

Sam squared her shoulders and marched straight through the hallway of the downstairs and toward the front doors, with a smile beaming with her intent.

The Sinclair home built in the great bend of the river stood silent, as the two horsemen approached. The noise of prosperous years that Morgan remembered was gone, and the sparkling beauty that once welcomed visitors had vanished with the ravage of time. Convinced the place was vacant, he guided his horse slowly toward the front of the house and its double oak doors. What he saw nailed to the exquisite doors enflamed his rage, and, without a thought about anything else but to rid the door of the offensive notice, he dismounted Zeus without a word to Haygood, rushed up the steps, and, reaching out with his right hand, he jerked the paper into his fist. As he crumpled the offensive notice in his hand, unexpected sounds of angry words caught Morgan's ears.

"I will not only tear that notice into shreds; I will also burn every scrap."

The voice of an angry female was what Morgan thought he had heard from just beyond the doors. He forgot, for a moment, the paper crumpled in his fist, and, with his left hand, he lifted his hat, preparing to meet a lady, when a person of indescribable origin blasted out the doors and into his presence.

Caught up in her defiant outburst against the Yankee eviction order, Sam had not heard the arrival of horses. She was prepared to defy the whole Yankee army, but she was not prepared to meet the Yankee that stood before her as she opened the door.

The sight of broad shoulders covered in a dark gray coat filled her eyes, and those shoulders were attached to a giant of a man. He seemed to have been occupied with something in his right hand, but as she stepped onto the veranda, he jerked off his hat and raised his head.

Her heart slammed against her ribs with a jolt she felt to the ends of her toes. She knew that face as well as she knew her own. It filled her dreams at night and her thoughts during the day, but, in her wildest fantasies, she never imagined she would ever look on that face again. For a moment, she was sure she had died and gone to heaven or hell, she wasn't sure which, her emotions were in such a state. Yet this handsome man stood before her, his expression as nonchalant, as if he had never laid eyes on her before. One moment, her heart was racing with glee, because he had come back to Riverbend. Then she had thoughts of what could happen if he ever recognized her, and those thoughts made her want to run and hide. But her desire to feast her eyes on him and to drink in every inch was stronger for the moment than her fear of being recognized.

She allowed her eyes to travel freely over him, savoring every morsel. He stood tall as a Georgia pine. His wounds were healed; his body was fit. Carefully trimmed, raven-black hair lined his collar, but the fullness of his thick locks were pressed down from having worn the hat he held in his left hand. His chiseled features and set of strong jaws reflected the inner strength that brought him to Riverbend that May night and equaled the strength of his muscular frame. The only flaw, if you could call it a flaw, was the hint of a dark beard just below the surface of his bronze skin. Her eyes moved up from lips that gave her her first kiss, passed a perfect nose, and met bold pools of ebony that held her spellbound, as they stared hard at her. To her surprise, he now did the same to her as she had done to him.

His eyes deliberately moved over her nose, mouth, and chin, not lingering on her face, since it was partly shaded with the floppy hat covering her hair. His eyes moved quickly down her body, as he took in her shabby ill-fitting boy's clothing. She drew in a breath, as she became conscious of how brazen she had been with her ogling of him.

Shocked by the appearance of this man at Riverbend and by his openly insulting behavior, she struggled for words to hurl at him. She realized that he could not recognize her features but that he would be able to recognize her voice. He had heard her voice for two days and two nights. She would have to guard against letting him hear her normal voice.

"What are you doing on our veranda?" she demanded, lowering the tone of here voice a notch and trying to speak through her nose. She began to gain a little of her composure with her demand, only to lose it again, as his lips spread in a lazy grin.

"Exactly what you intended to do," he replied, as he lifted his right hand, revealing the crumpled eviction notice. "But I believe you also mentioned something about burning every last scrap."

She was embarrassed that he had heard her declaration and enraged that he would taunt her with her own words. The denied release of her anger toward the eviction notice surfaced and found a new target. *How dare he deny me the satisfaction I craved!* she fumed inwardly.

"You have no right to remove that notice," she blurted out through clenched teeth. "By doing so, you have broken a Yankee law and will bring reprisal on this household."

Morgan was offended by the weird character's sneering tone and by the insinuation that he had acted recklessly, and replied, "By what right would you have to remove and burn the same notice? You are not a Sinclair."

"How do you know I am not a member of the Sinclair family?" she asked. "Are you acquainted with the whole Sinclair family?" Her questions were combative, her tone unduly irate. Pulling herself up to her full five feet, eight inches, and thrusting her chin up at a haughty angle, she glared up at him, with eyes spitting sparks of fire that would have warned anyone who knew her of the tiger that went with those cat eyes. But her adversary did not seem to notice, as he blasted back, "Yes,

I am acquainted with both Mac and Robert. My family has been friends of the Sinclair family for years, and you, tomcat, are not a member of that family. Now stop your caterwauling and fetch an adult with whom I can converse. I have no patience with an impertinent and brash infantile who has no manners."

With each volley of words, their voices grew louder, alerting everyone within earshot that Sam was venting her pent-up anger on some poor soul. Keowee hurried toward the uproar, ready to come to Sam's aid, if necessary.

How dare he call me impertinent and a brash infantile, Sam fumed, taking in a deep breath, and stomped her foot. Sam readied herself to put this arrogant, asinine man back on his horse and on his way, when Keowee bounced through the door, ready to take care of whoever was swapping words with her Sam.

"Lordy, Lordy can this be Mr. Morgan?" Keowee cried, as she pushed past Sam and rushed into the Yankee's arms.

Haygood had sat quietly on his horse, watching the exchange of barbs with interest. He was intrigued with the scene that played out in front of him, thinking, *Morgan might not have found the angel he is searching for, but this is one lady with whom to be reckoned. She is some gal.*

What was more intriguing and downright funny to Haygood was Morgan being so embroiled in the ardent volley of words being bandied back and forth between him and his tomcat that he did not realize his tomcat was really a she-cat.

As he grinned from ear to ear with this knowledge, a sneaky little idea popped into his mind: *I think I will just sit back and see how long it will take the old man to find out the true gender of his tomcat. It will serve him right for me to keep this little secret. A little payback never hurt anyone, and he will think twice next time before he puts me back in the army.*

By the time Keowee finished greeting Morgan and fussing over him, Santee, Lovie, and the boys joined the bevy on the veranda. Santee recognized Morgan right away and was relieved to see him looking so healthy and fit. He also noticed the man with the red hair. He had seen him before. It was the Yankee who was looking for the missing Yankee officer several weeks back.

Morgan introduced Haygood to Keowee, turned to greet Santee and to introduce Haygood, but he remembered the two had met. "Santee, I believe you encountered my friend, Haygood, a while back, when he was searching for me."

"Yes sir, that be the truth, Mr. Morgan. I had a bad feeling about that meeting. I feared he might be looking for you, and I couldn't understand that if it be you, why you hadn't come to us. I'm shore nuff glad to see you were all right and not harmed."

Hearing all this happy reunion, Sam was fit to be tied. *The cussed Yankee could have saved me a lot of worry and work if he had just explained he knew Mr. Mac. I would have been happy to turn him over to Santee and Keowee. It would have saved me a big headache, the cussed man.*

"Oh, but I was wounded, Santee. I was lucky to have found a sympathetic young lady who tended to my wounds, saved my life, and kept me safe till I was able to return to my men. I was shot on my way to check on Mac for my stepmother. I promised her to do so if I was near Riverbend at the end of the war. I was sorry to hear that Mac died. My Southern angel told me."

Sam listened with more than a little interest to the words of this Yankee she now knew as Morgan, as she eased back behind her family, trying to stay on the fringe of the group, out of the Yankee's line of sight, and to make herself as inconspicuous as possible.

Afraid Keowee or Santee would expose her gender, rendering her disguise useless, she again felt the urgency to run and hide, but she wanted to hear the Yankee's account of his two days in hiding, and she smiled with joy as she heard Morgan call her his angel. The seesawing of her fear of her gender being discovered and her desire to stay were appeased temporarily by Lovie's greeting and invitation.

"Lordy mercy, Mr. Morgan," Lovie chimed in, as she pushed by her parents to greet the Yankee. "We's just so glad to see you and to know you be all right we have plum forgot our manners. Please, you and your friend do come in. The house ain't exactly as you remember, but we does real well."

Haygood's payback plan was getting more interesting by the minute, as he watched the she-cat slip to the back of the veranda when the black servants emerged. He saw she was pulling in her claws, as she lingered in the doorway, tempted to flee but reluctant to leave. The canvas of her shadowy countenance became alive with a realm of interesting emotions at the greetings of the servants and Morgan's explanation of being shot and finding his angel. As he watched the play of these different expressions, he glimpsed a complexity of emotions. A face of beauty and strength brought to his mind a more intriguing thought: *Morgan's angel might be right under his nose. If I was a betting man, which I am at times, I would not be betting against that possibility. I like a sure thing when I wager.*

Entering the house, Morgan was stunned as he noticed the bare walls and the missing pieces of furniture. Keowee did not bother with excuses for the lack of furnishings, but she told Santee to show Mr. Morgan and his friend to the guest rooms upstairs, and she informed the gentlemen that the noon meal would be a mite late but that there would be plenty for all.

Sam was waiting for Keowee in the kitchen. She had to gain Keowee's promise to keep her gender a secret. As soon as Keowee and Lovie entered the room, she approached them.

"Keowee, promise me you will not reveal to either of these Yankees that I am a female. Please."

"Honey child, you don't have to be afraid of Mr. Morgan," Keowee replied.

"Please, Keowee," Sam pleaded. "Give me your word that neither you nor Santee will betray me. You, too, Lovie."

Keowee nodded her head and replied, "Sam, I promise we's all will keep your secret, but there might come a time when you will need Mr. Morgan's help and protection. He just might be the miracle we prayed for."

Keowee's halfway prediction did not set well with Sam, but she made no reply.

Keowee was good as her word. The meal was plentiful, and, from the aroma, it would also be tasteful.

Sam fixed her plate, while Keowee and Lovie were putting the meal on the table, and she dashed to the back stairs, where she could spy on the group while she ate.

However, getting Floyd and David to join the two Yankees at the table proved to be impossible. Through the crack in the staircase door and the wall, Sam could see and hear everything that went on in the kitchen. She watched with pride, as Floyd flat out refused to be seated.

"I will not eat with men who killed my pa," David said, siding with his brother and refusing to be seated.

Morgan and Haygood did not seem to be offended by Floyd's statement. They remained quiet, as Keowee tried to encourage the young boys to put their hatred of the Yankee army aside for now. She asked them not to blame these two men; even though they were from the North, they were not soldiers now. Keowee's words were of no effect on the boys, and Morgan said, to no one in particular, "I know how it hurts to lose a parent. I was about the age of this lad when my father died, but a good bit younger when I lost my mother." Morgan's next words, however, were directed to the two boys.

"The loss of your father during a battle far from home has to have been a very traumatic time, but whether a father was killed or just died, the loss is still there, and, with that loss, comes pain—pain you now bear. Young fellows, you might not believe what I am about to tell you, and it might not help you at all, but I feel I must say what is in my heart. I do not know the battle your father was in when he was killed, but, during the war, there were a lot of battles, and many, many men on both sides were killed. I was a soldier; however, my part of the war was not necessarily fighting in the different campaigns. Haygood and the ten men that rode with me were used in covert missions. A great deal of those missions were carried out where there were no guns. At least none that were being fired. Namely, in ballrooms and at soirees or in the gutters of humanity. I will not try to tell you I never killed a man, but I will tell you every time I did, it was kill or be killed. The men that we were engaged with were not soldiers, and the majority of them had no allegiance to any color or army. Just to them-selves. The men who rode with Haygood and me fought for what we believed in, not because we hated the Rebel army or the South. Young lads, the war is over, and, in order for us to build back what has been destroyed, we have got to put aside our anger or hate, if we have any, and our pain to become one country again. It is going to take great men to be able to do this. Will you make a start by sitting with me and my friend as men, not as soldiers, and share this good meal?"

Santee listened to Morgan carefully, as he watched the boys also listening and saw the easing of Floyd's staunch posture, as the words he was hearing registered in his heart and mind. Getting up from his chair, he walked around to the spot where Floyd and David stood. He knew the pain and hatred Sam carried, because she had freely expressed her feelings, and he had always suspected that, to some degree, Floyd felt the same, but today was the first time Floyd had put his feelings into words.

He himself was hurting for the pain the three Hatcher siblings carried, but he knew they needed to start somewhere to rid themselves of their hatred. He encircled the boys in his long arms and softly spoke, "Let's show these men how big a man each of you boys can be. Keowee, Lovie, and me are right alongside of you all the way."

Removing his arms, he stepped a step away and motioned for them to join the table. David waited for Floyd to lead the way, and then he followed.

The meal continued without any other incident. While there was conversation, the usual laughing and joking were missing. Sam sat on the bottom step of the back stairs, with her ear pressed to the crack around the door to the kitchen. *What had Santee said to Floyd? Surely Floyd did not believe that bunch of lies Morgan Anderson tried to feed them. I wish Floyd was big enough to make him eat his every word.*

Sam managed to stay out of Morgan's direct field of vision that afternoon, that evening, and the next morning, eating her meals away from the kitchen.

Haygood observed the she-cat spying on Morgan and the boys several times during the afternoon and evening. Having not encountered her since the meeting on the porch, he was very intrigued by her disappearing act and was amused by her constant spying on Morgan when the boys were around him. *I wonder if Morgan knows who these children are why they are staying here on this plantation if they are not members of the Sinclair family, as he stated earlier.*

After the night meal, Morgan and Haygood moved to the front veranda to smoke in the cool evening breeze rolling in off the river. Haygood was bothered by questions regarding the boys and approached Morgan.

"If that person we encountered upon our arrival is not a member of the Sinclair family, are the boys also not members of the Sinclair family?"

"No, they are not, unless they are distant relatives. However, I do plan to find out just who they are before we leave in the morning. However, that tomcat that berated me so rudely when we first arrived seems to have disappeared. He bothers me more than the three boys being here. They are all probably orphans of the area, and, knowing Keowee and Santee as I do, they have taken them in. The South is bound to be teeming with numerous children left without parents."

Haygood finished his smoke, as Floyd and his shadow came through the door.

Saying good night to the three, Haygood left Morgan talking quietly with the boys and was not surprised to find the elusive kitty cat watching Morgan and the boys through the crack between the front door and the door casing.

"Would you not be able to *hear* what is being said more clearly out on the porch?" Haygood whispered, as he stepped around the door.

Sam jerked around, her face red with embarrassment at being caught eavesdropping. The embarrassment was soon replaced with a look of sheer terror.

Afraid she would be exposed to that cussed Yankee sitting

on the porch, Haygood smiled at the emotions playing across her beautiful face.

"Your secret is safe with me for now," he whispered again to Sam, as he started for the stairs, thinking, *This young lady would have to be very careful if and when she comes face to face with Morgan. He will be able to read her like a book. Her feelings show plainly on her face.*

Watching Haygood until he walked to his room, Sam felt it safe to leave her place of hiding and hurried to her bedchamber. As she closed the chamber door, Sam sighed, "Today has been something else."

"Morgan." Sam spoke the name softly, trying his name on her tongue. "It fits him," she smiled.

"Now I have a name to go with the face, but the cussed Yankee called me a brash, infantile and impertinent." Her anger, mixed with her curiosity, was churning, and the questions began: "I wonder why he has come back. He already had the news of Mr. Mac's death to report to his stepmother. Is he here to stay?" She turned these questions over in her mind, as she walked to the window seat.

What did that friend of his mean by my secret is safe with him? Surely he was referring to my spying. There is no way he could know I am a female. Is there?

The question filled her mind, as she walked to her window seat.

"If he is suspicious that I am not what I appear to be, he might even put two and two together and decide I am the one who tended to Morgan's wounds. *Please God, help to keep my secret safe.*

Her curiosity mill was not going to stay quiet, and she began to question the cussed Yankee's return.

Sam was not the only one with questions during the night.

Morgan left the veranda, hoping for a peaceful night of sleep. He had already made decisions regarding several things that needed tending to before leaving the plantation, but he could not get settled down and fall asleep.

"It is not the condition of the plantation," he said to himself. "I know that, with a good owner, some money, and work, the place will once again be a productive, beautiful place. Riverbend people, although few, seem to be faring well. There are a few things lacking. I will take care of that in Athens on the morrow. I also plan to find out more about Floyd and David before leaving for Athens. That seems to take care of everything. So why can I not get to sleep? Is it that rag bag of a tomcat? There is a distinct peculiarity about him, yet, oddly, there seems to be something familiar, and, for some reason, he has sparked an interest. There is something that just does not ring true. There are a lot of questions about that fellow that I need answered. What has happened to me? I am talking to myself?"

Laughing, he remembered someone else that had that habit and their time together, wondering, *Is it something Southern?* With his mind on his angel, he relaxed, closed his eyes, and, before long, he was dreaming of his angel.

The next morning before leaving the plantation, Morgan called Santee and Keowee into Mr. Mac's study and closed the door. This stirred Sam's curiosity almost beyond reason, and she wanted desperately to know what was being said, but she was afraid of being caught by the red-headed man again. Having gained Keowee's solemn promise not to reveal her gender to these two men, she knew her identity would not be revealed, but she wondered about the Yankee's seeming interest in Floyd. Again watching from a safe place, her waiting for the study's door to open seemed like an eternity, but, at last, the door opened.

The Yankee exited the room and walked out the double doors to the veranda, with a smiling Keowee in his wake, while Santee marched toward the warming kitchen. As Santee entered the kitchen, Lovie and the boys came hurrying up the hall to follow Keowee outside to say their good-byes. As soon as the hall was empty, Sam hightailed it to her bedchamber to watch the goings on at the drive. Watching from her lofty perch, Sam was surprised to see Santee bringing the barouche around from the barn and both of the men's horses tied to the back of the carriage. Bewildered by this and all of the events of the morning, Sam was eager to question Keowee and was determined to leave her bedchamber as soon as the wheels of the carriage had begun to turn.

She hurried out of her room and down the back stairs to await Keowee's return to the warming kitchen. The minute Keowee stepped foot inside the door, Sam confronted her, "Keowee, what was all the secrecy about? Why did that Yankee call you and Santee into Mr. Mac's study and close the door? If it concerns me or either of my brothers, I need to know. Another thing, why did Santee bring the barouche around with the Yankees' horses tied to the back? Surely, traveling by horseback would make for a faster trip."

Keowee smiled, knowing Sam's churning curiosity. "Child, don't you know that curiosity killed the cat? The meeting with Mr. Morgan in Mr. Mac's study didn't have anything to do with you or your brothers, directly. You gonna be happy to hear what he did say. Mr. Morgan's a good man. We's known him since he was a small boy, and he has a good heart. Him being a Yankee, he can take that notice you wanted to destroy so bad to the Yankee offices in Athens and pay 'em taxes and keep the plantation safe until Mr. Robert returns. If Mr. Robert don't come back home, then Mr. Morgan's done bought himself a plantation. His concern about Floyd and David only went as far as wanting to know who the boys are and why y'all be at Riverbend. I's told him y'all were brought here to Mr. Mac after your father was killed in the war and your mother died, giving birth to the baby. As for why Santee brought the barouche out, Mr. Morgan wanted Santee to come with them to Athens so as to bring back the proof that 'em taxes been paid. He said it best we keep it here, in case some other Yankee shows up, claiming the taxes need paying. You don't have to worry no more about not having a place to live. You and the boys gonna be right here with Santee, Lovie, and me. Mr. Morgan is shor nuff a good man."

"Did you include me with the boys when you was telling the cussed Yankee about Papa and Mama?"

"Only your name. Child, he only wanted to know if y'all were brothers."

Sam was furious. She stomped out of the kitchen, without a word, her face red as fire and her countenance hard as stone.

The barouche with Santee sitting on the driver's seat and Morgan and Haygood sitting in the back traveled, as Sam had mentioned to Keowee, much slower than riders on horseback, arriving in Athens at twilight.

Haygood was glad for the hours of reprieve from riding horseback. The only time he was happy to have a good horse and saddle was when the force behind him was larger in number and when the bullets were flying fast and furious. The carriage ride also gave him time to sort out his suspicions about the kitty cat.

Could Sam be short for Samantha? I hope so. But what about her odd behavior of spying on Morgan? Could it be she is protective of her brothers or afraid the boys might give her identity away? She never came anywhere near Morgan, as if she was afraid he might notice something about her that would give him a clue to her identity. Dear girl, your actions have persuaded me further that you are Morgan's angel.

Morgan directed Santee west of the town of Athens to the home of a friend on the outskirts of town. The house was large and ablaze with lights. Carriages were parked here and there along the long drive up to the house and in the yard, and several horses were tied to the hitching post out front. Santee was a little nervous, wondering if they might be intruding on a party of some kind, and he asked, "Mr. Morgan, who lives here? Will we be interrupting a gathering of some kind?"

Morgan chuckled, as he answered Santee, "Some kind of a gathering, but, not to worry, we will not be interrupting anything. You wait here with the horses. I will have my friend's man come and show you where to stable the animals and where you can get some food and a bed for the night. We will see you bright and early in the morning. Sleep well."

Shortly, the biggest black man Santee had ever laid eyes on walked from the house straight to him.

"I be Tiny, Miss Ruby's man. She told me to take care of you. Please follow me, and I'll show you where to stable the horses and where you can eat your supper and where to find a bed."

The next morning, the only horses in the stable, besides the ones that belonged to the house, were the ones Santee placed in stalls and the yard was empty of carriages and buggies. Morgan and Haygood appeared at the stables by the time Santee finished hitching up the barouche and saddling their horses.

"Good morning, gentlemen, are y'all ready to go?" Haygood groaned, and Morgan laughed. "Yes, Santee, we are ready to go on into town."

"We will go back the way we came a short distance. I will tell you when to make your turn into town. It is just a short distance into Athens."

Santee stood on the street by the horse and was surprised to spot a former slave from one of the bigger farms in Hart County, and he hailed the man. The man returned Santee's greeting and walked over to the place where Santee was standing.

"Zeb, what you doing in Athens? Have you left the Nix's farm?" Santee asked.

"No, Santee, I be here on behalf of Mr. Nix, and it sure is good to see a familiar face. Mr. Nix done returned to the farm a few days back, sick from a wound he got in the war, and he ain't able to travel any farther as yet. With Miss Alison missing, he is shor nuff in a bad way. He sent me here to see if I could find her, and I'm not doing so good. I cannot find no one who will try to help me find where she might be or even listen to me. She ran off to marry a Yankee soldier. She said that he was taking her to Athens to get married and that they would live there, but I cannot find out nothing about them. I be worry sick. If I don't find her, it's gonna kill Mr. Nix."

"Santee," Haygood called, after hearing part of the spiel the old black man was telling Santee. He was roused up enough to know this girl would be of interest to Morgan.

"Yes, Mr. Haygood," Santee answered, walking to the back of the carriage.

"Tell you friend there to wait until Morgan comes back and to tell him just what he has told you. Morgan will be interested to hear this, and maybe he can send the brother a good word."

Santee repeated what Haygood had said, and the old black man sighed a sigh of relief, knowing somebody was going to listen to him and maybe could point him in the right direction.

Morgan was more than a little interested in what the Nix's servant had to say and asked him several questions about the man the young lady had left home to wed.

After gaining what information he could from the family servant, he assured him he would do his best to locate the young lady and to get her home, and he sent the servant home with a written message to her brother.

After sending the Nix's servant on his way, Morgan turned to Santee. "Santee, these papers I am entrusting to you are very important. Keep them on your person until you reach Riverbend. You and Keowee put them in a secure place. I would suggest you not put them anywhere in Mac's study. Find a place in the house that only the two of you would know about and show them only if you are threatened again with eviction. I will be back to check on you in a month or two. Haygood and I are on our way to Louisiana. Look for us back around the middle or the last of August. By that time, Robert will surely be home."

"Yes sir, Mr. Morgan. I will do just as you say with these papers, but you knows Mr. Robert ain't never had no interest in Riverbend. He shor nuff will not now. Not now that it ain't making no money."

"Let's hope he grew up a little while across the big pond."

Morgan and Haygood left for the train station, and Santee started for home with several items for Keowee and the kitchen that Morgan placed in the barouche.

Sam and the boys finished hoeing out the last late patch of corn. Sam sent David into Keowee with an armful of roasting ears to have for the midday meal, as she and Floyd hoed the last few rows.

Sam was in a terrible mood, snapping at the boys all morning. Floyd, tired of getting his backsides chewed out, stopped in the middle of his row after David had left the field and confronted Sam. "What in blue blazes is wrong with you? Whatever you got stuck in your craw, spit it out before you wear David and me to a frazzle with your snapping."

"I do not like being beholden to that cussed Yankee," Sam spat back at Floyd through gritted teeth. He was the big shot Yankee and paid the cussed taxes. That cussed jackass removed that eviction notice, denying me that pleasure, the arrogant son of a Yankee snake. It is his fault and the fault of men like him that have put us in this mess, and I do not like you cozying up to that Yankee jackanapes. There. Now, does that answer your question?"

"Morgan is a Yankee," Floyd said, "but he had nothing more to do with starting this war than Papa did. Papa did not want to fight in the war, and I do not as yet understand why he did. I think Morgan is like Papa. He did not want a war, and I do not think he wanted to fight, either. I think Morgan is basically a good man. He is very intelligent and smart, and he has a good heart. Since talking with him several times yesterday, I like him and respect him."

"A good man! Floyd, I did not think you could be so easily taken in. You think he did not want to fight in that war? Did you not hear him say he and his men were fighting for what they believed in? Papa did not believe in the war or anything about it. You cannot compare that Yankee to Papa. He fed you a bunch of pretty words that does not amount to a hill of beans." Sam was angry and so beset with an array of emotions since the arrival of the cussed Yankee. Her words sounded even somewhat hollow to her, but she would not change her thoughts on the matter.

"You were listening yesterday," Floyd said, "while we ate the noon meal. I knew you would be eavesdropping. You heard the same words I did, and if you would be honest with yourself, you would see the truth in his words and the goodness in his heart. You spied on him all day. You could not stay ten feet from him even if you were too scared to show your face."

Sam spun around and hoed the last two rows with a frenzy, directing her ire away from Floyd and down her hoe handle. Floyd watched his sister for a minute or two, finally turning to his row and shaking his head in disbelief. He had seen his sister angry, mad, and hurt, but never acting like this. *There is something else besides her temper that is causing this show of emotions. There is something all mixed up inside of her.*

Floyd mulled that little tidbit over for some time and thought he might know "the what."

Midday found Keowee, Lovie, Sam, and the boys eating their meal for the first time without the presence of Santee. Sam was extremely quiet during the meal.

Keowee and Lovie noticed her unusual mood and wondered at the cause. As forks were placed in their plates and chairs pushed back from the table, Keowee could stand Sam's silence no longer.

"Sam, what has struck you dumb? You ain't said two words the whole meal. Are you sick? It ain't like you to be like this."

"Floyd said she is mad at Mr. Morgan," David informed Keowee.

"Sam, is that true? What you got to be mad at Mr. Morgan about?" Keowee asked.

"I think part of the trouble," Floyd said, "is that she likes him more than she hates him." He grinned, as he put his napkin on top of his fork.

David sniggered at Floyd's remarks, and Sam shot daggers at both of them, as she looked across the table with her fiery cat's eyes. Without turning her eyes from her brothers, she spat out the words, "I do not like being beholden to a cussed Yankee. I told you this already."

"You ain't beholden to Mr. Morgan," Keowee replied. "He would have paid them taxes if you be here or not."

"He's playing the big moneyman by paying the cussed taxes," Sam said. "I had rather have been put in the road than having him pay those taxes."

"Child, you ain't making no sense at all," Keowee said. "Mr. Morgan didn't pay them taxes so anybody would be beholden to him. He's a good man. Always has been. I've known him since he was a little fellow. He's always had a big heart, and he's gonna pay them taxes because he thinks it's the right thing to do. You're wrong being mad at him. We's all ought to be thankful that we's don't have to worry no more about not having no place to live. I'm ashamed of you. Mad at that good man. He's done nothing to harm you. Just helped us all."

Adding to Keowee's praise of Morgan, Lovie said, "Mr. Morgan's a much nicer man than Mr. Robert. He's always been kind and helpful. Everybody on the plantation was always glad to see him and his family visit."

Giggling, David repeated Floyd's comment, "I think Sam likes him more than she hates him."

"That's crazy! He is a cussed Yankee," Sam advised the whole lot and left the table for the back stairs. She heard Lovie's sassy words, as she walked by her: "He's a mighty good-looking, young Yankee man, and he's available. He could be the one!"

Embarrassed and with a heavy heart, Sam ran to her room and away from the discerning eyes of Keowee.

No one has to tell me my behavior has been somewhat irrational these last two days, Sam admitted. Entering her bedchamber, she continued, "I know I am not my usual self. I have not been since when?" So she asked the empty room.

"What started all this churning of my emotions, turning me upside down and inside out?" The thought, *That's a foolish question,* popped into her mind. *It's not what, but who?*

"It's that cussed Yankee," she fumed. "And I do not know how to deal with it." So she confessed.

"It is not fair," she whispered, and she continued to plead about the issue.

"I will not feel kindly toward any Yankee or anything from the North or its people. In my mind and heart, all the people in the North are responsible for the destruction of my family. It took four years for the North to destroy the Confederacy, but only three months to dismantle our family, causing the death of Papa and Mama and making the four of us orphans, with no one to love and care about us except Keowee, Santee, and Lovie."

Before the last sentence was complete, her heart was breaking, and the tears were falling. Climbing up on the bed, she stretched out, with her head on the pillow, and cried herself to sleep, remembering, as her eyes closed, *He called me his angel.*

CHAPTER 7

After securing their horses in a box car, Morgan and Haygood relaxed in their compartment, each to his own pleasure. Haygood, nursing a bad case of last evening's too-much enjoyment, found a pillow to rest his aching head upon and closed his eyes, hoping for a little sleep.

Morgan mulled over what the Nix's servant had told him and the incidents he had heard about the night before at Ruby's house party, and his thoughts were filled with the magnitude of the problem. *There are charlatan soldiers operating in more states than Louisiana. News of young women missing in Louisiana has already reached Washington, and, according to what I heard last evening and today, the same is happening in Georgia and possibly South Carolina. Young women leaving home to wed Union soldiers and never to be heard from again in three states is not a coincidence. These men are not working on their own. There is an organized ring at work. There is someone who takes these women off the soldiers' hands. This someone has to have housing to hold the young women and available transportation to move the cargo of women. I am sure New Orleans is the headquarters for the ring. White slavery has always been a big moneymaker, and the South is now fertile ground.*

Hundreds of young women all over the South are without

fathers, brothers, or guardians and are ripe for the taking. Offer them a little attention with a promise of love and security, and you have your slave ready for market. We will need to move fast, and, hopefully, we can stop the next shipment from leaving U.S. soil. When I left Washington, I had no idea the problem was this widespread, and neither was President Johnson aware of the scope of this lawless depravity. He only had reports of young ladies missing in Louisiana. I will need to send him a wire also, after I get a feel of things.

***

Sam was sound asleep when Keowee tapped lightly on her chamber door and quietly eased the door open. Seeing Sam lying in bed, she tiptoed to the bed to make sure she was truly sleeping, and she spied the dried tears lining her cheeks.

The poor baby's all mixed up. There's something more than Mr. Morgan paying 'em taxes that's got her tied in knots. I wonder if Floyd could be right, but that don't ring true. She just seen Mr. Morgan yesterday. Unless! Lord have mercy. Could she be this angel Mr. Morgan be hunting for? Oh, my soul, I've got to think on this.

Slipping out of Sam's room, she checked on Lemuel and found him waking from his afternoon nap. She took him downstairs with her so he would not call out and wake Sam. Handing him over to David, she sent Floyd to the springhouse for a jug of milk, sliced several pieces of bread, spreading butter over the warm bread, and smeared a good, thick coat of scuppernong jelly. Floyd, David, Keowee, and Lovie joined Lemuel in his afternoon treat of butter-and-jelly bread and a cool glass of milk.

"Did you see Sam when you went up for Lemuel?" Floyd asked, as they sat down to eat.

"I peeped in on her," Keowee said, "and she was sound asleep. She was sleeping so soundly I didn't have the heart to wake her. Since there's nothing that needs her attention this afternoon, I just let her sleep."

"Sam sleeping in the day time?" Floyd asked. "She rarely sleeps during the night."

"Sam has a lot on her mind of late, worrying over that eviction notice," Keowee said. "Afraid y'all wouldn't have a place to live. I guess she's plumb tuckered out. Worry will do that to you. That's why I didn't wake her. She needs to rest."

"There is something bothering her other than those taxes, for sure," Floyd offered. "She was not herself today or yesterday, come to think of it. There is something other than Morgan paying those taxes and him being a Yankee that has her all rattled. I haven't got it all figured out as yet, but I'm working on it."

"The best thing we's can do for Sam is put her in our prayers and ask God to help her," Keowee said. "He knows just what's the matter and just how to fix it. We's just gonna have to trust God to work things out for Sam."

"That would be a good thing to do," Floyd agreed, as he mulled over his sister's behavior since yesterday morning. "God does know everything." Then, he added, "I am still going to think on it."

***

It was near midnight when Santee guided the horse and the barouche into the barn. After stabling the horse and unloading the items Morgan had bought and sent to Keowee for the kitchen, he started to the house, with the rewards from his trip to Athens in his arms.

"Santee," Keowee said, "I'm shor glad you be home. I've

been a little uneasy about you coming all that way back here by yourself."

"You needs not to be fretting," Santee said, as he placed his bundles on the table.

Waiting till morning to check the bundles, Santee and Keowee climbed into their bed. Both tired and sleepy, Keowee knew she'd have to wait till morning to talk with Santee about Sam.

Sam woke from her haven of sleep before old Red crowed the arrival of the new day. At first, she thought she was waking up as night was falling, but as she listened for the sounds of her family, she realized the old house was empty of the sounds of her family moving about. Walking to her favorite window, she perched on bended knees and looked out at the blackness before dawn. It was not long before the pink edge of a new day broke the eastern horizon and faithful Red crowed his welcome.

Shaking her head in amazement, she pondered, *I have slept the whole night, plus the afternoon of yesterday. I wonder what the family will think of that?* She giggled and admitted, *They are probably glad I stayed in my room, keeping my erratic behavior to myself.*

"God, my heavenly Father, help me. I know you know everything that is in my heart. Help me to find the answer. I pray in the name of Jesus."

She sat for a few minutes after praying, watching the coming day erasing the night. As the sun rose up the eastern sky, she left her lofty perch in lieu of the washstand and the basin of water to rinse the sleep from her eyes. Dressed in her boy's attire, she left her room and entered Lemuel's room, as he was beginning to stir from his night's sleep. With Lemuel dressed and ready for the day, she stopped next by Floyd and David's room, shaking each of them awake. "It is time to dress for the day and to hurry down for the morning meal."

"You finally decided to wake up?" Floyd asked in a sleepy voice, as he raised up on his elbow and looked at Sam with half-open eyes.

"No. I am sleepwalking, nosey," she threw back at him, as she closed the door.

Keowee was late getting to the kitchen after her late night. She and Lovie were rushing to get the meal on the table and barely grunted a reply to Sam's "Good morning," as she entered the kitchen. Putting Lemuel in his high chair, Sam gathered plates from the cupboard and began placing one at each chair. Finished with setting the table, Sam turned to Keowee.

"Is there anything I can do to help you?" Sam asked.

There was only one thing in particular Keowee wanted help with, but first she had to get the morning meal over and to find Santee alone so she could talk to him about Sam. However, she needed to answer Sam. "The meal will be ready in a few minutes; for now you can check the oven for me. The biscuits should be done. Be careful; don't get burned."

I'll get the biscuits," Lovie offered. "If you'll finish breaking these eggs for Mama. I'm used to messing with that hot oven."

Sam took over cracking the eggs, while Lovie moved to the oven.

While the family ate their meal of sausage, eggs, grits, and biscuits, enriched by the refills of cups of hot coffee, Sam was curious to know about the trip to Athens; however, she was not curious about the coffee they were enjoying after being so long without either the sugar or the salt that was on the table. *I am sure the coffee is from the rich Yankee, as well as the sugar and the salt, and I am not so prideful as to object to having hot coffee again with a little added sugar. Coffee, sugar, and salt are little payment for what the cussed Yankees caused.*

"Where did you sleep the night you were in Athens, Santee?" Floyd asked.

"Mr. Morgan, Mr. Haygood, and me stayed the night with a friend of Mr. Morgan," Santee replied. "Miss Ruby lived on the outskirts of Athens."

The name, Miss Ruby, kept popping into Sam's mind, as Floyd talked with Santee. The name was playing havoc with her thoughts, making her wonder, *How good a friend is this Miss Ruby to the cussed Yankee? How long has he known her, and how old is this Miss Ruby?*

After fixing a pan of hot, soapy water to wash dishes from the morning meal, Keowee joined the others. Sam and Santee began discussing the patches of corn they had planted late in the season and wondered if the patches were ready for harvesting.

Sam offered her opinion. "The ears are not filled out yet. I had to go over all three patches yesterday before I could find twelve ears for Keowee to fix for the noon meal, and there would have been more corn in the pan if the ears had been a few days older. I believe that, in order to have a good bounty for canning, we need to wait a few days before we start gathering."

Keowee agreed, "She be right, Santee. The corn gonna take a few more days before it be ripe enough for us to start canning."

"We'll look at the first patch we planted tomorrow and every day after, till the ears be ready. We's don't want any to get hard on us. Not till we have all our jars filled. Then we'll leave the rest on the stalk, till we pull it for feed and to grind for our cornmeal."

Everyone agreed to start checking the corn the next morning, and then they all scattered. With Sam's instructions, Floyd and David were off to the Sinclair library for a morning of reading, while Sam stayed in the warming kitchen to help clear the table.

Santee and Keowee were sent back to bed by Sam and Lovie because of their late night. Keowee agreed to go only after getting a promise from both girls to wake her in plenty of time to start the noon meal.

No sooner had the black couple entered their room than Keowee said, "Santee, I can't rest until I talk to you about Sam."

"What's wrong with Sam? She looked fine to me this morning."

"You should have seen her yesterday. There's something wrong. Floyd even says as much. We's both seen Sam when she's mad, angry, or hurt, but neither of us ever seen her act the way she did yesterday."

"What'd she do?"

"It started in the corn patch. I'm not too clear on all that happened there, except she and Floyd had some words about Mr. Morgan, but, at the noon meal, she sat swelled up like a toad and quiet as a mouse. I stood that as long as I could, and I asked her what was wrong. Was she sick? The boys answered she was mad at Mr. Morgan, and then Floyd says he thought she liked Mr. Morgan more than she hated him. Then Sam says that she didn't like being beholden to a Yankee and that she was mad because Mr. Morgan gonna pay 'em taxes. Says she rather be put out in the road than have him pay 'em taxes. I tried to tell her what a good man Mr. Morgan be, and Lovie told her, too. Then David kidded her about liking Mr. Morgan, and that made her madder. She says that was crazy. That he was a cussed Yankee. And she left the table, going to her room. I checked on her later, and she was asleep, but she'd cried herself to sleep 'cause I saw dried tears on her cheeks. Floyd is worried about her, too. He says there is something other than Mr. Morgan paying 'em taxes on her mind. He thinks it has something else to do with Mr. Morgan. I do, too. I'm wondering if she's not the one that helped Mr. Morgan when he was shot, not knowing who he was. And now he shows up here, and we's all are acquainted with him. There is that gun. It could belong to Mr. Morgan. There's something other than what happened on the veranda, and all the time they were here, she never spoke another word around him. She didn't eat at the table with us or enter any of the rooms Mr. Morgan was in. She stayed away from Mr. Morgan. Sam's not bashful; I would have thought she would have lit into 'em two Yankees with both feet, giving them more than a piece of her mind, unloading her anger and hatred on 'em, but, no, she just disappeared from their eyes."

"Lordy, Lordy, do you suppose that child tended to Mr. Morgan's wounds, a Yankee soldier, not knowing who he was? No. He didn't recognize her; surely he knows what the girl looks like that took care of him while he was wounded."

"I don't think so. Knowing Sam, she wouldn't have allowed him to get a good look at her face. She wouldn't have taken a chance of him being able to recognize her later, and she made me promise not to tell either of 'em she wasn't a boy. Besides, since she was dressed in her boy's clothing and that hat pulled down over her head, hiding her hair and most of her face, Mr. Morgan wouldn't have even noticed she was female yesterday. Oh, my goodness. Santee, the only thing Mr. Morgan might have recognized would have been her voice. That's why she stayed away from him. She recognized him and disguised her voice somehow on the veranda, but she wouldn't chance us hearing her. Santee, she's Mr. Morgan's angel. I'm sure of it."

"Well, I'll be a monkey's uncle. You think Sam's the one

who saved Mr. Morgan's life and her always talking about killing the first Yankee she sees."

"Yes, but Sam has a kind and tender heart. She would have helped a wounded man, even a Yankee, thinking she would never see him again, but there is something regarding that, other than her helping a Yankee. Whatever it is, it's lying heavy on her mind and more likely on her heart. She's not dealing with it easy. That's what scares me, the hatred she holds for 'em Yankee folk. And if her heart is affected, I'm a-feared what holding that hatred in her heart might do to her. Especially after all the hurt she's experienced in her young life."

Santee and Keowee pondered on these possibilities and, if they were true, what they could do to help Sam, as they closed their eyes for a short nap.

New Orleans, Louisiana

Upon arriving in New Orleans, Morgan and Haygood made themselves known to the commanding officer of the garrison occupying the town and, to the person, feeding information about the missing young women to the president. Later that evening, the two visited a taproom on the waterfront, as suggested by their contact, and, upon entering the barroom, Morgan decided that the far end of the bar would be to his advantage. Scanning the room, as he slowly made his way through the crowd, he noticed a mixture of gentry, travelers, and the common man. He was pleased with the array of the different patrons, and he was sure that Haygood would fit right in, playing his part of a friendly, fun-loving Northern visitor.

From what Morgan was able to glean from conversations, plus from what he had overheard from conversations of others, he was sure he knew what part of town the young women were being held.

Just before dawn, Morgan engaged a porter to help him and the inebriated Haygood to a hired hack. Trying to give the impression they both were well into their cups, Morgan wobbled along beside the very unsteady Haygood, as they walked from the taproom and climbed into the waiting hack.

Next morning, over coffee, Morgan was astonished by the amount of detailed information Haygood offered.

"I should not be surprised, but I am," Morgan laughed, as he scoffed. "You surely did not consume the amount of alcohol it appeared you were drinking, or you would not have been able to ascertain and to remember all this that you are reporting."

"Now, now, old man, you know it takes a heap of liquor to make this big man drunk and not aware of his surroundings or what is being said. You have to remember my size. Just for the record and your information, I am very observant. In fact, I would venture to say more so than you, and, in time, I will prove that to you."

Still chuckling, Morgan shook his head, wanting to know what Haygood was referring to, but he chose instead to remain on the subject of the young women stolen from their homes.

Haygood stuck to the subject of the missing young women, asking, "When do you expect the three musketeers? We will definitely need the boys."

"I expect Bishop, Jameson, and Whitfield tomorrow, but no later than the day after. I sent wires before we left Athens. I realized this was a larger problem than the president had thought. I am sure the young ladies are being held not far from where we were last night. From all that I heard, that is the only part of New Orleans feasible for housing and shipping. We just need to locate the house and watch the routine of the place as to when would be the best time to hit."

The three musketeers, as Haygood called them, arrived the

following day. The three former Union soldiers were to quietly blend in with the locals in the area of town Morgan wanted watched, becoming as inconspicuous as possible, while vigilantly keeping around-the-clock surveillance of the area. Any information gathered would be slipped under Morgan's door during the night. A face-to-face meeting would occur only if there was a crisis needing Morgan's attention or a break in the case.

Riverbend Plantation

July days were sunny and hot, and, by the third week of July, the corn patches were producing all they needed to fill their jars for the winter, with some to spare. They had cream corn or corn on the cob with every meal, except for the morning meal. Fresh corn, along with vegetables from the kitchen garden, were an added enjoyment to Keowee's good meals, and they had more than enough vegetables to fill their jars.

These jars would sit alongside the jars of jellies and preserves, as well as jars of blackberries, peaches, and apples.

They were anxiously awaiting the big patch of peas, and they were digging Irish potatoes to store in the hill of river sand that Keowee and the boys would make in the barn. Sweet potatoes were dug and laid out in the sun to cure. Santee and the Boys would put in a good-size patch of collards and turnips the first day of August so the greens would be ready for cooking and canning after the first frost. With their hard work and the bountiful blessings from God, they would make it through another winter.

They were all hoping the crop of peas would bring in enough money to buy everyone new boots for the winter—if there were boots in the stores to be had. If not, they would try to buy some leather, and Santee would make the boys each a pair. They were completely without boots. Either they had outgrown their old boots, or their boots were beyond repair.

August was hotter than July, and more humid, but after the sun set in the western sky and night covered the land, a cool breeze would roll in off the river. The house would fill with fresh cool air, giving the family a pleasant night of slumber after their hot, sticky day of work in the August sun.

The river was a reservoir of sources; it gave them food for their table, when Floyd and David pulled plump catfish from the river; it provided a place for frolicking, swimming, and bathing after a hot day's work; and it shared its cool breeze at night, refreshing their stifling bedchambers.

August 1865
New Orleans, Louisiana

Several days and nights of constant watching led the five men to suspect a large, old Spanish house on the outskirts of the area. The house was conveniently located near the waterfront, with direct access to a shipping dock. During another twenty-four-hour surveillance, the group noted and timed the coming and going of the people entering or exiting the house. With this time sheet, Morgan worked out the best time to raid the house, and he planned the rescue to begin at dawn, before the two guards and the old women who took care of the women at night were relieved by a larger force.

Not knowing the condition the women would be in, Morgan arranged for army conveyances to be waiting a short distance from the house. Morgan and Haygood entered by the front door after a well-placed kick by Haygood, and the former cavalrymen entered by the back door. The two guards were taken completely by surprise and were quickly subdued and carted off to jail. The older woman was bound and then taken right along with the two men.

Most of the young women were able to leave on their own, but several had to be helped. More arrests were being made in other parts of town and in Georgia and South Carolina, as the young women were being rescued.

The rescue of this house of young women was joyous, but it left the rescuers wondering about other young ladies that had been shipped to places around the world and if any would ever find their way back home.

Morgan, Haygood, and the three musketeers were tying up the few loose ends of their mission, as the men posing as Union soldiers, while wooing young women of the South with false promises of marriage, were jailed. The current group, enticed into this trap were being readied for shipment out of the country and, with this group, were a number of women who were scheduled to be disposed of because they were sick or were considered damaged goods.

Morgan made arrangements for all the young ladies to be escorted back to their respective homes, if it was impossible for a member of their family or a guardian to come for them. In the case of Miss Nix, Morgan sent a wire to the Union offices in Athens, Georgia, with instructions for the news of Miss Nix's rescue to be forwarded immediately to her brother, Mr. Nicholas Nix, in Hart County, informing him she would be returning home shortly in the company of Colonel Anderson and Captain Haygood.

Although a local madam was arrested as the head of the operation, Morgan was not completely sure she was the leader. For some unknown reason, he felt there was someone with more worldly connections behind all this mess. The more he analyzed the setup and studied the few records found in the madam's office, the more he was sure someone else was in charge. Someone moving among New Orleans high society, who was either from across the ocean or who traveled back and forth, was most likely the head of this atrocity. His intuition was working overtime, with a nagging sense that he was missing something, that there was something or someone on the outer fringe of this whole affair that he should know—something that he should recognize that would lead him to this person. And he was determined to smoke him out before he and Haygood left New Orleans.

"Haygood, I don't think we have accomplished all that we came to do. We have the tail and the body of the snake in jail, but the head is still out there somewhere. I have missed something, but I am determined to discover this evil, deranged parasite and to bring him to justice. We need to visit Madam Fifi's house of pleasure."

"What do you expect to find? The place is closed. There won't be any customers present at this time of day, even if it was still open."

"I do not expect to find men in attendance, but there has to be something there that will connect Madam Fifi to this man I am seeking."

"You are sure it is a man you are looking for and not a female?"

"Yes, a very erotic, lecherous man."

"All right let's go. We have today, tonight, tomorrow, and tomorrow night, before our ship sails."

Approaching Madam Fifi's house of pleasure, Morgan spied a person of great interest, a man who, from all reports, was supposed to still be in Europe. Tapping on the ceiling of the carriage, signaling the driver to stop a few feet shy of their destination, he watched this person of interest from the inside the carriage. The man, unaware that his movements were being observed, entered the empty place of business, using a key to unlock the door. This was very interesting to Morgan.

I wonder how he came to be in possession of a key and what his reason is for entering this place of business.

Morgan's curiosity was at a peak, as he jumped from the carriage, cautioning Haygood to remain inside. Encountering his former sergeant, as he approached from the opposite side of the building, Morgan hurriedly gave Bishop instructions and rushed him into the house; then, he returned to the parked carriage.

Inside the building, Bishop startled the man, coming upon him so quickly after the man entered the house.

Bishop immediately showed his military identification and began to quiz the man.

"Are you by chance part owner of this establishment?"

"No. I am, however, a patron and a frequent visitor, and I have misplaced a quite expensive object. I thought perhaps I had left it here on my last visit, and I came to look for it. I think that, under the circumstances, looking for it would be permissible."

"No. That will not be permitted. This place is still under investigation. I would also like to know how you came to be in possession of the key you used to open the locked door."

"A lot of Madam Fifi's valued customers have keys. I hope that is not a crime."

"No, provided you are telling the truth," Bishop said. "I will have to ask you for the key, until which time we can investigate your claim." So did Bishop demand, holding out his hand until the man reluctantly laid the key in his hand.

"Now if you would be so kind as to leave the premises," Bishop ordered the man.

The man was a little hesitant to leave, but he finally turned on his heels and left in a huff.

Morgan and Haygood watched the man leaving the house of pleasure and walking back up the street several yards behind them to a waiting carriage and entering it. From the structure of the carriage, it appeared to be personally owned. Whoever was waiting in the carriage surely saw Morgan alighting from his carriage and meeting with Bishop before Bishop entered the house. Morgan was not surprised to see the carriage turning around in the street and traveling away, in the opposite direction from Morgan and Haygood.

Evidently, the person traveling with Robert Sinclair did not want Morgan to get a look at the crest on the door of the carriage. This action gave credence to Morgan's intuition of a man's involvement and that the person was someone with social prominence.

"Zach, my intuition was right again. Whoever the other person is in that carriage, the crest on the door would have been recognizable. That is why he instructed his driver to turn around—so we could not identify the crest. The carriage belongs either to him or to the family where he is in residence.

"Whatever, I think we will find the answer inside Madam Fifi's establishment, but what is puzzling is that Robert Sinclair is somehow involved."

"Robert Sinclair? Would he be related to the Sinclairs of Riverbend?"

"Yes, Zach; Robert is the heir to Riverbend."

"Well, I will be a hog-tied jackass. Who would have thought there would be a connection to him? Do you think he is the one you are looking for?"

"No; Robert doesn't have the brains to organize something like this. Now, he might be knee-deep, or even neck-deep, involved, but he is not the man I am looking for. It will be someone with more money than Robert has and someone more depraved than Robert. Robert is as immoral as they come, and a coward, to boot. The kidnapping of young ladies would not turn his stomach. Now that I have witnessed him entering that house with a key and his return to the mysterious carriage after his meeting with Bishop, I am sure he knows all there is to know about this. It is my guess, and it is really more than just a guess. Robert was sent into that house by the person in that carriage to get something that person does not want found by us."

Entering the house, Morgan and Haygood found Bishop waiting to give Morgan a report of his meeting with the man he had followed into Madam Fifi's house of pleasure.

"First, I want to know what Robert had to say about the key, then what he said was the reason for his visit this morning."

"He claimed all valued customers of Madam Fifi have keys. He also claimed to have misplaced an expensive object. He did not say what the object was, only that he thought he might have left it here and was here looking for it. He left peacefully, but he was not pleased."

Morgan chuckled at the last sentence of Bishop's report, knowing the nature of the Sinclair heir.

"Thank you, Bishop; you carried that off well. I suppose you might need to get some sleep if you were here all night."

"No, I relieved Jameson around 7:30 this morning. I imagine Whitfield will relieve me later this afternoon, if you still need for this place watched."

"It all depends on what we find, if we find anything at all. In any case, Whitfield will need to watch from a hiding place inside the house tonight. I think that the person interested in getting whatever it is that ties him to this plot might be back and that he will not wait too long."

Morgan entered Madam Fifi's office, and Bishop went to the cellar.

Morgan's first target was the large desk occupying the center of the madam's office. After several hours of tearing the room apart, as well as Madam Fifi's living quarters, he found only one item he considered useful: a large envelope containing an old wanted poster from France for an Irvetta Cur and an accounting ledger listing money paid to someone Madam Fifi called "the bastard."

The name "Bastard" was written in the place designated for the payee's name, and, totaling the listed amounts, Morgan realized a lot of money had gone to this bastard over the past years. The dates told of a long history. *The connection between this person and Madam Fifi did not begin with this scheme.* Madam Fifi was paying this man regularly before the first young lady disappeared. However, the time span that coincided with the estimated time the young ladies began disappearing was the most interesting. The amount Madam Fifi had paid decreased after that time. Whatever Madam Fifi had earned for her participation in this evil ploy had gone to lessen the debt she had owed "Bastard." *There must be something more dangerous to Madam Fifi's well-being than what she is facing on these charges of kidnapping young ladies for a white slavery trade, or she would name the bastard. It probably has something to do with this wanted poster.*

While Morgan was pondering his find, he heard sounds of Bishop running up the cellar steps. Hoping Bishop's hurry to quit the cellar indicated a find and not his wish for fresh air, Morgan left Madam Fifi's office, and as he turned down the hall, he saw Bishop stepping through the cellar doorway, carrying a rusty metal box covered in dust.

"The box is locked. I tried forcing the lock open, but it

would not give," Bishop informed Morgan, as he handed the box over to him. This was the only thing I saw in my search of the cellar that looked the least bit as if it could mean anything to this quagmire."

Haygood was the last to call his search complete, as he walked down the stairs from the floor above.

"I looked over all the rooms upstairs, as with a fine-tooth comb. I checked the ones on this floor, as well. I have found nothing that would tie in with this wickedness."

"I found a large envelope with a couple of interesting items that's going to require some thought and investigation," Morgan said. "This box that Bishop uncovered could hold the key to this mystery man. I found no key in Madam Fifi's office or quarters. Which is strange. Surely, she would have a key somewhere for this box, if it belonged to her, but we will not wait for a key. I will have the smithy at headquarters cut the lock. I am confident he will be able to accommodate us and remove the lock."

Turning his thoughts to other matters, Morgan spoke to Bishop, "When Whitfield relieves you, have him continue the watch from inside and explain why he needs to do this. Before you retire to your quarters, check the train depot and the shipping office. I need to know if the man we encountered here earlier has bought a ticket or booked passage on a ship. The name of the man is Robert Sinclair, and he will possibly be leaving New Orleans for Savannah. You might also need to describe him to the gentleman you speak to, in case he used a different name. Whatever information you get, I need to know of it, as well as the time and dates, if any, as soon as possible. Write it all down and slip it under the door of my hotel room before you retire. Thanks for your good work, and maybe you and the others can head home in a few days. I'll be in touch."

The smithy was successful in cutting the lock off the metal box, but Morgan left the box closed until he and Haygood were in their quarters.

Bishop did as he was ordered, and Morgan found a sealed envelope on the floor of his hotel room the moment he entered. A detailed account of the information gathered at the shipping office was carefully noted—as follows: "Robert Sinclair is still in New Orleans. However, he tried to obtain passage today after his visit to Madam Fifi's. The ship was making ready to depart at that time, but, to his displeasure, the ship's cabins were all taken. He then asked to book passage on the ship leaving the day after tomorrow, but, after looking over the passenger list for the sailing, he decided to wait until the next ship for Savannah, which will leave in four days. The manager seemed to think there must have been someone on the passenger list of the ship leaving the day after tomorrow that changed his mind, because it was only after looking over the list of passengers that he expressed his desire to change his booking. Do you suppose your name and Haygood's had anything to do with this change? His passage is booked under the name of Count Luis La Cur and includes La Cur, Lady La Cur, and Robert Sinclair."

After he read the last sentence of Bishop's report, Morgan's face turned red as a beet, and he swore, "I be xxxx! I should have suspected the SOB was involved in this. The nature of this atrocity is descriptive of the corrupt bastard. This is what has been nagging at me. I knew I was missing something. The appearance of Robert Sinclair and knowing he sat the war out in France—I should have known!"

Haygood sat silent, while Morgan voiced his revelation, but as Morgan took a breath, he asked questions he was sure he knew the answers to but wanted to hear the how. "You know this man? Do you? Do you know him well enough to know he is the head of the snake without further proof?"

"Yes! I know him!"

"A little explanation would be nice."

"He is a SOB, as I said earlier! I am just surprised he is back on American soil and heading toward Riverbend. News of Mac's death must have reached France somehow. No. On second thought, they have been here long before Mac's death to have organized this well-run racket. Now that Mac's dead and we've arrested his New Orleans crew, the bastard feels free to visit Riverbend either to lie low or to start anew."

"How would Mr. Sinclair's death have anything to do with whether or not he visits Riverbend?"

"Luis is a relative of the late Mrs. Sinclair. Mac's wife was French, and, at the time of their meeting and their wedding, she was from New Orleans. Some of La Cur's relatives still live here. I do not know how many times Luis visited America after the Sinclair wedding, but I do know about his last visit. He arrived here in the fall of 1860, and he stayed until the last of March 1861. He left just prior to the start of the war. During his visit at Riverbend, he misused and abused two young slave girls, leaving the two in his bed for Keowee to find. One of the girls was Keowee's baby sister. Mac made it plain at that time that Luis was not welcome at Riverbend in the future, and he ordered him off Riverbend land at gunpoint, threatening his life if he ever returned. He came to New Orleans from Riverbend and remained there until just prior to the start of the war."

Speechless for several moments, Haygood just looked at Morgan with a look of pure malevolence. Finally, with a scornful sneer, he exploded, "You called him only an SOB. The term is too mild to describe this lowlife's character and behavior. I do not know if there is a word in the English language that would come anywhere near describing him. How in the world could Mr. Sinclair's wife be related to this man?"

"I agree that the adjective I used referring to Luis La Cur is a bit mild. However, I am truly surprised that Mac allowed Robert's visit to France, knowing Luis's character. There has to be something other than the war that made that visit necessary. It's common knowledge Mac hired a man to fight in Robert's place, so there was no need for Robert to leave the South on the war's account. Enough about family history. We need to examine the contents of the box."

The contents were baffling. There was a drawing of an ancient family crest and a lot of words supposedly referring to the drawing, all scribbled in French. The papers were old, and most of the writing was almost illegible.

"We will need an expert in old documents to unscramble these clues."

As he closed the box lid and turned to place the box in his valise, he hesitated keeping the box in his grasp. Looking back at Haygood, he informed him and spoke almost as if he were informing himself.

"I would be willing to bet that this is what Robert was sent to retrieve and that Luis La Cur was the man in the carriage behind us. If I am not mistaken, Robert knows by now that it was I who sent Bishop into Madam Fifi's after him. I am the one Luis La Cur is running from. France is where this whole scheme was hatched. Luis has probably been in this business for some time and has an organization in Europe. This is a larger setup than we first thought. Luis perceived the outcome of the war would be fertile ground for him. Using Madam Fifi and her henchmen, he acquired the men he needed to carry out this scheme and put them to work entrapping these unsuspecting young ladies who were without fathers, brothers, guardians, or the proper protection."

Haygood made a few circles around the room, while digesting Morgan's theory of the working of the evil, illicit crime. Scratching his head, he wanted more information on how they would proceed. "What now? We have no judicial authority in France or any foreign country."

"We will leave that to President Johnson and his ambassadors," Morgan answered. "However, we have the head of the snake in our sights, and our aim had better be true. Just knowing that Luis is the mastermind of the crime against these young ladies is not enough; we will need to have concrete evidence in order to see this man put where he belongs and he gets what he deserves. We had better be able to catch him with his hands in the cookie jar, so to speak. I am confident that once we are able to decipher the contents of the box, tie it in with the wanted poster, plus the ledger, we will have the nails to close his coffin."

"I am aware that nine times out of ten your projections are correct. I hope this is not the tenth," Haygood offered Morgan, as his thoughts turned to Riverbend: *If the depraved SOB is headed to the Sinclair Plantation, Angel will be right in his sights. Who will be her protector? Lord, I am between a rock and a hard place. Should I tell Morgan that his tomcat is really a female and more than likely his Angel and that if Luis La Cur ends up at Riverbend, she is going to be right in the midst of this mess?*

"Keowee?" Haygood asked.

What about Keowee?" Morgan asked.

"I am sure she has not forgotten the bastard. How will his arrival at Riverbend affect her? Shouldn't we at least warn her that this person is on his way back to the plantation? Surely, you are not going to let him just show up without giving her an advance notice."

"Haygood, I would never consider not telling Keowee and Santee that Luis La Cur is again on American soil, and with Robert soon to be on his way to Riverbend. I just do not know how I am going to tell them. No matter how I word it, the past history of La Cur will automatic emerge, along with the memory of Sadie Keowee' baby sister."

CHAPTER 8

August days began early and warm on the river plantation. This day everyone but Keowee and Lemuel were early visitors to the pea patch. Hoping to gather all the ripe pods before the midday sun became scorching hot, the group entered the patch, as the light of day broke through the vanishing night, and they gathered eight bushels. Sam and Santee were over-joyed by the bountiful yield of their first picking, and they allotted two bushels for family use and six bushels to be sold in Athens.

Tomorrow would be another early day for everyone, except for David and Lemuel. Sam, Santee, and Floyd, would need to be on the road to Athens before the sun was up.

The afternoon was spent shelling and canning peas for the winter to come. The task of shelling was carried out in the cool shade of the oak trees surrounding the warming kitchen. All had their laps full of pea pods and a pan to empty the shelled peas into, with the exception of Lemuel, who played on a quilt spread out between Sam and Keowee.

When the large dishpan in the middle of their circle was full of shelled peas, Keowee would move to the warming kitchen and start her sorting, picking out the peas not fit for canning. This chore of shelling and canning would take the better part of the afternoon, and, eventually, Lovie would move to the warming kitchen to help with the canning process.

After a few hours, Floyd and David became restless and headed to the river, with poles and a jar of worms. Sam and Santee were left to finish the bushels allotted for family use.

Late in the afternoon, Sam's shelling slowed, and her mind wandered. Her thoughts turned to her Yankee, as they would when it was quiet. As she struggled with her thoughts, Sam became aware of her name being called.

"Sam, Sam, Samantha Hatcher!" Santee's loud voice invaded her thoughts, startling her. And she yelled, "What!"

"I had to call you five times before you heard me, and you were sitting just across from me," Santee scolded. "You feeling poorly this afternoon? Did you get too hot in the pea patch? The drooping of that pretty face tells old Santee you ain't up to snuff."

When Santee stopped to catch his breath, Sam readied her answer. Sam set her pan of shelled peas down on the ground beside her chair, stood, stretching her back, and replied, "Truth is, I am a little drowsy. I am used to moving about, not sitting in one place for hours. I was just having trouble keeping my eyes open. I'll be back to finish the last basket," Sam threw over her shoulders as she lumbered off toward the river."

"Hmmmm," Santee mumbled. He decided he'd give the devil her due, because something or somebody was sure on her mind. Whatever or whoever it be was playing on her mind, and she didn't want no prying.

Sam was deep in thought, as she walked to the river bank, *If God would only hasten the return of the Sinclair heir.*

Robert Sinclair's homecoming would take the responsibility of Riverbend and the welfare of the boys and me out of that cussed Yankee's hand and would send the Yankee back north.

Keowee's thoughts, for some reason, turned to the return of the Sinclair heir, and she gasped, as a cold hand of fear tightened around her heart.

True to her word, Sam returned with the boys and their stringer of fish. She sat back down in her chair across from Santee, as the boys carried their fish into Keowee. Rid of her thoughts of the cussed Yankee for the moment, she relished the coming supper of fried fish.

The last bushel empty, Sam moved to the kitchen to help Keowee and Lovie. Later, with all the jars filled and Sealed, Keowee placed a platter of fried catfish on the table.

"Mmmmm, those fish smell good," Sam called. "We'll enjoy eating those tasty morsels as much as, if not more than, Floyd and David enjoyed catching them this afternoon."

"I don't know about that," Keowee chuckled. "'Em two brothers of yours sure do like to fish, and it's a good thing they do. They bring a stringer of good-size fish once or twice a week, and that helps keep good, fresh meat on the table.

The picking, shelling, and canning of peas finished for the day, they gathered around the long table for their evening meal. Sitting around the table during the evening meal was a favorable time for them, and they lingered until the dwindling sunlight forced them from the room.

As Sam, Santee, and Keowee planned for an early rising for the coming morning, Morgan Anderson and Zach Haygood looked forward to their ship reaching Savannah, come the morrow.

Arriving in Savannah, Georgia, Morgan did not linger. Despite Haygood's plea for a day without travel, he booked passage for them on the train to Athens, leaving within the hour after their debarkation. Morgan's recollection of the university that existed in Athens prior to the war and his hopefulness that he would find a professor or a scholar knowledgeable in French documents hastened his travel onto Athens the moment his feet touched Georgia soil.

After seeing to Miss Nix's comfort, Morgan took his seat across the aisle. Sitting next to a sullen Haygood, Morgan tried to explain his hurry.

"There is bound to be someone connected to the university who can decipher these documents or who can direct us to a scholar who can. You know that deciphering these documents found in the tin box could be the key to arresting La Cur."

Haygood's silence in response to Morgan's explanation and his childish attempt to ignore him as he stared out the window of the moving train, for some reason, presented a comical picture to Morgan, and his soft chuckles became full-blown heehaws, as he leaned his head back against the top of his seat.

"Okay, okay, you have made your point, I guess," Haygood finally replied.

Upon arriving in Athens, the pair deposited Miss Nix in a private room in the Lumpkin House and made their way to the headquarters of the Union Army. A message was sent posthaste to Mr. Nicholas Nix, advising him of his sister's safe arrival in Athens and asking him or a trusted member of his household to travel to Athens to escort Miss Nix home. Assured the message was on the way, Morgan turned to the reason he would be spending the next few days in Athens. Finding Captain Cree, commanding officer of the Iowa Twenty-Second Volunteers, the Union Army now occupying the town of Athens, he asked, "Where can I find the offices of the University of Georgia that was here prior to the war?"

"Colonel Anderson, I have no knowledge of a university operating at this time in this area. I have been told that our headquarters is in the building of what was once the university."

"Thanks, Captain. I'll see what I can find out from the local merchants."

Captain Cree cautioned, "The town was occupied by the Tennessee Thirteenth until the Iowa Twenty-Second relieved that army on the twenty-ninth of May. The Tennessee regiment, commanded by General William J. Palmer came into the town on May 5, looking for the Confederate President Jefferson Davis and, for two weeks, the soldiers plundered the defenseless city. It was two weeks of chaos, and the people here have been anything but friendly. "Good luck," was Captain Cree's final words.

Visiting merchants and shop owners, Morgan and Haygood began their quest, inquiring about teachers or professors who had taught at the university prior to the war, but they found no shop owner or merchant willing to divulge the first name.

With the shop doors closed to them—rather, slammed shut—they returned to the hotel. After arranging for a midday meal to be sent to Miss Nix, Morgan and Haygood adjourned to the hotel dining hall for their noon meal.

While Morgan was later sitting with Miss Nix in the lobby of the hotel, awaiting the arrival of the person to escort her home to Hart County, his mind was on only one thing, the documents. And he and Haygood were discussing their disappointment in receiving no information from the shop owners.

"What information are you seeking, if I am not too forward in asking?" Miss Nix inquired timidly.

"We were asking around town for information regarding the names and the whereabouts of former professors of the university that was housed in Athens prior to the war. I was hoping to find a scholar that might be able to help us decipher some old drawings we found in our investigation in New

Orleans."

"Oh! Is that all? Nicholas will be able to help you. I am sure he will be glad to share information of that nature with you."

"Your brother is acquainted with the teaching staff of the university?"

"He was a student there before the war and became, if I am not mistaken, acquainted with all the professors at one time or another. I am sure he will know enough of them to get you started on your search."

It was late afternoon when Nicholas Nix arrived in Athens and relieved Morgan and Haygood of the care of his sister, and Alison Nix was correct in assuring Morgan and Haygood that her brother would give them the information they wanted.

Nix was so grateful for the safe return of his baby sister that he was more than willing to give Morgan the name and location of a professor Nicholas named "Farmer" because he spent his vacations digging in the dirt, looking for relics.

The sun was midway down the western sky by the time Morgan discovered the name and location of Professor Neeley.

However late the hour, Morgan was ready to make a call. He was more than anxious to see if this former professor could shed some light on the items in the box, and he made a visit to the "farmer" at once.

With Nix's detailed directions to the "farmer's" residence, Morgan and Haygood rode straight to the man's door. The home was smaller than the houses in the same vicinity, but the yard and the flower beds were neat and well-manicured.

After several knocks, a dignified and stately older Negro man opened the door, asking, "Gentlemen, may I help you?"

He also inquired, "Since you are strangers, may I ask who you are and why you are calling on the professor?"

Morgan quickly furnished the old servant with his card,

asking if they could step inside, while the servant inquired if the good professor would see them.

Bowing slightly and stepping aside, the servant pointed to the room on their right. "Make yourselves comfortable in the parlor. I'll see if the professor is at home."

Five or ten minutes passed before they heard the sliding steps of the old servant approaching the parlor.

"Gentlemen, the professor has agreed to give you an audience. He's just finishing his evening meal and will meet you shortly in his study."

Bowing to the men, he again requested, "Please follow me."

After another five or ten minutes' wait, the door opened, and in walked an image of the past, a perfect reflection of a Southern gentleman of 1861. The clothes were a little worn and outdated, and a little loose, in places. However, Morgan knew that, at one time, they were the top of the style, and he was sure that the fit had been perfect. The man was, perhaps, sixty years old; his hair was white as snow; and he had a handlebar mustache to match. His white hair hinted at his age, yet his eyes, bright blue as the sea on a clear day, sparkled with interest and intelligent curiosity.

"I am Professor Neeley. How may I be of service to you gentlemen?"

"How do you do, Professor? I am Colonel Morgan Anderson, and the gentleman at my side is Captain Zachery Haygood.

We were sent to the south by President Johnson on a special assignment. During our investigation, we discovered some old drawings and inscriptions that have us baffled. They could prove to be helpful in bringing the prime suspect in this terrible crime to justice. A former student of yours, Mr. Nicholas Nix, was kind enough to steer us in your direction, and we are here tonight, urgently asking for your help. We will gladly pay for your services."

"First, Colonel Anderson, I see you are not in uniform, yet you introduced yourself and your companion with military titles. Why is that? Second, before I agree to help you, I must know if this assignment or mission of yours involves investigating the conquered Confederate States?"

"Your questions are legitimate and well received. I will be happy to answer them. We are not in uniform because we are working undercover, as it were. Our assignment has nothing to do with the Confederacy. However, it does have something to do with crimes being rendered against Southern people. So far, we have been able to ascertain that only three Southern states are affected by these crimes: South Carolina, Georgia, and Louisiana. We were successful in arresting what I call the body and the tail of the snake, but not the head, and that is why we have sought your help."

"You are not going to tell me the nature of this crime, are you?" asked the professor solemnly.

"Not as yet. You have not said if you are willing to help nail this SOB, and I can assure you that he is not Southern or Northern, although he has connections with people of the South. As of now, I do not know if the people in Louisiana that he is visiting in their homes are knowledgeable of this crime. He did have men working in the scheme from both parts of our country. These men are already behind bars. I am sure that the man traveling with him from France to New Orleans and that will travel in his company from New Orleans to Georgia knows of what he is involved in. Hearing what I have just told you, will you help us?"

"I would like to know the nature of the man's crime," the professor said, continuing to dig for answers that would satisfy his ethical principles. Morgan had watched the interest and concern growing in the old gentleman's eyes and felt sure he was eager to help, so he answered, "Kidnapping."

"Was it the kidnapping of young Southern women, and was it done for monetary gain?'

"Yes."

"How can I be of assistance?"

Morgan, still standing, produced the box from the chair to the left of where he stood. He carried the box to the desk of the professor, who was now sitting behind it and placed it in front of the man he hoped would solve the mystery of the documents.

Haygood had long since found a comfortable chair, on which to deposit his large frame, and he watched Morgan's words sparring with the professor.

Morgan watched, as the professor removed the papers from the box and laid them side by side across the desk.

The papers were old and needed to be handled with the uttermost care. The professor was most meticulous in the handling of the papers, and Morgan realized, within a short time, that these were not the first ancient documents the professor had worked with.

"As you suspect, Colonel, it will take some time to work this out, and as you probably guessed, the wording is old French and very poorly written. The author of the documents either wrote in a very big hurry or was not well-educated. Will you leave the documents with me, or will you transport them back and forth, while we work on deciphering these missives?"

Haygood watched as Morgan warred within himself, wanting the answers the documents would provide but not being completely sure he wanted them out from under his protection. Haygood was not the only one watching Morgan's hesitant reaction to the professor's question.

"If you would feel more comfortable taking the papers back with you tonight, Colonel," the professor offered, "I understand. Perhaps after we have worked a while together, you will feel more secure in leaving the papers in my care. I can assure you no one will be able to snatch them out of my hands."

His decision made Morgan inform the professor of the urgency, "We are in a hurry, to say the least, to know what these documents can mean to our investigation. If any. We believe the man that is the head of the snake we are dedicated to arresting will soon be on Georgia soil, and we desperately need this information to stop him from harming any more young Southern ladies. I would like to begin this project early tomorrow morning, if that is agreeable with you. We will arrive shortly after breaking our fast. If it is not convenient for the two of us to be in your home while you are deciphering, we shall rent a room in the hotel for you to use as your work room."

"No need to go to that added expense. My home will suffice; so good-bye till the morning, gentlemen. Abraham will see you out."

The old servant opened the door as soon as the professor's last words were spoken.

Haygood and Morgan looked at each other in surprise, but they smiled as they realized the old servant was listening at the door all the time, making sure his friend and former master was safe in the company of the two strangers.

***

Later that night, in the darkness of the country road, no windows shared their candlelight or lamp light, as a wagon rolled slowly along. The new moon gave very little light to the three weary people carefully watching the road for a familiar pasture fence or a patch of woods, telling them they were near their destination. Sam sat on the seat with Santee, watching the road ahead, and Floyd watched the right side of the road from the wagon bed. They had left Athens in the early afternoon and had eaten their biscuits and sausage as they crossed the covered bridge over the Oconee River. This was turning into a very long day, as they had left Riverbend early in the morning before the sun was up. Their trip to Athens had been successful; they had sold all six baskets of peas. With money from the sale of four bushels, Santee had visited a store and had bought ready-made boots to fit Floyd and David, while Sam and Floyd had sold the last two baskets of peas. The boys would have new boots to start the winter.

Santee was still laughing about their last customer, as he guided the old plow horse up the dark road. "Sam, that lady shor-nuff wanted that basket; I believe she wanted that basket more than she wanted the peas, but you showed her when you came up with that sack. I shor wish I'd seen it all. I just got in on the last as y'all were filling that sack with peas and you was grabbing that dollar. Yes sirree, I would like to have seen it all. We'll have a good one to tell Keowee and Lovie tomorrow."

"Santee," Floyd called. "Our turnoff is just up a little ways. I recognized that old oak tree growing almost in the road, which that big, old bobcat jumped out of and ran across the road in front of us, as we were coming back from Bull Snort. Remember?"

"You shor nuff right, Floyd, and here's our turnoff," Santee said. "We's almost home. Praise the Lord. That's been a might long road." So did Santee acknowledge as he pulled the reins to the right, giving the old mare the reins.

"We's finally on Riverbend land, and old Maud knows it as

sure as we does."

The dawn of the new day broke the eastern sky, and old Red's welcome to the new day came too early for Sam, waking her from a sound sleep.

"That cussed rooster sits right below my window, crowing his silly head off the minute the sun breaks the eastern sky," Sam grumbled. She rolled out of bed, still fussing, as the effect of yesterday's long hours and short night's sleep left her temper raw.

Squawking, "I wish that cussed bird would find some other place to perform his duties," as she made her way to the wash-stand in the dim light, she stumped her little toe on the edge of the modesty screen and said words she would have washed the boys' mouths out with soap if they uttered such words. Washing the sleep from her eyes, she donned her boy's attire and left the chamber for the warming kitchen.

Coals from the previous evening's cooking fire smoldered in the back of the chimney, and Sam quickly pulled the hot embers to the front of the fireplace. From the wood box, she laid on pine knots and wood onto the fire that would be needed to cook the morning meal. Soon, flames licked upward, and the blaze gave forth both warmth and light.

Pulling a chair near the stone hearth, she propped her feet on it and waited for the warmth to chase away the chill of the early morning. As usual, the tranquility of the room in the early hours were enhanced by the crackling and popping, as the blaze rumbled over and around the logs, leaping upward and racing the smoke up the chimney.

Now wide awake, Sam was ready for her day to get started, and it wasn't long till she heard Keowee coming from her bed.

"Morning, Keowee; I've made the fire, and I'm ready to help you get the morning meal started before I go up to get the boys."

Keowee cast a discerning eye Sam's way, looking for signs of a sleepless night, but she found none. Sam looked as fresh as a daisy.

"Child what has you up before old Keowee?"

"Old Red. He has taken to sitting below my window every morning for the last few months and crows his welcome to the day. He wakes me every morning, and this morning he was extra loud."

"He used to roost in that old tree at the south corner of the warming kitchen. I wonder what's chased him from that tree? We'll have to think on that."

This day began as early as the two days before on the Riverbend Plantation. All, but Keowee and Lemuel, were again visitors to the pea patch, hoping to gather all the newly ripe pods before the midday sun became scorching hot.

By midday, the baskets were filled to the brim with ripe pods.

After enjoying a delicious meal of fresh vegetables, with blackberry cobbler for desert, the pickers relaxed and rested their backs for a spell. The afternoon was again spent with shelling and canning.

***

After days of watching Professor Neeley's painstaking method of working with the documents, Morgan and Haygood prepared to leave Athens for Riverbend. As Morgan was settling their hotel bill, Professor Neeley entered the hotel lobby. Stopping short of the desk, he waited for Morgan to complete his business. Morgan knew, from the look on the professor's face, that there was a break in the deciphering, and he hurried to him.

"Where can we talk privately?" Professor Neeley asked excitedly."

Morgan motioned for Haygood and led the two men into an anteroom off the lobby. Before the professor could speak, Morgan asked, closing the door, "You have some news?"

"Not exactly news you are awaiting, but a break in the deciphering. Some of the documents are old family documents regarding a family crest. The others are a record or an accounting of some possible misdeed against the family endowed with this crest. I am sorry, but I feel I will need help, especially with these documents regarding the history of the crest. I have been able to translate a portion of the documents and the wanted poster, but how they affect the lineage of the family endowed with the crest I am afraid I will need help. I corresponded regularly over the years before the war with a professor in France, who is an expert in French family crests and the history of such. I wanted to talk to you about possibly writing to him, giving him a copy of the crest and asking for the history of any gossip or suspected illegalities pertaining to the crest. It will take a couple of months or more to receive his reply, but I know of no one else who could help with this particular puzzle."

"You are sure that some of these documents more or less tell a story of some kind of wrongdoings regarding this crest?"

"Yes, the family names involved are Cur and La Cur. I have deciphered both names, but which family did what I am still working on. As you know, some of the words are faded almost to the point of being unreadable. Someone who knows the history of the French nobles will know what is suspected and who the crest originally and legally belongs to and the how or what happened to the true owner."

"Is there not a scholar of French history in America that

we could contact and get a faster reply than going overseas?" Morgan asked, wanting the puzzle solved faster than the several months Professor Neeley spoke of.

"I have no idea. As soon as I realized what you had, I thought of my letter-writing acquaintance and his expertise." Morgan mulled over all the professor told him for a while, thinking of all possibilities, and finally asked, "How long will it take you to make copies of the crest that we would send to France?"

"Several days."

"In the meantime, I will send a wire to Washington, inquiring if there is a person in the States with the expertise we need. I will have the answer to whether or not one can be found by the time the documents are ready to send either to France or to somewhere in the States. Fair enough?"

"Yes."

Two things Morgan needed to do before heading north to Riverbend could be accomplished at the Union Army headquarters. First was a wire sent to President Johnson, asking if anyone in his office knew of a scholar whose expertise was French history, particularly pertaining to French family crests, and asking for a quick reply. Second,

Morgan impressed upon Captain Cree the importance of getting messages to him posthaste.

"As soon as I receive a reply to this wire, rush it to Riverbend Plantation. Also, if one of your men placed in the railroad station spots a man fitting Robert Sinclair's description arriving, I need to know immediately. I would appreciate your sending your fastest horse and best rider with either the reply to my wire or the spotting of Robert Sinclair."

Morgan and Haygood mounted their horses and rode north out of Athens and over the Oconee River and onto the road leading to Danielsville, Hart County, and Riverbend.

Hoping to reach Riverbend by midafternoon, Morgan and Haygood set a steady pace out of Athens, but, the farther they rode away from the town, conditions of the roadway at times made it impossible to keep the fast pace Morgan had desired. However, when they found the roadway moderately clear, they rode hard and fast, as if a troop of Reb cavalry were racing behind them. After several grueling hours of hard riding and walking their mounts, Morgan began recognizing familiar landmarks and knew the turnoff to the plantation was near.

While their mission had stretched into more days than Morgan had anticipated when heading to Riverbend, he was not looking forward to today's visit. The items crammed into his and Haygood's saddlebags would be appreciated by Keowee and Santee, but the items would not soften the news he was obligated to bring them.

As the empty, overgrown fields of Riverbend gave way to the vista of the sun-blistered walls of the old home, anger flared in Morgan's chest, but as he rode closer to the house, the anger turned to a sense of anguish and loss that almost consumed him. Astonished by the degree his emotions were affected by the ruined condition of the once-beautiful home, he increased the speed of his mount, racing to the barn, as if he could outrun what caused these feelings.

Haygood, not to be left in Morgan's dust, spurred his horse on. Both men raced around the Sinclair home and into the backyard and toward the stables, causing the occupants of the warming kitchen to stare at each other in alarm. Seeing the fright on the faces of the women, Santee headed to the yard through the kitchen door. Keowee ran to Santee, catching his arm before he could exit the door and pleading for him to stay in the kitchen, not noticing Sam fleeing up the back stairs.

Sam did not flee up the back stairs to get away from the strangers on horseback but to get the Yankee pistol hid in her room.

Taking the gun from the lair, she was down the front stairs, out the front doors, and around the house as fast as her feet would take her, stopping as the stables came into view. She crouched behind the large fig bush at the corner of the warming kitchen. She could hear sounds of men talking and knew they would be coming out in a few minutes.

Considering herself in the right place to get a good shot at the men as they exited the barn and to protect her family from them, she readied herself to shoot; her hands resting on the trigger, she waited. The men, dusty from their ride, walked into view, and Sam pulled the trigger.

Morgan's hat flew from his head, and both men hit the dirt. Sam, seeing whom she shot, turned and ran, retracing her steps. Locked in her room, she stood looking at the gun in her shaking hand, while, below the stairs, there was chaos.

Morgan and Haygood slowly came to their feet. Picking up his hat, Morgan stared at the hole a couple of inches above the hatband. Turning to show it to Haygood, he found his friend investigating a fig bush several yards away. Stunned, he turned toward the warming kitchen and spied Santee peeking out the door.

"Lordy mercy, Mr. Morgan, is that you?" Morgan heard Santee ask.

"If the aim of the person pulling that trigger was a better shot, I would not be standing," Morgan answered, as he walked toward the warming kitchen door.

"Santee, who around here would take a shot at Haygood and me? Do you know anyone close by that would have a pistol?"

The color drained from his face, but Santee met Morgan halfway between the kitchen door and the stables, shaking his head, "No."

Finding his voice, he finally spoke, "Mr. Morgan, nobody at Riverbend wishes you harm. That shot has left me dumbfounded."

By the time Santee had reached Morgan, Keowee followed in Santee's footsteps. She was also lacking color in her face.

She asked, "Mr. Morgan, could somebody have followed you and snuck onto the yard while y'all was in the stable, shooting at you when you came out?"

"Possibly," Morgan admitted. "They would have had to have known where we were heading, because no one ever gets close enough to us on the road to follow us without our noticing and being aware of that person's presence. I do not recall anyone trailing behind us. Do you, Haygood?"

Turning with his words, he saw Haygood still checking the large fig bush.

Haygood answered in the negative. He joined the group, as everyone from the house surrounded Morgan, and Haygood quickly noticed Morgan's tomcat was missing. *Surely she could not be the one who shot at us?* Haygood thought. *Where on earth would she come by a pistol?* With that thought, Haygood almost swallowed his tongue, as he remembered Morgan's missing sidearm when he returned to camp after being wounded. *Well, I'll be that little tiger. What was her reason? Why would she want to shoot Morgan? I'm thankful her aim was off. Or was that shot a warning? I've got to waylay her away from the boys and ask some pointed questions before this can go any farther.*

The two Yankees walked to the house, seemingly unnerved. In the warming kitchen, Keowee and Lovie busied themselves with setting out refreshments for Morgan and Haygood, while the boys got a chance to approach Morgan.

They gave him their welcome and expressed their sorrow that someone would try to harm him. Haygood watched the two, wondering how the boys could warm to Morgan if they were related to the she-cat. He decided there was something between the kitty cat and Morgan, besides his being a Yankee. The more he thought on that, the more he liked it. So the grin that had annoyed Morgan, while they both were riding north, returned.

After visiting with everyone, Morgan knew it was time to talk with Keowee and Santee. There was no need for him to delay telling them the news he carried.

"Keowee, Santee, I need a few minutes of your time. If now suits you?"

"Yes, sir. There ain't nothing pressing. You want us to go to Mr. Mac's study?" asked Santee.

"Yes."

Haygood watched Morgan lead the couple through the door and down the hall, knowing he did this with a heavy heart.

As Morgan and the two former slaves left the room, Haygood motioned for Floyd and David to follow him outside.

Under the large oak trees, Haygood turned to the boys and asked, "Would you two fellows happen to be kin to Sam?"

David stood silent, as was his habit, waiting for Floyd to speak. Floyd was suspicious of Haygood's question, but he was not going to disown being Sam's brother. "Sam is the oldest of our family. Our papa and mama are both dead. Sam, being the oldest, carries a heavy load and does not feel kindly toward Yankees. Why do you ask?"

"Just my Yankee curiosity, trying to place everyone,"

Haygood replied. "You two seem to have accepted Morgan and me, but I have noticed Sam does not join the family at meals or at any time. Is this something Sam does only when we two Yankees are visiting?"

Floyd answered, but he did not elaborate, "As I said, Sam does not take kindly to Yankees." Not ready to explain further, Floyd walked away from Haygood, and David followed.

Morgan opened the door to Mac's study and motioned for the couple to go in ahead of him. Closing the door behind him, Morgan suggested they all sit. Keowee sat down first, and Santee pulled a chair up beside her, while Morgan placed a chair in front of them both.

"I have a couple of things to tell you and thought it best if you two hear the news alone. First, I saw Robert in New Orleans, and I am sure he will be making his way here before long. I did not have an opportunity to speak with him, but, from what I was able to observe, I do not believe his stay in France caused any improvement in his self-centeredness or his irresponsibility. I also have another bit of news, and I would rather take a whipping than lay this on you. I just do not know of any other way to handle this, but know it hurts me to tell you. Robert's traveling companion is Luis La Cur."

Morgan thought he would be able to hold his composure when Keowee and Santee heard the terrible news. However, the cry of anguish that escaped Keowee tore at his heart, and tears of grief that he had not shed since the death of his father filled his eyes. He wanted to throw his arms around the couple and promise that all would be well, that they would not have to come face to face with the bastard, but he was limited to what he could do at the present time. He did know what he had in the works, and he was going to do his best to expunge the bastard from the South, if not the Earth.

Hearing Keowee's mournful wails subsiding to sobs, Morgan reached across and placed a hand on Santee's knee.

He brought Santee's attention back to him and took hold of Keowee's hand, and, looking her in the eyes, he began to speak. He told them some of the reasons why he was in the South.

"Keowee, I do not want to promise you something I am not 100 percent sure I can do; however, I will do my best to make sure you will never have to fear seeing the bastard again. What you plan to do to ready Riverbend for Robert's homecoming is your business, but I would suggest you make sure Lovie is not present when he arrives.

I have no idea why they are traveling to Riverbend, unless to lie low for a while. Nor am I sure that they know I will be in the vicinity. But once they become aware of my and Haygood's presence, they might change their mind about coming to Riverbend. However, be assured, if at all possible, that if La Cur heads this way, I will not be far behind him, if not in his company."

Santee spoke with a ring of authority, as he spoke his mind, "The man won't get nowhere near my Lovie, Mr. Morgan. I's be a free man now. I no longer have to buckle to the Mr. La Curs' of this world, and I's knows how to protect my womenfolk."

"Santee, you are right in saying you are a free man, but you know that, here in the South, if you were to harm the bastard, it would be hard for me to protect you. So promise me you will try to keep a cool head around this man, and let me and Haygood take care of him. I still say the best plan right now is to hide Lovie or send her to a neighbor, until I can get what I need to arrest the bastard. I also want to caution you not to arouse Robert's suspicion. You might have to revert back to the days before Mac's death for a while. Do I have your promise? I told you my business to help you deal with this situation, so you can be my eyes and ears when I am not around. Can you promise me?"

Keowee's eyes were dry, even though her face was wet with her tears. She looked at Morgan with sadness, as she spoke. "Mr. Morgan, we's knows you will do all you can to help us. You've always had a good heart, even as a boy.

I promise I'll do anything I can to help you get this evil man, and I'll see that Santee does the same." Looking at Santee, she waited for his nod of agreement before she looked back at Morgan.

Keowee asked, "Would one of the slave cabins be safe enough to hide Lovie in? That's the only place I's can think of that could keep her sheltered away from the house. I's don't knows any neighbors now that we's could ask for help."

Morgan shook his head, saying, "That is not far enough away from the plantation."

As they readied to leave the room, Morgan chuckled and patted Santee on the back, knowing Keowee was able to bring about what she had promised.

"I will take Keowee's words to include you, too, Santee."

He added, "I appreciate you both understanding my need for your promises."

All eyes were on the three, as they returned to the warming kitchen, but Morgan was certain very little would be told to Lovie to satisfy the curiosity beaming in her eyes. Keowee was quick to turn her attention to preparing herself to start the night meal. After washing her hands, she motioned for Lovie to do the same. Pots and pans were brought forth, and the men and the boys were shooed out the door, and Keowee promised to call them when the meal was on the table. Morgan remained only a moment, emptying the saddlebags.

Turning to Keowee, Morgan said, "I thought you might be running low on a few items." Keowee nodded, smiling her appreciation.

"Why did Mr. Morgan want you and Papa in Mr. Mac's study? Why all the secrets?" Lovie asked.

"Slow down, Missy," Keowee cautioned. "You sounding like Sam."

"Sam!" With Sam's name came a revelation. *I's not seen her since I heard the loud sound of running horses racing around the house, followed by the gun shot.* Keowee staggered with that thought.

Terrified, Keowee asked Lovie, "Have you seen Sam? Where's she gone?"

"Sam be around somewhere. Hiding, I guess, since Mr. Morgan's returned. Now answer me about Mr. Morgan's secrets."

"Child, ain't no secrets. Mr. Morgan just brought news he saw Mr. Robert in New Orleans and thought we might want to know ahead of time that he might be home soon and see if we might need something to prepare for his homecoming.

That's all. Now run up to Sam's room, and check on her, and tell her I wants to see her."

Keowee was so disturbed by her thoughts it was hard to keep her mind on fixing the meal the men and the boys were waiting on.

Lovie was gone only a few minutes; however, it seemed a long time before she returned to the kitchen.

Where she be? Ain't she with you?" Keowee wanted to know, as soon as one of Lovie's feet stepped inside the kitchen.

"She ain't in her room," Lovie answered. "I suppose she be snooping around, watching Mr. Morgan. She shor has a fascination with him, to hate him as much as she says she does."

175

"Just as soon as we get this to cooking, I's want you to check around outside and see if you can find her. I's want you to tell her I really needs to see her, and I's don't want any excuse."

Keowee caught hold of Lovie's arm and added, "Is that clear? If so, make it clear to Sam when you find her."

"Yes ma'am," Lovie replied softly. "I'll do what you ask, but I's don't see what's so wrong with Sam disappearing. She did the same when Mr. Morgan was here last time."

"You never mind the why. Just do as I say."

"Yes ma'am."

As soon as the pots and pans were full and simmering, the table set with the plates and things, Keowee sent Lovie to check on Sam's room again and to look around outside, if she didn't find Sam upstairs. Lovie's search proved in vain; Sam was nowhere to be found. Of course, not knowing about the granite cave and not mentioning Sam's disappearance to the boys, Keowee and Lovie had no idea where she was.

The moment Sam realized whom she had shot, a pain hit her in the chest, as though the bullet had gone through her.

Running to her room and locking the chamber door was a spontaneous act of preservation, mixed with anguish. She did not know why, but as soon as the sound of the gun blast stopped echoing in her brain, her hands stopped shaking, and her mind could hold a rational thought. The need to be in the cave overwhelmed her. She opened her door, slipped from her room and out the front doors, and ran to the river. The cave was dark, but Sam lit no candle. She walked slowly across the granite floor to the straw mattress her soldier had used for a bed as she had tended to his wounds. She sat down, stretched out on the pallet, and cried herself to sleep.

None of the family, except Keowee, thought anything about Sam's failure to join them for the meal. Keowee's concern showed on her face, but Santee and Morgan thought only of her pain upon her hearing of La Cur. Santee had no idea Sam was the cause.

Eating little, Keowee was the first to leave the table, and she began the task of washing and storing the pots and pans.

Before long, Morgan and Haygood gave their thanks for the delicious meal and asked to be excused. They made their way to the front veranda for a smoke and the cool breeze that would soon roll off the flowing river. Floyd and David followed the two men, like little puppy dogs. They perched on the top step of the veranda and occasionally joined in the conversation, with questions for the two Yankees.

Santee made his nightly walk around the buildings and the yard, checking to see if all was well, and he soon walked back through the kitchen to the front veranda. After asking Morgan and Haygood if they needed anything before he and Keowee retired, he found the visitors comfortable, needing nothing. After sending the boys upstairs to prepare for bed, Santee wished the men good night.

After Santee left, Haygood questioned Morgan about Keowee's and Santee's reaction to the news they had brought. Morgan's answer included his suggestion for the couple to send Lovie to a neighbor or to hide her, while the nefarious visitors were at Riverbend. Morgan's mention of Lovie and his thoughts on protecting her gave Haygood a good opening to mention the news he had obtained from Floyd.

"While you were talking with Keowee and Santee earlier, I spoke with Floyd and David. Are you aware that the boys are the younger brothers to Sam?"

This bit of news gave Morgan a start, causing him to respond, "What! You mean they are related to the tomcat? I had no idea. When I asked Keowee and Santee about the boys, their reply was they were all orphans. To be honest, I thought the tomcat was a loner and only showed up occasionally. How could that person be related to Floyd and David?"

Haygood grinned and replied, "If you are thinking of the difference between Floyd's and Sam's attitudes toward you, I can only repeat Floyd's words: 'Sam does not take kindly to Yankees.' Here again, Haygood's aggravating grin was in place, as he stood. Walking to the door, he asked, "Do you think there might be something else behind Sam's immediately intense dislike of you? Especially since it was a first meeting. Or do you have Yankee written across your forehead?"

Returning to the kitchen, Santee found the room empty. He banked the dying coals in the fireplace to the back of the chimney, snuffed out the lamps, and made his way to their room. Most often, he and Keowee left the kitchen at night together, but tonight Keowee had not waited for him. Santee contributed her going to their room ahead of him to the jolt Morgan's news gave her. However, he was soon to hear something that would add to the sorrow and the fright that the afternoon had held.

Keowee was sitting on the bed, not lying down asleep. She was waiting to talk to Santee about Sam and her additional fears.

She allowed him to sit and to take off his shoes before she shared her fears with him.

"Santee, when did you last see Sam?" Puzzled by her question, he looked at Keowee in the dim candlelight without answering, trying to read her face.

"Was she in the kitchen when we all heard the sound of fast-galloping horses?" Keowee asked, still not giving any hint as to why she was bothering Santee with these questions.

Santee felt that there was something bothering Keowee,

but, like Lovie, he could not understand why Keowee was concerned with Sam's disappearing.

"Keowee, what's this about Sam that got you upset? You knows she would keep herself hidden away while Mr. Morgan be here."

"I wish that was all. She didn't sneak down to fix her plate of food before I called y'all to supper. Lovie has looked all over—her room, the yard, the outbuildings—and there was no sign of her anywhere. I can't recollect when I last saw her. You be running to the back door, intending to rush outside, after we hear them horses, and me be hurrying to stop you. I don't know if she left by the backstairs then or later, when we's all went out to greet Mr. Morgan after the gunshot. I be worried Sam's the one what shot at Mr. Morgan with that pistol she's got hidden in her room, with her disappearing like she has. Once she realized who she shot, maybe even thinking she killed him, I'm afraid of what she might have done."

"Lord, have mercy on that sweet child," Santee prayed, as Keowee words rang true. He sat with his head in his hands, while begging the good Lord for mercy.

"I have no idea as to where to start to look for her. Do you? Did Lovie search the cabins?"

"I don't think so. She wasn't gone that long, and I'm sure she didn't, thinking she be seen walking that way. Y'all menfolks and the boys might have wanted to know why she was heading that way."

"Well, that be a place to start," Santee said, as he put his shoes back on and stood.

"You think to go now?"

"Yes; that child can't spend the night down there alone, without a candle or a lantern."

"Wait; let me check her room one more time. Wait right

here; I'll tip up the back stairs without disturbing the men or the boys. You wait, you hear?"

Santee waited, and Keowee was back in a few minutes, shaking her head. "Give me time to get on my shoes. I'm going with you."

Santee had a lantern lit by the time Keowee entered the kitchen, and the two quietly slipped out the back door and walked the path to the empty slave cabins. They stopped in front of each cabin. One by one, Santee stuck his head into the door of a cabin, using the lantern to light the inside of it, but they found no sign of Sam. More worried than ever, they made their way back to the warming kitchen, hoping that, by morning, Sam's need for food would bring her to the warming kitchen for something to eat. Keowee lit a new candle and placed it on the table, just in case Sam came in during the night for food.

With nowhere else to look, the couple returned to their bed.

Morning came, and Keowee was late leaving her bed, after a restless and sleepless night. The sun was already up over the eastern tree tops when she entered the kitchen and saw there was no sign of Sam having visited during the night.

With a sad heart, she turned to the fireplace, adding pine knots and logs, and she began to prepare food for the household to break their night's fast.

The first meal of the day was served and eaten without any mention of Sam and her absences. Santee, Keowee, and Lovie were the only ones concerned and wondering where she might be. Floyd and David did not expect to see Sam at the morning meal, and they diverted Lemuel's unuttered questions as to Sam's whereabouts by playing with him and amusing him.

Keowee sent Lovie to Sam's room as soon as she finished

her meal, and Lovie returned and gently shook her head at her mama's questioning look.

Late morning brought another sound of racing horse hooves, and Morgan was on the veranda to greet the soldier in blue, as he reined in his mount. The corporal called to Morgan, as his lathered mount came to a stop.

"Colonel Anderson, sir. I have a message from Captain Cree."

Hearing a Southern accent coming from the mouth of a young man wearing Union blue seemed a little strange, but Morgan ignored the soldier's manner of speech, preferring to receive the message.

"Thank you, Corporal. There is a watering trough around the corner there."

He pointed to the soldier's right.

"I know you know to walk your horse, letting it cool down before you allow it to have water, so I will not mention it," Morgan said, with a grin, as he waved the soldier away.

With a smile on his face, Morgan informed Haygood, "One of our men of interest has arrived in Athens from Savannah.

I think we need to return to Athens ourselves and have a chance meeting of sorts with Robert Sinclair. What do you think?"

"This chance meeting will involve some physical contact, I hope."

"We'll just play it by ear, so to speak. As of now, let's join the corporal and offer him some refreshment. As soon as his horse is rested, we will ride back with the soldier."

Walking around the corner of the house, they spied the soldier near the stables, and as they passed the large fig bush, Morgan and Haygood looked hard in and around the large bush that played such a part in their arrival the day before.

Approaching the soldier, Morgan asked him about taking some refreshments, while his horse rested from his long ride.

Happy for the invitation, the young man walked with Morgan and Haygood toward the kitchen door.

"Corporal, I believe I heard a very distinct Southern accent when you approached me. That seems a little odd, since you wear Union blue. Of course, I am aware there were Southerners fighting for the North, and I suppose you are one of them."

"Yes sir, I was born and raised in Virginia. After April of 1862, when I would have been made to fight in the Confederate Army, my parents, not able to pay a substitute for me, told me to choose the army I would be most comfortable fighting in, so I joined the Union Army."

"I know that must have been a hard decision to make, having lived your whole life in a Southern state. I am sure you had friends and relatives fighting for the South."

"Yes sir."

Morgan was sure the corporal's two words answered both his statements and turned the conversation to horses, as they entered the kitchen.

"You are a good horseman. I asked Captain Cree to send his best rider and fastest horse with the message I had hoped to receive."

"Well, sir, I learned to sit a horse before I could walk. Most Southerners do. We learn to ride and to shoot younger than most Yankees."

"That you do, son. That you do."

A tomblike quietness fell over the kitchen, as Morgan and the soldier walked through the door. Except for the two men's conversation, there was no other sound. It took Morgan several minutes to realize why there was no usual kitchen racket, and he felt like a fool.

"Keowee, Santee, Lovie, and the boys, let me introduce a young man who has just ridden from Athens to deliver a message.

Folk, this is— sorry, son, I do not know your name."

"Calhoun, sir."

"Corporal Calhoun," Morgan said. "Folks, please make him welcome. Haygood and I will be riding back to Athens with him, as soon as his horse is rested. I have offered the corporal a light repast, Keowee. I hope this will not cause a problem." Morgan spoke while looking at Keowee with a plea in his eyes.

"No sir. No problem, Mr. Morgan," Keowee offered. "I's heard a pleasant Southern drawl coming from his lips, and I knows just what the young man will like. Y'all just set yourselves down at the table. It just gonna take me and Lovie a minute."

Good as her word, sweet potato cobbler, apple pie, and glasses of cool, sweet milk were set before the men.

"Mr. Morgan, you and Mr. Haygood better eat up, too. It be a long ride to Athens, and you be needing more vittles."

Chuckling, Santee added, "You won't find none as good as what my Keowee cooks." He heaped his plate with vittles after the other men were served.

Morgan watched Floyd and David sidle toward the door and leave the kitchen. He was sorry he had added to the pain they carried, but he was not sorry he offered the young soldier food and drink. It was the right thing to do, but he regretted not having talked to the boys first, preparing them for the soldier's appearance. He felt bad for that slipup.

Finishing his pie and milk, before Haygood and Corporal Calhoun could finish theirs, he stood and asked Keowee and Santee to follow him to the front of the house. After entering Mac's study and closing the door, he said, "The message I received was from Captain Cree. He informed me that Robert arrived in Athens midmorning by train. He was alone, and he seems to be staying the night. I have no way of knowing his plans, even if he will ride out of Athens for Riverbend come morning. But it is not likely he will ride before morning. I do not believe he would want to be caught on the road at night.

Do you think so, Santee, knowing Robert?"

"No sir; he would not chance riding alone on a darkened road all the way from Athens."

"I have received no news as to La Cur. However, should I do so after I reach Athens, I will try to keep you informed. For now, I can only advise you to be on your watch. Robert might try making a trip by horseback during the day.

Do you have any questions or anything you need to tell me while we are alone?"

Keowee asked, "When the devil comes to Athens and heads this way, will you be coming, too, or will you and Mr. Haygood have to stay in Athens?"

"Keowee, if I am not able to ride in La Cur's company, Haygood will not be far behind. He is well aware of all I have told you and of what happened here years ago. Rest assured that if I turned him loose, La Cur would never live to step foot on Riverbend land. In saying this, I want you to know that if something happens, you would come to me for help. You can also go to Haygood."

Haygood and Corporal Calhoun were awaiting Morgan at the watering trough, having already saddled the horses. Morgan waved to the two and stopped, turning to look for Floyd and David. Santee understood Morgan's hesitation.

"You looking for the boys, Mr. Morgan?"

Morgan looked around to the place where Santee stood and nodded his head.

"They probably be at the river," Santee said.

Morgan smiled his thanks and ran toward the river. He needed to talk to Floyd before leaving. The boys sitting on the bank with their poles came into sight, as Morgan cleared the front yard.

Morgan called their names, and they both turned toward him.

Boys, I had to see you before I left," Morgan began. "Haygood and I are riding back to Athens with Corporal Calhoun.

The message he brought me requires me to go, but I could not leave without first telling you I am sorry I brought Corporal Calhoun into the kitchen before I talked to you about him. I apologize for handling the situation wrong. I would never intentionally hurt you. Will you forgive me?"

David looked at Floyd, waiting for his lead. Floyd looked into Morgan's face and then at his outstretched hand, wanting to forgive him, but holding back. The sight of the Yankee soldier in the blue uniform walking into the warming kitchen still registered too painfully in his mind. Morgan waited, not wanting to push the boys but wanting their forgiveness desperately.

Morgan realized, after several long minutes, that Floyd was not going to move and that David would follow Floyd's lead. He bid them good-bye. As he turned toward the house, the path in front of him seemed very long and lonely, and his feet moved very slowly. Halfway to the house, he heard running feet behind him. Turning, he saw the boys running toward him.

Morgan stopped and waited.

Floyd stopped running a short distance away and walked to Morgan with his hand outstretched. Morgan grabbed

Floyd's hand and pulled him into his arms, with tears in his eyes. Never had he been so glad to see an outstretched hand.

"I want to shake your hand, too, Morgan," David said.

Morgan laughed, and, releasing Floyd, he grabbed David's hand and pulled David into his arms for a bear hug. Unbeknown to the three, their reunion was being watched with mixed emotions and with sad, weary eyes.

Morgan, Floyd, and David walked together toward the house. The path no longer seemed long and lonely for Morgan and seemed a whole lot happier. Morgan stopped near the front veranda, and, turning to Floyd, he said, "Floyd, Haygood, along with Corporal Calhoun, is waiting for me at the stables. If you and David had rather not walk with me further, we will say our farewells here, and I will understand."

Floyd smiled at Morgan's words, but, with his decision to forgive Morgan, came the need to look the soldier in the eye.

"I believe we will just walk with you all the way. Don't want you to get lost."

Haygood wondered why Morgan's jaws didn't split wide open from the pressure of the grin he spied on his face, as he and the boys walked to the stables.

"Are you ready, Colonel," Haygood asked, sneeringly.

Morgan mounted, and, waving good-bye to the people that somehow had found a solid, unmovable place in his heart, he said, "Let's ride for Athens."

"Lead the way, Colonel. I am at your back, as always," Haygood yelled, as they left the yard.

*Floyd Hatcher, my great grandfather
the oldest of the four orphans of 1862.*

*In the Savannah River between Hart County, Ga. and
Anderson county, S.C. is Geneveive Island.*

Cokesbury United Methodist

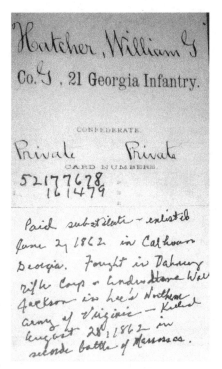

William Hatcher, father of the four orphans of 1862.

CHAPTER 9

The three riders rode through the cedar grove and passed the empty fields, and soon a cloud of dust was all that gave tangible proof that Morgan, Haygood, and the young Union soldier were ever visitors to Riverbend. Lovie walked back to the kitchen to finish preparing the noon meal. Keowee slowly followed, her usual liveliness hindered by the constant uneasiness of Sam's disappearance and the worry that Sam was the one who had shot at Morgan. Morgan and Keowee was not the only ones with Sam on their mind. As Santee walked away toward the barn, Floyd stood with a mind full of uncertainty. Having checked Sam's room several times during the night after David slept, he knew Sam was hiding away from the house. Being unable to figure out why she would stay away from the house day and night worried him. David stood quietly by Floyd's side, waiting, and not liking the way Floyd was acting, but he figured he could handle whatever was bothering him.

Deciding to visit the cave, Floyd turned to David. "You'd best be helping Keowee and Lovie with Lemuel. They are going to be busy with the cooking from now until it's time to eat, and Lemuel might get into some mischief." Floyd's suggestion was all David needed. He was still enough of a child to enjoy entertaining his baby brother. He did not hesitate; rather, he ran to the warming kitchen.

Floyd waited until he was sure no one was around to question him while he was walking to the river alone. After he passed the corner of the veranda, his steps increased. He was running by the time he reached the riverbank; buttons on his overalls were unbuttoned, and his overalls were slipping down his legs. All he had to do was step from the overalls, wad them up, and step into the water. Walking the ledge slowed his steps.

Wanting to find Sam brought him to the river. What he would say and her reaction to his finding her now occupied his thoughts. Their meeting could turn into another battle of words, like the heated discussion in the corn patch after Morgan's last visit.

As soon as Floyd was near enough to hear Sam without her yelling, she spoke, "I figured you would be showing up after the Yankees rode away."

Grinning, as Sam's word proved him correct, Floyd replied, "Do you think it's time you came to the house? Keowee will have the midday meal on the table by now, and I am hungry."

For the first time in two days, Sam chuckled, and suggested, "You go to the house alone. We don't want the others knowing you knew where to find me. I'll be along shortly."

Floyd knew Sam was right in her not wanting questions. However, Sam's eyes confirmed what he had been thinking. She was not hiding so much from the family and Morgan as she was for some other reason. He hoped she would work out whatever the problem was and would find peace. Closing the few steps between them, he put his arms around her and squeezed her.

"I'll run along. I'll look for you to appear on your own soon, say, in time to eat your share of the meal."

Sam wondered how Keowee and Santee would react to her disappearing act. She knew, by now, that they were thinking she might be the person shooting at the Yankees, and she dreaded their questioning. She had never told them a lie, and she did not want to start doing so. She decided that if they asked straight out whether she shot at the two men, she would tell the truth and suffer the consequences.

She had enough bothering her without adding lying to two of the people she held dear.

Sam's entering the warming kitchen caused little stir; heads turned, and eyes looked, but no one expressed surprise to her coming to the table. A plate was set at her regular place. She sat down, and bowls and platters were passed her way.

True to her prediction, after Santee and the boys left the kitchen, Keowee asked Sam to help her get Lemuel down for a nap, leaving Lovie to clean up from the meal. Keowee was quiet, as she followed Sam carrying Lemuel up the stairs. As usual, Lemuel was ready for a nap and was asleep by the time Sam laid his head on his pillow.

Sam left the nursey, without a word from Keowee, and led the way to her room. Sam, who was sitting across from Keowee, awaited her questions. The wait was not long.

"Child, where have you been? Santee, Lovie, and me looked this place over and could not find hide nor hair of you. We's been worried sick."

"I am sorry to have caused either of you a moment of worry. I knew my complete absences would probable make you wonder— "

A soft knock interrupted Sam's confession. The door opened, and Santee eased into the room. Sam smiled, as the tall, proud figure came across the room to sit by his wife.

"Santee, I was just apologizing to Keowee for causing y'all

to worry. I knew you would wonder why I stayed away from the house. I hoped you would know I would be safe. After all, the only thing I feared was under the same roof as you two." This last statement was said with a chuckle.

Sam's lightheartedness referring to Morgan and Haygood as her feared Yankee foes did not amuse Keowee or Santee. Keowee wanted more from Sam, so she said, "When Mr. Morgan visited last time, you only kept hidden from him, not from us. This time, you never came for a bite of food for three meals. I's wants to know why you acted different than the last time Mr. Morgan be here. Did something happen to make you hide from us?"

Sam hesitated a minute before answering Keowee, wanting to be honest in her answer but wanting to leave out Morgan's name as far as any personal connection to her was concerned. "You both know of my feelings toward Yankees. I find myself in a very awkward position, through no fault of you two. Morgan Anderson really has more ties to Riverbend than I do, since he has been a friend of the Sinclair family for years. In addition to this, I seem to be at odds with my own brothers when it comes to Mr. Anderson. I cannot blame you two, Lovie, or the boys for your feelings, but it is hard to be the only one who does not welcome his visits, and, being aware of all this, I thought it best to separate myself from the house while he was here. I know this seems like I was hiding from you, but I was really hiding from the Yankee."

Hoping her explanation would appease Keowee, she started to rise, but Santee had a question. "Missy, we's known your feelings toward the Yankee folk, and we understand. Knowing the kind of person Mr. Morgan be, it's hard for us to understand you putting him in with the other Yankee folk. But I's not too worried over that. I just want to know if you was the one that shot at Mr. Morgan and Mr. Haygood when they arrived yesterday. I's wants the truth, Missy."

She hoped she would not have to face that question, but since Santee stated his concern plainly and expected the truth, Sam had no other recourse than to answer him truthfully. Standing and taking a deep breath, she said, "Yes."

Looking into shocked faces and realizing they had rather have heard anything else than the word, "yes," she continued, "I honestly did not know who they were until after I pulled the trigger, if that will help your feelings. I gather our meeting is over. If so, will you excuse me? I believe I will take a nap."

***

After arriving back in Athens, Morgan and Haygood rode straight to the office of Captain Cree to obtain the where-abouts of Robert Sinclair. He thanked the captain for getting word to him posthaste, and he asked for the use of a man to keep tabs on Robert while he was in Athens. He added, "This man needs to shed his uniform and to dress in clothing similar to the clothing of the locals. I do not want Robert to become aware he is under surveillance. Even Robert would immediately notice a soldier in uniform mingling around and would know he is being watched. A man in local dress would not be noticed by Robert and would not raise his suspicion."

Morgan went on, "Captain Cree, it would help if this soldier happened to have a true Southern accent, and I happen to know that Corporal Calhoun is truly a Southerner. Would you be able to spare him a few days?"

"Yes. I will inform Calhoun of his new duties at once and have him contact you."

It was no surprise to Morgan that the last report placed Robert in a tavern north of town on the banks of the Oconee

River. Two of Captain Cree's finest were still at the establishment, engaged in surveillance. Morgan dismissed the soldiers and found a place of concealmentdirectly across the road from the front entrance, and Haygood entered the tavern.

Haygood found the tavern empty, except for Robert and a man behind the bar. Approaching the man, he asked for a glass of beer. Upon the delivery of the beer, he tried to engage the man in conversation. The man did not tarry to chat; rather, he returned to his chores, not interested in idle conversation.

Haygood spoke his appeal loud enough for both men to hear, hoping his words would spark an invitation from Robert. Thinking of joining Morgan, he heard the scraping of chair legs against the floor, and, in seconds, he felt the movement of a body beside him. Robert had taken the bait.

"You are a stranger to these parts, or you would know this place is not open for the pleasures you mentioned until dark," the man beside Haygood said. "Where are you from, friend?"

The word "friend" was said with a note of cynicism, but Haygood turned, smiling at the man at his side, giving the impression that he had not noticed the man's inflection on the word, "friend."

"I confess I am a stranger to Athens," Haygood said. "However, it seems we are both in the same boat, so to speak. Alone in a tavern without the usual accommodations one would expect to find."

"I believe that you are not only a stranger to Athens, Georgia, but that you are also not from the South. Am I correct, sir?" Robert quizzed.

"Yes, you are correct. I am not from the South. I came to the South with a friend. I'm sure my friend would have enlightened me, had I mentioned my desire for some company, shall we say? However, with all the soldiers in this town, I thought that a place offering the expert pleasures that I'm sure can be found here would be open around the clock."

"Is your friend from Athens?"

"No. He is, however, familiar with the area."

"Does he have family in the area?"

"No. I'll be glad to introduce my friend to you. I'm sure he will be tracking me down soon, but, in the meantime, I think that another beer would be what the doctor's ordered, me being the doctor."

"Are you a physician?"

"Heavens no! But may I prescribe you another ale? My treat."

"Yes, thank you. Choyce, old man, our friend here would like another beer, and so would I."

Haygood noticed the old man's hesitation, but as the man heard Haygood's gold piece hit the bar, he turned without a word and filled two clean glasses. He placed the glasses in front of the men, giving Haygood the change that was due.

As he picked up his glass, Haygood turned and walked across the room to a table, saying over his shoulder, "I am tired of standing. Shall we sit and relax, while we enjoy our drink?"

Robert followed like a puppy dog, wanting to be near Haygood if another treat was offered. Haygood sat facing the door, placing Robert across the table from him, with his back to the door.

Morgan, leaning back against a large tree, waited the arrival of the newest member of their team. Hearing feet hitting the packed-dirt roadway alerted Morgan someone was approaching his place of concealment. Crouching down behind the bushes between him and the roadway, he watched, as a young man sauntered along, seemingly without a care in the world. The man passed within an arm's reach of Morgan and was halfway to the covered bridge before it registered with Morgan that the man was Corporal Calhoun.

"Young man, could I have a word?" Gaining the corporal's attention, he stepped back into his cover and awaited the young man. "Colonel, sir," Corporal Calhoun whispered, slipping into the cover of the bushes and the trees. "I was not expecting you to be where you are, thinking you would be in the tavern."

"Captain Haygood is the one in the tavern. I thought it best if we spoke first in private. I want you to watch a man from a distance, close enough for you to know what places he visits and with whom he converses. Try not to get near enough to raise his awareness of you, making him suspect he is being watched. In order for you to know what this man looks like, I want you to go into the tavern, buy a drink, and sit, relaxing but observing, the sandy-haired man sitting with Haygood. I will enter a short while later and join Haygood. Finish your drink, leave, taking up this place of concealment, and wait for Robert to leave. I do not expect him to stay in Athens long after my meeting with him."

While Robert was speaking, Haygood noticed a young man, dressed in clothes slightly out of fashion and slightly small for his size, entering the tavern. On close examination, he realized it was the corporal.

Morgan entered the front door, calling as he spied Haygood, "There you are, friend. When I found you gone from our lodging, I figured you would be out, looking for a watering hole with fringe benefits, but it seems you were disappointed." So Morgan continued speaking, as he neared the table.

"I see you have managed to find a drinking companion," he commented, as he turned to make the acquaintance of Haygood's tablemate. Morgan's look of surprise upon facing Robert was purely theatrical. There was no way the man would know this was a planned meeting. The two spoke the other's name at the same time, but Morgan allowed Robert to ask the first question, positive that he knew what the question would be.

"Morgan Anderson! You are this man's friend?"

"Guilty as charged. Not to change the subject, but Santee said you were in Europe. But that was several weeks ago, when we came by Riverbend to check on Mac for Evalyn. I was sorry to hear of Mac's death. Evalyn will be saddened to hear of it. I have not written her, waiting to tell her in person."

The color had not as yet returned to Robert's face, and his countenance expressed his desire to be anywhere but at that table in that tavern. Morgan did not give him time to gain his composure before he began to apply a little pressure.

"Did your ship happen to dock in New Orleans a week or so back? If so, it must have been you I spied while we were in New Orleans. You remember, Haygood, that I mentioned about seeing someone who resembled Robert Sinclair, Mac's son. You do know whom you are sharing a table with?"

Haygood assumed a puzzled look and answered, "No. We have not bothered with names. I complained about the place being empty and expressed my desire for conversation, and the gentleman answered my appeal. I hope your association has not been affected by the happenings of the last four years."

Calhoun was intrigued by the playacting going on at the table across the way, but he made himself stand up and left for the spot across the road.

"We did fight, or, at least, *I* fought on the opposite side of where Robert's loyalties were, but I hope we can put that behind us. I hold no animosity toward any Southerner or his or her beliefs." Morgan looked Robert straight in the eyes, as he made his statement, and waited for Robert's reaction.

Still not able to regain his composure completely, Robert waited a few moments, while forming his reply, and finally replied, "Although I felt a loyalty to the South, I went to Europe so that I would not be required to fight my fellow Americans." Robert was not as good an actor as the two men he gave those words to.

Pulling a chair away from the table, Morgan sat and again mentioned New Orleans, "You never said if your ship docked in New Orleans or Savannah. I am curious to know if you have a twin walking around the streets of New Orleans."

Taking a gulp of his beer, Robert nodded his head, "Yes, our ship docked in New Orleans. You know I have relatives in that fair city."

"Were you in the company of relatives while sailing from Europe? Your traveling companions, I take it, were members of your French relatives. Is that true?" "Not that it is any of your business. My uncle, Count Luis La Cur, and his wife were traveling with me."

Robert realized, at once, his mindless error in admitting his uncle and aunt were his traveling companions, and he realized the need to distance himself from the nosy, interfering Morgan Anderson, so he became overwhelmed and spluttered, "You will have to excuse me; I have to attend to business."

In his hurry to leave the table, he knocked over his chair and all but ran from the building. With a knowing grin, Haygood asked, "Would you say we have the gentleman somewhat flustered?"

"Considerably," Morgan replied. "I hope I haven't frightened him to the point of fleeing. Robert does not have the fiber to withstand much pressure. By the way, how do you like the beer?"

"It's rather a different taste than I am accustomed to drinking, but it is wet and refreshing."

"It is a local brand that is homemade, using the fruit of the locust tree. Of course, there are several other ingredients added, and they vary, depending on the maker. Be forewarned that if you drink enough of the brew, it will make you drunk, the effects slipping up on you without notice."

Robert hurried back toward Athens, his mind racing with thoughts of escaping Morgan Anderson's interfering presence. Unaware of the young man slipping from a cluster of trees as he approached the crest of the hill just outside of the town limits, he did not slow his steps.

Suddenly, Robert's thoughts concerning Morgan were interrupted, as the face of his uncle popped clear and frightening into his mind, making him wonder, *How will Luis take the news that the man he thought left New Orleans for Washington D.C., is in Athens and possibly visiting Riverbend?*

"These thoughts are getting me nowhere," he spoke into the air, as he neared the Lumpkin House. Entering the hotel, he rushed across the lobby, hurrying for the stairs and the security of his room, without acknowledging anyone.

Robert's swift passage through the lobby and up the stairs was not fast enough to take him out of the sight of Corporal Calhoun. Hearing the sound of a door being slammed, as he near the top step, the corporal smiled. He thought, *From what little I overheard of the conversation in the tavern and by observing the man's reaction to Colonel Anderson, I know the colonel really ruffled this man's feathers. I have never seen a man run away from a tavern. It is usually the other way around.* Corporal Calhoun smiled, even after the thought left his mind.

Inside his door, Robert Sinclair was more disturbed than

just flustered. Afraid of his uncle's temper and concerned with Morgan being in Athens, he paced the floor, not knowing what Luis La Cur would do if he arrived without first knowing of Morgan's presence. He was also afraid to try to set up things, as Luis had ordered, with Morgan in the area.

"If I could get a message to Luis in Savannah," he said to the room, "before his departure, maybe he would postpone his departure? His postponement could possibly make Morgan think that Luis did not intend to come to Athens and could make Morgan leave for Washington."

"How will I be able to get word to Luis without funds?" he asked the room. *If not for my shortage of funds, he thought, I would never have paid attention to that loud, talkative Yankee, and I could have slipped into the back room upon Morgan's entrance and escaped a meeting with him.*

CHAPTER 10

After an exhausted and fearful night of alarming memories of his uncle's temper and thoughts of possibly fatal consequences, Robert arose, with only one thought: escape to Riverbend. But there was a snag. He had no transportation. However, a ray of hope flourished among all the troubling thoughts of Morgan Anderson and his uncle Luis: Phillip R. Whitfield, Esquire, his father's long-time attorney.

Robert was determined to leave Athens, but the possibility of walking all the way to Hart County did not set well with him. He was sure he could talk Phillip Whitfield into the loan of a horse, even if there was none of his father's money left.

"Surely there is something left of the old man's fortune," he spoke aloud, trying to enliven his lacking confidence, as he prepared to leave his room.

While Haygood and Morgan sat in the dining room, awaiting their morning meal to be served, Haygood happened to glance toward the room's entrance and spied Robert hurrying toward the hotel's front entrance. Nodding toward the door, Haygood whispered to Morgan, "There goes our pigeon. Calhoun should be close behind."

No sooner had Morgan turned to look in the direction toward which Haygood had nodded than Corporal Calhoun passed slowly through his line of vision. Smiling, he confirmed Haygood's prediction, "Right on cue, and in no hurry. Good chap."

"Robert seems to still be in a hurry," Haygood offered. "Where do you suppose he is headed? Riverbend?"

"First, he will have to obtain some form of transportation. There was no report of a horse arriving by train with him, and I cannot picture Robert Sinclair walking to Hart County. In the past, the furthest he has ever walked was to the stables, unless a groom saddled his horse and brought it to the front veranda, which happened most of the time. Mac had an attorney in Athens, if I am not mistaken, and that is where he is headed."

A couple of hours passed before Corporal Calhoun found Morgan and Haygood, sitting on the porch of the Lumpkin House.

"Good morning, Colonel; the man you had me watching has left Athens, as you had predicted."

"Traveling north?" Morgan inquired.

"Yes sir. I followed him outside the city, to be sure he was long gone," the corporal offered, smiling.

"Did he make any stops before leaving?" Morgan questioned further.

"Yes sir. He first visited the offices of a Mr. Phillip R. Whitfield, Esquire. He left that office in the company of Mr. Whitfield and proceeded to the stable where Mr. Whitfield housed his two horses. Neither horse looked very serviceable, and your man was not the least bit appreciable for the nag he was loaned, the horse being the worse of the two. He also sent a wire before leaving Athens. The wire was sent to a Count La Cur in Savannah, Georgia."

Satisfied with the corporal's report, Morgan stood, offering his hand, "Corporal Calhoun, you have done a superb job, and I am sure Robert was never the least bit aware of your observing him."

"If there is nothing else I can do, I will return to headquarters, and I thank you, sir, for your compliment." Saluting, Corporal Calhoun turned and left the porch.

"What is next, Colonel?" Haygood asked, grinning.

"We wait and see what happens next, Captain," Morgan answered, sneeringly.

He added, "It appears that Robert not only begged a horse from Mac's former attorney but that he also begged enough money to send a wire."

***

Santee and Keowee talked off and on, after Morgan had explained the situation that they would soon face. They were not only wondering where to hide Lovie, but they also knew they had to keep Sam hidden so that neither Robert nor the count would ever know about her. Late in the night, after Morgan and Haygood had left Riverbend, they agreed they had to tell the girls about the dangerous situation that soon would be coming to Riverbend.

The next morning, after breaking their fast and after the kitchen was put to order, Keowee told the girls to come with her to Sam's bedchamber.

Wondering the whole time, as they climbed the stairs, why they were being summoned upstairs, the girls entered Sam's room and sat down without a word.

Santee joined them a few minutes later. Pacing back and forth in front of the place where Keowee and the girls sat, he finally spoke, "Girls, we's were told some disturbing news when Mr. Morgan and his friend arrived from New Orleans, and the message Mr. Morgan received yesterday will cause the two of you to leave Riverbend for a spell."

Sam screamed, "What in the world could Morgan Anderson have to say that would make me have to leave Riverbend?"

"Mr. Robert is in Athens and will be coming here, maybe today. Mr. Robert's uncle, Count La Cur, sailed from France with Mr. Robert, and he will likely be following Mr. Robert to Riverbend."

"No!" Lovie screamed, and the look of terror on her face scared Sam, but she still wanted to know, "What does Mr. Anderson have to do with this? Sam added, "Riverbend is not his yet. I know that you all have known this man a long time and that you place a lot of store in him, but Robert Sinclair is the heir to this plantation. He will be the one to say who comes and who leaves, not the high and mighty Mr. Morgan Anderson."

"Yes, Missy," Santee answered. "We's known Mr. Morgan a long time, and we's known Mr. Robert all his life. We's also known his mother and her uncle. We's was greatly disturbed by the news Mr. Morgan brought, and as you claimed, we put a lot of store in what Mr. Morgan say. Partly 'cause he's a truthful man, but partly 'cause we's knows the others. Without betraying all that Mr. Morgan told us, I'll just say he feared for Lovie's safety. 'Course, him not knowing you were a female did not suggest we send you away, while Mr. Robert and the count visited, but we's know that if Lovie ain't safe, neither is you. Even with Mr. Robert, there would be no one to protect you or Lovie from the Count 'cause no one says no to him. From what's them two men be doing, you would not be safe from either Mr. Robert or the count."

"What in the name of all that is good did Morgan Anderson accuse Robert and this count of doing?" she asked. "Did he have proof? In my mind, if he's so informed, he surely offered proof."

"He had proof, and we's has proof also," was all that Santee would say.

Aggravated that Morgan was once again meddling in her life, she would not accept Santee's words. Not wanting to be convinced that what she was hearing was the truth, she stated, "Well, I, for one, would like to see this proof before I go traipsing across Hart County, away from the only home I now have. Anyway, what kind of proof did he offer?"

Lovie found her voice, saying, "Mr. Morgan's word be enough for me, even if I didn't know Mr. Robert."

Wanting to discredit Morgan, Sam questioned again, but she braced her question with an apology, "I am sorry to ask, but could your acceptance of Morgan's words against Robert Sinclair's be tainted, because the Sinclairs once owned you?"

Keowee, having sat silent, allowing Santee to speak to the girls, finally turned to Sam. Sam's attention had been directed to Santee, while she had listened to him and had stated her questions, but, sensing Keowee's movement, she now turned to her. Tears filled Sam's eyes, as she looked upon the painful anguish marring Keowee's usually pleasant face. Not able to hold her tears or her tongue, she fell on her knees in front of her friend and pleaded, "Keowee, what is the matter? Santee, help her."

"You want proof?" Santee asked. "Keowee has proof in her heart and soul. I was hoping she would not have to suffer the pain of telling her story."

"Child, raise yourself," Keowee all but whispered to Sam. With Sam seated back in her chair, Keowee began her story. "The evil goings on happened way before you were born. I gonna tell you 'cause I want you to be gone from Riverbend while these men are here." The pain the old housekeeper felt and the seriousness of what she was about to tell were mirrored in her eyes and on her face, as she struggled with the memories she was about to disclose.

"Just the mention of a man's name done put this fear and pain into my old heart, and don't you be taking lightly what I'm about to tell you. Too many young girls done been hurt because of the count's cruel ways, until Mr. Mac stopped him coming to visit. He's an evil man, and it appears that the three years Mr. Robert lived under his influence done brought out Mr. Robert's dark side."

"Keowee, I know."

Before Sam could say more, Keowee was up, grabbing her by the arms pulling her up out of her chair and shaking her with a force that made Sam's head bob back and forth, until she thought her head would leave her shoulders. Surprised at Keowee's actions, she hollered for her to stop.

Santee, understanding Keowee's actions, calmly eased her hands from Sam' arms and helped her back to her chair; turning to Sam, he said, "Be patient, Missy, and listen."

As Sam saw the tears rolling down the dear woman's face, Sam's shock turned to compassion. She was still not convinced there was danger, but if the pending visit of the count could frighten Keowee to the extent of tears and the reaction she had just witnessed, she would at least hear her out.

"I will listen; I will listen," Sam repeated, with her own tears wetting her face.

Keowee was beside herself with concern for these two. Calming herself, Keowee sat for several minutes before continuing. Wiping the tears from her eyes and face, the old black woman sat back and spoke, "Samantha Hatcher, I've lived on this plantation all my life, and I was here when Master Mac brought Miss Alicia, the count's niece and Mr. Robert's mother to Riverbend. That was the first time the count visited. We's were used to a few white men, visitors coming to the slave quarters occasionally or having them a young slave brought to their bedchambers, but the black women of Riverbend had never been treated brutally. Two young slave girls were beaten, used, and died on the count's visit. Mr. Mac denied the count the pleasure of visiting the plantation again. One of those girls was my younger sister."

"Now do you see why we want you and Lovie to leave Riverbend and to stay gone till the count returns to France or Mr. Morgan takes care of him?"

Keowee now had Sam's full attention. Sam sat in shocked silence, numb with reluctant disbelief, trying to comprehend how such evil killings that Keowee had revealed could have happened, not once, but twice, at Riverbend. She hated the images unfolding across her mind's eye, as she came to terms with the plight they faced.

Her eyes rounded with fear and a countenance saddened by the reality of her situation, she whispered, "Santee, Keowee, have you forgotten that I have no place to run to and that no one who will offer me protection? What will happen to the boys if I leave? They will think I have abandoned them."

"The boys will be fine," Santee assured Sam. "Floyd and David will be with me, and they will understand you leaving, if they know it was Mr. Morgan's doings. Have no fear about Lemuel. Keowee will see to him."

The old housekeeper would not be deterred, saying, "You and Lovie are leaving now as soon as you can gather a few things. Santee will leave first, claiming he needs to see someone up the road. I will tell the boys I need for them to catch some fresh fish for supper, and that will keep them from wanting to go with Santee. Santee will wait for you two up the road, out of sight of the house and the river. Without bringing notice to your leaving, the two of you will quietly slip out through the front doors. Walk quickly away from the house around the cedar grove and out the road to where Santee will be waiting, and he will drive you to Reverend Henry in Hartwell. We knows the Henrys will not turn you away. Leaving now will give Santee time to get back here about midday and be here if Mr. Robert decides to pay us a visit today. When the boys come in from the river, I will explain to Floyd that you have gone to visit the Henrys upon hearing of Mrs. Henry being sick and that Lovie went along to help. I will also caution Floyd and David about mentioning their sister and Lovie, should we have visitors. Taking Floyd aside while David is busy with Lemuel, I will empress on him the need for this caution, since Mr. Morgan thought this is what we should do, since the visitors we might have are not the kind of men to be trusted around young ladies."

"Lovie, is something wrong? Are you having second thoughts about leaving home?"

"No; not about leaving the plantation, but afraid for Mama and Papa when Mr. Robert comes and there ain't nobody else there except the boys. Mr. Robert can have bad temper fits if there ain't people to wait on him hand and foot. I fear him finding all the slaves gone and nobody left but Papa and Mama. He might blame them."

"He's been back in the country long enough to see and hear what has happened in the South and what has happened to the slave populace," Sam said. "Riverbend is not the only plantation slaves walked away from. He might have a temper fit, as you say, but no harm will come to Keowee and Santee." So did Sam promise, wanting to calm Lovie's fears.

"What you girls whispering about?" Santee asked. "You not planning mischief now? You both be on your best behavior and no trying to slip back to Riverbend. You both promise me right now you will stay with the reverend till I comes for you. Only me or Mr. Morgan." Santee finished his firm request, and waited.

After several seconds, he spoke again, "I be waiting."

"Papa, I promise," Lovie said, as she put her arms around Santee's shoulders and squeezed them.

"Thank you, baby," Santee sniffed, adding, "I ain't heard from you, Missy."

"I am not sitting near enough to hug you," Sam joked. However, I promise I will be on my best behavior while visiting the Henrys."

After a little more than two hours, the wagon from Riverbend pulled into the yard of the Henrys. They were welcomed with smiles and words of greetings in the yard. Santee quickly asked for a word with the reverend, and Mrs. Henry ushered the girls into the house. The house smelled of bread baking, and Sam's mouth watered for the taste of hot bread smeared with butter and jam. Mrs. Henry bid them to follow her to the kitchen, and as if she had read Sam's thoughts, she suggested a treat of bread and jam.

Before Mrs. Henry and the girls finished their treat, Santee followed Reverend Henry through the back door, carrying Sam's and Lovie's bags. Sam saw Mrs. Henry noticing the bags, but she never asked why the bags only instructed Santee to set them down inside the door to the dining room. Offering the reverend and Santee bread and jam, with a cool glass of milk, she rose from her chair to prepare the treat.

Santee turned from the place he had placed the bags said, "I's thank you for your offer, Mistress, but I need to be on my way back to Riverbend at once. I will only take time to tell my Lovie and Sam good-bye."

Hearing his words, Sam and Lovie both hurried to Santee for their good-bye hug and a few parting words. Tears clouded Sam's and Lovie's eyes, as they left Santee's embrace, and he quickly turned from the room, not wanting anyone to notice the tears swimming in his eyes.

Reverend Henry, adding to his welcome in the yard, spoke to the girls, "We are very happy you have chosen our home for a visit. I assured Santee that Mrs. Henry and I would be proper chaperons for you and would keep you safe."

"Thank you, Reverend Henry," Sam said. "It seems I will once again be in your and Mrs. Henry's debt. I thank you not only for myself but for my friend's care, as well. We will try not to be trouble and will be more than willing to do more than our share of cleaning and cooking while we are here. I have not as yet become an expert in cooking, but I am good at washing dishes, sweeping, mopping, and making beds."

"Lovie is an expert in all things." She added this last sentence with a grin and a jab at Lovie, trying to soothe her pain of having to say good-bye to her parents for the first time.

Her little tease brought a chuckle from Lovie and laughter from the couple who so willingly opened their home and their arms to the girls.

Santee arrived back at Riverbend in time to unhitch the horse, turn it out in the lot, and eat the midday meal, before they heard the slow trot of a horse on the gravel drive. Before anyone could leave the warming kitchen, the loud sound of riding boots hit the floor of the front hall, telling of Robert Sinclair's homecoming.

Robert's heated voice carried down the hall, "Where is everybody? There is a horse out front that needs tending to, and I need some food. What is the matter with all of you? Just because McMullan Sinclair is dead does not mean you can become lazy!"

Santee caught Keowee's arm and pulled her behind him as he walked through the door and into the front hall.

"Welcome home, Mr. Robert. I'll see to your horse shortly, and Keowee will heat you up some food. You'll have to make do with the two of us. The others be gone. Our people began leaving when Mr. Mac became too ill to see to them. Keowee and me have been here alone with the Hatcher boys for over a year. The South losing the war freed the slaves. Keowee and I felt we couldn't leave Riverbend unattended or leave the boys alone. You been gone a long time, and a lot has changed."

Robert made no reply to Santee's words, as he pushed by him on his way to the warming kitchen, ordering Keowee to fix him something to eat.

CHAPTER 11

The morning found Sam and Lovie up early and in the kitchen with Mrs. Henry, offering to help prepare the morning meal. Sam put out the plates, eating utensils, and cups. Lovie busied herself with watching the biscuits in the oven, while cracking and beating the eggs for Mrs. Henry to cook in a little of the sausage drippings. The girls were determined to be useful and not to be a burden. Mrs. Henry smiled, as she watched each young lady take on a specific task without being told what to do. The two young ladies were at home in the kitchen, going about their chore with ease, revealing a routine she was sure was practiced every morning. Never having had help in the kitchen while cooking, she was amazed that Lovie never once got in her way but always had whatever she needed right at hand. Her thoughts ran, *Too much of this, and I will become spoiled.*

Enjoying her second cup of coffee that Santee brought from the plantation, along with other supplies, Sam debated whether to address an outing she had hoped to make while visiting the Henrys' home. Finally deciding that now was as good a time as any, she directed her words to Reverend Henry, using the title her family used.

"Pastor, do you think it might be possible to take an afternoon ride out to our old home place? I would like to collect a few of Mama's and Papa's things. That is, if no one has taken shelter there or pilfered our belongings."

Reverend Henry looked at his wife, as if soliciting her help, and waited a minute before answering. He could see in Sam's eyes the need and the longing for anything of her parents. He knew that if there were items still there that belonged to William and Martha, they would be a treasure Sam would value.

"Sam, I will give your wish to visit your family farm some thought. Let's see how the next few days go. Does that seem fair?"

"Yes sir. I do not wish to cause a problem," Sam informed the reverend. "Lovie and I being away from the plantation at this time is very important to Keowee and Santee, and I am very appreciative that you and Mrs. Henry opened your doors to us."

Lovie listened to Sam's words to the reverend with a tad of relief, hoping Sam was not sugarcoating her reply.

The day went quietly, as the girls helped with chores and spent time in the Henrys' guest room. The evening meal was eaten with little conversation, as both girls were still pondering their afternoon. However, the Henrys were concerned that Sam's low spirits were due to having to wait for an answer to her plea to travel to her old home place.

The girls insisted they would clear the table and put the kitchen in order, while Mrs. Henry relaxed in the parlor.

Mrs. Henry retired to the parlor with her husband, and a soft, but intense, conversation regarding Sam's request for an outing ensued. They both agreed to pray about the request and to sleep on the matter, making their decision in the morning.

***

Robert's homecoming to Riverbend turned out to be unprofitable moneywise. He could find nothing in the house worth selling. However, being away from the prying eyes of Morgan Anderson, he had relaxed and had enjoyed a peaceful afternoon nap. Late in the afternoon, after searching the old house from top to bottom, he questioned Santee and Keowee firmly about Mac's personal items and the things that were missing from the house, as well. He received very little information, except to be told that Mr. Mac contributed freely to the Confederate cause and that soldiers in gray were regular visitors.

After a disappointing morning and afternoon that left his pockets empty of cash and that left him with no valuables to sell, he paced his father's study in an angry, childish rage, shouting, "There is not even a bottle of brandy left in this godforsaken house. I need some libation. Surely there is some hard liquor in one of Hartwell's taprooms and someone willing to take my marker."

Leaving the study, Robert yelled, "Santee!" and he continued to call at the top of his voice, as he climbed the stairs to his room, while instructing Santee.

His instruction, "Have my horse saddled and brought around to the front veranda," vibrated through the hall downstairs.

Hearing the racket coming from the front of the house, Keowee wrinkled her nose in disgust. Honoring her promise to Morgan Anderson, she lifted Lemuel into her arms and left the house in search of Santee. She found Santee and the boys in the barn sharpening hoes and mattocks.

"The young master wishes his horse saddled and brought

to the front of the house," Keowee informed Santee.

Santee could tell by Keowee's tone of voice that she was riled by Robert's request.

"Did he come to the kitchen and ask you to fetch me?" Santee asked.

"No. He bellowed his order from the front stairs. Robert Sinclair has the manners of a field hand."

"Calm down. He won't be here long. He's most likely going to Hartwell to the taprooms. He won't find what he's looking for in town. Not now, and he'll be heading back to Athens if he can find a way to get a hold of some money."

Santee was busy saddling Robert's horse, as he talked to Keowee, not wanting to cause Robert to have to wait for his horse. After all, he and Keowee promised Mr. Morgan.

True to Santee's prediction, Robert's hurried ride into Hartwell was proving to be unsatisfactory. No one was willing to take his marker, nor were any of his old friends offering to buy him a drink. Having been subjected to their rude neglect since the first helloes, he was considering leaving the Red Top in lieu of Matheson's Tap Room, when the conversation of two strangers near him sparked an interest.

"Excuse me gentlemen. I had no intention of eavesdropping on your conversation," Robert apologized, moving closer to the men and lowering his voice.

"The mention of bonding out children left without parents because of the war caught my ear. Could you or would you mind explaining this process? I know of several young boys who might profit from this program."

Being strangers to the town, the two men looked Robert over very cautiously before answering.

"Would these boys be kin of yours?" the older and the largest of the two finally asked.

"No. Not really kin, but their father left them in the care of my father when he joined the Confederate Army.

They have no mother; their father was killed; and my father is now dead. I have no way of taking care of them."

"From your manner of speech and the looks of your clothes, I take you to be a gentleman farmer or a plantation owner," the man said. Do you live in this area?"

"I am afraid my clothing has given you the wrong impression, gentlemen," Robert answered. "Although I was born into a family of a somewhat large plantation and am now the owner, I do not have the people or the means to put the place back into operation. Therefore, I am not in a position to provide the proper care for the boys."

Robert hoped that his statement would help him find out how he could make some money off the boys.

"Well, use them to replace some of your slaves what ran away," the younger of the two men said, with a sneer on his face. He added, "That's what the farmers who buy the children are doing. They are replacing their black slaves with white orphans. Ain't it a shame the brave men of the South fought and lost their lives to keep their slaves? And now, thanks to Mr. Lincoln, their children are going to be used to replace the slaves he freed."

"That's enough," the older man cautioned. "This here man don't want to hear your idea of how this bonding works; he just wants to know how you go about it. Ain't that right, young fellow?" The older man looked at Robert, and grinned. Robert, afraid that the young man spoke too loudly and that his words would draw the attention of his acquaintances, looked around the room and noticed the loud words were causing a few of the men to look their way. He did not want the townspeople to suspect what he had in mind.

"Do the two of you handle any of the bonding?" Robert asked, lowering his voice.

The men smiled and, not wanting to advertise their purpose for being in the town, they nodded their reply.

Robert bid them good night and left the taproom. He slowly walked to the place where he had left his horse, hoping the men would soon follow. He wanted to strike a deal for the two older boys, and he wanted to know if there was a market for the baby. He stood on a spot where he could see the door to the taproom. He did not have long to wait. The two men he was waiting for came out into the street and turned toward the place where he was standing. Robert engaged the two men in conversation, while sharing their jug of corn whiskey. A deal struck, Robert left the two men and rode back to Riverbend. His only obstacle to having money in his pocket at the moment was getting the boys away from his former slaves without them interfering. Ways of how to quietly expedite this ploy ran in and out of his murky, alcohol-soaked mind all the way back to Riverbend.

Early morning found Robert hung over and still abed, sleeping off the ill effects of his overindulgence of the jug of corn whiskey he had shared with his newly found cohorts.

Sam, on the other hand, was happily helping Mrs. Henry and Lovie prepare a picnic basket for their trip west to her family home.

The morning ride away from Hartwell was quiet and unnoticed, the streets being empty. The sun had barely begun its travels up the eastern sky, and the grass was still damp with the night's dew. Sam, dressed in her male attire, with her floppy hat pulled down low over her brow, sat quietly beside Lovie, as the buggy's wheels rattled along.

Unaware that her tears were falling from her chin, she was

startled by Lovie's arms slipping around her shoulders.

"What makes you cry?" Lovie whispered, as she drew Sam against her. "I thought you would be happy to get to make this trip."

"I am happy to make this trip, Lovie," Sam said, smiling through her tears. "I'm just remembering."

The house was open, the lock broken, showing signs of uninvited visitors. The front room and the three small bedrooms looked untouched. However, the kitchen and the pantry revealed they were the target of an uninvited guest. The shelves were empty.

"Sam, why don't you and Lovie check out the other rooms for the items you would like to have, while Mrs. Henry and I set out our picnic here in the kitchen?" Reverend Henry suggested.

Sam and Lovie returned to the front of the small house. Reverend Henry brought in the basket of food from the buggy, while Mrs. Henry found a pan to hold water and a cloth and soap to clean the dust from the table and the chairs.

As Lovie waited for Sam to tell her what to look for and if she wanted to start a pile of items, Sam slipped beneath her parents' bed and crawled to the back wall, leaving Lovie with a startled look of befuddlement.

Rolling to the side of the notched board at the head of the bed and sliding back away from the wall, she pulled hard on the notched board. Without a sound, the wide square lifted up into her hands. She had no light by which to search out the hole, so she lowered her hand into the dark square hole. The first thing she felt was shaped like a book, and when she brought it up to a place where she could get a look at it, she immediately knew what she had.

"Mama's Bible," she whispered. "This is why I have Papa's

Bible and not Mama's at Riverbend. On our hurried trip into Hartwell on that fateful day after hearing of Papa's death, I picked up the Bible lying on the table by Papa's and Mama's bed, thinking I was bringing Mama's Bible with us. *I wonder why Mama's Bible needed to be put into their secret hiding place. Mama must have placed it in there soon after Papa left for the war. No. Mama was too big with Lemuel to crawl under here even then. Papa placed the Bible here before he left. But why?*

Again, she slipped her hand into the hole, which was not very large, and she found a small box. After retrieving the box, she once again put her hand into the hiding place, sweeping her hand from corner to corner, finding nothing else. Convinced the hiding place was empty, she replaced the board and crawled out from under the bed, clutching her find in her left arm and hand.

Finding Lovie standing in the center of the room, staring at her with a bewildered look, Sam laughed. She knew that her hasty dive under the bed, without a word of explanation, had caused her friend to think she had finally lost what little sense she had. Chuckling, Sam spoke, "I am not batty. I was told by Papa before he left to fight them cussed Yankees about their secret place, and I was told to open it if something happened to him and if Mama was not able to do the opening. I am sorry for leaving you standing in the middle of the room without a word, but I have waited almost three years to come back here and see what Papa felt was important enough to put in a secret place.

"Well, it looks like you have an armful," Lovie answered.

Sam laid the items she found on the bed and started gathering up quilts and some of Floyd's clothes that would fit David. She added the books her family owned to the pile.

Her mama's locket she found in the bureau and fastened it around her neck.

Other keepsakes of Martha she also found in the top drawer of the chest. Martha's treasures, along with her sewing basket, were placed with the collection on the bed. There were not many of her papa's personal items, for he had carried his shaving mug, soap brush, razor, and strap with him. She did find a pipe and a tobacco pouch she knew Floyd would want.

"Something for David and Lemuel," she reminded herself. "I have to find something of Papa for them."

She was determined not to leave without an item for David and Lemuel, but she did not come across anything suitable for keepsakes, as she gathered up a few of their parents' clothes. However, after she returned to the kitchen and as she washed her hands at the pump in the kitchen, she spied her papa's mustache cup. "Perfect," she explained. "Now, if I can find one more thing?"

"Maybe there will be a tool or something he used every day in the barn," Reverend Henry mentioned. "We can look after we finish our picnic."

Sam was pleased with Reverend Henry's mention of the barn, and she told him so, as she sat down at the table.

Looking in the barn had slipped her mind completely. The barn would have a number of things her papa treasured.

The buggy was loaded with Sam's findings soon after the four finished their meal, and the ride back to the Henrys' home was quiet. All of them respected Sam's doleful countenance, as they drove away from her childhood home, and they kept their comments on the day to themselves.

The sun fell below the western horizon before they approached the town of Hartwell, and they rode through the streets of town to the Henrys' home in the evening twilight. There was no one on the streets that late in the day, as Reverend Henry guided the buggy safely home, and as far as they could tell, no one was even aware of their travels. But the night always has eyes.

CHAPTER 12

Her mind full of racing thoughts, Sam lay on her comfortable bed in the upstairs bedroom she shared with Lovie. Since saying good night, she tried to turn her thoughts to the items she had found in her parents' secret hiding place, but her thoughts kept straying. Without her bidding, her mind turned to Morgan Anderson. Disgusted, she admitted, *It seems that cussed Yankee is going to rule my thoughts, as well as my life. I should not be surprised he has wormed his way into my thoughts tonight. The cussed man has become a constant visitor since the night I saved his cussed life, especially when I am alone and everything is quiet. Now I have another perplexing facet to the cussed man that I do not understand. His concern for Lovie's safety. Why would a cussed Yankee even care? Every blessed thing I have observed of Morgan Anderson since his return to Riverbend has been completely different from what I had expected from a cussed Yankee, and I cannot help being skeptical.*

"There must be some kind of unsavory motive behind his goody-goody behavior," she whispered to the darkness. "Oh, I miss my window seat. I can always clear my head and come to rational conclusions as I watch the night."

"*That's a joke,* popped into her mind. *You are just as upside down about your feelings toward Morgan at Riverbend as you are here. Why don't you just admit that he is one Yankee that does not fit neatly into your opinion of Yankees?*

As Sam tossed and turned in a bed that had grown uncomfortable by the hour, her brain would not turn off and let her drift off to sleep. Along with all the thoughts of Morgan running through her mind was a nagging disquiet that she was becoming more of a traitor. She was afraid that her unwanted thoughts and feeling about the cussed Yankee had betrayed her family, especially her papa. A Yankee soldier killed Papa, and Morgan Anderson had been a Yankee soldier, and, in her mind, he should be held in contempt, not with favor.

She knew hate for the first time in her lift on October 2, 1862. After receiving news of her papa's death, she allowed the hate for Yankees that she felt on that day, especially for Yankee soldiers, to grow. She fed her anger and hate over the last years by constantly reminding herself that Yankees were responsible for not only the death of her father but also for the death of her mother and the destruction of their home life.

Sam awoke with a heavy heart and a need to talk with someone. She purposed in her heart, as she dressed, to not let the day pass without a discussion of sorts about Southern people's plight with Yankees occupying and trespassing on good, Southern family land.

Lovie noticed Sam's sour mood, as they dressed for the day, and she contributed her low spirits to their visit yesterday to the Hatcher home place. Knowing Sam as she did, she did not even offer a good morning to her friend but busied herself with making her bed and tidying up her few pieces of clothing.

As was the girls' practice since arriving at the Henrys' home, Sam and Lovie immediately and without instructions from Mrs. Henry shared in preparing breakfast. As the food was being placed on the table, Reverend Henry joined the ladies. Sitting at the table, Sam and Lovie bowed their heads for the blessing, as was the custom at Riverbend and as was the same in the Henrys' home. Reverend Henry blessed the food, as usual, but he did not stop with just the blessing. Instead of saying, "Amen," he prayed for the people hurting in the South and in the North. Sam's head jerked up at the reverend's words asking God to help the North.

Upon saying, "Amen," Reverend Henry raised his head, letting his eyes rest first on Sam. He had wrestled with the words he would use this morning. The need to use them in prayer laid heavy on his heart since the day of the girls' arrival, and God had not removed the need for him to speak this prayer within Sam's hearing. He had hoped that, during her stay in their home, he could, in some way, help her to start to heal and to rid her heart of hate.

Reverend Henry and Mrs. Henry both noticed Sam's bewildered stare at the end of the blessing. Her eyes stayed glued on the reverend for several moments after he said, "Amen."

Reverend Henry braced himself for the onslaught of Sam's words that he was sure would come, words denying the need or the duty to pray for the Northern people. He knew that, even as a child, Sam was never bashful in speaking her piece or in asking questions, and he knew that once the shock of his words subsided, she would once again use her God-given voice. However, the barrage of questions and denials he was expecting from Sam did not come right away. Instead, Sam quietly rose from the table and began her usual help of clearing the table and of washing the dishes, but Reverend Henry was not too disappointed. The time would come when Sam was ready, and not before.

Along with what she had planned to use in her argument

against the need to pray for the Northern people, Sam was sorting out questions she wanted to ask—questions regarding one Yankee, in particular, and the turmoil he was causing her, without mentioning the uninvited feelings that accompanied seeing him or thinking about him. She desperately wanted to know how to handle this cussed Yankee and to get rid of him, shy of committing murder. These thoughts kept her quiet and sullen, while she washed and rinsed the breakfast dishes. Mrs. Henry talked quietly to both girls, as the three worked, putting the kitchen to order, but only Lovie was responsive to her. By the time Sam had washed all the dishes, the pots, and the pans, Lovie had them dried and stacked to be put back into the cupboard. Sam dried her hands on the towel that hung by the dishpan, and, without a word to either Mrs. Henry or Lovie, she turned and left the room on her way to Reverend Henry's study.

A light rapping on the study door alerted Reverend Henry to Sam's arrival. He had spent the time since returning to his study from breakfast in prayer, asking God for help in dealing with Sam. Rising from his knees, he walked over and opened the door, smiling and bidding Sam to enter with outstretched hands.

Sam entered the study, without meeting Reverend Henry's eyes or acknowledging his outstretched hands. She sat in a chair opposite his desk, expecting him to sit behind his desk, but he pulled a chair from the other side of the room and placed it in front of his desk. Turning the chair so he could face Sam, he sat and waited for Sam to speak. Reverend Henry's taking a seat beside her instead of going to the chair behind his desk rattled Sam, and, for a few moments, she sat quietly, as though she were hesitant to start the conversation, seemingly waiting for Reverend Henry. Thinking Sam was hesitant to speak first,

Reverend Henry invited her to speak, saying, "Whenever you are ready Sam, say your piece. I'll listen, and then maybe we can discuss some of your thoughts."

Taking a deep breath and steadying herself, Sam turned and opened her mouth, and out came, "We are the vanquished, the beaten, the killed, and the robbed. Why should we ask God to help the North? They are the ones who killed our fathers, our brothers, and our sons and who destroyed our families and burned Southern homes and crops, leaving women and children to starve. What have we done to them that they should forgive us? They are the ones in the wrong. They have stolen all that the South had. They are a people without mercy. They have no heart or feelings. They are hard and mean. We will be wasting our prayers. There is no way God could reach their hard hearts. They would have to have a heart first, and people who commit the acts that the North has committed could not have a heart. I hate them!"

Tears that she swore she would not shed flowed from her eyes with her last three words. Reverend Henry's heart was breaking, as he listened to her words, knowing they attested to the pain and the hurt she carried.

When the tears began to roll down her pretty, rosy cheeks, he reached for her hands, placing both in one of his large hands and softly patted her hands with his other, while letting her cry out her sorrow.

"God, our heavenly Father, help me to help this sweet, young lady, and help her give her hate to you. She is hurting and has carried a heavy load since losing both parents within a short time span."

Sam listened in earnest to Reverend Henry's whispered words, as tears washed her face. "Give my hate for Yankees to God," she blurted out, as she pulled her hands free of the comforting hand that had held hers so compassionately. Sam's outburst caused Reverend Henry to stop praying and to turn his eyes to her.

"You want to finally drown in your hate for the Yankees?" Reverend Henry asked. "That is surely what you will end up doing. Destroying yourself and maybe one or more of your brothers. The hate you hold for Yankees is not hurting the first Northerner; it is only hurting you. That is why the Bible tells us not to hold malice toward others in our hearts. God knows it does not affect the person or persons we are hating, but holding hate in our hearts only hurts us, causing us to become sick in many ways. He tells us this because he loves us and wants the best for us, and that includes you."

"Okay," Sam said, "so God does not want us to hate because it is bad for us, but that does not mean I have to pray for the Northern people, who are sitting comfortably in their nice and pretty home, enjoying the bountiful love of their family. Why do they need prayer? They have not lost their parents, their homes, and the loving care that abounds in their homes. Lemuel will never know the loving touch of Mama or the secure feeling that came with Papa's strong arms wrapped around him. The last few years of Floyd's and David's childhood that should have been carefree were swept away by a Yankee's rifle ball and replaced with working from sunup to sundown, helping scratch out of the earth enough food to keep us all alive. My days that could have been spent attending church socials, barn raisings, and dates with nice beaus were taken from me by that same rifle ball."

Reverend Henry watched Sam carefully, as she sincerely rendered the painful facts that caused her hate of anyone or anything to do with the North. A lovely, young lady sat before him, not dressed in her usual male attire but dressed in her mother's plain cotton day dress that Mrs. Henry had altered after they had returned home from the Hatcher farm. The pain and sorrow the young lady felt was easy to hear in her words and to see in her countenance. There was no doubt in Reverend Henry's mind that Sam was confident that the traumatic events surrounding the loss of her mother and her father and her home gave her the God-given right to hate the ones she held responsible.

Seeing Sam out of the male attire she had worn for protection on the plantation and now dressed in a young lady's dress gave credence to how her years should have been spent. However, he knew that for Sam to have any kind of a love-filled life that all young ladies wanted, she had to clear her heart of hate so there would be room for the love she deserved. With compassion and words contrary to her beliefs, he continued to try to bring Sam to a path leading to forgiveness of the North and the Northern people for her loss and the pain she carried and to rid herself of the hate that filled her heart and her life. So, after several minutes of quiet following Sam's last remarks, Reverend Henry spoke.

"Sam, Mrs. Henry and I know you have lost more than your share, so we do not blame you for your feelings of hate. This reaction to the cause of your losses is natural. Anyone in your shoes who did not experience these same emotions would be less than human. However, in my years, and I have had a good many more than you, I have seen terrible things happen to people who hold onto their hate and who allow it to grow and to fester till it destroys everything they hold dear. Mrs. Henry and I do not want to see this happen to you, and neither would your mother and father. William and Martha wanted the best for you and the boys. William left here with a heavy heart, because he did not want to fight and kill his fellow Americans, but since he had to go, he was confident he had secured a safe and secure life for his wife and children. He would not want the aftermath of this horrible war to cause you more loss. War is horrible. No one really wins. I dare say there were as many, if not more, Union soldiers killed during this atrocity than Southern. The South ran circles around the North in most conflicts, until we gave out of men and supplies, and, of course, Sherman's fiery march through the South did not help. It is natural for you to think that the people up North have not suffered as you, but many Union soldiers were killed, and there were many who had mothers, fathers, wives, and children. Northern families were also torn apart, just like your family. Numerous Northern children were left without parents, the same as you. The only difference between the North and the South at the end of the war that I can see is that, first of all, the North won. The South lost, and the North did not experience any kind of fiery march like the South. But pain and loss know no color. Men in blue and men in gray were both killed, and the loved ones of the blue and of the gray suffered the same loss and the same pain. So you see the Northern people are struggling with their hatred of the South, and they will have to work to forgive us just as we struggle to forgive the North here in the South."

"Sam," the reverend continued, "you are a dear, sweet Christian. I was there when you made your decision to accept Jesus as your Lord and Savior, and you know, as I know, that this same Jesus stands ready to help you. Although you are a very strong young lady and have survived and have helped your brothers to do the same, you cannot release this hate on your own. All people need help at some point in their lives, and this will be a time in your life when you will need a stronger power than yourself. I am trusting Jesus to help you decide to release your hate and to start changing how you feel toward the people from the North. When the times come when you want and need Jesus' help with this, ask him to help you, and then trust him to do what you have asked. Let's bow our heads in prayer." However, before he could bow his head, Sam spoke.

"I have a few questions."

Not completely convinced to stop hating Yankees as yet, Sam thought that now might be a good time to see if she could ask some roundabout questions and maybe get some help with her problems with the cussed Yankee named Morgan Anderson.

"I have plenty of time to answer your questions," the reverend answered, adding, "Ask away."

"Well, where do I start?"

"Just how are we to tolerate Yankees that are wandering around and coming uninvited onto Southern-owned property?"

"Santee did not mention that," the reverend said. "Have Yankee soldiers visited Riverbend?" He felt a tinge of uneasiness.

"Well, he wouldn't," Sam said. "You see, this particular Yankee was not in uniform, although he is a Yankee soldier and he happens to be connected somehow to Mr. Mac."

"Connected to Mac?" the reverend asked. "Through Mac's cousin? Who happens to be the stepmother of this said Yankee soldier?"

"Yes," Sam said, "and don't tell me you know this cussed Yankee and hold him in high esteem. If you do, I'll just lay down and die."

"Please don't do that," the reverend said, in alarm. "Mrs. Henry would never forgive me if I caused you to die in her home. But I will have to confess to knowing Morgan. I am sure he was a member of the Union Army at some time. He is, after all, a graduate of West Point. Sam, this should not upset you. Even though he was a Yankee soldier, he is a very good and kind young man. He would never harm you or anyone on the plantation. I am sure he holds no malice toward the South or the men who fought for the South. Are you afraid of him? If so, let me put your mind at ease. There is no danger to you or anyone at Riverbend from Morgan Anderson."

Well, this certainly not going as I had wanted, Sam thought. Maybe I should just let them put a halo on the cussed Yankee and be done with it. Disappointed and not really knowing what she had expected Reverend Henry to say, she thought to approach the matter from a different angle.

"I am not exactly afraid for my life when this Yankee visits, but I do not feel comfortable around him, so I find other places to spend my time rather than with the members of the household and this visitor. I do seem to be in the minority. Floyd and David even follow him around like little puppy dogs. I just want him to stay away from Riverbend, but I have no authority to order him to do this. Now he has Lovie and me banished from Riverbend. I have not even had a chance to meet Robert Sinclair and to form my own opinion of him. I think this is all a farce. I think the cussed Yankee wants to own Riverbend."

"Sam," the reverend said, "Morgan Anderson is a wealthy man in his own right, and I understand he even paid the back taxes on Riverbend for Robert in order to keep it from being sold for the back taxes, probably to some Northerner. If Morgan said there was danger in you and Lovie being at Riverbend when Robert returned, I would take it to heart, without asking questions, and believe him. From what you have told me about the way Floyd and David are reacting to

Morgan, I have— " Reverend Henry paused, a smile gracing his face, as he thought, *Could there be some underlying reason for Sam's reaction to Morgan other than him being a Yankee? Of course, if that is true, her hatred for Yankees is the problem. That must be it, knowing Sam as I do. If it was just that he was a Yankee, she'd be in his face, giving him a piece of her mind, instead of distancing herself from him.* This thought also brought a chuckle with his smile. A chuckle that he tried to disguise as a cough while finishing his sentence.

"I have often heard it said you can trust a child's opinion if a person is good or bad. David and Floyd's liking of the gent should erase all of your disquieted feelings. On his next visit, I suggest you try to get to know him. Ask him to tell you his true feelings on the war and how he feels now toward the South. This might help you begin to tone down your disregard for Yankees."

Sam almost laughed in Reverend Henry's face, and she would have if she had not been so distraught after receiving no help at all with what to do with her confounded feelings. Feeling a bit discontented with their whole talk, she stood and started to leave the room, but she remembered her manners before reaching the door. Forcing a smile, she turned to face the reverend.

"Thank you for your time. I will give some thought to your words on forgiveness." She said this with her arms and fingers crossed behind her back.

After Sam left the study, Reverend Henry continued to ponder Sam's problem with Morgan Anderson. Most of the people of the South shared her feelings, to some extent, and they would look down on a young Southern girl, should she fall in love with and marry a Yankee soldier or a man who was a member of the Union Army during the fighting. However, this insight into the temperament of the South at this time did not dissuade Reverend Henry's resolve to encourage Sam to deal with her hate and, with God's help, to rid herself of the hatred that consumed her.

CHAPTER 13

A wire from Washington was delivered to Morgan at the Lumpkin House in Athens. After reading the wire, he stood and motioned to Haygood, saying, "Let's take a walk."

Hearing Morgan's invitation, Haygood rose from his chair and followed Morgan out of the building.

"We have the information regarding La Cur," Morgan advised quietly, and he shared the gist of the wire.

"It seems the old count sired two sons, one legitimate, Luis, and one illegitimate, Phillip. Both were born in 1810, a few weeks apart and the spitting image of their father. The only thing that identifies the heir is the La Cur birthmark on his right buttock. Luis inherited the title at his father's death. Sometime after the old count expired, talk in the village surrounding the La Cur castle hinted that something was wrong in the castle. Longtime servants were mystified by the changes in the new lord's manners, among other things. Also missing was Phillip, the illegitimate son in the village. Phillip's mother, when questioned about Phillip, reported he had left the country soon after the death of his father to seek his fortune. A good many men in the French Government had suspicions of a change of identity, perhaps by murder, but they could not prove a crime without asking a lord of the realm to bare his buttocks, just on suspicions. When we apprehend La Cur on American soil, we will not be barred from baring the man's behind. Should we prove the man to be Phillip, the French government will be most appreciative."

Taking a breath, Morgan continued, "This information is certainly worth the time it took to obtain it. You can be sure that when I get my hands on the SOB, I will do more than bare his bottom."

"Well, if that don't beat old bob," Haygood said. "They think that Luis is really Phillip, who is not only a kidnapper but also a murderer?" Haygood asked his question with a shake of his head. Then he went on, "Colonel, we not only have a plot to sell women into slavery; we also have the intrigue of a French murder on our hands."

"Let's pay our friend, Professor Neely, a visit," Morgan said. "We have news to share."

***

A light, early September rain was falling in Hartwell, as the Henry household finished their midday meal. Sam and Lovie laughingly shooed Mrs. Henry out of the kitchen, promising to clean up from the meal and to leave the kitchen shining clean. Sam was quiet during the dish washing, and Lovie wondered why. In fact, Sam had been extremely quiet ever since she had returned from the talk with Reverend Henry.

With the last dish placed in the cupboard, the girls left the kitchen for the upstairs bedroom they shared. The soft rain pitter-pattering against the window brought a tranquil and sleepy atmosphere to the room, causing Lovie to say, "I'm going to take a nap."

Sam lay quiet, replaying her talk with Pastor Henry in her mind: his recounting of God's desire for his children to keep hate from their heart. She could not argue with that. She had been taught, from the time she had been a small child, about God's love. *Hate was never a part of my life until Papa's and Mama's death. I never heard my parents speak a harsh word toward anyone. The war did more than kill and destroy; it changed the way we feel toward people, especially how I feel about the people of the North. And I am supposed to just forgive them.*

"I cannot do that," she whispered, as tears filled her eyes.

"They took everything from the boys and me. I cannot do it. God, I cannot do it." *Ask God for help, if you are ready.* She heard Reverend Henry's voice enter her thoughts.

"Am I ready?" she whispered. *Pastor said I would not be able to do this on my own.*

"Do I want to stop hating?" She lay quiet and dry-eyed, considering what she had just asked herself. *If you could begin to forgive the Northern people, you might be able to begin to understand the emotions and feelings toward one cussed Yankee.*

She sat straight up in the bed and muttered, "Does that cussed man have to stick himself into every conversation I have with myself?"

"At least you're at the point of calling Mr. Morgan 'that cussed man' and not 'that cussed Yankee.'" Lovie sleepily commented. "What has brought that about? You're finally realizing he's a pretty nice fellow."

"What are you talking about?" Sam asked.

"You woke me with your complaint about a cussed man sticking himself into all of your conversations," Lovie said, "and I have no doubt you were referring to Mr. Morgan. There has been no other man making himself at home in your life. Has there?" Lovie asked wide awake now, as she turned on her side, facing Sam.

Miffed with herself that she had spoken loud enough to wake Lovie, she hit back with her usual displeasure with Morgan Anderson, "Of course, you think he's so grand he should be sporting a halo, but I cannot and do not appreciate his interfering in my life."

"Are you still angry because he told Mama and Papa to make us leave Riverbend?" Lovie asked. "Are you mad because of something the Reverend said or 'cause he knows Mr. Morgan? I guess everybody that's anybody around here knows Mr. Morgan and likes him."

"Pastor Henry did mention he knew the cussed man," Sam mumbled. "He talked mostly about me forgiving the Yankees and that I should not hold hate in my heart because it could make me sick and bad things could happen to me."

"Really!" Lovie squeaked, as she slid to the edge of the bed, coming quickly to a sitting position.

"What bad things?" she asked.

Sam grinned at her friend's anxious glare, knowing she had touched a nerve with her mention of bad things happening and thought to sooth Lovie's nerves, explaining further her talk with Pastor Henry.

"Pastor referred to a Bible verse I remember hearing Papa quote, 1 Peter 2:1. Pastor told me to ask God to help me. Since he has told us not to hate, God would surely help me when I was ready to stop hating Yankees.

I don't know if I am ready."

"Lovie," Sam went on softly, "pray for God to help me to want to stop hating."

Hearing the helplessness in Sam's plea, Lovie dropped to her knees beside her friend's bed.

"Sam, I's pray by whispering in my heart to God. I's guess I can whisper a prayer for you in my heart. I's can do that for you. If you want me to."

"Lovie, that's about the sweetest thing anyone could do for me. I would love being included in your whispered prayer to God."

A little uncomfortable with having shared her most private and personal relationship with God and a little uncomfortable with Sam's words of praise, Lovie was feeling embarrassed. Wanting to lighten the effect of their talk, she informed Sam in an unwavering firmness that reminded Sam of Keowee's no-nonsense tone.

"All right, Miss Southern Gal Full of Hate, get yourself ready to give that hate to God. Do not dillydally if you want my help. Do it now! Today!"

"Please be a little patient and have compassion for me, as I struggle to bring myself to do this," Sam pleaded. "You, of all people, know how hard it is for me to make myself do something I do not want to do."

"I shor nuff do," Lovie huffed, as she walked to the rain-splattered window.

Sam folded her hands under her head and again starred at the ceiling. Her thoughts came in a battle of wanting and not wanting. *I guess I need to approach this rationally, she suggested. List what is good about my hate of Yankees and of what is bad. Could that help me find a reason to want to rid myself of this hate? The one good thing I can think of right now is that my hatred of Yankees keeps a barrier between me and that cussed Morgan Anderson, and, because of my hate, no one will ever know that I became a traitor to Papa and the South by helping a cussed Yankee soldier. The one and only bad thing I can think of is the effects God says hate will have on the person that hates.*

Before Sam could add to her list of good and bad, Lovie interrupted her thoughts and said, "Sam, I think it be time we help start the evening meal. I heard Mrs. Henry clanking pots. That's usually a good sign."

The girls entered the kitchen, as Mrs. Henry finished adding wood to the fire.

"You girls always know when to come to the kitchen," she said. "Do you have a built in clock?" She chuckled.

"No, ma'am," Sam replied, with chuckles mingling with Mrs. Henry's. "However, Lovie does have great hearing."

The geyser of light laughter added a jovial flavor to the mundane cooking of a meal. The gayety continued through the placing of the food on the table, calling the reverend to the consumption of the meal. Sam's mood was dampened by Reverend Henry's request for her to join him in his study shortly.

After putting the kitchen to order, the girls walked toward the stairs, Lovie climbing the stairs, as Sam walked to the pastor's study. With a light tap, she opened the door, but she hesitated a moment before entering uneasy about what might be forthcoming. However, Sam did not have long to wait. Reverend Henry started speaking, as he drew a chair from across the room.

"Sam, I have prayed about our earlier conversation off and on all day, wanting to offer you something that might help you. Something that would ease the struggle you are bound to have. Would making a list help you?"

The reverend's last statement gained Sam's interest, and she wondered, *Has he been reading my mind?* Taking a deep breath, Sam ventured to ask, "What kind of list?"

"Usually when making a list to help you reach a decision, you list the good and the bad of the decision. List the good effects and the bad effects of holding hate in your heart. Does that sound reasonable?"

He's saying my thoughts almost word for word. I wonder what he would put on this list. Only one way to find out. "If you were to make such a list, Pastor, what would you list under 'good'? I know what you would list under 'bad.'"

"I would be hard pressed to put anything under 'good,'" the pastor said. "However, trying to put myself in the shoes of a person who has hate in his or her heart, I would think hate has to give the person some kind of pleasure or that person would not hold onto the hate. Since you know what God says about holding hate in your heart, his words would be in the bad column. The good column would require some thought, unless you know this without thinking. I hope you will put a great deal of thought to the good column."

The soft rain of the day turned to pouring rain, as the Henry household prepared to take to their beds for the night. Thunder rumbled loudly, and sharp cracks of lighting flashed across the night, but Sam paid little attention to the noise of the storm. Dressed in her mama's nightgown that she had salvaged from her home place, she said good night to Lovie and crawled beneath the bedcovers. Her brain would not stop replaying words of her chat with Pastor Henry, until she finally relented. Wishing for her window seat at Riverbend, she sat up and rested against the pillow and the headboard. Mentally, she began to wrestle with the reverend's counsel, examining and discarding, always coming back to the suggestion of making a list.

"I will make him a list, since I had the idea first," she whispered to the night. She decided to list the good things about her hate first, and she was struck with just one: the barrier between her and her cussed Yankee. *Unless,* she thought, *I count the fact that hating Yankees gives me a way to deal with the loss of Papa, Mama, and our home?* As she pondered this thought, another question butted in, *Will I be able to endure the grief of losing Mama and Papa without my hate? Before I can go any further with this list, I need to consider how ridding myself of hate for the ones responsible for our loss will affect me.* As she pondered these thoughts, she became sure of one thing. *Pastor Henry is wrong as to why someone holds hate in his or her heart. There is no pleasure, at least not for me. The hate that I feel is mixed with grief. I take no pleasure in hating. In fact, there is pain in my hatred.* With this admission, Sam began to pray. Unaware of what had become a nightly custom, she reached for and grabbed the pendant hanging around her neck.

Saying, "Amen," Sam snuggled beneath the sheet and closed her eyes in sleep.

The pounding rain kept Robert Sinclair closeted in his father's study with a jug of homemade whiskey, compliments of his newly found friends. The jug bolstered his courage to continue with his idea of bonding out the boys, therefore obtaining the money he needed to sustain him until his uncle arrived from Savannah.

As he drank and thought of the money he would soon have in his pockets, a plan for abduction began to emerge. Remembering the buggy he had observed pulling into the home of Reverend Henry a night or two ago and knowing that the couple had no children caused him to speculate on who the other two occupants could be. *There is no kin that would account for the boy,* he surmised. *The young black female could only be in the Henrys' home because of the boy. With no family ties, the boy must be an orphan from the area. I am sure that two extra mouths to feed puts a strain on the reverend's pockets. It would be the Christian thing to do to relieve the good reverend of this added burden. I will therefore add these two to the two boys from Riverbend. I will not be able to bond out the black girl, but Uncle Luis will be mighty generous because of my thoughtfulness when I present her to him.*

The empty jug fell to the floor, and Robert staggered out of the study and to the stairs.

CHAPTER 14

As the fields and the roads began to dry, people began to stir. Late morning found Robert Sinclair up and dressed for a ride into Hartwell, but, before leaving Riverbend, he told Keowee to have fresh fish for the midday meal. Floyd and David were happy to spend a morning on the bank of the river, engaged in their favorite pastime.

The Henrys prepared for their planned morning of visiting the sick and the homebound of their flock. Sam and Lovie agreed to stay inside, while enjoying a morning of their choosing. Watching from a stand of trees separating the church yard from the home of the reverend, Robert observed the Henrys' departure and smiled in anticipation. He had all he needed to carry out the abductions, except for his two new friends, their wagon, and their horses.

Directing the man handling the horses to the Henrys' yard, he motioned for the larger of the two men to follow him to the back door. After knocking, Robert took a couple of steps to the side of the door and waited. Upon hearing the knocking, Lovie walked to the back door, cautioning Sam to remain in the dining room. Lovie continued to the door, and, looking through the small window in the door, she saw the wagon and a man sitting on the wagon bench. Unlocking and slightly opening the door, she leaned out to ask the man if he needed the reverend, and she was grabbed by her arm. Dragged from the door, Lovie came face to face with Robert Sinclair and opened her mouth to scream for Sam to run, giving Robert the opportunity to stick a gag in her mouth, along with a cloth soaked in chloroform over her nose.

Sam grew tired of waiting for Lovie to return to the dining room, and, unaware of the danger, followed her to the door. Finding the door ajar but no sign of Lovie, she stepped out of the door and into the waiting hands of Robert Sinclair and the same fate that awaited Lovie.

The wagon left the yard of the Henrys' home, traveling out of town toward the Savannah River. Sam lay on her back, gagged and hog-tied. Waking from her drug-induced sleep, she struggled to get off her back. Finally able to roll onto her side, she found Lovie staring at her with tear-filled eyes. Neither were able to utter a word, the gags still securely stuffed in their mouths.

Sam's mind slowly began to clear, and she remembered a smelly rag being clamped over her nose, making her lose conscious, and she figured she had been asleep only long enough for the man to get her in the wagon and to tie her up. *Now I know what happened to Lovie. Whatever the reason this man took us from the Henry home is not in Hartwell. Our fate awaits us either in Anderson or in Athens.*

Either town means a long ride. I wish I could talk to Lovie. From the look of fear in her eyes, I believe she knows something I don't. Maybe a hint as to why we were taken, or maybe she recognized who did this. Oh, sweet Jesus! Could the man I saw be Robert Sinclair? No. He knows nothing about Lovie and me. God, please help us. Keep Lovie and me from harm. In Jesus' name, I pray.

Lovie wanted to tell Sam that Robert Sinclair was behind this, but she could not even smile, much less speak. She was scared out of her mind. Awakening to find Sam in the wagon she had seen out the back door, she had no idea where they were being taken or what was to be their fate. However, having seen Robert Sinclair before the cloth was placed over her nose and mouth, she was sure of one thing. It was not good. Watching Sam, she saw Sam's confused frown turning to a look she saw hundreds of times before, and she knew Sam's mind was beginning to work.

She be trying to figure out a way to get out of this wagon and this mess, but she don't know it gonna take a miracle for us to get safely away from Robert Sinclair.

The covered top made Sam unable to see the sky and to judge the time of day. With no sense of time or directions, she wondered, *Are we traveling west out Hartwell or toward the river? Examining the situation, our only chance of escape or getting help would be at our destination; until then, we best lay quiet and conserve our energy. We will need all the strength we can muster when the time comes to make our escape.*

Later, the wagon began slowing, and the conversation on the wagon seat livened up. Sam heard one man giving instructions to turn onto another road, and she felt the wagon turn to the left. A short time later, it came to a complete stop. The same man instructed the driver to drive into some trees and to stay hidden until he returned. Sam saw Lovie eyes opening wide at the man's words and a frown creasing her forehead. Sam was sure that Lovie was wondering the same as she. *Why are we stopping here, and who were the men hiding from?*

Robert knew that Floyd and David would be on the river, where he had planned for them to be. Walking the short distance from the wagon to the river, he congratulated himself for having told Keowee to have fish for the midday meal.

The boys were right where he had planned, out of sight of the house and the yard. He approached, smiling, and, pretending interest in their fishing, he asked, "Are you boys having any luck?"

Robert stepped to David's side, motioning for the big man to move toward Floyd. While informing the boys about the midday meal, Robert and his helper each grabbed a boy. The boys were caught, just as Sam and Lovie had been caught. The unconscious boys were easily carried to the wagon and placed across the wagon bed, at the feet of their sister and Lovie.

Sam's screams were not heard, but she screamed with all her might, seeing the limp bodies of her brothers in the hands of the two men.

Lovie, afraid for the fate of the two boys and for the terror her mama and papa would feel, when they found the boys missing, cried silent tears.

Tears rolled from Sam's eyes, as she realized how frightened Floyd and David would be when they woke from their sleep. She would have no way of letting them know that they were not alone but that she and Lovie were with them.

Fearing for Lovie and herself was bad enough, but knowing that, without a miracle, her brothers would share the same fate, was almost unbearable.

To accommodate the width of the wagon Floyd lay on his side, his legs bent at the knees. He woke first and saw David lying on his back, at the feet of someone. Blinking his eyes, he looked hard, squinting to see, in the dim light, whether he saw one set of feet or two. Whether he had seen one or two, he knew they were not alone. There was someone else in this. Becoming aware of the bumps, he knew they were in a wagon.

Why is Robert taking us away from Riverbend, along with this other person? Pushing up slightly with his shoulders, he was able to get a better look at the boots on the feet near David's head, and he ecognized them. *Those are Sam's boots. Robert has stolen Sam away from Pastor Henry's house. If he got Sam, he also got Lovie.. So there are two pair of feet. How did Robert find them? We never mentioned Sam or Lovie when he was at Riverbend. He might not know whom he has. He just happened upon two unprotected girls. Morgan was right; Robert Sinclair is not a man to be trusted. I'm glad Sam is with us. She'll think of some way to get us out of this mess. I wish I could tell David; he will be so afraid when he wakes up. What in the world made us go to sleep? I bet it was something on that rag that man held against my nose.*

David began to stir, and Floyd bent at his waist and nudged David in the side with his head. He continued nudging him until he turned his head to face him. Tears slipped from the corners of David's eyes, as he became fully awake. Floyd motioned with his head for David to look the other way, hoping he would see and recognize Sam's boots and would know she was with them. After looking at Floyd for a long time, David turned his head to look on his other side.

Floyd knew that David's natural curiosity had kicked in and that he wanted to look things over. It did not take long. David jerked his head back around toward Floyd and widened his eyes. Floyd nodded. Floyd could tell, by David's expression, that he had recognized Sam's boots.

Sam felt movement at the bottom of her feet and knew David was awake. Hoping he had seen Floyd upon opening his eyes, she knew his brother would give him comfort. Sam's thoughts began to run in familiar territory. *I have one more evil deed to lay at the feet of the Yankees. You would think that killing Papa would have been enough to satisfy the bloodthirsty Yankees.*

Amidst this bout of bad-mouthing the Yankees came a startling recollection that jolted Sam to her feet. *These men are Southerners, not Yankees.* On the heels of that truth, another truth followed. *A Yankee, Morgan Anderson, warned Keowee and Santee against Robert Sinclair. Well, that'll beat the old bob. I guess I will have to give Mr. Anderson credit for trying to keep Lovie safe.*

But, even with her attempt to put some blame on Morgan, she began to consider, *If they take us to Athens and I can get to Morgan or Haygood, they'd help.* Smiling at that thought, she began to see a way of foiling Robert Sinclair's plans.

Lovie strained her eyes to keep a watch on the boys, and she realized that she could see David's face below Sam's feet. She hoped that she could make eye contact with him, letting him know that she was with him, so she kept her eyes on his face. After several minutes, she realized that his eyes had never left Sam's boots. Taking a hard look at his face, she was surprised to see a face not twisted with fear but relaxed, as if he was pleased. Not seeing the fear she had expected, she watched and wondered. All at once, the reason why hit her, *That young'un done recognized Sam's boots. If that don't beat all. No one but David would have done that. That little rascal.*

The wagon had made a semicircle, going back the way it came from, and turned left out of what the girls knew was the road to the Sinclair home. With the turn, Sam knew their destination. Convinced they were being taken to Athens, Sam had a little light of hope, as she decided, *No matter how it will gall me to ask a Yankee for help, I will do so for Lovie and my brothers.*

Robert directed the man handling the horses to the rear of

the Oconee River Tavern. After cautioning the men to keep their goods quiet, he left the wagon and entered the back door of the building. Within minutes, Robert returned and climbed the stairs leading up to an upstairs room. With a key, he unlocked the door, opening it wide.

Floyd and David were unloaded first and placed on a bed in the upstairs room. Next, Sam was heaved over the shoulder of the large man; Robert noticed a gold chain falling from beneath her shirt and hanging loosely down from her neck and called to the man, "Hold on a minute. I just spied something that will buy us plenty of drinks."

Walking to the man's back, where Sam's head bobbed, he reached for and unfastened the chain and told the man, "You can take him up the stairs."

Throwing Lovie over his shoulder, he followed Sam up the steps, and the two girls were placed on the other bed. Leaving the four bound and gagged, Robert locked the door, and the three men entered the back room of the tavern.

Sam twisted until she was near the edge of the bed. She moved her feet off the bed, wanting to bend her knees and bringing her feet to the floor. Struggling to raise her body to a sitting position, she felt movement on the mattress, and the next thing she felt was Lovie slipping beneath her back. Together they raised Sam up, till she sat on the side of the bed.

Standing, Sam hopped to the bed that held the boys, motioning with her head for Floyd to stand.

Repeating what he watched Sam do, he slid to the edge of the bed and, with little effort, stood beside her. Sam turned her back to him, knowing what she aimed for him to do. Back to back, Floyd's fingers found the knot of the rope around Sam's wrist and untied the knot. Hands free, Sam jerked the gag from her mouth and turned to untie Floyd. Once Floyd and

Sam were free of ropes, they moved to free Lovie and David.

With hugs and tears, Sam cautioned the others with her finger against her lips. Taring sheets from the two beds, Sam quietly began to share her plan. Hurriedly, the four tied the sheets together. Sam tied an end to the nearest bed and pushed the bed to the window. With Lovie and the boys sitting on that bed, Sam threw the rope of sheets out the window and made her way down the side of the building.

As Sam ran into Athens, her thoughts were to find her cussed Yankee. The first person she saw was an old man hobbling along.

"Excuse me, sir. Can you point me in the direction of the cussed Yankee headquarters?"

Her description of the occupying forces brought a smile to the old man's face, and he gladly gave her the directions she craved.

Again running, Sam approached the building, and as if divine hands were guiding her way, a soldier coming out of the building looked familiar. She soon recognized him as the one who had come to Riverbend several days earlier.

She stepped to block his path, and, none too sweetly, she told him, "Take me to Morgan Anderson at once! Now!"

Corporal Calhoun stepped back, asking, "Who are you?"

With her fist on her hips, not moving an inch, she informed him, "The lives of the boys from Riverbend are at stake."

The name of the plantation caught his attention, and he motioned for Sam to follow him. Reaching the Lumpkin House, Corporal Calhoun paused and said, "You wait here, and I will see if he is here."

Not to be left behind, Sam hurried past the soldier and up the steps. The corporal caught Sam, just as she opened the door. Together, they approached the desk.

The gentleman behind the desk tried not to show how appalled he was at Sam's mode of dress and asked, "Can I help you?"

Sam answered, "I need to see Morgan Anderson."

Haygood reaching the bottom step of the stairs and heard Sam's loud and forceful statement and recognized the little she-cat.

"I'll take this creature off your hands," he informed the flustered man.

Hearing a familiar voice, Sam turned thankful eyes on the Yankee and smiled, "Haygood, you and that other cussed Yankee have got to come with me. The boys and Lovie are in danger."

Hearing the fear in her voice, he put his arm around her shoulder and yelled Morgan's name.

Hearing Haygood's loud call, Morgan turned to face the doorway and blinked his eyes at the sight of Haygood with the tomcat and his friend was motioning for him to follow them.

More than a little confused, Morgan exited the room, seeing Haygood, Sam, and the corporal going out the front door. He stepped out onto the porch, expecting to find the three and was surprised to see them hurrying down the street and toward the river. After catching up with the three, Morgan asked, "What is the hurry?"

Haygood stopped and explained, "Lovie and the boys are being held in a locked room near the river. It seems our friend, Robert Sinclair, is the one that locked them in the room."

Before Haygood finished his explanation, Morgan was giving orders to Corporal Calhoun, "I need a squad of men on the double, including you.

Bring them to the Riverside Tavern. Place half in front and half in the back. They are to allow no one in or out and are not to enter the establishment until I call. With his orders, Corporal Calhoun ran toward headquarters, and Morgan ran toward the river and the man he wanted to hang.

Morgan slowed his steps, as he neared the tavern, and waited for Sam to lead the way. Walking to the back, Sam informed them that the door was locked, but Morgan assured Sam that Haygood had a key.

Once at the door, Haygood stepped forward, and, with one of his big feet, he kicked the door open.

"Are you all all right?" Morgan softly asked, signaling Lovie and the boys to be quiet.

Bringing nods from all three, Morgan was satisfied that Lovie and the boys were not harmed, and he motioned for two of the soldiers below to come to the room and ordered them to stay in the room with Floyd, David, Lovie, and Sam.

"I will not stay here," Sam informed Morgan. "I have a bone to pick with Robert Sinclair. He stole something from me and I intend to get back what belongs to me."

Morgan nodded his okay, but added, "You will wait until Haygood and I have confronted him and you have pointed out the other two men. After you have done this and they are under arrest, you can demand what belongs to you. Understand?"

Sam nodded her head and followed Morgan from the room.

CHAPTER 15

Morgan, Haygood, and Sam entered by the back door of the tavern. The big room was dimly lit, with only a few candles lighting the area. Morgan spotted Robert, as soon as his eyes adjusted to the poor lighting; then he turned to Sam and asked, "Do you see the other two men?"

She nodded her head and pointed to the two men sitting at the table with Robert. That was all the identification Morgan needed. Telling Sam to remain by the door, Morgan made his way to the table, stopping directly in front of Robert Sinclair, and Haygood stood behind Robert.

Sam had a clear view of Robert and the table. The three men were deep in conversation, enjoying their beer, and did not at first notice Morgan. The moment they became aware of someone standing at their table, the conversation stopped, and Robert looked up to confront the person. Robert's look of insufferable irritation at the intrusion changed in a flash to disbelief and then to a stricken look of horror, when his eyes looked into Morgan's angry face.

Recognizing Morgan Anderson, Robert pushed back his chair and started to stand up, intending to run, but not aware of Haygood until big, strong hands seized his shoulders, pushing him down hard.

By this time, the other two men were aware of Morgan and Haygood and the anger radiating from them. The two looked as if they wished to be in any other place than Athens, Georgia, not to mention the Riverside Tavern. They both began to push back their chairs to take their leave, but Morgan loudly ordered, "Soldiers advance!" And the two halted their movement, as both entrances of the tavern open and armed Yankee soldiers entered.

"What's the meaning of this?" came loudly from behind the bar, as the patrons of the taproom began to rise from their chairs, reacting to the presence of the Yankee soldiers.

"You are harboring three criminals," Morgan calmly answered, indicating the table in front of him and without turning to face the man.

"These men are being arrested and charged with kidnapping!" he shouted.

The charge of criminal kidnapping from Morgan brought loud words of disbelief and claims of false charges from the other patrons.

"These men took by force, gagged, and hog-tied three Hart County boys and a young black woman who was with the three at the time. These boys were stolen away from their home and brought to Athens. The boys were orphans whose father died in the Second Battle of Manassas as a substitute in the Confederate Army." Not missing a beat, Morgan stuck his hand across the table, stabbing Robert Sinclair in the chest, and continued, "A substitute for this man!"

Morgan went on, "The four were taken for no other purpose than monetary gain. If you doubt my words, I have the oldest boys with me. The others are in an upstairs room, where I found the door bolted."

"Robert Sinclair was recognized at the time of the kidnapping, and the oldest boy pointed out the two other men to me, when we entered the room. They are the two men sitting at this table with Robert Sinclair.

Now whether this satisfies your disbelief of my charges or not, these men are under arrest and will be escorted by these soldiers to the Union Army headquarters and jailed.

They will stand trial for the crime of kidnapping, along with any other crimes they may have committed."

Hearing that her papa was fighting in the Confederate Army as a substitute for Robert Sinclair, Sam clasped her hand over her mouth, stifling a cry of anguish at Morgan's words. She began to inch toward Robert Sinclair, with murder in her heart.

By the time Morgan finished explaining the charges against Robert and his henchmen, Sam was standing beside Haygood. She balled up the fingers of her right hand, as she stepped to Robert's side, and, without saying a word, she hit Robert in the face with all her might, landing a blow between his chin and his cheek bone and knocking him from his chair. He landed flat on his back, and Sam's foot stomped hard into his chest, as she called out, "You son of a bitch! You are the one responsible for my papa's death, not the cussed Yankees, and you had the gall to kidnap me and my brothers in order to sell us. I hope you hang, but before you leave this place, I want the gold chain you stole from me. You murdering thief!"

"I don't have it any longer," Robert confessed. "I gave the chain to Choyce in payment for our drinks."

The confession did not smooth Sam's anger, nor did the rough handling of Robert by the soldier that had pulled him to his feet.

Stomping toward the man behind the bar before Morgan or Haygood could stop her, she verbally attacked him. "You are in possession of stolen goods. The murdering thief, Robert Sinclair, named you as having accepted my gold chain as payment for their drinks. Give me that gold chain now!"

Choyce was angry enough to box Sam's ears by the time she finished her accusatorial request, but, leery of the situation, he tried ignoring the boy, instead, hoping he would leave or would stop implying that he had unlawfully accepted the chain.

While Morgan was busy giving instructions to the sergeant, regarding the prisoners, Haygood followed Sam to the bar. Knowing that the chain was worth more than a few glasses of beer and thinking that the chain was a keepsake of Sam's mother, he thought to offer to pay the cost of the beer the men had drunk.

"Would you be willing to give Sam the chain if I pay you the cost of the beer the chain covered?" Haygood asked.

"No!" Sam screamed. "This man knew the chain was stolen."

"Sam, it is not uncommon these days for men and women of the South to use valuable possessions as a means of buying things they need or want," Haygood offered, trying to calm Sam. "I'm sure Robert is not the first man to buy his beer or his liquor with family jewelry."

"Am I not correct, Choyce?" Haygood continued.

The man nodded his head in agreement, but he still did not offer to relinquish Sam's gold chain.

Morgan got in on the last of Haygood's discussion with the proprietor of the tavern and added his two cents.

"Choyce, Robert Sinclair named you as having taken this boy's gold chain as payment for the beer. I disagree with my friend, in part. I suspect—and I might even be convinced to prove my suspicions—that you were well aware that the chain was stolen and that you were well aware that the boys and the young black woman were in the upstairs room of your establishment. I am sure you do not want me to close the doors of this tavern while I conduct a thorough investigation into my suspicions. I know that you were aware that the chain was stolen. Now, are you going to do the right thing and give the chain to the rightful owner, or am I— "

"Who gave you the authority to arrest and jail us? You are not the sheriff," the large man with Robert shouted, distracting Morgan's attention and preventing him from seeing the chain that Sam had fought so hard to recover.

"I am Colonel Morgan Anderson of the Union Army," Morgan enlightened the man, "and I was sent by President Johnson to investigate reports of young Southern women being kidnapped. I was given the authority to arrest and to bring to trial any and all guilty parties. I even have the authority to shoot any who resist arrest, and I can guarantee you that these arrests will not be overturned and that others will follow."

Halfway through Morgan's threat, Choyce was digging the gold chain out of his pocket. As his hand brought the chain up to eye level Sam reached for and snatched the chain from his hand, but not before Haygood saw the small medallion on the chain and recognized it as the one Morgan had worn. He remembered he had not seen it since Morgan had been shot last May. Catching Sam's eye, he raised his eyebrows and smiled, thinking, You are, without question, Morgan's angel, and there is no need denying that to me.

Sam hurriedly stuffed the chain in her pocket and looked up to see Haygood smiling, with raised eyebrows. Sam knew that he'd recognized Morgan's chain and that he knew, at once, where and how she had come to have the chain. She turned and ran from the room, before Haygood could stop her. After climbing the stairs to the boys and Lovie, she spoke to them, "We need to get started back to Riverbend. Robert and the two men were arrested and are being taken to jail. They are no longer a danger to us. Keowee, Santee, and the Henrys will be worried sick. The faster we get back to Riverbend, the sooner they will be relieved."

The three stood looking at Sam with befuddled stares. Finally, Floyd asked, "How are we to get back to Hart County? Walk?"

"Haygood and I will take you to Riverbend after we are through questioning Robert and the men who kidnapped you," Morgan answered. He had heard Floyd's question, as he and Haygood entered the room.

Sam was inching toward the door, as Morgan was speaking, planning to make her way back to Hart County alone, if she had to. Haygood blocked her way before she reached the door, shaking his head.

Lovie, thinking Sam's only reason to hurry back to Riverbend was to let her parents and the Henrys know they were safe, wondered why Sam didn't speak up and tell Mr. Morgan that they needed to go now. Not waiting for Sam to speak up, Lovie pleaded, "We's needs to hurry and get home, Mr. Morgan, just as Sam said. If you could get us some way to travel, we would be thanking you. We's no longer have to fear Mr. Robert."

"Lovie, I have already sent a messenger to Riverbend" Morgan said. "I sent Corporal Calhoun and three other soldiers with him before I entered the tavern. They are traveling on fast horses, and they are accustomed to riding hard and fast. The news of you four being safe and in my care should be told to Keowee and Santee shortly. The officials who will be handling the trial of Robert and the other two men need to hear from you what happened to you. I will feel better with all of you staying with me and Haygood until we can take you to Riverbend. Besides, I know you are hungry and tired, so we'll go to the Union Army headquarters. They will have food and a place you can rest, while I question Robert and the men with him. I want more information from Robert than I was able to obtain in the tavern; after you have eaten and rested, you can tell your stories to the provost marshal."

While Morgan explained to Lovie and the boys the need for them to stay in Athens, Haygood watched Sam and realized, *The kitty cat is not ready for Morgan to know she is his angel. That's strange, in light of him rescuing her and her brothers from Robert Sinclair. Surely, she is not afraid of him. I wonder: Did something happen while she was hiding him that caused her not to want Morgan to know she is his angel?*

"Haygood," Morgan called, interrupting his musing, and he quickly answered, "Here, Colonel."

"I could see you are here in body, but I was not sure you were here in spirit. You look as if you were hundreds of miles away. We need to get these children loaded into the wagon that brought them to Athens." Haygood answered, "Okay, Colonel."

Traveling in the old wagon that had brought them to Athens, Sam, Lovie, and David sat in the bed of the wagon, propped against the sides, with Morgan, Haygood, and Floyd sitting on the wagon seat.

A hard jolt of the wagon rolling in and out of a washed-out hole told Sam they were near the top of the hill leading into Athens. In the twilight of early evening, lit candles and lamps could be spotted in the windows of the few houses they passed. Only a few people were on the streets, because the time for evening meals was near. All the other people would soon be putting their feet beneath their tables. The growl of Sam's stomach was echoed by growls from Lovie and David. Sniggering, Sam looked around at the two and asked, "Would the noise I heard mean you two are hungry?"

"I ain't eaten since early morning," David sang out. "My stomach thinks my throat's been cut. I hope there will be some food at the army house."

"You poor baby," Lovie cooed, as she pulled David into her arms. "You've had a bad day. 'Em awful men needs to be whipped with the lash before they be jailed, treating you and Floyd the way they did."

"Lovie," Sam reminded her, "do not forget that David and Floyd were not the only ones in this wagon. I seem to remember being tied and gagged, and if my memory is correct, you lay beside me in the same fix. I also do not remember us being offered food during our trip into Athens."

"Shame on you, Samantha Hatcher," Lovie scolded. Before Lovie could finish scolding, Sam placed a hand over Lovie's mouth and pressed her finger to her lips. She was afraid that Morgan or Haygood had heard Lovie call her by her full name. Her playful mood was at an end. She whispered, "You called me 'Samantha.' The cussed Yankee might hear. Please be careful. I still do not want him or Haygood knowing who I really am."

"Why in the world do you still not trust Mr. Morgan?" Lovie whispered. "He done saved us from what evil thing Mr. Robert had in mind for us."

Sam had no answer for Lovie. If the truth be known, she had no answer for herself. She did not want to think about why she still did not want Morgan to know she was the one who had tended to his wounds, and she did not want to dwell on the changing roles of Robert Sinclair and Morgan Anderson. She just wanted this day to be over so she could go to Riverbend, be alone in her room, and sit in her window.

Morgan directed Floyd to the back of the building housing the army headquarters. Soldiers were present to take charge of the horses, while Morgan and Haygood ushered their four guests into the Union Army's office. Morgan spoke with a soldier.

The soldier left the room, to return almost immediately with an officer older than Morgan. The officer talked with Morgan for a moment; as he turned to acknowledge Haygood, his eyes fell on the four by the door.

"Corporal," he called to the soldier behind the desk. "These young people are in need of food; see to their needs."

Sam looked at Haygood with questioning eyes. He walked to the place where she and Lovie stood. "You will be perfectly safe in the company of the corporal. He will take you to a private room. There will be water for you to wash your hands and face. The room will have table and chairs. Food will be brought to you. No one will harm you. They will all be informed that you four are under the protection of Colonel Morgan Anderson. Later, if Morgan is still occupied with the prisoners, I will come back and supervise the addition of cots to the room for your sleeping accommodations."

"Mr. Haygood, we's thank you and Mr. Morgan for all you be doing for us, and we will be just fine. Pay no never mind to Sam. Sam be fine, or Sam would done be letting you know. As long as there be plenty of food, the boys will be fine."

Sam, Lovie, and the boys were led by the corporal to a large room. Sam stood inside the door, as she looked the room over, and she admitted that Haygood's words about the room were correct. The only thing that bothered her was the absence of an outside door.

The corporal walked to the long table; picking up the silver bell from the table, he shook it, saying, "Should you need anything other than what is in the room or some additional food, ring this bell. Someone will attend to whatever you need. Do not hesitate, should you require something other than what is given."

Food was furnished, and the hour grew late. Heads were bobbing on chests, as sleep fought to claim tired bodies. Sam thought, *If we'd been allowed to travel back to Riverbend when I wanted, we would be in our beds by now.* Turning, Sam decided to let her displeasure be known and started to the table to ring the bell. The door opened before she reached the table, and Haygood's big body filled the doorway.

"Are you children sleepy and ready for a place to lay your heads?" Haygood asked as he came into the room, followed by a gang of Yankee soldiers. Four soldiers carried army cots, and four carried pillows, sheets, and blankets.

Lovie became busy spreading sheets and blankets so Floyd and David could lie down before they fell down. Sam pitched in and had Lovie's and her cot covered with a sheet and a blanket by the time Lovie finished with the boys.

Sam lay awake long after she heard the soft breathing of Floyd and David, telling her the boys were asleep.

"Do you think maybe the kindness we's got from these Yankee folk can help you with your hate?" Lovie asked.

Sam lay perfectly still and quiet as a mouse on her Yankee cot, with her head resting on a Yankee pillow, with her body covered in a Yankee sheet and a Yankee blanket, and listened to Lovie's spiel. Her conscious mind dictated that she should agree with Lovie's assessment of the Yankees' kindness and their seeming eagerness to please them.

Her vote on that was still not forthcoming. After all, they still wore the hated Yankee soldier's blue uniform.

Morgan's questioning Robert's two companions was short and enlightening. The men proved to have been tricked into helping Robert take the boys, having been told they were part of the plantation property and legally his to bond out.

Robert gave the location of La Cur, the address of where to send a wire, and how to word the message. After sending a wire to the address Robert had furnished, Morgan and Haygood were elated with their night's work and with the trap they'd set for La Cur. Everything was set to arrest La Cur in the Athens train station the minute he stepped off the train from Savannah.

Thinking to peek in on their four Southern troopers while they slept securely in the Union Army headquarters before Morgan and Haygood retired for the night, Haygood took hold of the doorknob and was able to turn the knob, but the door seemed to be stuck. Pushing gently on the door, but without success, he looked at Morgan with a smile and explained.

"It appears that one of our Southern troopers does not feel as safe in Union Army headquarters as we would like. You care to wager on the culprit? My vote would be Sam. Do I hear a yea?"

"You have to give him credit for trying to take care of the boys and Lovie." So did Haygood praise Sam, chuckling.

"I am sure he does his best," Morgan said. "He still worries me. He was almost civil this time. At least, he was genuinely doing his best to help Lovie and the boys. Do you know if he followed the wagon to Athens or if he was kidnapped? I failed to ask him how he came to be in Athens."

"Sam must have been kidnapped, the same as the others," Haygood suggested. "I don't think it's likely Sam would have watched and not tried to stop the kidnapping, whether Sam was a target of this kidnapping or was taken because he had interfered with it."

"Everything will be made clear tomorrow, when they tell us how and where they were taken," Morgan said. "I am ready for my bed and a few hours of sleep." He stifled a yawn.

Morgan woke to a banging on his door, and, coming wide awake, he yelled, "Haygood, is that you?"

"Yes; are you alive?"

"Go back downstairs. I shall be with you shortly."

Morgan and Haygood listened as, one by one, the four "Southern troopers" recounted what took place the morning they were kidnapped. The only thing that needed an explanation was what was on the cloth they all mentioned being placed on their noses and mouths.

The naming of chloroform by Morgan made every adult male in the room sick to think a man could stoop so low as to nesthetize children and a young woman in order to do them harm.

Sam quietly approached Haygood, asking, "How long before we can leave Athens? We are all in a hurry to get back home to Riverbend."

Haygood knew he and Morgan would not leave Athens until La Cur was safely locked in jail. He hated to tell Sam they would have to stay in Athens a little longer, knowing Sam wanted an answer now.

"Sam, why are you asking me about when you will leave Athens? Morgan is the one who told you he would take you to Riverbend when things were settled here."

"We have done as that cussed Yankee wanted us to do. Why are you reneging on your word? I should not be surprised. After all, you both are cussed Yankees."

Stomping her foot, Sam turned to leave. Reaching out, Haygood caught Sam's arm.

"I am just a captain. Morgan is a colonel and is in charge of this mission. I will tell you that arresting Robert gave us what we needed to apprehend the man we were sent south to arrest. When Morgan will be free to do what he promised I do not know. He is the one who will decide when we leave for Riverbend. Why don't you ask him? Are you afraid of him? You should know he would not hurt you. You saved his life. He owes you his life. He is not a man who would treat that great gift lightly. I try to respect your wishes, but I care a lot for that cussed Yankee. So have mercy on each of us."

Whether Sam intended to answer Haygood or not, Morgan was calling, and he left in a run. The last she saw of either man, they were hightailing it out the door of army headquarters. For some reason, she felt a sense of alarm, and, without conscious intent, she thought, *Please God, keep them safe.* She knew, without question at that moment, that was her deepest desire and prayer.

She walked slowly back to where Lovie and the boys stood, waiting to hear when they would be leaving Athens.

Lovie saved her the misery of having to tell them they would not be leaving anytime soon, as she commented, "Mr. Morgan and Mr. Haygood was shore nuff in a big hurry. You have any idea where they might be headed and what caused all that hurry?"

"I only heard the cussed Yankee bellow," Sam replied.

CHAPTER 16

As Morgan placed La Cur under arrest, the Frenchman shouted his outrage at being manhandled and insulted in a public place. Claiming his status as a member of the noble families of France, he raved, promising to report to the French Embassy the abusing disregard of his station and to bring down harsh punishment upon the ones responsible for this humiliating disrespect of a French nobleman. The man's threats and complaints did not deter Morgan's actions in any way.

A self-satisfying smile graced Morgan's face, as he brought La Cur's arms behind his back, placed restraints on his wrist, and ordered the soldiers to take into custody the remaining members of the man's party. He led the head of the snake he was sent south to find and to exterminate out of the station and up the hill to army headquarters.

Haygood followed in Morgan's wake, after making sure the La Cur woman and their supposed servants were secured and on their way to jail. He was as anxious to witness the disrobing of La Cur as Morgan. There was no doubt, in either of their minds, that the La Cur now in custody was not Luis, the legitimate son of the late Count La Cur, but Phillip, the illegitimate son. Following the noise of the loudmouthed Frenchman,

Haygood had no trouble locating the man's cell and was not surprised to find soldiers in the act of stripping off the man's trousers.

With the Frenchman's buttocks bare as the day he was born, Morgan asked all that were present, "Gentlemen, do you see any kind of birthmark on the man's bottom? From where I am standing, his cheeks are without blemish. Sorry, La Cur, you have just been demoted to a nonentity in the presence of all these witnesses, and you will not have to notify the French Embassy. According to the wire I received from the ambassador, he was more anxious for your disrobing than we were. It seems the French government suspected you were an impostor from the first. I promised the ambassador I would send him the results of the baring of your buttocks as soon as we had you in custody and had performed the deed.

Morgan was first to speak, directing his words to Haygood, "It's over for us, or will be, as soon as I send a wire to President Johnson and a wire to the French ambassador. We will be free to gather our four guests and head toward Hart County and Riverbend. Tomorrow, I can begin my hunt for my angel.

Jotting down the message he wanted send to President Johnson and composing the message to the French ambassador, he handed them to the telegrapher.

"Will you be waiting for answers to these wires, sir?" the soldier asked. "No, Corporal, but I will be advising Captain Cree to send any answer forthcoming to me in Hart County, so be sure you are alert to messages arriving from Washington that are addressed to me."

Finding Haygood, Morgan suggested, "Get Lovie and the boys. Are you ready to put Athens behind us?"

Heading north, the wagon rumbled across the wooden bridge over the Oconee River, and smiles spread across the faces of the occupants. They were at last going home to the place they feared never to see again. Floyd was handling the horses, and Sam sat on the seat beside him. Lovie and David sat in the bed of the wagon, propped against the sides.

Morgan and Haygood rode a safe distance behind the wagon, watchful for any possible danger that could threaten the four.

Sam was as happy to be on the way back to Riverbend, but she was concerned about their escorts. If the two men stayed very long, it would be next to impossible to keep her true gender hidden. She knew Haygood already suspected she was the female that saved the cussed Yankee's life.

With the constant bumping and swaying of the wagon and the happy chatter of the others, Sam's mind became entangled with thoughts. *I realize I need to separate how I think of this cussed Yankee from the way I think of other Yankees. Although I haven't as yet completely rationalized the two Yankees' concern for Southern boys and a young black girl or their quick rush to rescue them. The urge to kill that I saw on their faces when they confronted Robert dumbfounds me.*

Now that I am free of the fear I felt during my encounter with Robert Sinclair and our ride into Athens, I am beginning to see the merit of this cussed Yankee and Haygood. How do I equate the concern these two men have shown to my usual opinion of Yankees? Will it be possible for me to separate my opinion of Morgan Anderson from my hatred of Yankees? With that thought came the voice of Reverend Henry: *When you are ready to relinquish the hate, ask God to help.*

Recalling Reverend Henry's words, Sam began to ask God to help her to see and know the true character of Morgan Anderson. With the prayer came a sense of relief, as if a heavy weight were being lifted from her.

As the night wore on, Santee and Keowee lay wide awake in their bed, praying the night would bring their Lovie and the Hatcher siblings safely home. A familiar sound brought them to their feet, and Keowee asked, "Santee, do my ears hear what I think I be hearing?

"If you be hearing the sound of a wagon coming into the backyard, you be right," Santee answered, as he was pulling on his shoes.

Morgan had long since taken over the handling of the horses. Floyd's head rested against Haygood's shoulder, as he had fallen sound asleep. The long ride at an end, Morgan brought the wagon to a stop in front of the barn and was not surprised to hear the door to the house open and to see two figures appear in the moonlight.

"That be you, Mr. Morgan?" Santee asked.

"Yes, Santee, and I have a wagonload of sleepy passengers."

"Do they all be all right, Mr. Morgan?" were the first words out of Keowee's mouth.

"Be assured, Keowee; they are as right as rain. A little tired and a whole lot sleepy."

Hearing the sound of conversation and realizing the wagon was no longer moving, two sleepyheads in the back of the wagon began to stir, coming out from beneath the blanket that covered them.

Haygood motioned for Morgan to assist him, as he gently raised Floyd's head from his shoulder and lifted the soundly sleeping youth from the wagon seat and into Morgan's waiting arms.

Lovie and Sam slowly stumbled from the wagon, and as their feet touched the ground, each was encased in hungry arms, welcoming the girls home. Haygood hoisted a sleeping David into his arms and followed Morgan to the house.

Keowee was late coming to the kitchen the next morning, but the coffee was made, biscuits were in the oven, and meat was sizzling in the pan when their two guests came through the door.

"Good morning. I believe there will be a few empty places at the table this morning, if I am any judge of sleeping boys. I peeped in on Floyd and David before coming downstairs. They were dead to the world."

Morgan's predictions came true. They ate their morning meal, with Lemuel being the only youngster in attendance.

The absence of the boys and the girls gave Keowee and Santee a chance to question Morgan in depth regarding how and why the kidnapping had taken place.

"Mr. Morgan," Keowee began, "what did Robert Sinclair intend to do with our Lovie and the boys, and how did he know Lovie and Sam be at the home of Reverend and Mrs. Henry?"

Morgan waited a couple of minutes before answering Keowee, wanting to be as truthful as he could, but not hurtful.

"Keowee, as to how Robert knew Lovie and Sam were at the Henrys, I do not believe he knew who Lovie and Sam really were. His answer to my question of why he stole the two from the home of the Henrys was that he knew the Henrys had no children or young male relatives and that he figured Sam an orphan and was free for the taking. Lovie was just in the wrong place at the wrong time. In taking Sam, he had to take Lovie. In fact, Lovie's account of the incident was she answered the knock on the back door and was taken when she opened the door. She awoke in the wagon bed and saw Sam. If Sam had opened the door first, it is possible he would not have bothered with Lovie. In answer to your question about what he intended to do with the boys, let me first tell you something

273

that will help you understand Robert's thinking. There is an undertaking by the government to find places for the orphans of the South who have no one to care for them. The process is called 'bonding.' The government's plan is to find good permanent homes for these children. The majority will be used to replace freed slaves. Robert and the two men arrested with him heard about this plan and planned on doing their own bonding. In other words, selling them to the highest bidder."

CHAPTER 17

The kitchen of Riverbend Plantation was almost back to normal this morning, since the return of the Hatcher siblings and Lovie two nights past. Keowee and Lovie were busy cooking the morning meal, while keeping an eye out for Sam. Santee and Haygood were deep in conversation. Morgan, trying not to be noticed, was eyeing the door to the back stairs, watching for Sam. For some reason, that enigma had sparked an interest during the trip from Athens, but he could not put a finger on why.

Morgan and the family were anxious to see if Sam would break her habit of hiding, while the two Yankees were here, and make an appearance, but no one was as watchful for Sam as Morgan.

The door to the back stairs opened, with a loud swoosh, and everything came to a halt, until David bounced through the door, followed by a more sedate Floyd. Hungry as ever, the two boys greeted the room with a "Good morning, all," and took their seats at the table. Lovie placed a platter of sausage and eggs and a bowl of grits on the table. A platter of hot biscuits completed the morning fare. The meal was on the table, and the men and the boys were seated and ready to eat, but there was still no sign of Sam. Keowee stood behind her chair, looking at Sam's empty chair, but she hesitated only a moment, before sitting.

"Let's have the blessing," Keowee stated, as she took her seat.

As everyone bowed their heads, the door to the back stairs quietly opened, and Sam walked in, dressed in her male attire, hat and all. Without a word to anyone, she sat in the only empty chair, the one next to Morgan.

"Sam, we's about to have the blessing," Keowee explained. "We's all here now, so let's ask God to bless the food and thank our heavenly Father for our blessings."

Keowee said a quick prayer, and as soon as she said, "Amen," Morgan grabbed the hat from Sam's head and threw it to the floor.

"A gentleman always removes his— ", He stopped, before adding, "Hat at the table."

A face glowing with contempt turned to him, and before Morgan could process all he was seeing, Sam jumped to her feet, overturning her chair, scrambled to retrieve her hat, and ran from the room.

Morgan's eyes fell on thick, dark braids wrapped around the top of Sam's head, as she bent to snatch her hat from the floor, and as the door slammed behind her, his loud, booming voice aimed at the table full of people demanded, "What is going on here?"

Not waiting for an answer to his loud demand, he turned to Haygood and asked, "Did I see female braids on that boy's head?"

The antagonizing grin that Morgan hated spread across Haygood's face, as he nodded his head.

"You do not look surprised," Morgan said. "What do you know that I don't know? Haygood, wipe that blasted grin from your face. I want answers, and I want them now!" Puzzled at Haygood's calm, unaffected nod and getting no further reply, he turned and rose from his chair, intending to follow Sam.

"Mr. Morgan, what you wants to know?" Keowee called out.

Stopping short of the door, Morgan turned to Keowee. "Who the devil is that person? Why does that boy have female braids pinned to the top of his head?"

Shaking his head, Morgan stood in complete bewilderment and asked, "You are hiding a female in boy's clothing?"

"Sam be one of the Hatcher orphans, oldest of the four children of Miss Martha and Mr. William, as I told you on your first visit. Sam, Miss Samantha, be dressed in Mr. Robert's cast-off clothing because of me. We's had no white gentleman on the plantation to protect her, since Mr. Mac passed. I be afraid for her if some ruffians showed up here, aiming to do mischief or harm. I didn't know nothing else to do, Mr. Morgan. Santee would have been killed if he tried to protect her, and, besides that, the child don't have no young lady's clothes now what fits her. She be only a girl a few months shy of her sixteenth birthday when they were brought here. She outgrew what few dresses she had with her before Mr. Mac passed."

Unable to understand why Keowee did not explain this to him when he and Haygood first arrived, he pleaded, "Why did you not tell me this on my first visit? Did you feel you needed to keep her true gender from me? Surely, you knew we would not harm her."

"Yes sir, I be knowing that," Keowee admitted.

She went on, "You got to understand Sam's feelings toward Yankee folk, Mr. Morgan. She blames them for both her papa's and her mama's deaths and for her and the boys not having a home. She made Lovie, me and Santee promise not to reveal who she was to y'all. She's kept herself away from us and the house whiles you and Mr. Haygood be here until now. She loves these boys and us. She works hard, helping to keep us all fed. She means you and Mr. Haygood no harm."

Beginning to understand a few things but still wanting more information, Morgan questioned, "You said Sam is a young woman. How old is she?"

"Nineteen, Morgan," Floyd said. "She is my sister, and as Keowee said, Sam means you and Haygood no harm, but since Papa and Mama's death, she considered all Yankees mean and evil. Things are a little mixed up for Sam right now, after being kidnapped by a Southerner and hearing of crimes she would never have imagined a Southerner committing. She's also having trouble understanding how you and Haygood, Yankees, came to our rescue so easily. I know how Sam thinks, and she's trying to satisfy in her mind why you and Haygood helped. Knowing all this, she's having to rethink how she measures two Yankees' worth. That is why she came down to eat with us, and 'us' includes you and Haygood, but she is not yet ready to show who she really is. Sam has a good heart and a good sense of right and wrong. She usually does not form her opinions without weighing all aspects, but us losing both Papa and Mama and being brought to this plantation in a matter of hours—that was a lot for all of us to handle, and the only people Sam knew to blame for her loss and pain were Yankees. Don't judge her too badly. Give her time, and she'll come around."

"Where is she, Floyd? I need to talk with her," Morgan said, as he turned to go up the back stairs.

"You'll not find her," Floyd cautioned, stopping Morgan before he could leave the room.

"I knows Sam's temper, too, Mr. Morgan," Keowee said, "and

it gonna take her some time to cool down, as Floyd done said. We might as well eat whiles she be getting her fuming over with." So did Keowee plead, as she began breathing calmly.

"Besides, you trying to talk to her right now would not be a good thing to do," Floyd added. "Sam does have a wee temper, and she's probably mad as a wet hen. I best talk to her first."

"When we finish the meal, I think the time will be right for that discussion you mentioned you wanted to have in private," Morgan suggested, turning to Haygood with a knowing look.

Looking forward to ragging Morgan on his lack of perception and trying not to choke on his chuckles, Haygood complied between chuckles, "Yes sir, Colonel!"

Finished with his meal and refusing another cup of coffee, Morgan rose from his chair and, turning to Haygood, said, "Okay, Mr. Know-It-All. It is time you talked.Follow me."

During all that had happened during the morning, Keowee and Santee were left staring after the two men, wondering what would happen next and if the outcome of Mr. Morgan's confronting Sam would be what he wanted.

Morgan's steps did not slow until he entered the hall of the barn. Spying a line of empty barrels against the wall, he selected one and moved it to the center of the hall and sat down on it. Haygood entered closely behind him, and Morgan motioned for him to take a barrel and said, in the same tone of voice as the tone of his invitation, "Spill it! You seem to think you know some things that I do not. So let's have it."

Haygood took his time placing the barrel of his choice, where he could look Morgan in the face, and, with the grin on his face that had antagonized Morgan for weeks, he perched atop the barrel. "It's I who am more observant than you and who seems to know more about females than you."

"Haygood, you have not told me anything but your assumption of your abilities. I want facts, if you have any, and I want them now! Explain! I am tired of that silly grin, and if I do not hear something worthwhile, I am going to wipe it off your ugly face."

"Morgan, I will be honest and say I was surprised you did not notice what I saw when we had first arrived in June. You were so intensively involved in sparring with Sam that you failed to see or to recognize her femininity."

"Thanks a lot. Did you ever consider that Sam could very well be my angel? In all that time, you never once thought I might appreciate knowing this. You can just keep your mouth shut from now on."

"Yes, Colonel. However, you might want to hear something else that I know. I saw something before we left Athens that will be hard to dispute."

"What else can you possibly know that I don't?"

"Something about a gold chain."

"The gold chain Robert took from Sam? I am sure that chain was something that belonged to her mother."

"I thought that at first, but it was not."

"Haygood, why do you drag things out? It's like pulling teeth to get you to say whatever it is that you know. If you have something of value to say, please say it."

"I happened to get a look at that chain as Sam grabbed it from Choyce's hand. The chain had a small medallion attached to it, and I had seen that medallion before. I am positive it is the one you wore for years, but I haven't seen it on you since you were shot here in Hart County that May night. Now am I forgiven?"

"Are you sure?" a breathless Morgan asked. "I was standing right beside you, and I do not recall seeing anything of that."

Still grinning, but not quite as aggravating to Morgan as

before, Haygood reminded Morgan, "At the time you were looking away from Sam, you were busy informing one of Robert's partners in crime of your authority to put his carcass in jail."

"If that chain is mine, that will cinch it, Haygood: Sam is my angel. I left my chain behind, because I wanted her to have something of mine to remember me by, and that was all I had to leave. Knowing that Sam has the chain and the medallion makes me confident that she is my angel. I can't understand why she hides from me. Surely, she recognizes me."

"I also have wondered why she continued to keep her identity a secret, because I was sure she recognized you that first morning."

Suddenly, Morgan's elation that came with Haygood's news of his gold chain and medallion began to ebb.

"Could she dislike me because I was a Union soldier, blaming me for her father's death? Goodness, Haygood, if that is the problem, how will I ever be able to talk to her and express my gratitude?" Softly he spoke his fears.

Floyd did not tarry in the keeping room after the two men left. He circled around the house on the opposite side from the barn and headed for the river, hoping Sam's temper had cooled. Wading over the ledge, he started climbing the bank to the cave. He spotted Sam sitting cross-legged at the entrance.

Sam was expecting Floyd and was surprised he waited as long as he did.

"You waited, knowing my temper would be riled. Well, I am still mad, and if you do not want to hear me rant and rave about your friend, Morgan, you'd best leave."

Floyd shook his head, knowing Sam was still a little hot under the collar, but he continued his climb until he was beside her. Sitting down on the dirt bank, he took a deep breath and reminded her, "Papa would have done the same thing Morgan did, and you know it. Papa never wore his hat, while he was at the table, especially not during prayer, and he would have corrected either of us, had we sat down to eat, not removing our hat. You know this, and you should not have come to the table with your hat on. You never wore your hat at the table before. Why did you today? Were you trying to start a quarrel with Morgan?"

Sam sat silent, not looking at Floyd, knowing that what he was saying about their papa was true and that she had no excuse for wearing the hat at the table. *I don't know why I did what I did. Hearing Morgan tell about the young women he and Haygood rescued and that Robert Sinclair and his evil uncle were the ones who schemed to have those young ladies kidnapped, I wanted to see Morgan this morning, hoping that, by seeing him, I could . . . I don't know. What? I had to see him. How do I explain this to Floyd when I can't explain it to myself?*

Floyd kept quiet, knowing Sam was giving his words some thought. Sam finally turned to face Floyd, and, with tears wetting her eyes, she nodded her head and said, "You are right about Papa. I cannot disagree. I have no answer for you as to why I wore that cussed hat to the table. I wear it to conceal my hair, and I am not ready to shed my boy image. I can only say I should have stayed in my room. I'm at fault."

"Well, I hate to tell you, but the fact that you are a girl is out in the open. Morgan got a look at your braids. He was a little disturbed, you might say, demanding answers. It's good you left the room, or you would have been the one answering his questions. Keowee told him she was the one that had you dress in Robert's clothes and why. That helped a little, but then he seemed to be hurt because she did not tell him upon his arrival that you were a girl."

While Floyd related what went on in the kitchen after she ran out, Sam watched the flowing river and realized that, from what Floyd was telling her, Morgan would be asking her if she was the one who had tended to his wounds that May night.

Do you want to talk to Morgan or not?" Floyd finally gained the courage to ask after walking around in a circle a few times and clearing his throat.

"Not," was all Sam answered.

Floyd did not linger on the riverbank. He left Sam just where he had found her, sitting on the ground by the cave. He was more confused than ever, thinking there was a lot more between Sam and Morgan than what he or anyone else had thought.

Haygood watched his friend wrestle with Sam's dislike of Yankees and if that dislike was keeping her from acknowledging she was his angel. Leaving his friend with his demons, Haygood walked out of the barn and met Floyd at the door to the kitchen.

"You been to check on Sam?" Haygood asked Floyd. It was more of a statement than a question, and he added, "Will she agree to see Morgan?" With his hand on the door handle and shaking his head, Floyd turned to Haygood and asked, "Where is Morgan?"

"I left him in the barn, moping."

Thinking that he and Floyd had better put their heads together and see if they could come up with something to get the two talking, Haygood turned toward the old swing in the oak tree behind the house.

"Floyd, let's walk over to that swing. I want to ask you something and to tell you something else."

Floyd hesitated a moment, but he decided that if Haygood could tell him something that would help him understand

Sam's behavior toward Morgan, he would listen.

"What do you think of all that has happened, Floyd?" Haygood asked "I know you were aware of Sam being a girl and why she dressed as a boy. I admit I also knew Sam was female, dressed in boy's clothing, but not why."

"You knew Sam was a girl. How?" Floyd blurted out.

"I saw through her disguise the first day we arrived here," Haygood admitted.

Haygood went on, "Your sister has a very pretty face, and I recognize a pretty female face when I see one, even if a few smudges of dirt cover a portion of it. I have wondered why she kept her true identity hidden, after she learned who we were. Keowee's explanation this morning has Morgan and me concerned. I thought you might be able to answer a question or two for me, since Sam does not want to talk to Morgan. You have told her that her true identity has been revealed."

"I told her everything that went on after she left the table," Floyd confessed. "I may not have given her enough time to cool down, because I left her still a little riled."

Haygood chuckled at Floyd's attempt to lessen the state of Sam's anger, after he had witnessed her unloading her anger on Morgan the first day.

"I had wondered," Haygood said, "if Sam was distancing herself from Morgan because she was mad at Morgan for something she thought he had done. After Keowee's explanation about Sam's dislike for all Yankees, I have considered the reason could be her dislike for Yankees, but she doesn't seem to dislike me. I have never felt any ill will from her. Floyd, do you think her dislike for Yankee soldiers goes somewhat deeper than dislike? Maybe hate? Can you shed some light on this? 'Cause Morgan and I are both thinking that Sam could be Morgan's angel—the young lady that saved his life last May."

Floyd wanted to answer Haygood as truthfully as he could, but his saying that Sam might be Morgan's angel added to the puzzle of Sam's reactions toward Morgan that he'd been trying to figure out. *If Haygood and I talk enough, maybe we can sort all this out. I thought all the time there was more to Sam's odd behavior toward Morgan. Him being a Yankee would not have made her hide from him. She would be storming at him every time he appeared on Riverbend land.* Satisfied with his deductions, Floyd was ready to tell Haygood all he knew or thought.

"Haygood, Sam blames the Yankees for everything that has happened to us. She makes no bones about that, telling everyone she hates Yankees. If her feelings are hate and not dislike, I do not know. I have been puzzled by her reactions toward Morgan from the start. Knowing Sam's temper, if it was hate or dislike for Yankees, she would have been in his face every time he visited, leaving no doubt as to her opinion of him. Her odd behavior has dumbfounded me. The mention of his name will send her into a frenzy, raving about the cussed Yankee. I am at a loss as to why she was not ranting and raving in the cussed Yankee's face. I'm think there is something else besides her dislike of Yankees. It could be her being Morgan's angel. What do you think?"

"I listened to everything you said, and, to be honest, some of the things gave me more to think about, but knowing you have been puzzled by Sam's odd behavior from the beginning is somewhat comforting. I agree with you I think there is more to this than what we know. You know your sister better than anyone on this plantation. Do you think she is capable of hating Morgan so

fiercely she would keep the truth from him just because he is a Yankee, making him wonder for the rest of his life who saved his life?"

"No!" Floyd answered right away. "Sam is not vindictive. She proved that the night she helped Morgan. If her hate was that strong, she would have let him die that May night."

"I'm with you on that. As long as I have known Sam, I know she would not hurt anyone intentionally. I had wondered about her dislike for Yankees. I have not felt no hate or dislike from Sam. I think we have eliminated Sam's dislike for Yankees as the reason for her not talking to Morgan. Could it be she's embarrassed for us to know she is a young lady dressed as a boy?"

"She has worn Robert's clothes for so long I don't know. Mrs. Henry did some sewing on some of Mama's dresses so they would fit Sam. I just thought of something else. Knowing Papa was killed by Yankees, Sam might be feeling like she is a traitor to Papa and Mama by saving Morgan's life and is ashamed to admit she is the one that helped Morgan."

"I will give some thoughts to Sam's feelings of betrayal," Haygood said, as he rose from the swing and headed to the barn and Morgan.

His entrance startled Morgan out of his reminiscing. He had spent the time going over all he could remember of the days and nights he spent with Sam, and the only thing he could recall that might cause her to be a little timid and to stay away from him was their kiss.

Haygood flopped down on the top of the empty barrel and began relating the results of his conversation with Floyd. "I have spent the last thirty or forty minutes with Floyd. The two of us has discussed and discussed the problem you seem to face with Sam. That boy knows his sister better than anyone on this Earth. Floyd said Sam's dislike for Yankees would not be the reason she has hidden from you. He is positive there is something else, or she would be in your face, bombarding you with her dislike every time you visited. After thinking of and discarding several things, we have come to the opinion there could be one or two things causing Sam to hide from you. She could be feeling she has betrayed her papa by aiding a Yankee soldier, or it could be her clothing. Both could be part of the reason. While at the Henrys, they made a trip to the Hatcher's home place, and Sam brought some dresses of her mama back to the Henrys. Mrs. Henry altered them to fit Sam."

Morgan listened to Haygood without interrupting, but as soon as Haygood took a breath, he wanted to know: "Floyd has found Sam and talked to her, and I take it she is not ready to see me. Thus, you think it's her female pride that is keeping her from facing me. You did mention a second reason. Floyd thought Sam might be feeling she betrayed her papa with her good deed."

Haygood watched Morgan, as Floyd's words registered, and he realized Morgan was thinking the same as he was. If this was the reason for Sam's actions, it could prove to be the worst of the two.

"Would you care to elaborate on this second reason you and Floyd came up with, or are you in need of a gallop into Hartwell. I do not think that Sam's manner of dress is the reason she is staying away from me, but since she refused to see me, we might as well do something, and riding into Hartwell is better than sitting here and doing nothing."

"I'll go inform Santee and Keowee we are going to Hartwell, while you saddle the horses," Morgan called from the barn door.

Sam watched the two men ride through the cedar grove and away from the plantation, keeping their cloud of dust in sight all the way to the pine woodland. Confident the Yankees were leaving Riverbend for Athens, she hurried to the house.

The family was not surprised by her return to the kitchen, knowing she would be aware of the comings and goings of Morgan and Haygood. The food left from the morning meal was waiting for her on the table, with a plate, a fork, and a glass of cool milk.

Sam's apologetic smile greeted the family, as she came through the door, and the first person she embraced was Keowee.

"Keowee, please do not fret," Sam whispered, while she continued to embrace Keowee. "I am not upset with you. I know you had no choice. You had to tell the cussed man I was a female and to explain why I was dressed as a male."

As she turned from Keowee, Sam smilingly assured the rest of the family, "Floyd has told me all that happened after I fled the room. I apologize for fleeing the warming kitchen, leaving you all to face the cussed man's temper and to answer his questions. I have come to terms with the cussed man knowing who I am, and I will deal with him when needed. So please do not be concerned. However, right now, I feel I am in need of a head-to-foot crubbing, and after I put a few kettles of water on to heat, I am going to partake of the food you have graciously set out for me."

Floyd spoke up, telling her to go ahead and eat and that he would draw the water and fill the kettles.

Keowee and Lovie, pleased that Sam's temper was smoothed and that she was not upset with anyone for having told Morgan her true gender, returned to the preparation of the midday meal. Santee sat down to keep Sam company.

"I have had a lot to think about since we were kidnapped," Sam said. "I learned a fearful lesson during that time. I now know that it is not the part of the nation that you come from that makes a mean and evil person, but what is inside of the person. Maybe I should have said I was reminded of Papa's principle rule of thought: Do not judge a person by the color of the skin, the kind of home the person lived in, the person's clothing or the person's wealth. You judge by what is inside of the person, his or her character. I know the bullet that killed Papa was fired from a Yankee gun and the trigger was pulled by a Yankee soldier, but I now know Papa was in that battle because Robert Sinclair was a coward. Robert refused to fight, and, somehow, Papa was made to fight in his place, as a substitute. I cannot imagine what would have made Papa do that, because he was against the war. Santee, would you or Keowee know what made Papa go to war in Robert's place?"

Sam's question was asked as Floyd came through the back door, and, hearing that his papa was made to fight in the war in the place of Robert Sinclair, he jerked to a stop, sloughing water from the two buckets he carried.

"What do you mean Papa was made to go to war in Robert's place?" Floyd demanded.

Santee turned to face Keowee, wondering how on earth Sam learned this shameful news and, they both waited for the other to tell the children the truth. Sam, seeing their hesitation, urged, "If you know, please tell us. It will be easier for us to understand if we know the reason. Please Keowee, Santee. One of you tell us."

By this time, Floyd had filled the kettles and set the buckets down on the hearth, and he walked to the table and sat down beside Sam. David, as usual, followed Floyd's lead, and he, too, sat down at the table.

"You tell them," Keowee said to Santee. "You were privy to some of Mr. Mac's and Mr. Robert's plans."

Since Sam had asked and, at Keowee's urging, Santee knew it was time to tell the children, but he thought to soften his words, withholding the whole truth of why Mr. Mac badgered their father into being a substitute for Mr. Robert. Santee directed his words to Sam.

"Missy, Mr. Mac was wholeheartedly for that war, but he did not want Mr. Robert facing no bullets. Mr. Robert didn't want to be in the war, either. He didn't want his life disturbed by having to join the Confederate Army. The two of 'em discussed this for a while and came up with the idea of getting someone to join the army in Mr. Robert's place. Mr. Mac was acquainted with Mr. William and Miss Martha, and Mr. William being the best shot in the county, Mr. Mac set his eyes on your papa to be the one to join the army in Mr. Robert's place. The two of them visited your papa several times, and he refused every time, until the last time in June. Now just what was said that made Mr. William go in Mr. Robert's place, I don't rightly know, but I do know it was not the offer of money. His payment was to be the care of Miss Martha and you children. That be the reason Reverend Henry done brung y'all to Riverbend. Him, Reverend Henry, knew all about how this was arranged. After hearing the news of Mr. William being killed and Miss Martha's death the next night, he loaded y'all in that wagon and brung y'all to us."

Keowee stood as still and as quiet as a mouse, waiting for the hurtful words that were sure to come, and she was thankful to God for Santee's way of telling that spared the children more pain. Not hearing a word about the reason her papa went to war and not able to hide her disappointment, Sam protested "Santee, you have told us why Mr. Mac wanted Papa to be a substitute for Robert. And you have told us why we were brought here to Riverbend, but we still do not know the reason Papa agreed to be Robert's substitute."

"Sam," Floyd said, "it may have something to do with army

rules. I bet Morgan or Haygood will know what would have caused Papa to agree to be a substitute for Robert. Would you mind if I asked them? Hey, how did you come by the knowledge that Papa was a substitute for Robert?"

Floyd's interruption saved Santee from having to comment on Sam's rebuke, and he was thankful in his quiet manner.

"I heard Morgan tell the men in the tavern that Robert was guilty of kidnapping the children of the man who fought, as a substitute for him, in the Confederate Army," Sam softly admitted.

"I don't mind if you question the cussed man about army rules," Sam told Floyd, giving her okay. "Maybe he can shed some light on why Papa agreed to fight in a war he did not believe was right."

"None of you have mentioned that Morgan will probably be the owner of Riverbend, now that Robert is in jail and will be there for a long, long time," Floyd stated excitedly. "He did pay those back taxes. Does that not give him ownership of the plantation? I just thought of that."

Hearing Floyd's excited spiel, Sam placed her elbows on the table and dropped her head into her hands. His words brought to mind a predicament that would affect their lives and one that she had not realized as yet but that she knew they would be facing, making her wonder, *What will happen to us now? His home is in the North, and he will be going home soon. Surely, he will not want to stay in the South and run a plantation. Will he sell the plantation?*

The rest of the morning passed without conversation, each member of the family lost in his or her thoughts. Keowee and Lovie managed to get the midday meal on the table, and the seven ate their meal without guests, as they had since Mr. Mac's illness and death. No one mentioned the absent two

Yankees. Santee and Keowee knew that the two men would be getting their meal somewhere in Hartwell and that the two would enjoy the bond of kinship that had formed over the years.

CHAPTER 18

Before retiring for the night, Morgan asked Lovie if Sam was in her room when she carried the items from the Henrys upstairs, and she sadly shook her head. Morgan tossed and turned all night, listening for sounds of Sam sneaking up to her bedchamber. He kept telling himself his only concern was knowing she was safely in for the night, but way before the rooster crowed, he admitted that, lying heavy on his mind and heart, was the fear Sam would again stay away from him. The admission that his need to see his angel was more than expressing his gratitude for saving his life and making sure she was safe. He could no longer deny that his heart held more than just gratitude toward the young woman he had met on that May night. For this Southern spitfire had snuck into his heart.

Floyd's and Haygood's idea that Sam's male attire was the reason she stayed hidden was wrong. The realization my feeling for Sam goes deeper than gratitude; I now know why my angel stays away from me. She is dealing with what I have finally admitted to myself, but there are more things for her to satisfy in her heart and mind. Among other things, how she could feel anything but hate toward a Yankee soldier, and she's having difficulty picturing me other than in a Yankee blue uniform. The same uniform worn by the man who killed her father;that is what has kept her from me. When she comes to me, the uniform will need to be discussed.

Haygood's knocking on Morgan's door interrupted his musing and told him it was time to go down for the morning meal.

Sam sat in her window seat, wide awake, since old Red had crowed his welcome to the new day. She'd spent the last hours at the window, trying to decide how to face the day. She was pulled between wanting to go down for the morning meal and the uneasiness she felt at the thought of facing Morgan Anderson. Her struggles ceased, as the red ball of the morning sun rose over the tree tops on the east bank of the Savannah River. The sunlight of the new day pushed away the night, along with her doubts, bringing a calmness to her nerves.

Coming to the house in the wee hours of the morning, Sam was surprised to find things from her home. She was convinced that Lovie had opened her mouth about their visit and that the arrival of her things was the result of the departure of the two men she had witnessed leaving Riverbend yesterday.

Her earlier indecision eliminated, she now faced another— how to dress for her encounter with the cussed man. She realized, by now, that he knew that the young lady that had saved his life that May night lived on Riverbend right under his nose. Walking to her bed, she held up each dress, discarding all of them.

Turning to the armoire, she removed a freshly ironed boy's shirt, slipped her arms into the sleeves, and buttoned all the buttons, except the last one at her neck. Next, she pulled on clean trousers; tucking the shirttail in the waist band, she tied the rope around her waist and slipped on a pair of her mother's shoes. Taking a last look in the mirror, she thought *He won't have any trouble knowing I am a female this morning.* She then acknowledged, with a smile, *I left my breast unbound.*

Morgan did not try to conceal his impatient watching of the door to the back stairs. His eyes were glued to the area, and everyone in the room was aware of his wondering if Sam would make an appearance.

Haygood was affected more than the other people in the room by Morgan's complete focus on the door to the back stairs. Having known Morgan since they were six years old, he could not remember ever seeing Morgan so consumed with a personal problem. He suddenly realized that Morgan's need to see and talk with Sam was more than expressing his gratitude and that finding his angel was more important to Morgan than anything he had ever done.

The back staircase door opened, and Haygood sighed a sigh of relief, as a young woman dressed in male attire entered the warming kitchen. Her family, not knowing Sam was even in the house, were relieved her hiding was at an end. However, her coming to the warming kitchen put looks of total surprise on their faces, but smiles soon replaced their looks of surprise.

The two Yankees were speechless, seeing the pretty, young lady walk through the door and to the table, but they were relieved and happy.

After apologizing to Keowee and Lovie for not doing her share of the morning work, Sam pulled out the chair next to Morgan and sat down. Looking first at Haygood across from her, she turned to the cussed man. Smiling, she said, "Morning, gentlemen. I hope you both enjoyed a peaceful night of sleep."

Seeing the look of complete astonishment on both men's faces gave her the pleasure that knowing her presence and actions caused exactly what she had intended. Turning away from the two Yankee idiots, she found that her greeting to

Morgan and Haygood had replaced the smiles on her family's faces with absolute shock. It was all she could do to retain her pose of genteel mannerism, afraid she was either going to start laughing or to turn and slap the cussed man's silly face. *I wonder which would give me the most satisfaction.* Deciding she'd better not do either, Sam sat back in her chair and waited.

Santee spoke, "Sam, since you be back in the folds of the family, after a time of keeping yourself from us, you need to ask God's blessing on our morning meal."

Assured there was no need to protest Santee's way of letting her know he recognized her mischief, Sam bowed her head, asking God's blessing on the food he so graciously gave them. The meal progressed without any further shenanigans on Sam's part. The talk and laughter that usually accompanied the family meals gradually found a way into the clinking sound of forks against plates.

Morgan sat spellbound the first few minutes after Sam's entrance. He could not believe his eyes. The young woman, his angel that had passed herself off as a male, was beautiful beyond his imagination.

The dark hair with streaks of fire that he remembered fell in waves down her back, and one long curl hung over her left shoulder. He now knew her eyes were the color of emeralds, and they sparkled with irksome fire, even while she was wishing him and Haygood a good morning. Smiling, he was sure those sparks testified to the wee temper she so easily concealed in her morning greeting. She was still dressed in her trousers and boy's shirt, but there was no denying she was a beautiful, young lady.

I named her correctly. Not only was her ministering to my wounds that of an angel, but her face is one fashioned from the pattern of angels. I hope when we have our private face-to-face meeting, I can calm that wee temper and have her responding like an angel. Before he could clear his mind and direct a word to Sam, the horrible thought, *Robert Sinclair had her in his grasp!* passed through his mind, leaving him shaken and breathless far longer than he realized.

Haygood noticed Morgan's smile of pleasure turn to a frown and a look he had never seen before on his friend's face. Fright. Punching Morgan in the side, Haygood asked, "Are you all right?"

Nodding his head, Morgan steadied himself, without having to tell Haygood the disturbing thought that had flashed through his mind.

Haygood was not completely sure Morgan's nod told the whole truth, but he let the dog lie for the time being, keeping a cautious eye on Morgan.

"Sam, or should I address you as Miss Samantha?" Morgan softly asked.

Hearing the sound of her name in that now-familiar Yankee accent sent goosebumps up her spine andbutterflies to her stomach. Hoping to calm the butterflies and shake away the goose bumps, Sam waited until the food on her fork was in her mouth, properly chewed and swallowed, before turning to face the cussed man.

Morgan was too impatient to look Sam in the face again and spoke before she could speak, "Are you afraid to look me in the face? You know I do not bite, and I do not think my face will spoil your meal."

If he only knew what looking at his face does to me, she thought, as she calmed her nerves. Turning to him, she replied, as she aimed her eyes on the cussed man's handsome face, "I am not sure about the biting or the spoiling of my meal, but I can assure you I am not afraid of you, Yankee."

Her answer to his verbal missive brought a hearty laugh from Morgan and a memory of her quick retorts to his words of May. A smile followed his laughter and spread across the handsome face she saw every night in her dreams. His laughter and smile brought the cussed butterflies back and a familiar sensation to her chest, but she held her ground and never wavered.

Enjoying their little verbal jousting more than he would care to admit to Haygood, he offered a request. "Since you are not afraid of this Yankee, may I invite you to walk with me at the end of the meal?"

Lowering his voice almost to a whisper, he added another baited sentence, "Please allow me to put your mind at ease, since you seem to have forgotten. I do not bite."

Before Sam could lower her head, a blush colored her face at Morgan's attempt to remind her of their kiss. She felt the heat of her blush and knew her face was red as a beet. Hoping no one was paying close attention to their conversation, she looked up through her eyelashes and looked straight into the smiling face of Haygood.

"The cussed man was listening to our every word," she fumed. Ready to give Haygood a wallop like the one she had given Robert Sinclair, she squeezed her hands into fists, but she hesitated, knowing she would never hear the last of it if she lunged to the end of the table, knocking the cussed man out of his chair. She was mad enough to spit, thinking, *It would probably be worth the tongue-lashing to wipe that knowing smile off the cussed man's face.*

Haygood heard Morgan's whispered words, but he did not understand their meaning or if they even had a meaning, until he saw the blush covering Sam's face. *That crazy Yankee. I knew there was something that happened while Sam tended to his wounds.*

Sam kept her attention on her food for the remainder of the meal, but she was having no success condemning to Purgatory the butterflies the cussed man caused. *What do I do? I told him I was not afraid of him. If I refuse his invitation, he will think I am afraid.* Stiffening her spine mentally, she assured herself, *I will not cower before the cussed man. Surely, I can walk and talk.*

Morgan watched Sam move her food around on her plate, knowing she was in a battle regarding his invitation to walk with him. Confident the fortitude of his angel would not allow herself to cower before a Yankee, he leaned back in his chair, arms folded, enjoying watching her mental battle.

The noise of chairs being pushed away from the table brought Sam's attention to the room and the fact everyone was finished eating. Pushing back her chair, Sam stood. Wanting to wait as long as possible before walking with the cussed man, she turned to Morgan and said, "Colonel Anderson, I need to help clear the table before I can join you for a walk."

Morgan listened to Sam's words, hoping Keowee would come to his aid. There was no way he would accept Sam's refusal. Hoping Keowee would come to his aid, he waited patiently.

Keowee had kept a watchful eye on Sam during the meal, wondering how the meal would end. Sam taking a walk with Mr. Morgan had not entered her mind.

"Sam, no need to wait for the walk," Keowee offered. "Lovie will be all the help I's need. Y'all go on and enjoy the cool morning air."

Morgan's smile spread further across his face, as he watched his angel stiffening her spine and turning to face him. Standing by his chair, he bowed slightly and motioned for Sam to precede him.

Stepping out the door onto the whistling path, Morgan took hold of Sam's arm, stopping her in her tracks and multiplying the butterflies.

"In what direction would you like to walk, Samantha?" Morgan asked, continuing to hold her arm.

"Please release my arm. You may call me Sam, the name my family uses. The direction we take makes no difference to me."

Morgan felt the slight quivering in Sam that his hand had caused and reluctantly complied with her request.

"Let's walk toward the river," Morgan suggested, "and as far as to how I address you is concerned, I would like to call you 'Angel.' That's how I remembered you these last months. You are an angel, at least in my mind."

Sam was surprised that the cussed man would refer to her as his "angel" so soon and was determined to steer him away from thinking she was the one that tended to his wounds.

"What makes you so sure that I am your angel? You could be mistaken."

Sam's response stopped Morgan in his tracks, but the thought came to him, *Why am I surprised that this stubborn, Yankee-hating woman would claim that I am mistaken. That's my angel, holding out to the last.*

"There is no other," Morgan replied. "Even though you would not allow me a clear look at your face during the time you tended to my wounds, I have a perfect memory of the sound of your voice, and your dark hair, streaked with fire when the light hits just right, remains in my memory. You probably still do not want to admit that you kept a Yankee soldier from dying, but you cannot deny the compassion you showed to a wounded man. I remember your truthful words of hate for Yankees while you saved my life and they make me regret that your first memory of me is the uniform of your hated enemy. Angel, I cannot apologize for being a Union soldier or for being in the war that caused the death of your father. Your losses caused by this war were severe, and I am sorry for your losses. I had hoped our first meeting would be amiable and would consist of talk of pleasantries. I had hoped it would be a time for you to begin to know me as a person, not Yankee soldier, but I knew that, in time, we would need to discuss your feelings toward the North."

Feeling a little embarrassed for talking at length without allowing Sam a comment, Morgan said, "I seem to be doing all of the talking; please forgive me. Feel free to speak up at any time. I remember you are not the least bashful to have your say. I will end my spiel with assuring you there is no doubt in my mind that I have found my angel."

Sam watched Morgan's face while he spoke and saw the truth of his words in his eyes. Her heart felt the empathy she heard in the words that came from the Yankee's heart, but her stubborn mind would not allow the tears that threatened to flow.

She would shed her tears in private. Not only did his empathy touch her heart; his regret that he was dressed in a Yankee uniform at the time of their first meeting also cut deep into her emotions. Struggling not to show the effects, she tried to ask in a normal voice, "Why is it so important that you find your angel? Could you not go on with your life, saying the deed was done by a Southern Samaritan?"

Morgan stopped, standing motionless until Sam became aware he was no longer walking beside her, and then he turned around. Looking Sam straight in the eyes, he replied with a flat, emphatic, "No!"

Sam waited, hoping Morgan would add to his one word.

She wanted him to tell her why, but he stood still, looking at her with disbelief.

"Why is it so important to you?" she asked again.

As he came to stand in front of her, their bodies almost touching, Morgan took hold of her arms, and finally spoke.

"Do you not know? When my touch or just my smile causes you to experience feelings or emotions that mystify you, feelings and emotions that have bothered you all these months, I can imagine the turmoil you must have experienced, trying to come to terms with your emotions because of your hatred of Yankees. I, too, have been dealing with some of the same emotions ever since I woke in bright sunlight and you were gone. I have had a driven need to find you. I have not had to deal with hatred of Southerners because I have never had a reason to hate anyone from the South. But there is one Southerner I would like to put an end to his life with my bare hands. This morning at the table, the thought that Robert Sinclair had you in his power flashed through my mind and affected me, as nothing else ever has. I was sick to my stomach and felt both anger and fear all at once. I despise him for the crimes he has committed against young Southern ladies, but that does not compare to what I felt toward him for attempting to harm you."

"I'd hoped you'd become more at ease in my presence and see me as a man, not as a Yankee before this discussion arose."

Smiling and looking down, he realized he was still holding Sam by the arms and was filled with a strong desire to pull her into his arms. Immediately, he dropped his hands and stepped back.

"I seem to have developed a loose tongue," Morgan stated. Sam stood in stunned confusion, hearing Morgan's words regarding his emotional state of the last months.

Mentally talking to herself, she silently assured herself, *The cussed man's words came from his own egotistical opinion of his Yankee self. He has not the least idea of my emotional state.*

While Sam was busy finding fault with Morgan's words and her emotional battles, Morgan hoped his thought to take her into his arms was not as apparent in his eyes as what he was seeing in Sam's face and eyes. He was reading her like a book and knew the moment her stunned confusion at his confession turned to skepticism.

He was not the least bit surprised that Sam would question his words after the shock of their meaning had begun to sink in, but he knew that even though Sam wanted to doubt the truth of his words, they would later haunt her. She would have questions, and her questions would be asked of him, and he would share his knowledge. He fought to keep a cousin to Haygood's lopsided grin from covering his face.

Sam's thoughts were not only jumbled, but being near Morgan and hearing his voice were also playing havoc with her emotions and her ability to think rationally. She was able to form the notion she needed to leave the cussed man.

Still reading Sam's thoughts, Morgan began to feel a little compassion for her confusion. "Angel, let's take advantage of the rockers on the veranda and sit a spell."

Reaching the rockers, Morgan released Sam's arm. While Morgan gained his seat, Sam collected a little of her good senses and decided, *I will put the cussed man in his place. I will give him a smile, and before he can recover, I will be gone.* Turning to face the cussed man, Sam smiled a beaming smile she knew he would feel to his toes.

"Please, excuse me; I have a chore that needs my attention," she stated and then walked through the front doors before Morgan could recover.

Although Morgan was shaken to his toes by his angel's smile, he also saw the sparks of ire in her beautiful emerald eyes, as she spoke so pleasantly, and his chuckles filled the air as the door closed behind her. Morgan's chuckles ended, and thoughts of what was ahead filled his mind.

CHAPTER 19

The sun was nearing midday, and no one had laid eyes on Sam and Morgan since they had left the warming kitchen. Keowee and Lovie tried to concentrate on preparing the midday meal, but their thoughts kept turning to Morgan and Sam.

All would be relieved to learn the couple's walk could be described as a little strained at times, but mostly pleasantly polite. The whereabouts of each would not surprise the majority.

The Yankee colonel sat on the front veranda, rocking quietly, his mind full of their walk and when he would next see his angel. The Southern rebel entered her bedchamber, churning with anger. Two mad to stay long in her favorite window, she paced the length and breath of the bedchamber, furious that she allowed the cussed man to affect her to the point of not being able to think straight. Angry at herself more than at Morgan, Sam paced, berating herself with a tongue-lashing. Her angry conversation raged. If any of her family happened to hear the angry words bouncing off the chamber walls, they would not doubt that Sam's temper was riled and that some poor soul would soon be the recipient of her anger. Sam's angry words and thoughts as to how to handle the cussed man, now that he thought he had figured out she was his angel, became heavy and tiring.

She fell onto her bed, exhausted. As she found her pillow, she thought, *I knew the cussed man would know my voice; that's why I tried to disguise it the morning he showed up on the front veranda.* With that reminder, forbidden tears she had refused to shed earlier washed her face and dampened her pillow. When she was empty of tears, a thought she was unable to deny registered in her weary mind: *Those tears were not shed for Papa or Mama but were the result of the words Morgan sincerely offered in empathy for the loss of my parents. I cannot understand how I can let the words of a Yankee touch my heart, however sincerely spoken.*

Wanting to shut out all the disturbing thoughts of the whys that she could not answer or understand, she rolled onto her side and curled into a fetal position. Turning to the only way she knew to find the solace and answers she wanted and needed, Sam began to silently ask God to help her. As the "amen" to her prayer slipped from her lips, the thought, *He seems to be a good and ethical Yankee,* slipped through her mind, as she drifted off to sleep.

Keowee announced the midday meal would be on the table soon and asked Floyd to find Mr. Morgan and Sam.

Haygood and Floyd set off around the house and toward the river, without a word. Haygood was anxious to check on the emotional state of his friend, and Floyd was hoping that Sam had held her temper and had behaved. After they found Morgan sitting calmly and alone on the veranda, their concern turned to Sam, since she was nowhere in sight.

Floyd looked Morgan over carefully, thinking he could not have restrained an angry Sam without her getting in her licks and leaving scratches and bruises. Not finding any telltale marks, Floyd was satisfied and asked, "Where is Sam?"

"You have not thrown Sam in the river, I hope? Haygood asked before Morgan could answer. Amused by Haygood's concern for Sam and by Floyd's careful examining of him, Morgan almost laughed in their faces.

He smiled and said, "Relax, you two; Angel and I enjoyed a peaceful walk. The walk ended on the veranda, and Angel excused herself, saying there was a chore that needed her attention. Now, does the overview of our walk calm your fear that I threw Angel in the river?"

After Floyd heard Morgan refer to Sam as his angel, his eyes almost popped out of his head. "Morgan, you think Sam is your angel?

"No doubt about it; your Yankee-hating sister is definitely my angel. I do not as yet know where she had hidden me or how she had kept all of you from knowing what she was doing, but I know she is definitely my angel."

"But Morgan," Floyd fired back, "you said you did not know what your angel looked like. Sam does have a tender heart, but I just cannot see her hiding you and tending to your wounds."

"Floyd," Morgan said, "your sister is an amazing young woman. I confess I never saw a clear image of her face, but I heard her voice clearly. The sound of her voice has stayed with me all these months. Several other things have remained in my memory all this time. Yes, Floyd, I am positive your sister is my angel."

"Well, I'll be a suck-egg dog," was all Floyd could say to Morgan's declaration.

Haygood finally remembered Keowee's announcement and said, "We came to get you for the midday meal."

"Floyd, would you know where to find Sam?" he asked, as he turned from Morgan. Tapping Floyd on the top of his head, Haygood asked, "Would you know where to find Sam and would you tell her to come to the kitchen?"

"Maybe," Floyd replied. Then, turning to Morgan, he asked, "Which way did she go when she left to attend to her chore?"

Morgan pointed and said, "Through the front doors."

Since she was not in the warming kitchen when Keowee had asked them to find Sam, Floyd knew there was only one other place she could be in the house. Floyd walked through the front doors, thinking, *Morgan might have thought their walk was peaceful, but I know Sam. She was pleasant, at a cost. I bet she left the veranda mad as a wet hen, and I'll find her still fuming.*

Knocking on Sam's bedchamber door, Floyd waited a minute before entering. Floyd was surprised at what he found. Instead of Sam's meeting him with loud, angry words, she was curled up on her bed, sleeping like a baby.

He hesitated only a few minutes, before taking hold of Sam's shoulders and shaking her awake. He braced for her fist to come flying, and he did not have long to wait. Sam came up, with her fists ready, but she lowered her hands when she recognized Floyd.

"What are you doing, waking me?" Sam asked, rubbing her eyes.

"It's meal time, and Keowee wanted me to get you down to the table. I'm hungry."

Sam smiled, knowing Floyd was always hungry and was usually the first to pull out a chair. "Go on down. I'll be right behind you. I need to wash the sleep out of my eyes."

"I guess you'd better," Floyd threw over his shoulders, as he walked out the door. "You wouldn't want Morgan to know the chore you needed to attend to was a nap."

Floyd, mentally and emotionally older than his sixteen years, left Sam's bedchamber, troubled. Having seen the dried tears on her face, he feared for Sam for the first time in his life. Morgan's cheerful announcement that Sam was absolutely his angel and Floyd's finding Sam asleep in the middle of the day was earthshattering for him. *Sam is aware Morgan is naming her his angel and, for some reason, it has made her cry, rather than flying at him with walloping fists and kicking feet. Sam never cries. Not since Papa's and Mama's death and we were brought to Riverbend. Her tears tell me she is facing something she has come up against and doesn't know how or what to do, and it has brought her to tears. If she is truly Morgan's angel, there is more bothering her than admitting she saved a Yankee's life. Sam has always owned up to anything and everything she's done.*

Opening the door to the warming kitchen, Floyd placed an unfelt smile on his face and announced, "Only me. Sam will be down shortly."

As Floyd found his seat at the table, the downstairs' door opened, and Sam entered the room. Dressed in her male attire, but not as chipper as she was for the morning meal, she took her seat by Morgan without a word.

After the blessing was said, the only sounds heard in the otherwise silent room were those of utensils striking dishes. The silence became deafening, and Lovie, thinking that Sam would appreciate knowing that Mr. Morgan might be leaving the plantation after the meal, broke the silence.

"Mr. Morgan, do you plan to continue your search for your angel this afternoon?"

Morgan looked up at the faces around the table and could see that more faces than Lovie's were waiting for his answer, but, before answering, he looked down at Sam and smiled at her.

"Lovie, I have no need to look further for my angel. As fate would have it, I know the whereabouts of my angel and, in time, I will be delighted to introduce the beautiful young lady that saved my life in May to all of you."

Morgan's words left everyone at the table with slack jaws, with the exception of Haygood and Floyd. Sam showed her surprise differently than the others.

She turned to face Morgan, with murder in her eyes, and, of course, the cussed man only smiled.

David was the first to speak, "Morgan, I know the lady is very special."

Still smiling, Morgan answered David with an aura of pleasure that made it impossible for anyone in the room to doubt his words. "She is very special, and it is my deepest desire to be able to do this in the very near future, as soon as the lady is ready for me to make this announcement."

Watching Sam during all this talk, Keowee was shaken to her bones by what she saw. Her suspicions had been right. *Lord, have mercy. Mr. Morgan done figured out Sam be his angel.*

Wanting to ease the situation, Keowee suggested, "If we don't eat our food, it's gonna be cold, and we's be eating cold vittles."

No one dared disobey Keowee when sitting at her table, so the talk turned to more everyday subjects. Sam hardly tasted her vittles, and she was the first to push back her chair.

Morgan gently placed his hand on her arm before she could stand and quietly whispered, "Please don't run and hide. I thought we could take a ride after we ate. We have two fine horses."

Sam was startled by Morgan's quick actions and did not at once try to remove his hand, but she said, quietly, "Yankee, if I choose not to ride, I will not be riding. I will be enjoying an afternoon, reading."

Still holding her arm, Morgan pleaded, "Do not try to convince me that spending the afternoon in your room would not be your way of hiding from me. Please let's behave like the adults that we are. We have already wasted too much time.

All I am asking is for you to spend the afternoon with me. If not riding, perhaps in pleasant conversation."

Sam was once again touched by the sincerity she could see in the cussed man's eyes and the captivating way he had of letting her know he knew she was shaving the truth in her reply to his suggestion. She continued to look the cussed man in the eyes.

"I do not recall saying I would remain in my room," Sam quickly replied.

Thinking she would need to yank on her arm in order to remove it from Morgan's hand, Sam was surprised at how easily her arm slipped from his grip. Sam turned suddenly from the table and walked quickly from the room, hoping she could reach her room before the tears filling her eyes began to fall.

Running up the stairs and down the hall, she was again perplexed by her reaction to the cussed man. *I am as angry as I have ever been, but, instead of yelling my head off, I am becoming a complete watering pot.* When she was halfway down the hallway, Sam's tears began slipping from her eyes. Entering her bedchamber, she did not take time to close her door, as she rushed to get a handkerchief.

Morgan, having followed in her wake, was up the stairs, and, nearing her room, he heard her sniffles. He observed that she had not taken the time to close the door. In a matter of seconds, he asked, "Angel, what is the matter? What has upset you to tears?"

Taking a step inside Sam's bedchamber door, he pleaded,

"Sweetlin', please tell me I am not the cause of your tears. I would not hurt you for the world."

At the sound of Morgan's voice, Sam whirled around, coming face to face with him, and the helpless look on her tear-wet face almost brought him to his knees, and her words added to his dismay.

"You cussed Yankee," Sam threw at him. "Was it not enough that Yankees took my papa's life and caused my mama's death and the loss of our home. No! You rode into my life, bleeding, and my tender heart would not allow me to turn you away, but saving your life was not enough. You had to ride back into my world, turning the life I had gleaned from the shambles of war upside down, to the point that I am not myself. I should be unloading my anger on you, as I would have months ago. Instead, I am reduced to tears."

Stopping to blow her nose and trying to stifle her tears gave Morgan time to walk to her. He put his arm around her waist and led his seemingly distraught angel out of her room, down the front stairs, and into the parlor before she could thaw his intent.

Steering Sam to a seat on the settee, Morgan sat beside her and took her hands in his before she could refuse them.

"Angel, I feel like a heel," he began. "I need to be horse-whipped. If I could, I would do that task for you. I am truly sorry for causing your tears.

Please be sure I would never hurt you intentionally. I do have good intentions. From the day I woke in the camp with my men, I wanted to find you. Having been informed by you of your hatred for Yankees, I promised myself that when I found you, I would not approach you as the Yankee soldier whose life you saved, but as a friend of the Sinclair family. I wanted us to become better acquainted before I told you I knew you were my angel. I wanted you to get to know me as a person, instead of seeing me as a Yankee soldier. My plan was slowly to bring you to the knowledge that I recognized you, but sometimes things have a way of not working out like we would want."

"Being told the person I thought to be male was female and a permanent resident of Riverbend rattled my ability to think rationally," Morgan continued. "The conundrum of why a young lady knew we were Yankees having never met or seen us in uniforms. The sense of de ja vu I felt during the trip from Athens when you spoke. Haygood revealing the chain you retrieved from Choyce was mine. You having the gold chain and medallion I left for my angel proved to me you were my angel and thrilled me. Then I wrestled with why you hid from me until old Red crowed his welcome to the coming morning. The reason hit me. You struggled with your memories, because they were of a Yankee soldier. A man wearing the same blue uniform the man wore that killed your father. That is why you hid from me. You have not been able to come to terms with your lingering emotional feelings of that Yankee soldier."

Morgan continued, "I told myself I had all this figured out and I would act accordingly. But this morning, when you walked into the warming kitchen, and I saw a beautiful, young lady, named Samantha, knowing without a shadow of a doubt that you were my angel. At that moment, what little sense left in my head after finding out a Yankee-hating female lived on the plantation disappeared, but realizing I had not seen through your disguise was crushing. I am to blame for my plans going astray. I should not have acted the idiot and called you angel at first, but, to be honest, if I had had all the sense in the world, it would not have mattered. Do you have any idea how beautiful you are? I acted like a schoolboy with his first sweetheart."

Hearing Morgan say she was beautiful made Sam perk up. She turned to face him and realized that he held both of her hands and that, earlier, his arm had been around her waist. *Gracious me! What am I to do now? Maybe it is about time we have that down-to-earth talk and get to the nitty-gritty. Maybe this cussed man can help me understand what is happening to me or what has happened to me. I hate to get help from a cussed Yankee, but I have no other choice right now. With her mind made up, Sam took a deep breath.*

"All right, Yankee, tell me about yourself and these feelings and emotions you say you have been having."

CHAPTER 20

Taken back slightly by Sam's request, Morgan mentally shook his head and happily began, "You are aware of the fact I was born in the North. My father was a man of the North, but my mother was born and raised in Virginia. I lost my mother at the age of four. I met Haygood two years later, and we became inseparable from day one. Haygood had just lost both mother and father, and he was lost. You might say we were in the same boat, and our friendship grew. Papa and I struggled in our misery caused by my mother's death until I was eleven. Papa met a lady by the name of Evalyn. Miss Evalyn was also from the South, New Orleans. I loved this lady very much, and after Papa and Miss Evalyn married, as a family we visited Riverbend. Miss Evalyn and Mac were kin, and we visited over the years. Robert and I were near in age, but we never became friends. I tolerated Robert, and I imagine it was the same with Robert."

"When Haygood and I came of age," Morgan continued, "Papa enrolled us in West Point. I found a second home. I had a wonderful teacher, who became not only a beloved instructor but a very close friend, by the name of Robert E. Lee. He is another person whose departure from my life left a place hard to fill. I lost Papa the same year.

"In 1860," Morgan went on, "I graduated from West Point, receiving the rank of lieutenant. In April 1861, after the South seceded from the Union, I faced the hardest decision I have ever had to make. Angel, half of the men I studied with, roughhoused with, ate my meals with, and lived with for four years were from the South. I either had to turn my back on the government I had sworn to uphold or to take up arms against men, friends that I loved and respected. In the end, I could not forget, nor could I dishonor the oath I had taken at my commencement. I was fortunate to be assigned duties that, most of the time, kept me out of the regular fighting, and, only a few times, did I have to aim my rifle at Southern troops."

I came to Riverbend on that May night to see Mac," Morgan spoke further. "I promised I would check on him, should I be anywhere near the plantation when the war ended. You know what happened on that visit. I would have died from my wounds, had I not found an angel. A young Southern lady that would not leave my memory, even though I saw only a face in shadows, a shapely figure with a soft, sweet voice like my mother and hands compassionate and gentle, even though they were calloused by work that should have fallen to a male. My angel made no bones as to her feelings toward Yankees. She plainly stated she wanted no Yankees at her home or around her family. There was no mistaking her hatred for the army that had killed her papa, but she showed a mountain of kindness to me, a man wearing the blue uniform of that hated army. The morning I woke in bright sunlight, I knew I was no longer in the place you had hidden me. We were already behind schedule, reporting to Washington, and so I had to leave, not knowing where you were or how you fared. I kept telling myself I owed you a debt, and that was why it was so important for me to find you. But, deep down,

I felt something was missing in my life from the moment I opened my eyes and you were gone. I tried to deny the emptiness I felt, telling myself my need to find you was to satisfy myself that you were safe in the war-torn land. After President Johnson sent Haygood and me south because of the reports of missing young ladies, I became more anxious to find you. There was one memory that filled my dreams and thoughts. This memory caused emotions and feelings that would leave me breathless and that sometimes would happen at the most inopportune time. The memory of the kiss we shared and the feelings it kindled were the catalyst that finally made me admit there was more to my need to find you than just to say, 'Thank you.' There was a longing in my heart to not only see you but also to hear your voice. There was an emptiness that only you could fill. The heart does not hearken to the dictates of a person's wants or of a person's dislikes. The heart loves, without instructions."

Sam sat perfectly still, listening to Morgan's account of his life. However, his open and free avowal of the true reason behind his search to find his angel gave Sam more than just a warm feeling. Hearing he felt an emptiness when he found her gone, memories of her voice and her touch and constantly seeing her in his dreams. His feelings and thoughts described the dilemmas she was cursed with since that May night, and they left her speechless. All she could do was stare at the cussed man.

Understanding the look of dismay on Sam's face, Morgan tried not to show too much exuberance in his questioning, "Have I mentioned occurrences or effects that sounded familiar? If so, I would welcome the opportunity to discuss our said emotions."

Morgan waited, hoping Sam would agree for them to talk

freely about their feelings, but the only response he received was a slow shaking of her head, as she withdrew her hands from his and walked from the room.

Morgan watched her leave the parlor and climb the stairs, and he was left with only the hope that Sam would find the strength to admit she had feelings for the man, not for a hated enemy.

Twice in the same day, Sam entered her bedchamber in tears. These tears were not of anger but of heaviness of heart. Slowly she closed the door, eyes brimming with tears that freely washed her face.

With eyes open but not focusing, she kept hearing Morgan's voice saying over and over, "There is a place in my life only you can fill, and the heart cannot be told whom to love."

Above all else, that Morgan said those words would not leave her. The window seat was a welcome solace, and later she became aware of the dampness on the front of her shirt and aware of her dripping nose. Blowing her nose, she crawled up on her knees. She automatically looked at the cedar grove where she first saw the grey horse that May night.

Sam sat deep in thought, recalling Morgan's account of his life and, with these insights, there came the truth of why he had worn the blue Yankee uniform. She knew his words were true.

In her mind's eye, Sam followed the route of the grey horse that May night, recalling the fear and the anger she had felt at the sight of Yankee blue. *I struggled with my hatred of Yankees that night, but the fear left. The hate of Yankees that filled me before and after May fifth was never aimed at the man I now know as Morgan Anderson. Only hatred toward my feelings and emotions that were repulsive to me because he was a Yankee soldier.*

Dumbfounded, she realized, *I was never conscious that I did not feel hate toward him until now.* Pausing for a few moments to consider that revelation, she searched her heart to see if her hatred included the cussed man. Finding no hate in her heart for the cussed man or Haygood, she wondered, *Is God answering my prayer? Will I in time be free of the hate I now have toward the North?*

Feeling as if a weight of stone had been lifted off her, she leaned back against the window alcove, and a soft peace filled her. A peace she'd lost on October 2, 1862.

Basking in the newly found peace, Sam did not want to think of things that might rob her of the peace she'd found, but the cussed man's words, "There's a place in my life that only you can fill," crept into her thoughts, and tears again threatened to flow. The moisture appearing in her eyes needled her wee temper, and she raved at the empty room.

"Why does the cussed man's words of his need to find me turn me into a watering pot? The cussed man has made me cry more this day than I have in a coon's age. I should march down the stairs and give him a piece of my mind, along with the feel of a few jabs of my fist."

"Gracious me! I cry at his sad words. He's a Yankee, and I don't want to hurt him. What is wrong with me?"

The last question caused her to pause not only her outburst but also her pacing.

Walking back to the window, Sam sat leaning back against the alcove. Her emotions having run the gamut of sad tears to angry words, Sam knew the time had come for her to face the truth. She had to come to terms with the emotions this man from the North had evoked in her from the first time she had looked upon his face.

"I have been in a chastising turmoil since that May night

because of the feelings and emotions for a man in a Yankee uniform I can't seem to help. Maybe the cussed man is right: you can't dictate to the heart whom to like or to dislike. Was it that I hated the Yankee uniform but not the man? Evidently, my hate of the Yankee uniform did not penetrate his uniform."

With a smile gracing her face, she had to stop and ponder her last two admissions. As she let those words sink in, she was reminded of another truth.

"There is the fact that Morgan is still a Yankee, even though I have come to know he is a good man from the North. I know that I am still having trouble being comfortable acknowledging that my feelings are for the man, not a Yankee soldier." Before she drew a breath, there flashed through her mind the thought, *What about the cussed man claiming to know of my emotional turmoil?* She didn't have time to digest that thought, until another thought, *Was he serious about all that he admitted?* raised more what-ifs. Those questions left her breathless for another few moments.

"Is it possible that I could have affected him in the same manner? Did he speak the truth about his turmoil?" *Why question his words when you watched his face while he spoke? What did you see in his eyes?*

"His words were truthful."

She jumped from the window seat as quickly as she had the night she saw the beautiful horse standing in the moonlight, and then she was out the door, running down the stairs in search of answers to questions forming in her head, giving no thought to Morgan's not being in the parlor. Sam was stunned to find the parlor empty. Uncertain as to what she should do now, she walked slowly up the stairs and hesitated outside of her bedchamber's door. Not wanting to return to her bedchamber, she continued down hallway and down the back stairs. Entering the warming kitchen, she was pleased to find Keowee and Lovie finishing up the evening meal, and she welcomed the distractions of setting the table and of helping to place bowls and platters of food on the table.

CHAPTER 21

Morgan left the parlor soon after Sam and found his friend deep in conversation with Santee. "I see you have found a person of great knowledge of this area. I hope you have paid attention to his words. I also wish to gain some insight from Santee, as to some events that transpired in the halls of Riverbend."

Santee quickly explained, "We's just talking about horse breeding, Mr. Morgan, and the value of the horses what was bred and raised at Riverbend before the war."

Morgan chuckled at Santee's statement, and he turned to Haygood. "Did I hear Santee correctly? You interested in horses? I do not believe my ears. You hate horses."

"I hate the *riding* of horses, not the breeding and the selling. There is bound to be a big demand for fine horseflesh after the country rebounds a little. The loss of horses in this war was as great as the loss of men, if not more so. I am just thinking of the future and a honest way to put money in this man's pockets."

"I agree we will need to put some thought into our future after we once again resign from the army." Turning to Santee, Morgan changed the subject.

"Santee, I wonder if you might know the answer to a question that is bothering me. Robert was exempt from fighting because Mac paid a man to take his place. That man was William Hatcher; am I correct?"

"Yes sir, Mr. Morgan, that be right." Santee was nodding his head as he answered.

"I thought the rumors I had heard were true, but I am mystified by Robert traveling to France. Was there a reason for this other than the war?"

"I's don't rightly know the reason, Mr. Morgan. I knows I was rousted from bed about midnight. Mr. Mac was in an awful state, hollering at Mr. Robert loud enough to raise the dead and ordering me to hurry and pack Mr. Robert's clothes in the same breath. Mr. Mac went to the safe, as I started to leave the room, but before I could leave the room, Mr. Robert was pulling on my arm, telling me what horse to have saddled and to hurry. Before I got out of the room, I saw Mr. Mac pulling out a heap of money. I suppose the money was for Mr. Robert. As I brung Mr. Robert's bag down, Mr. Robert left the plantation in a mighty big hurry, and he never came back to Riverbend until now."

"Knowing Robert and Mac as I do," Morgan continued, "I am sure there was something that happened that made it necessary for Robert to leave not only the plantation but the country." Hesitating again, Morgan looked at Santee, "One more question, Santee."

"Did Robert leave the plantation before the children arrived, or afterward?"

"Sam and the boys arrived on the day after Mr. Robert left," Santee answered right away, but he was looking at Morgan with growing concern. Again, Morgan questioned Santee.

"Did news of any trouble in or around the county reach Riverbend that could account for Robert's and Mac's actions?"

"No sir, Mr. Morgan. The children arriving was the only

thing unusual, and it took us a few days to get 'em settled in."

"Mr. Mac's loud ranting and raving at that good preacher was not unusual," Santee went on, "but it shor did unsettle Keowee. What you want to know all this for, Mr. Morgan? If I'm overstepping by asking?"

Morgan hesitated a few moments before answering Santee, but he finally assured Santee, "You are not overstepping, Santee. You have answered my questions as truthfully as you could, and I am obliged. Am I to understand Mac was not pleased with the children being brought here?"

"Well, Mr. Morgan," Santee thoughtfully replied. "Mr. Mac didn't mistreat the children bodily. His treatment of 'em did upset Keowee. She didn't think it right that the children be given chores like the slave children and that Mr. Mac did not allow 'em to eat with him. The children didn't complain. They did their chores, and Sam still found the time for them to do their schooling."

Morgan patted Santee on the back and again thanked him for his time and his truthfulness.

"Haygood, we need to saddle the horses," Morgan said. "I would like a word with Reverend Henry." After Morgan explained what he wanted to do, he walked to the barn.

There were two empty chairs at the midday meal, and all that were there, but Santee, were wondering where the two Yankees could be. Keowee was the first to ask, "Santee, where be Mr. Morgan and Mr. Haygood?"

"A short time before you sent word for us to come to eat, Mr. Morgan informed Mr. Haygood he had business in Hartwell, and the two saddled their horses and left without another word." Santee did not feel he should repeat Mr. Morgan's words.

Cloistered in her bedchamber, sitting in her favorite window, and deep in thought, Sam was surprised to hear a knock on her door. Thinking it to be Floyd again, she took her time opening the door and was shocked to see Keowee.

"Have you lost your tongue completely?" Keowee asked, as she pushed by Sam and walked to a chair and sat down.

"No," Sam answered. She was unsure what could have brought Keowee to her room so soon after the midday meal, but, for whatever the reason, it must have been important for her to leave the kitchen to Lovie. Bracing herself for the reason, she joined Keowee by the fireplace.

"Child, you have me and Santee worried. You be acting strange, and we's want to know why. It cannot still be Mr. Morgan and Mr. Haygood being Yankees. I thought, for sure, that after 'em two men done helped you, Lovie, and the boys, you would be thinking different about 'em."

"You are right. I do look at Haygood and your Mr. Morgan in a different light after they rescued us. However, you will have to understand that, with a Southerner kidnapping us and with Yankees saving us, my mind has been flip-flopping. A Southern man, raised to be a gentleman, committed a mean and hurtful crime, and then Yankees saved us. I have a lot of sorting out of my old way of thinking. I apologize if I have caused you and Santee any worry." She hoped that her explanation would suffice and that Keowee would not ask about her and Morgan's walk.

Keowee was not completely convinced that Sam's sorting out and rethinking was all that was causing her unusual behavior, and she continued to sit, looking at Sam with prying eyes.

"Sam, I have another question, and you will probably think I be prying where I have no business, but I wants to know if you be the angel Mr. Morgan be looking for and if you be upset because he be knowing now that you are his angel."

Calling her "Sam" and not "child" alerted her to what Keowee might be asking, but Sam was not ready to tell all. Not wanting to lie but not knowing how to describe being the cussed man's angel, she decided to just tell all and let it be. Keowee waited, knowing Sam was trying to decide just how to answer, but she had no mind to leave the room until Sam gave her some kind of an answer.

"Keowee, I ask you to keep whatever I tell you a secret, for now. Will you promise?"

Keowee nodded her head.

"This man that I now know as Morgan Anderson appeared out of the darkness of night of May fifth. By the time I arrived on the veranda, the moonlight gave me enough light to see his Union-blue trouser leg. I tended to his wounds, after my hatred battled with my Christian teaching and my hatred lost the battle. I did not want anyone to know I was helping a Yankee, not even y'all. Hiding him those two days and nights, I was afraid that helping him would cause Riverbend to be burnt to the ground by the home guard. I was more afraid that if Yankees found him here wounded, they might kill us all. After Santee and Floyd ran into the Yankees looking for the cussed man, I put him on his horse and led him to the camp of Yankees after y'all were asleep. I had no knowledge he was a friend of Mr. Mac. If I had, I would have turned him over to you and Santee and washed my hands of him. I am still having trouble admitting to anyone that I aided a Yankee soldier, because I still feel I have, in some way, betrayed Papa, and I am ashamed." The last sentence was said with sadness.

Keowee sat in utter silence, wondering how on earth this child did all that she did and none of them were the wiser.

"Child, there be nothing for you to be ashamed of doing.

I knows your mama and papa, and they would be proud of you. You saved a good man's life. I just wish you had not carried this secret all by yourself. You should have come to me and Santee for help, knowing we's would have kept the secret of the Yankee being here, and we would have recognized Mr. Morgan."

"I know all that now. Keowee, if you feel you have to tell Santee, it will be all right, but please do not tell anyone else."

"Mr. Morgan done said he gonna introduce his angel to all of us."

"I heard him, but he does not know what I have just told you. He thinks he knows what he needs to know to identify me as his angel."

With Sam's last words, Keowee rose from the chair, satisfied that she now really knew what was keeping Sam quiet—whether or not to admit to Mr. Morgan just what she had told her. Leaving the room, Keowee stopped at the door.

"God bless you, Samantha Hatcher, for saving that Yankee soldier's life."

Sam smiled at Keowee's blessing and sat back in her window seat, hoping to unscramble all the thoughts running through her head and her web of emotions.

The ride to Hartwell took a little over an hour. Morgan had set a fast gallop, as they left the plantation, and they did not let up until they were inside the small town.

Reverend and Mrs. Henry welcomed the two men into their home and at once asked how Sam, Lovie, and the boys fared. At first, Morgan was a little taken aback by the inquiry, but he soon came to realize that the Henrys had known the family for a long time. Realizing this increased Morgan's confidence that Reverend Henry would be able to give him more information on William and Martha Hatcher. After several minutes of polite chitchat, Mrs. Henry excused herself to the kitchen to prepare some refreshments, and Morgan turned to Reverend Henry. "Reverend Henry, I have come seeking information. I hope you will be able to supply answers to some questions. First, I would like to know how William and Martha Hatcher became involved with Mac Sinclair. Also how the agreement came about, what the agreement was, and why Mac chose William Hatcher? Can you help me with any of this?"

"Yes, Morgan I think I can give you the answer you are looking for. I have known William and Martha Hatcher since they came to Hart County from South Carolina. The children were all born here. We respected William and Martha, counting them among our dearest friends." Pausing for a moment, the reverend began again.

"Mac, as you know, was a very wealthy man, with a big plantation and numerous slaves. Even before the first shot was fired, Mac expressed his opinions, stating openly his favor for seceding from the Union. During the forming of companies of men to fight, Mac badgered William about his refusal to join or, more to the point, to fight, with questions and comments. I never understood why Mac and Robert singled out William for their badgering and cannot say for sure what pointed Mac in

William's direction to be a substitute for Robert. It could have been because of William's reputation. You see, William was an expert marksman. He won most of the shooting events in and round the county. The marksmanship might have enticed Mac to want him to represent the family. I also do not know why Mac would not accept William's refusal at first. There were plenty of men in the area who would have jumped at being paid to join the Confederate Army. I do know that, from day one of the conscription law, Mac was a regular visitor to the Hatcher farm with offers. At first, William was not interested in becoming a part of the war. He also expressed his beliefs to Mac, as he did to everyone else."

The reverend went on, "The deciding factor I believe that caused William to agree to be a substitute for Robert was the care and welfare of his wife and children. Since it was a fact that he would, in time, be conscripted to fight and to leave his family alone, he chose to take Mac's offer of a substitute for Robert. He made it plain to Mac he would not take money for shooting his fellow Americans. The agreement stated that while William was serving in the army, Martha and the children would be seen after and that if a need arose that Martha could not handle, Mac would take care of the need. If he, William, was killed, this care would extend until the oldest boy reached manhood. He also included a request for the boys' education to continue.

The three men were silent after Reverend Henry concluded his answers to Morgan's questions. Morgan sat, still digesting Reverend Henry's statement. All that Reverend Henry explained halfway answered Morgan's questions, except for Robert's going to France. Mac's not allowing the children to eat with him told Morgan that Mac did not want them to be considered by the slaves as his equal, as well as giving them chores. Morgan thought to ask the reverend about this, but before he could ask his question, Mrs. Henry came through the door with a tray.

"I thought you gentlemen might be in need of some tea, after your ride from Riverbend. I also took the liberty to include my lemon squares. I am always asked to bring lemon squares to all our socials. Everyone here in our town loves them. I hope they are to your liking."

Morgan was not comfortable with questioning Reverend Henry in front of Mrs. Henry, so he remained quiet on his last question. He was glad Reverend Henry had not asked him for an explanation as to why he wanted this information. But it was well and good that he had not, for he was not sure he could have given a sound reason. He could not give himself one. There was something that kept nibbling at him, and he could not brush it off.

Morgan and Haygood enjoyed a pleasant visit with the lovable couple, while enjoying Mrs. Henry's famous lemon squares, but all good things have to come to an end, especially if they wanted to arrive back at Riverbend in time for the evening meal.

Wishing Mrs. Henry a pleasant evening and thanking her for her hospitality, Morgan and Haygood left the cozy home. The chance to ask the reverend about Mac's treatment of the children came, as he walked the pair to their horses. Morgan stopped before mounting, stuck out his hand, and as he shook the reverend's hand, Morgan thanked him for his information and mentioned Mac's treatment of the children.

"Reverend, I really do not have a sound reason for bothering you with my questions, but something keeps stirring me to dig into this, and there are a couple more questions."

"Would you have any idea why Mac would order Keowee to feed the children in the warming kitchen, refusing to allow the children to eat with him? Especially since he put forth such effort to get William to comply with his offer? I would also like to know a little more about Martha's death."

"I am sorry to say that I have known for some time that Mac Sinclair was a hard man, but I never dreamed he would be capable of mistreating the children, especially the children whose father was killed while fighting as a substitute for his son and who were left without a mother. As to Martha's death, the afternoon after hearing of William's death, she came with the children to Hartwell.

Her explanation was she wanted to confront the man she considered responsible for William's death. I do not know if she was referring to Mac, Robert Sinclair, or someone else. She never named the man. She left the children with Mrs. Henry and myself a little after sunset and walked to town. Later that night, we became concerned because of the lateness. I engaged a neighbor,

Doctor Webb, to accompany me on my search for Martha."

The memory of what they found filled Reverend Henry's mind, and his eyes filled with tears, so it took him a while to compose himself so he could continue, "We found Martha, after much searching, lying in the mule lot behind the Red Top Store. She was badly beaten and barely alive. She lived long enough to give birth to her son. The birth was early, caused by the beating. The baby was big and healthy and survived."

Thanking him again for his help, Morgan mounted Zeus for the return trip to Riverbend, but before Morgan and Haygood cleared the yard of the Henry home, Morgan heard his name being called.

Turning in his saddle, he saw the reverend hurrying toward them, and before he was abreast of Morgan's horse, Reverend Henry was speaking, "Morgan, I just thought of something. I do not know if it is important, but I felt strongly the necessity to tell you. Soon after William's and Martha's arrival in Hart County, William or Martha once mentioned, in a moment of conversation, that Martha's maiden name was Sinclair. Since that time, there was never any other mention of that by either William or Martha. You can be sure that if Mac was aware of this, he would never have mentioned she was a Sinclair before marriage. I am sorry I almost forgot this. I heard the statement so long ago, and it was said with so little to-do."

Hearing the reverend's confession, Morgan felt he was now truly onto something, and he could not wait until he could get Keowee and Santee alone and could ply them with questions. He again reached for the reverend's hand and shook the man's arm almost from his shoulder.

"Thank you," Morgan said. "I, too, do not know if there is a connection, but you have given me a lead to follow. Do not feel bad or apologize for not thinking of this earlier. This time, tardy is better than never. Thanks again, Reverend. You and Mrs. Henry, take care, and thank Mrs. Henry for her hospitality. Especially for the lemon squares."

With a salute, Morgan galloped past Haygood. Haygood recognized the look on Morgan's face; he had seen it before, and it reminded him of a hound dog holding a bone between his teeth he was unwilling to give up.

CHAPTER 22

As the former slaves and the Hatcher siblings prepared to sit down for the evening meal, galloping horses echoed in the warming kitchen. Not yet at ease with that sound, all widened their eyes in question. Floyd was the first to offer an explanation.

"No need to be alarmed. It is Morgan and Haygood returning from Hartwell; that's what we hear."

True to Floyd's words, the familiar laughter of the two men filled the air and flowed into the room. Soon, the two Yankees were scrubbing the bottom of their boots clean on the moss-covered brick whistling path.

"We made it,", were the first words out of Haygood's mouth upon the two men entering the room. Grinning, he slapped Morgan on the back.

After all were, seated, their heads bowed, and a prayer of thanks was offered to God for their food and a plea for continued blessings for all. After "Amen" was said,

Morgan asked to be excused along, with Haygood, so they could wash their face and hands before partaking of the food. Giggles and chuckles were heard around the table, as the two men exited the room almost as fast as they had entered.

As chairs were pushed away from the table, Sam asked,

"Yankee, could I impose on you for a moment or two of your time?"

Morgan's shock of Sam asking for his time was well-hidden behind a familiar grin that graced his face of late. "You are more than welcome to any and all of my time Sam." He stopped, then called her "Angel."

"Good. I would like to speak to you on a matter and thought to engage you in another walk." After stating her reason for speaking to him, Sam pushed back her chair and walked to the back door.

Morgan was quick to follow, and he soon was walking by Sam's side, but he did not speak, waiting for Sam to tell him what was on her mind. He hoped that she had used the afternoon to ponder the confession of his feelings and that she was now ready to speak freely of her emotions. Walking almost to the river, Morgan felt that whatever was on his angel's mind was probably going to be difficult for her to share with him.

"Yankee, I have two things to tell you. First, I feel I need to discuss the hatred that I have, and, second, I have decided to tell you something I think you want to know. First, I want your solemn promise not to reveal what I tell you to anyone, and that includes Haygood. Will you give me your word?"

Sam's asking for his word to keep secret what she told him concerned Morgan. He could not imagine what his angel could know that she would have to have his promise not to tell anyone else about it, but, no matter what she was ready to tell him, he would keep her secret.

"Sam, you can feel free to tell me anything, and I will always respect your privacy. Whatever you share with me today or in the future, I promise to keep to myself."

"If that means you won't tell anyone, here goes. With the happenings of late, I have had to adjust my thinking. I should have been able to discern and put my hate where it belonged all along. But! Never mind. The boys and I were taught by our parents to judge persons by what was inside them, not the color of their skin, the kind of clothes they wore, the house they lived in, or the amount of money they had. However, that teaching was blotted out by the pain and confusion of losing Papa and Mama

within a few hours. I am not trying to make excuses. Even before Robert kidnapped us, I had a couple of conversations withReverend Henry, and he reminded me what the Bible said about hate. I was struggling with his reminders before we were kidnapped. So, you see, I have had a lot on my mind." She smiled as she spoke those last words.

"Sweetlin', I cannot blame you for your hatred toward the Yankee Army. I know the pain of losing a parent, and I cannot comprehend the pain that came with the loss that you experienced. Since you were the oldest of four siblings, the responsibility of what was left of your family fell on your shoulders, which would have been hard for an adult to carry. Angel, you were not consumed by your hate. You proved that by saving the life of a soldier wearing the uniform of the army that killed your papa."

Taking her hand, he said, "Have I monopolized the conversation again? Please forgive me. Would there be more that you want to share?"

"To continue, I have come to terms with my hate. I think. Maybe I should say I know now that my hate was not aimed at a person. I hated the Union army. Some of my turmoil has been why I did not hate you or Haygood."

She hesitated for a moment, trying to decide how to proceed.

"I now know the focus of my hate. Not so much hating

a person but the cussed Yankee army. I also have to admit Robert Sinclair made me better understand it does not matter where a man is from, North or South; rather, it is what is in the man's heart. I have been occupied for days sorting all this out. As soon as I had a clear picture of my problem, I wanted you to know."

"I am happy you have all this settled in your mind and heart. Your confession or explanation does not surprise me, because I have never felt that you hate. I have only heard that you hated Yankees. I also know you felt no hatred toward me while you tended to my wounds. Your hands were too tender and your voice too soothing. The care I received from you could not have come from a person full of hate. Now that we have the hate all straightened out, we can talk about the two days and nights you tended to my wounds."

I knew the cussed man would get around to asking me about that before this day was over. I do not know if I am ready to tell him all of what he wants to know. He has tried to be patient, but everyone has a limit to the length of their patience. After walking to the end of the path and the edge of the river, she decided to start. How much she would be able to tell she did not know. But she began, pointing down the river.

"There is a granite bolder that is on the downriver side of the bend in the river. You might already know that, but you probably do not know there is a cave in the upper part of that bolder. I mention this because I thought you would like to know where you were hidden during the time of your absence from your men." Morgan interrupted Sam before she could continue.

"Are you telling me you carried me to that cave by yourself and hid me there while you tended to my wounds? How on earth were you able to do this? I know you do not lie, but what you are saying defies logic."

Sam had to smile at Morgan's disbelief.

"Your being hidden in a granite cave on a riverbank defies logic, yet your being completely sure I am your angel is logical?" That was Sam's only reply.

"I know you are my angel, and your telling me I was hidden in that cave does not change my mind. I only want to know how you managed the feat."

Sam was silent a long time, following Morgan's declaration.

"Me knowing where you were hidden does not show that I am your angel; it only shows that I am privy to where you were hidden."

Morgan was beginning to tire of her efforts to dissuade him she was his angel. This was not what he wanted.

"I had hoped that you used some of the afternoon to ponder the conversation in the parlor and that you would see things differently, hoping the Union-blue uniform I was wearing the night we met would become less damning after I opened my heart and laid bare my emotions and feelings for you. But I see that your hatred of the Yankee blue-uniformed army still rules. Does it not?"

"I cannot deny I still have unfriendly feelings toward the Union Army, but I thought I made myself clear as to not holding any hate for you. Did I not?"

Looking to the heavens, Morgan breathed a loud, long sigh. While Morgan's eyes were fixed on the sky, Sam walked to the stump she used often in May. Removing her shoes, she rolled her trouser legs up to her knees, but when Morgan looked back at the river, he found her standing. Sam pointed to the stump, saying, "Sit; take off your shoes and socks; and roll up your pants' legs to your knees. Yankee, I am going to show you how your angel got you to the cave."

Sam stepped into the water and waded out to the ledge and stopped, waiting for Morgan to join her. With Morgan walking behind her this time and not slumped over his horse, Sam led the way up the dirt bank to the entrance to the cave. After she found a candle and a flint, a dim candlelight lit the way to a straw mattress. Sam did not say a word; she stood watching Morgan searching

every inch outlined in candlelight. His eyes stayed for a long time on the pallet. When he finally turned to Sam, there was a look on his face of recognition, but more a look of disbelief.

"The last memory I have of that pallet is a pleasant, lingering memory. There are vague memories of the rest. It is hard for me to understand or believe you could have brought me here by yourself. I do not remember getting here."

"You still think I am your angel?"

"Sam, I do not *think* you are my angel. I feel that you are my angel. The only thing that has me questioning you is that I am a large man, and as far as I know, no one but you knows I was on Sinclair land."

"I am the only one that knows you spent two days and nights in this cave."

"Angel, won't you please admit to me what I already know? I have already promised to keep your secrets. I won't tell anyone that you have admitted having saved my life until you are ready for me to do so. Please."

Sam made an about-face and hurried from the cave, leaving Morgan in the dark. Hurrying, Morgan hoped to catch Sam before she entered the water and was bewildered to not see Sam in the river.

"I am here." The three words were all she could say at the moment, and she wondered why she had even spoken. Morgan turned to find Sam sitting on the ground, her back against the granite bolder, and before he spoke, he thought, *That is where she has spent a lot of her time of late while hiding from me.* That insight brought a question, *Has she spent her nights alone in that cave?* A solemn Morgan walked over and sat beside Sam. Taking her hand in his and bringing it to his lips, he placed a kiss on one of the hands that saved his life. Still holding her hand, he leaned back, resting against the granite bolder. Waiting.

All the unexplainable emotions started the moment the cussed man took her hand. *I need to know why this cussed man affects me this way and what I can do to stop the cussed feelings. Maybe the best person to ask is the one causing all this.* Her reasoning was seemingly logical. *I have always been told to go to the horse's mouth! So I will go to the cussed man.* However, she waited, trying to build up her courage to expose her problem.

Morgan could imagine the effect his kissing Sam's hand had on her, but he could not see her face. So he waited, hoping the kiss would bring a favorable response, but the moments were stretching and he was becoming impatient.

"All right, you cussed man, let's get this over with. I have questions, and you seem to be the one to seek answers from. Your holding my hand caused feelings I do not understand. I want to know why. Can you enlighten me?"

"Angel, I will start my answer with first explaining what happens when a man and a women are attracted to each other. This can happen at their meeting, or it can grow over time. The emotion of each can be turned upside down, and there can be confusion, especially if one or both have never been attracted to the opposite gender. Sometimes these feelings go away in a few days, and the man or woman is not affected any longer when seeing the person or hearing the person's voice. However, if the feelings continue indefinitely, these emotions will appear with each and every appearance of the person, with the sound of the person's voice or with the mention of the person's name. There is a reason for this affliction and a name for it. I am sorry to say there is no absolute cure, but there is a remedy that helps, and I feel I must tell you something before mentioning the remedy. I am knowledgeable of what you want answers to because I have been affected once or twice over the years, but, each time, only for a few days. I am glad to say this time that, for months, my emotions have been affected every time I think of a certain young lady; when I see her or if I get a chance to touch her, I experience the same feelings that you want explained, and there is a difference in this time than the others. All that I can tell you, sweetlin', is you are suffering from the same affliction as I. I have known for months that I was in love with my angel. Whether or not you want to accept the fact you are in love with this cussed Yankee, I do not know, but that is causing these unfamiliar feelings and your emotions being turned upside down."

Sam sat with her eyes widened and her mouth open. She was numb until her mind began to work, and she realized what the cussed man implied. *Me in love with this cussed man? Me in love with Morgan Anderson, a cussed Yankee? Never!* As the shock began to wear off, she was more confused than ever. Embarrassment would more accurately describe her mood now. *How am I going to be able to face the cussed man? Surely he does not think I am in love with him. Oh! Mercy me! He said he was in love with his angel. Me! God, my heavenly Father, help me. Please.* She continued to sit silently. For once in her life, she really did not know what to do. She felt like running, but it was her fault she was in the predicament, and common courtesy called for a polite parting.

"Thank you for your explanation; I will give it some

thought. Please excuse me." Sam was running by the time she finished speaking, and she stepped into the water with little hesitation.

Morgan was not surprised by Sam's hasty departure, even though he hoped the end to his truthful explanation would have a different ending. Taking a deep breath and leaning back against the boulder, he decided this was a good place to spend the evening.

Haygood was up with the crowing of old Red and ready for Keowee's hardy morning meal, and he hurried to Morgan's room. Tapping on the bedchamber door, he opened the door, expecting to find Morgan still in bed. To his surprise, the bed was not mussed, and there was no sign of Morgan. Not finding Morgan already up, dressed, and downstairs was not what Haygood wondered about. Rather, he wondered about the unmussed bed, and he stood unsure of what to do—whether to sound an alarm, using Sam's name, or go in search of the cussed Yankee.

Entering the warming kitchen, Haygood searched the area, but he found no Morgan. Spying Floyd and David already seated, he hurried to the boys. Gaining Floyd's attention with a tap on the shoulder, he nodded toward the outside door and left the table for the door. Floyd quickly followed, aware that Haygood was usually as eager for food as he.

"Have you seen Morgan or Sam this morning?"

Haygood's question opened Floyd's mouth as if to speak, but he stared with eyes wide and finally said, "Why do you ask?"

"Morgan is not in his room, nor has his bed been slept in. The last time I saw Morgan, he was leaving the kitchen with Sam. At Sam's request. Morgan did not return to the house before I retired. So have you seen either Sam or Morgan since the evening meal?"

"No, but I am not concerned. Sam keeps to herself most of the time while you and Morgan are visiting. I am sure she will make an appearance for the morning meal. As for Morgan, you know him better than I."

"Knowing the cussed Yankee is why I am disturbed. Could Sam have pushed him in the river or something?" This question amused Floyd, and, with a smile, he shook his head.

"Days ago, I would not have been surprised, but today I can say no. Morgan says Sam is his angel, and if she had wanted him dead, she would not have saved his life. Let's eat. They will show up."

Haygood liked Floyd's line of reasoning and followed the boy back into the kitchen.

True to Floyd's words, Sam sat at the table. But Morgan's chair was empty. One by one, the other members of the family were noticing Morgan's empty chair, but Sam did not comment on the empty chair. Floyd spoke up before Haygood could and added to everyone's interest with his find of an empty bed and room.

"Morgan does not seem to be in the house. Sam, did he mention anything to you last night about leaving the plantation?"

Sam's heart leaped at Floyd's statement of the cussed man not being in the house, and a whim of worry flashed through her, *Could the cussed man have fallen off the ledge and into the deep and fast-moving water and drowned? Surely he could swim.*

Not waiting to ask about and to receive an answer to her thought, Sam pushed her chair back from the table, just as the noise of the door opening from the back stairs hit her ears.

"Morning, everyone; please excuse my late arrival. I took an early-morning walk, and the time seemed to slip by without my notice. I hope I have not caused you an unnecessary wait beginning the meal?"

Looking at Sam as Morgan pulled his chair from the table, he saw on her face what he considered a countenance of worry. *Maybe there is hope for me after all, if my angel was feeling a bit of concern caused by my late arrival.*

Morgan spoke to Keowee and Santee, as he took his seat, "Would the two of you be able to spare me a few minutes of your time? I would appreciate you meeting me in Mac's study."

"Yes sir, Mr. Morgan; Santee and I will be glad to meet you in Mr. Mac's study," Keowee answered, as she shot Santee a questioning look.

Santee and Keowee were not the only ones to notice the hint of urgency in Morgan's request, and Sam's inquisitive nature was racing faster than the Yankees' horses coming from Hartwell before. Sam's mind filled with questions. One thing was sure: she would not be left out of this meeting.

She was part of this family, even if she was not blood kin to the Sinclairs. With that decision made, she told Santee and Keowee,

"I will be meeting Morgan in Mr. Mac's study with you. I have a right to know what he will be asking you to do or what questions he might want answered."

This was said in a tone of voice that Santee and Keowee recognized, and they knew Sam would definitely be in Mr. Mac's study to greet Mr. Morgan. Without a word, they each decided that if this was not to Mr. Morgan's liking, they'd let him deal with Sam.

Sure enough, Sam was sitting in the chair in front of Mr. Mac's large desk when Keowee and Santee entered the study, and she'd pulled so close her knees were almost touching the desk. Santee and Keowee smiled at her ploy, knowing that if

Mr. Morgan did as he had in the past, he wouldn't be sitting behind Mr. Mac's desk. Keowee considered telling Sam this, but, here again, she thought to wait and to let Mr. Morgan handle Sam.

The three did not have long to wait. Trying to hid the grin that covered his face upon spying Sam, Morgan placed a hand over his mouth and faked a cough; gaining his composure, he spoke, "Sam, your presence is welcomed. Be assured I would have spoken to you about these issues after talking with Santee and Keowee, but you are indeed welcome to stay. Your joining us may help find the answers I seek more quickly."

Taking a chair from across the room, Morgan placed it to the left of Keowee and motioned for Sam to turn her chair to face the black couple. He wanted to bring her to his left. Morgan did not hide the grin that spread across his face at Sam's bewildered look when he failed to sit at Mac's desk.

Turning to Santee and Keowee, Morgan said, "I am sure you knew of Mac's desire for a substitute for Robert. Although Mac was 100 percent for war, he would not have wanted his only son in harm's way."

Santee answered by nodding his head, and Morgan continued, "Reverend Henry was not certain why Mac chose William, but he speculated the fact that William was a marksman could have been the reason." Again turning to Sam, he continued, "Sam, your father did not want to be involved in that war, as you know. However, during the first half of 1862, the Southern government

enacted a conscription law that made it mandatory for all able-bodied men to become soldiers in their army. The law also had a clause that entitled a man to pay a substitute. Robert's having a substitute did not whet my curiosity. What bothered me was why Robert found it necessary to hightail it to France." Turning to Santee, he directed a question to him, "Santee, on the night Robert left Riverbend, did you see any blood on Robert's clothing or hands? Any sign that he could have been in a fight?"

"No, Mr. Morgan; I was called from my bed, and Mr. Mac was in a fit, shouting at Mr. Robert and giving me orders. Mr. Robert was walking around like a crazed man. I didn't take a good look at him, and I can't say for sure."

"Morgan." Sam almost whispered the name, but Morgan heard her loud and clear. Even in the seriousness of the moment, he smiled. She did not call him "Yankee" or "cussed man," but, for the first time, she called him "Morgan." He waited for her to ask her question.

"Did Robert leave Riverbend the night my mother died, and do you think his leaving has something to do with her death?"

Keowee's groan shattered the silence that followed Sam's questions, but Morgan never took his eyes off Sam, as he nodded his head.

His desire to take her in his arms as her tears threatened to flow was almost more than he could resist. Keowee was up and out of her chair before Morgan could say a word, kneeling before Sam and throwing her arms around her hurting baby. Santee was the first to speak.

"Mr. Morgan, you be thinking Mr. Robert had something to do with Miss Martha's death? That be right, ain't it?"

Morgan waited a few minutes before he answered Santee, but knew he had to continue, so he nodded his head again, as he said, "Yes, Santee; I haven't been able to find another reason for him to leave Riverbend and Mac. In 1862, the South was doing well in the war, and things here would have still been to Robert's liking. Your description of Mac's temper that night and his rush to get Robert away from the plantation tells me there was something very bad that Robert was mixed up in—something Mac was not sure he would be able to keep Robert out off. Martha Hatcher's death is the only thing that happened at that time. The children being brought to Mac the next morning proved to me that Martha's death occurred the night Robert left Riverbend."

Sam spoke up, after Morgan ended his sentence, "We received the news of Papa's death, and Mama, me, and the boys left our farm at noon the next day for Reverend and Mrs. Henry's home. Mama was determined to find the man she said was responsible for Papa's death, and she left the Henrys' home after dark for town. Mama was found in the mule lot in town, and we were brought here the following morning. She had been beaten and bloodied. I heard Dr. Webb say a man had to have beaten her because the lot was empty of mules and horses. At the time, I did not know whom she wanted to find. Now I know, as you know, Morgan. She was looking for Robert Sinclair. He killed Mama with his own hands, and Papa died because he was at Manassas instead of Robert. I have hated and blamed Yankees all this time for nothing. I should have aimed by hatred closer to home. Thank you, Morgan, for uncovering the truth."

Keowee sat with her arms around Sam the whole time she was telling of her mother's tragic death; her voice was soft as raindrops on rose petals, but the listeners felt the hard, utter anguish caused by the evil wrong that had been committed that night. The air was thick with unspoken words, as the room became quiet. A dropped pin would have sounded like thunder. Keowee, heavy in heart, returned to her chair, and Santee was absorbing all that Morgan and Sam had said and was beginning to agree it all made sense. Mr. Robert could have been guilty of killing Miss Martha. Of course, no one saw him beat Miss Martha. All this was running through his mind, when Keowee spoke.

"Mr. Morgan, I have something to say. You might say I's gonna put another rock on Mr. Robert's grave. I be the one what saw the clothes Mr. Robert had on that night before he dressed to leave Riverbend. They had blood on 'em. I found 'em in his room that next morning. I told Mr. Mac the clothes were bloody, and I asked if I should get old Markie to see if she could wash the blood out. But Mr. Mac said I was to burn the clothes, and that's what I done."

Shaking his head, Santee added, "There be nothing else but that Mr. Robert beat Miss Martha and she died from his beating. God have mercy on his soul."

"Yes, Santee," Morgan said. "I am sure that's why Mac was in such a hurry for Robert to flee to France. But I cannot understand why Robert would have attacked the lady. The agreement between Mac and William was legal, and Mac would have kept his half of the bargain. I know Robert was a coward, showing his temper to blacks, lowly females, or weaklings. He loved to show his authoritative cruelty sometimes. I never knew him to act that way with a white lady. There had to have been something she threatened him with, or she had something that would have set him off. Could it have had something to do with the Sinclair name? Did either of you know that Martha's maiden name was Sinclair? If so, was there a connection to Mac and Robert?"

"Who told you my mama's maiden name was Sinclair?" Sam asked. "There is no way she could have been kin to Mr. Mac and that lowlife, Robert. She and Papa met and married in South Carolina. I know this because she told me. There is no way my mama's maiden name was Sinclair."

CHAPTER 23

The silence in the study of the deceased owner lingered, as the tick of the passing minutes sounded loudly from the clock on the mantle. Morgan's eyes remained glued on the housekeeper of Riverbend. He was confident that if anyone knew the answer to his last question, it would be Keowee. Sam fidgeted angrily in her chair, not understanding why the cussed man did not accept her explanation that her mother came from South Carolina and that her name could not possibly have been Sinclair. Santee sat beside Keowee, knowing the pain he and Keowee would feel having to say the words that would answer Mr. Morgan's question in front of Sam. Keowee was silently asking God to be with Sam, as she gave the information she was sure Mr. Morgan wanted.

Morgan's patience was coming to an end, and he was sure all the facts had not as yet been uncovered. Taking a deep breath, he broke the silence. "Keowee, please tell what was behind this quandary of evil plots orchestrated over the years by Mac's family; get it out in the open. I believe we need to give Sam and the boys all the facts pertaining to their family's tragedy. I understand your wanting to remain silent regarding certain events, because you are afraid you would put more pain on them. But you know that even though the truth may hurt, as you expect, in the end, it can bring a comforting understanding."

Keowee wiped her eyes with the scrap of clean cloth she always carried in her apron pocket, and, with a soft, trembling voice, she began. "Mr. Morgan, I's been on this plantation since birth. In the old days, we's knowed to keep our mouths shut about the happenings of the master and the mistress. We's mostly kept what we heard or saw to ourselves. Mr. Ulric was the father of Mr. Mac, as you know. Have you ever heard of Mr. Silas?" Morgan answered by shaking his head, not wanting to stop Keowee from speaking.

"The story from the old people what was here before I be born was two brothers, Mr. Silas and Mr. Ulric, came to this part of the country while the Cherokees still roamed the land. Mr. Silas was said to be the oldest, but each one of the brothers came with two hundred acres of land grants. In time, they bought a few slaves, mostly male. As the land produced and the men prospered, they bought more slaves. Santee's mother, my mother, and my papa were among that group. The brothers also bought more land and slaves, and more land was added, as the years went by. As they watched babies being born to the slaves, they began to talk about wives and children to share their good fortune. Neither man had family. According to Mama, Mr. Ulric began to seek a wife in 1805. Mr. Ulric left the plantation during that year and returned to the plantation several weeks later with a wife in tow. Miss Elizabeth was a spinster from Louisiana."

After taking a breath, Keowee went on, "Her family had fallen on hard times, and she had no expectation of receiving an offer of marriage, so she accepted an arranged marriage with Mr. Ulric. Miss Elizabeth was no beauty. She was somewhat plain, but Mr. Ulric seemed to be pleased with the match, and, in 1808, Mr. Mac was born. Mr. Silas helped his brother enlarge the house, and all was pleasant and congenial between the three. The brothers owned a number of slaves, but as the years went by, they needed more. Mr. Silas left the plantation late in 1811, this time for Savannah, to buy more slaves. Although Mr. Silas was the older of the two, he was also the better looking. Mr. Silas returned with a wagonload of slaves, along with an indentured white woman he bought with his money, as a gift for Miss Elizabeth. He thought the indentured woman could take some of the responsibility of running the house, giving Miss Elizabeth more time to spend with Mr. Mac. She was a little older than Miss Elizabeth, not quite as tall and slimmer, with long, curly, reddish-brown hair and big, green eyes."

Taking another breath, Keowee continued, "My mama said Miss Elizabeth formed a dislike for Miss Corrine from the start, even though Mr. Silas had bought Miss Corrine to be a help to her. It was plain from the start that Miss Corrine was taken with Mr. Silas, even though he was a good many years older than she, and it was not long, Mama said, till the feelings were the same for the two. Mr. Silas married Miss Corrine over the objections of Mr. Ulric and Miss Elizabeth. Not only did Miss Elizabeth object to the marriage; she also refused to allow them to live in her house. Miss Elizabeth's behavior caused a split between the brothers, and nothing was ever the same. Mr. Silas's heart was good, and the trouble over his marriage weighed heavily on him, but he built a nice house, smaller than Miss Elizabeth's, down about where the quarters end. Mr. Silas was maybe around fifty when Miss Martha was born. A prettier baby you've never seen, and Mr. Silas was the happiest man this side of heaven. In addition to the new baby for Miss Corrine and Mr. Silas, a man with reddish-brown hair, more red than brown, rode up one day, looking for his older sister by the name of Corrine. The man visited with the happy couple and the six-month-old baby for a few days before leaving for his land in South Carolina. Three weeks to the day after Mr. Thomas left for South Carolina, Mr. Silas and Mr. Ulric were clearing more land down the river, and a large tree jumped the stump, crushing Mr. Silas. A month after Mr. Silas was buried, Miss Corrine was told she was no longer welcome at Riverbend. Mr. Ulric did, however, arrange passage for Miss Corrine and Miss Martha to Miss Corrine's brother in South Carolina. Half of the plantation belonged to Mr. Silas, and, by rights, half should have gone to Miss Corrine and Miss Martha. But Miss Elizabeth's greedy jealousy and Mr. Ulric's doing her bidding robbed Mr. Silas's wife and child of their share."

The silence that followed Keowee's tale of begrudging greed, jealousy, and thievery had a life of its own, leaving the occupants of the room gasping for air. Sam was dumbfounded to hear her mother was part owner of Riverbend. Her earlier fidgeting stopped when she heard that she had a grandfather named Silas Sinclair and that Grandmother Corrine was really Corrine Sinclair. Keowee's description of Corrine could have been a description of Sam's mother. By the time Morgan found his voice, Sam's awe over hearing of her ancestors was turning to anger at the treatment of Corrine and her mother.

"Keowee, I take it there are now no documents that would prove Silas to be part owner of Riverbend. The documents were probably destroyed years ago."

"You can be sure that Miss Elizabeth, Mr. Ulric, and Mr. Mac did not leave anything what could be used to make them let go one inch of Riverbend."

"If that is true, why were Mac and Robert so afraid of

Martha and William as to get rid of them?" Morgan asked. No one noticed Sam leaving the study, but their attention focused on her when she arrived back into the study. "I believe there may be something in here that may be helpful," she said, as she handed her mother's Bible to Morgan and explained, "Papa told me to keep Mama's Bible safe, that it would be useful if something were to happen to him."

After hearing of William's charge to Sam, a charge he expected her to obey, Morgan became very interested in Martha's Bible.

"Sam," he asked, "have you inspected the book? Have you looked for pages glued together that could hold important papers or something?"

All Sam could do was shake her head in response to Morgan's question at the moment. She was hopeful that Morgan would find whatever her papa wanted her to have, yet she was afraid to know what the Bible would hold. She knew in her heart that whatever was hidden in the Bible was what got her mama and her papa killed.

She was filled with seething anger, as she paced the floor of the study, wanting to scream and to demolish the very house she occupied—to destroy all that was Mac's and Robert's precious Riverbend. Sam was oblivious to the others in the room, and no one noticed the tempest raging in her.

The former slaves sat quietly resting. Morgan was occupied with a careful examination of the Bible. But the peaceful quiet was interrupted by the cussed man's shout, "I've found something." The shout shook the rafters.

CHAPTER 24

Morgan' loud words stopped Sam in her tracks, rousted Keowee and Santee from their rest, and alerted the remaining household that something in the study needed their attention. Sam stood motionless in the spot where her feet landed, upon hearing Morgan's shout. Keowee and Santee, shaken from their sleep by the shout, sat in their chairs, eyes wide with shock. Morgan hurried to Mac's desk, needing a place to work on his find. Laying the Bible on the desktop, he began removing the stitching around the edge of the Bible. With the back cover free of the stitching, he pulled the material from the Bible, revealing paper yellow with age. Quickly he pulled the cover back into place and turned the Bible to remove the stitching from the front of the it. With the cover free of thread, he gently removed the whole cover, and the papers were free to be examined.

Scanning the papers he found hidden between the outer cover and the Bible, he hardly noticed the abrupt opening of the door or Floyd's and Haygood's hurried entrance into the room.

Finding Morgan bent over Mac's desk, intensely interested in papers spread out on the desk, Floyd and Haygood quickly looked at Sam, Santee, and Keowee.

The stunned expressions on their three faces quickly increased the pair's curiosity.

"Sam, why do you have that funny look on your face?" Floyd asked. Receiving no answer from Sam, Floyd approached the desk and Morgan, and, in a louder voice, he asked, "What's the hollering about? Does it have something to do with those papers you are reading?"

Floyd's voice being louder than usual brought Morgan's attention to the two new arrivals and gave movement to Sam's feet.

Sam came to stand beside her brother, as Morgan raised his head and stared at the boy.

Sam added to her brother's question, "Morgan, have you found something that you think explains why Papa and Mama were killed?"

Sam's referring to Martha as having been killed caused Floyd to do some hollering of his own. "What do you mean Mama killed?"

Floyd's agonizing cry got Morgan's and Sam's attention, but, at the moment, neither were able to give him an answer.

"Morgan, Sam, answer me!" Floyd yelled, with tears beginning to roll down his cheeks. "Answer me now!"

Sam threw her arms around her brother and pulled him close and looked to Morgan with pleading eyes.

Morgan drew in a deep breath and hesitated only a moment before answering, "Mac and Robert were afraid that your mother had legal papers, these papers, in her possession and that she and your papa might use them. The fear of what these papers could do to them and Riverbend was why they chose William to be Robert's substitute. I cannot prove without a doubt that was the reason, but it is very suspicious when they approached no other man and they hounded William until he agreed. The night after receiving news of William's death and out of her mind with grief, Martha sought Robert in town. Finding him, she probably threatened to use these papers, and Robert, in a fit of rage, attacked your mother, beating her almost to death. We know he beat someone the night your mother died, and we know he left the plantation in a hurry that same night on his way to France. Keowee found his bloody clothes the morning after he left. There was no other reason that I can find for Robert to leave Riverbend in a panic, much less leave the country. There were no other deaths, but Martha's."

Floyd listened to Morgan quietly and calmly, but he was not satisfied with what he had heard, and he said, "You have told me who you think beat Mama and that those papers you have were the reason, but you have not said what the papers are. Why are they so important that Mr. Mac would send Papa to war and that Robert would beat Mama?"

Morgan again took in a deep breath before answering, "Floyd, your grandfather was Silas Sinclair, brother to Mac's father, Ulric Sinclair." Sam nodded her head, as Floyd turned his eyes on her, and she tightened her arms around his shoulders. Morgan continued, "These papers give half ownership of Riverbend to Silas's descendants."

Morgan, Haygood, Santee, and Keowee waited, without speaking, to see Floyd's reaction. Sam knew how Floyd's mind worked and knew it would take more time than he needed to come to terms with the reason for their loss and to understand the significance of all Morgan's words. She was also sure Floyd would soon find his peace with their family history. Squeezing Floyd hard, she turned to Morgan and asked, "Morgan, will you explain to us what each of these papers mean?"

Keowee offered, "I wouldn't be surprised to know 'em two

men, Mr. Mac and Mr. Robert, visited Miss Martha's and Mr. William's home when they not be at home, looking for them papers. Mr. Mac probably visited after

Mr. Robert left, still trying to find 'em papers. I's know Miss Martha telling Mr. Robert she had 'em is what got her killed. You can be sure Mr. Mac went back there later and looked for 'em."

Santee offered, agreeing with Keowee, "You be right, Keowee. Mr. Mac would have looked for 'em papers till the day he died. You can also be sure of another thing: none of 'em Sinclair people of Riverbend lived peaceable, afraid 'em papers was somewhere they couldn't get 'em. Not Mr. Ulric, not Miss Elizabeth, not Mr. Mac, and not Mr. Robert. They worried about 'em papers every day they lived. Mr. Robert's still worrying about 'em. The poor, greedy people."

Morgan agreed with both Keowee and Santee. Their opinions proved once again the insight the two former slaves had of the workings of the minds of the past masters and mistresses of Riverbend The clock on the mantel struck the hour, and the chime of each hour registered in Morgan's mind the lateness of the day, and he suggested, "We need to postpone further discussion of the papers until after the midday meal."

Morgan carefully picked up the three sheets of paper, folded them,and placed them in the Bible. Then he left the room. Haygood followed Morgan.

Sam and Keowee again found Lovie in the keeping room, with the midday meal started, and soon the aroma was filling the room and the yard, making the menfolk anxious to put their feet under the table. The food was eaten with pleasure, but with little conversation. Lovie was bursting with curiosity; Sam and Floyd were anxious to return to Mr. Mac's study. No one again paid any attention to the lack of the usual talking and laughing.

As forks were placed and chairs pushed back, Morgan, Haygood, Santee, and the boys left for the yard, giving the womenfolk space to clean up the table before heading back to Mr. Mac's study.

Soon, Mr. Mac's study was again occupied. The same people who left for a midday meal were anxious to hear what the papers found in Martha's Bible could mean to their lives. Morgan hesitated again, which was unusual for him. He was one who came to the point of any meeting right away. But the people in this room were dear to his heart. What he discussed with them this afternoon would have a bearing on their lives.

Haygood noticed Morgan's behavior and wondered why he was deviating from his usual pattern. However, not wanting to rile the old man, he sat patiently for the explanation of the papers. Sam was also concerned by Morgan's fidgeting. He looked at one sheet and then at another. Floyd was the one to break the silence.

"Morgan, are you not as sure about the importance of those papers as you were earlier? Has something suspicious caught your eye?"

CHAPTER 25

Morgan's reply was directed to Floyd. "No, Floyd, there is nothing irregular about the papers. I was just reflecting on what these papers mean and how the contents could change the future for you and your siblings. How old are you Floyd?"

Sam asked, "Just what does Floyd's age have to do with these papers?"

"Please, Sam, just be patient a few more minutes. Before I proceed, I need to know the Floyd's age."

"I was seventeen this summer," Floyd admitted.

"Thank you, Floyd. I was hoping you were a few years older, but, knowing Sam is nineteen, I should have been able to calculate your age. Now to the papers you all need to hear about. As you might suspect, the papers are old. One in particular is quite old. The first paper I will explain dates back to the late seventeen hundreds. It is

Silas's land grant for two hundred acres, half of the acres that made up what began Riverbend Plantation. It is proof that he owned at least two hundred acres of this plantation at that time. The second paper, a deed to Riverbend, is dated January 27, 1803, and it states that the brothers owned equal shares of the plantation, including all buildings and improvements. This paper shows that Silas not only contributed two hundred acres to the beginning of this plantation but that he was also as responsible as Ulric for its growth and was equal owner of all that is Riverbend Plantation. The third paper is Silas's will, and it is dated September 16, 1822. The will gives his portion of Riverbend, at his death, as a right of dower to his wife, Corrine, and his daughter, Martha."

After Morgan finished explaining the three papers, no one in the room spoke for several minutes, and some were hardly breathing. Sam's curiosity was working, even at a time like this, and she finally spoke, softly and almost in a whisper, "What is a dower?" Morgan grinned, not surprised that Sam was the first to speak and that her words would be in a form of a question, and he replied, "The law does not allow women to own property in their name. Property can be given to a girl or a woman in a right of dower. Her right of dower can be sold to a male member of her family to hold in ownership or to be used at her marriage, as a dowry, passing the property to her husband, giving him ownership. There is no paper stating that Corrine ever sold her right of dower to Ulric. You can be sure that, had she done this, there would not have been a pressing need by Mac and Robert to get their hands on these papers. Corrine never remarried. These papers also entitled Martha to a right of dower and a right to give ownership of her half of Riverbend to her husband, William."

"You mean our papa could have owned half of this plantation all this time and he never made a claim to his share?" Floyd asked.

Before Morgan could give Floyd an answer, Sam offered, "Mama would not have wanted him to do that. She would not have wanted any part of this plantation while Papa lived. Keeping these papers hidden and out of Sinclair hands was her way of getting even with the Sinclair family for their greedy treatment of her mama. At Papa's death and in her grieving mind, the only way she had of making them pay for his death was to claim her share of this plantation, the only thing this line of the family held dear."

"You are right Sam," Floyd agreed, while nodding his head.

"Mama never wanted anything but us, Papa, and our farm. Having Papa and her children around was all she needed to make her happy. She had none of the Sinclair greed in her."

The two eldest children of Martha and William Hatcher embraced and let their tears of loss and admiration of their mama wash their faces. Keowee watched Sam and Floyd, hoping to the depth of her heart that the coming years would be kinder to the children of Martha Sinclair Hatcher. Morgan waited for Sam and Floyd to gain their composure before speaking again, but he finally informed them, "Sam, the reason I asked earlier about Floyd's age was that I was hoping he would be old enough to be given ownership of Martha's share of the plantation, but since you are the oldest, your mother's share will come to you as a right of dower. If, for some reason, you would not want anything to do with the ownership of dower of your mother's share of the plantation, I would suggest you sell your dower to Robert. However, considering his future, along with his lack of money, that would not be possible. You can hold your share of this property in a right of dower until you are married, or you can wait until Floyd is of age, selling the dower to him for a price of only a dollar. That would grant Floyd ownership. There is also an another factor to consider. Robert will surely be sent to the gallows, and there are no other relatives but you four, so the remaining share of Riverbend will also be yours, unless he wills his share to a male friend, just to keep you from owning all of Riverbend."

"Are you not forgetting something, Mr. Anderson?" Sam

asked. "You paid the back taxes on this plantation. Am I not correct in knowing that gives you ownership of Riverbend until you are reimbursed for your payment?

And, as you just stated, Robert Sinclair is in no way able financially or otherwise to pay you or anyone else. Without sounding flippant by stating the obvious, neither Floyd nor I have the means by which to repay you. Therefore, even though these papers have been found, they mean absolutely nothing to us in regard to ownership of any part of Riverbend. However, might you be able to enlighten us regarding our ability to regain our father's farm?" So did Sam boldly ask Morgan, after reminding him of his ownership of the plantation.

Morgan mentally shook his head, after hearing Sam reminding him of the payment of back taxes. He knew, at once, that Keowee must have told her of his intent to pay the back taxes in order to keep the plantation from being sold. Sam was not only smart; evidently, she also never forgot anything. Then Morgan spoke, "I could tell Sam that that act of kindness was not done for Robert Sinclair, but for Keowee, Santee, and Lovie to be able to remain on the plantation, along with the boys. I would be tempted to tell her just that, if I thought that, hearing that reason, she would not refer to me anymore as 'Mr. Anderson' or as 'the cussed Yankee' but that she would use my given name when addressing me."

"Lordy, child," Keowee pleaded. "You can't be thinking of leaving here? Mr. Morgan, tell her it ain't safe for her and 'em boys to live anywhere but here, where there is some protection."

Morgan saw Sam was steeling herself to argue with Keowee, and he spoke before she could say a word. "Keowee is right, Sam, all over the South, people, especially older adults, are being forced off their land. Women who are left without a father, a brother, or a husband are faring the worst."

"See, honey child, the safest place right now is still right here with Santee and me. We's done good. You, Floyd, and Santee has been able to keep food growing. Santee with his trapping and the boys with their fishing keeps us in meat. There be no need for y'all to go back to Mr. William's farm."

"Keowee," Sam said, having waited for the cussed man to say his piece and for the reminder by Keowee of their ability to keep food on the table. She stated her reason for leaving the plantation: "Have you not thought that the new owner will be looking for a buyer for Riverbend? Mr. Anderson will not want to remain in the South and to take care of an overgrown, nonproducing plantation. You and the rest will have no difficultly remaining here with a new owner, but the four of us will need to find a new place to call home. Hopefully, we can return to our home. Floyd, David, and I can work enough ground to feed us, plus to have a little to sell or to bargain with. You and Santee have taught us well. We will be able to manage."

Morgan had heard all that he was going to hear without putting his foot down. "Young lady, you will not leave this plantation, no matter how well you think you and the boys will fare. What kind of a man do you think I am to sell Riverbend, causing you and the boys to have to leave and to put Keowee, Santee, and Lovie in the care of strangers?" Taking a deep breath and trying to calm his anger, Morgan hesitated just a moment, and Sam took advantage of his pause.

"The kind of man you are has nothing to do with the fact you are from the North. Your home is in the North. Your stepmother lives in the North. All of your ties are in the North. Not to mention why, on God's green earth, would you choose to remain in the South, much less to be shouldered with the responsibility for us. You have only become acquainted with Floyd, David, and Lemuel in the past few months. The debt you may have felt for my having removed a rifle ball and a little lead from your flesh has been paid in full. You owe the Hatcher siblings nothing." Her last few words came at a cost, making tears fill her eyes, and she spun around, leaving the room quickly. Sam did not turn from Morgan fast enough. He glimpsed the dampness in her eyes, and he knew the reason she had fled from the room. Morgan spoke to no one, nor did he linger in the study. He climbed the stairs two at a time and took hold of Sam's arm, just as she reached for the latch on her bedchamber door.

Sam knew, without looking, that the hand on her arm belonged to Morgan, and she struggled to remove her arm from his grip. The more she struggled, the tighter Morgan's hold became, causing her to turn to look him in the face and to demand that he remove his hand.

One glimpse of the anguish etched on Sam's face and in her eyes was all Morgan needed. He pulled her to him, before she could utter a word, and he folded his arms tightly around her. He whispered, "Please, sweetlin', don't cry any more. There is a way to work this out. You and I need to talk about this in private. Will you trust me, knowing that I will do everything in my power to see to the welfare of you and the boys? Please trust me Sam. Let me take some of the responsibility for the boys you carry off your shoulders. My shoulders are bigger than yours."

Sam's face lay buried in the right side of Morgan's chest, just below his shoulder. She had not moved since he pressed her against his body with unyielding arms. The strength of his embrace afforded Sam little room for movement, but the words of endearment, whispered in the husky, emotional voice of the cussed man, erased all thoughts at the moment of leaving his arms. The security she felt in his strong, masculine arms was a comfort she had not felt since the morning her father had left the Hatcher farm in June of 1862.

Sam's right cheek was now laid against the wet cloth of the cussed man's shirt, a shirt wet by her tears. Sam's slight movement alerted Morgan to the strength by which he held her. Loosening his hold a tiny bit, he allowed Sam to raise her head so she could look him in the eyes, but not enough to allow her to escape his arms. Because Sam's head was now raised and because her tear-wet face was just inches from his, there was only one thing for Morgan to do. Once again, he lowered his head an inch or two and covered those tear-wet lips with his hungry lips.

Before Sam could say the words that were forming in her mind, her mouth was covered. Having been kissed before, she knew there was no mistaking the feel of this hard male mouth pressing on her lips. There was no doubt that they were the lips of the same culprit, her cusse Yankee. The same feelings she had experienced with the other kiss returned, and before she could resist or form a rational thought, she was kissing Morgan as passionately as he was kissing her.

Sam may not have been aware that she was kissing Morgan as fervently as Morgan was kissing her, but Morgan was certainly aware. Once again, Morgan's arms tightened around Sam, holding her firmly against him. The kiss lasted until they both were gasping for breath; then, their lips parted. Neither spoke; rather, they lingered in their embrace, gazing into each other's eyes, both of them lost in the moment.

Sam, confused and unable to form words, could only look into Morgan's eyes. Morgan, too satisfied to mar the mood with words, smiled and waited for Sam to come to terms with what had happened.

Coming to her senses and preferring not to remain in

Morgan's arms and not to converse with the cussed man, Sam pushed against Morgan's chest. Not yet ready to let her go, Morgan kept his arms taut. She was unable to gain her release from this awkward situation, as she was hoping, and an emotion she had felt only one other time in her life filled her. A sense of helplessness possessed her. Sensing a change in Sam's body, Morgan ordered, "Sam, look at me." Seeing a helpless Sam unable to speak touched Morgan's heart.

"Angel, would you like for me to release you? If so, there is no need for distress. All you need to do is ask, and I will let you go," he explained. "Please do not ever be afraid of me. Please know that I would never hurt you, but the feel of you in my arms was so wonderful and right that I held you too long. I apologize, and should I have the pleasure of holding you again, I promise I will try to be more sensitive to your feelings. If I have not frightened you too awfully much, will you be comfortable taking a walk with me now? I feel I need to discuss more fully some different views on dealing with the papers I found."

Sam's ability to speak returned. She was now ready to let him know what she thought about his ability to hold her against her will. "I was not frightened of you. You could not have kept me held in your arms much longer. You would have tired in time and released me. When you did, I would have opened the door to my bedchamber and entered. There would have been no way you could have kept me from doing so."

Morgan offered no reply, but, quickly, before Sam could react, he simply slid his left arm down her right side, beneath her knees, picked her up into his arms, and walked down the stairs. Reaching the entrance hall, they met Haygood and Floyd. Morgan simply motioned with his head to the front doors, and the two gladly opened the doors. By the time they stepped onto the veranda, Sam gained her voice, but laughter hindered her from speaking an objection to the cussed man's actions, because they had struck her funny bone.

"May I hope the laughter is your way of telling me that you would rather that I carried you on our walk than make you walk," Morgan said, around his chuckles.

Sam shook her head in reply to Morgan's question, her laughter preventing her from answering verbally. Gaining her feet and patting the shirt of her dress down, she admitted, "All you proved is that you are stronger than me," and before Sam could finish her sentence, Morgan once again picked her up.

Offering a rebuttal, Morgan said, "If that admission is your way of telling me that you enjoy being in my arms—if that is so—from now on, all you have to say is, 'Morgan, will you please put your arms around me?'"

Sam forgot that they had an audience, until she heard Haygood and Floyd's laughter. Because she was embarrassed by Floyd's and Haygood's witnessing their behavior, the wee temper she was famous for was riled again, and the tone of her voice revealed to one and all how she felt, as she said, "You cussed Yankee, put me down this minute, and stop your shenanigans."

Morgan did not at first do as Sam asked. He put his mouth next to her ear and whispered, "I could really give them something to witness. I could kiss you again. I know I'd rather do that, but should you say, 'Please put me down— '"

"Morgan, will you please put me down?" Sam said, before Morgan could say another word.

This time, loud chuckles came from Morgan, as he placed Sam on her feet, but he did not let her go. He took her hand in his and led her down the veranda steps, beginning the walk he wanted to have before the evening meal.

Haygood and Floyd were left on the veranda, exhibiting smiles and shaking their heads. Floyd was dumbfounded by Sam's and Morgan's behavior. Sam's actions were more baffling than Morgan's, at first, but as he thought more on what he had seen and heard, he was sure there was something wrong with both. Haygood was pretty sure he knew exactly what was taking place. Morgan had not only found his angel, but the need to find her was also more than to say thank you for saving his life. It was heartwarming for Haygood to see the old man's teasing of years past and the old man's showing the right kind of attention to a beautiful lady.

Floyd, still scratching his head in disbelief, turned to Haygood and asked, "Why are Morgan and Sam acting so strange? Do you think they might be getting sick or something?"

Haygood's loud burst of laughter puzzled Floyd further, and his answer didn't help much.

"Floyd, has anyone mentioned to you about the birds and bees? If not, I can see how you might be surprised and a little concerned by what we had just witnessed. However, I assure you that the sickness affecting those two is not a disease people usually die from."

CHAPTER 26

The pair walked hand in hand down the footpath leading from the time-ravaged house to the west bank of the Savannah River in complete silence. Morgan gave Sam's wee temper time to cool. Sam was dealing with the memory of Morgan's hands, arms, and lips of a moment ago and was too embarrassed by the memory to even look at the cussed man, much less to speak to him. So they continued to walk in silence, each with their own reason for remaining quiet. The only distractions were Sam's slight attempts several times to remove her hand from Morgan's hand. Determined not to let go of Sam's hand, Morgan would increase the strength of his hold a tiny bit with each attempt, but he would relax his hold once she let her hand lie gently in the fold of his fingers. Sam finally realized the cussed man was not going to let go of her hand, but she wondered if he was as affected by the touch of her hand as she was affected by his fingers encasing her hand.

Morgan finally broke the silence, "Angel, do you realize you announced to Keowee, Santee, Floyd, Haygood, and me that you are my angel? Of course, that was not news to me, but you might have left the others a little speechless." So did he remind Sam of this as soon as they were out of hearing of the veranda. Without missing a step, Sam responded, "Floyd and

Haygood might have been shocked, but Keowee and Santee already knew. They asked me point-blank earlier if I was the one that tended to your wounds that May night and if I was the one that shot at you and Haygood. I never lie to them, so I answered yes to both questions."

Sam's admitting she was the one that took a shot at him and Haygood stopped Morgan in his tracks, and he jerked hard on Sam's hand, turning her to face him. In painful disbelief, Morgan asked, "You despise me so much that you tried to kill me?"

The painful look on Morgan's face, as he asked the question, stabbed Sam in the heart as nothing had since learning of her parents' death. The emotion left her speechless for the moment, and all she could do was shake her head in denial. Morgan's shock and disbelief turned quickly to painful anger, and, in a hard, stern voice, he said,

"Explain yourself now before I turn you over my knee and tan your behind."

There was no doubt in Sam's mind that cussed man would do exactly as he had promised. She had heard that tone of voice once before, on the morning he had appeared on the front veranda, and she lost no time trying to form words that would appease Morgan.

"The sound of your galloping horses frightened me. Please understand that at that time, just as now, the quality of horses that could gallop at that speed usually meant trouble to Southern people. It never crossed my mind that you and Haygood would be returning to the plantation so soon after your departure. I was only trying to protect my family."

Morgan's anger was appeased slightly, not so much by Sam's words as by the truth of her statement that was written on her face. The strength by which Morgan had held Sam's hand lessened, as he waited to hear more. He knew Sam well enough by now to realize there was more she was struggling with. Sam never once tried to remove her hand from Morgan's grip. Strange as it seemed to her, the touch of the cussed man gave her the strength she needed to tell him more.

"I was more frightened," she began again, but she needed to take a breath before saying more. She drew in a breath and exhaled with the words, "When I realized it was you and Haygood and how close I came to hurting or even killing you, I thought I would die myself. I really do not know how to explain my feelings now or to myself at that time. I could only run. I only knew I did not want to face the family or anyone. So I hid. I found myself hiding in the place where I tended to your wounds that May night. If I could have hidden from myself, I would have, but I could not. I had to deal with what I had almost done. It was several days. I did not know how many days would pass before I could return to the house and look at my family. I returned to the house after you and Haygood had left for Athens again. Keowee and Santee were worried sick because of my behavior, and that caused me an additional pain. All I can say to you in a form of an apology is that, had I known the riders of the galloping horses were you and Haygood, I would have just gone into hiding. I would never have shot at you."

By the time Sam finished explaining why she shot at him and Haygood, Morgan's military stance was easing, but, hearing the effect the shooting had on Sam when she became aware of who was riding the galloping horses, he wanted to take her in his arms and console her, and not turn her over his knees and to spank her.

After taking several deep breaths and suppressing his desire to enfold Sam in his arms, he asked, smiling, "Angel, by any chance, did the gun you used to protect your family that day happen to be a Yankee pistol?"

She was surprised not only that she had admitted she had shot at him but also that she had explained why she had shot at him. She realized that her admission, together with relating the effects of finding out she had shot at him, made her want to ask for forgiveness. She was also dismayed at how easily she had included her feelings that occurred once she realized she had shot at him and almost killed him. All of this left her speechless, so all she could do was smile and nod her head. Near the end of the path was the stump that Sam had sat on to remove her shoes and trousers while she had kept Morgan hidden, and as they approached the riverbank, Morgan led Sam to the familiar stump.

"Why don't you sit while we talk? And I will lounge on the ground beside you."

As she sat on the stump, her mind tried to recall how many times she had sat on this stump, during those days and nights in May and over the months since. Sam was brought back to the present, with Morgan calling her name.

"Sam, Sam, Sam!"

"Sorry, I was woolgathering, you might say. This spot holds a special place in my heart and my memory."

Morgan was happy to hear that her leaving him in thought was due to memories of the spot. "Maybe sometime later, you will share with me why this spot is special, but now I want to talk about us."

"Talk about us!" The three words automatically raised Sam's guard, and, at once, the thought of running away came to her mind, but before the thought could bear fruit, Morgan added, "There is no reason for you to avoid this talk, and there is nothing for you to be embarrassed about. We are both adults, healthy human beings, but I can understand if you are a little embarrassed, even though kissing between a man and a woman is a natural event. An event that happens quite often when there is an attraction between the two, such as there seems to be between us."

Taking Sam's hand, he continued, "I hope the attraction is mutual. There are several things that tell me that is so. Would you like for me to name them? Then you can tell me if I have or have not imagined the basis for my claim."

Sam hesitated to answer Morgan's question and his idiotic statement because the cussed man held her hand and she was having difficulty forming a rational thought, much less putting words together in a sentence. Moments ticked by, and her lingering silence became very noticeable. She called on every fiber of strength in her body and somehow managed to say, "If you will let go of my hand, I will add my two cents regarding this event you claim not to be embarrassing."

A grin spread from ear to ear across Morgan's face with Sam's words, and he could not help mentioning, "My fingers wrapped around your hand are causing you somewhat of a disturbing but pleasant emotion, rendering you unable to give me your opinion. Angel, an emotion of that nature is one of the things I want to discuss with you, and I am happy to know I am not the only one having those feelings. However, if you will be able to talk with me about our kiss and other things if I remove my hand, I will do so, but I want you to know I do so with protest. Because I thoroughly enjoy the touch of your hand in mine." At the end of his last sentence, Morgan slid his hand from Sam's and leaned back on his forearm, ready to listen to her. Sam stared in disbelief. Her hand was free of the cussed man's hand, but his words and her looking at his handsome face unsettled her almost as much as his touch had unsettled her. Morgan waited patiently while Sam collected her thoughts, but the grin never left his handsome face.

"Yankee, I am not a dumb female from the South. If that is your opinion of me, you are wrong. I am well-read compared to some of my counterparts, but I missed out on the usual courting process of young people. Therefore, not having experienced the interactions with male callers and with parties, I am lacking in personal knowledge of the goings on of young, healthy adults. Do not misunderstand me. I am not apologizing for my embarrassment, and I am sure any lady would experience embarrassment with her first kiss. A Southern lady, that is."

Morgan's chuckle at Sam's distinction of a Southern lady caused a halt to Sam's explanation and gave Morgan a chance to ask a question, "Sam, are you saying that your lack of having boyfriends or male callers at the time you were becoming a young lady is what effects the way you regard what has and is happening between us? If so, I believe there might possibly be another reason, and you are shying away from admitting that reason. So I will ask another question, and I want an honest answer. On the night of May fifth, if the soldier you had aided had worn a gray uniform instead of a blue uniform and if you had become attracted to him, experiencing the same feelings you now have, would you be trying to deny the truth of those feelings, instead of dealing with them honestly? Does not the fact that I was a Yankee soldier and still, to some degree, a hated enemy in your mind have a bearing on what I am trying to get you to talk to me about? I want an honest answer."

Before Sam could answer, Morgan added, "The kiss this morning in front of your bedchamber is not our first kiss. I kissed you the night you took me to my men and left me. The feel and the taste of your lips were with me when I awoke the next day, and they have stayed with me all these months."

Morgan almost did not hear Sam's soft and teary and emotional question, "Why do you have to say things like that?"

It was not the tone of voice that prompted Morgan' reaching for his angel and pulling her into his arms for the second time today, but it was the emotions he heard in those soft spoken words. He whispered to her, as his arms crushed her to him, "I spoke the truth, sweetlin'. I may not have admitted the truth the morning I awoke looking into Haygood's face and not the face of my angel. However, the morning you walked into the warming kitchen as Samantha, I knew that my need to find my angel was not just to say thank you for savingmy life. I had to admit that my need to find you went much deeper and that I would not be able to live a happy life without you."

Smiling, he added, "Sam, sometimes the effect you have on me is very unsettling, and all my plans fly right out of my head. I planned to bring these facts to you slowly, not springing the fact that I am head over heels in love with you all at once."

Sam looked up from her place buried in Morgan's chest, reached up for and pulled his head down, and placed Southern lips on a cussed Yankee's lips. Morgan's pent-up passion and Sam's budding passion spoke louder than words. There would be no further questions to answer regarding their feelings and emotions. The lingering kiss answered any and all, as nothing else could. Their lips sliding limply apart left the two spent and listless in each other arms, drained of the will and the strength to move. However, it was not long before something other than their desire not to part brought to mind a need for a more comfortable arrangement. Morgan might have spent many a night sleeping on the ground or sitting around a campfire, but a rock gouging a hole in his back brought to mind a reminder he was on his back, and Sam lay in his arms atop him, and it was time to move.

"Sweetlin," Morgan whispered. "My heart is not willing for you to move, but my back is complaining fiercely about a rock gouging into my flesh, and, at the moment, my back wins the argument."

Sam opened her eyes and looked dreamingly into the cussed man's eyes and laughed. Unsure of just how to rise gracefully from her position atop Morgan, she did the only thing she was able to do. She rolled off the cussed man and onto the ground and her knees. Gaining her feet, she stood, but she found her legs to be a little unsteady. Morgan's strength and mobility were still a little shaky, as he stood, but he pulled his shoulders up, straightening and stiffening his spine. After they took a few deep breaths, the effects of their loving encounter lessened. He once again found Sam sitting on the stump; taking his foot, he swept a spot of ground clear of sticks and rocks, and he sat down in front of her, and, taking her hands and looking up into her sparkling green eyes, he asked, "Would you please answer my question?"

Sam hoped the cussed man was referring to his question regarding the color of uniforms. At the moment, she could not remember if there had been another question. Her mind was full of the fact she was the one that had initiated the kiss, this time. *What in the world possessed me to take the man's face in my hands and bring his lips to mine?*

Morgan recognized the look of confusion on Sam's face, and, if possible, the grin that occupied the lower part of his face for the past few minutes got bigger. He was sure it was not his question about the uniforms that had Sam in a bewildered but her remembering that she had instigated their last kiss.

"Sweetlin', answer my question regarding the uniforms. Put the kiss we just shared out of your mind, for now. Please. A lot of ladies kiss men, even Southern ladies. You can rest assured you are not the first, and be assured that I am pleased by the way our second kiss of the day happened."

Sam's condemnation of her actions was quickly overshadowed by her remembering Morgan's actions as he stood. The squaring of his shoulders, the stiffening of his spine, and his deep breaths told her of the lingering aftermath of her kiss on the cussed Yankee. The kiss affected the cussed man the same as it had affected her, and it mattered not who the instigator of the kiss was.

"Morgan," Sam said, using his given name again, instead of "cussed Yankee," gained his complete attention, and he relaxed, waiting for her to continue.

"Your question is nothing new to me. I wished several times during your stay in May that the uniform you were wearing was gray." Taking several deep breaths and making herself tell of the reasons, she continued, "From the moment I noticed the bloody leg encased in Yankee blue, I argued with myself as to whether to help you or not. There were two reasons for this argument. First was my hatred, at the time, of the whole Yankee Army, and, second, my fear of that army. The fear of what Yankees might do not only to me but my family, should you be discovered wounded on Sinclair land. As you know, my Christian faith won the battle. Later, the feelings and emotions you stirred in me and the effect on my actions caused me anguish. I could not understand how I could feel anything but hatred toward a Yankee. Not only was the color of your uniform mixed up in all this, but I also did not completely understand the feelings and emotions. I wondered if there was something terribly wrong with me. I felt like I was a traitor not only to the South but also to Papa and Mama. I tried picturing you in a Confederate uniform, but it was not you. Even after you returned, I fought against these feelings. However, still holding on to my hatred, I tried to discredit the feelings."

Sam stopped for a moment, trying to decide how to proceed; Morgan calmly waited, hoping she would continue, and he was soon awarded for his patience.

"While in the Henrys' home, I talked with Pastor Henry. During our talk, he reminded me of what my parents taught us and what God commanded about hate. I would not or could not see how that could, or would, apply to Yankees. I was struggling mentally with all this, when Lovie and I were kidnapped by Robert and those men."

Taking a breath, Sam went on, "However, the moment I saw David and Floyd being put in that wagon with Lovie and me and I realized the wagon turned left onto the road leading to the Athens, there was no difference between

Yankees or Confederates in my mind at that time, only the knowledge that you and Haygood were in Athens and that if I could get to you, you would rescue Lovie and the boys. There was no color of uniforms in those thoughts. In fact, I was on my way to the building housing the Union offices, when I met the young soldier that brought a message to Riverbend. He brought me to you."

Taking another breath, Sam continued, "After Athens, my hate and thoughts were a mess. You could say I had another mental battle. Even now, I do not know why I was so judgmental. We were taught not to judge people with anything but their character and their actions. Well, I have said a lot when I could have said simply, 'Yes, your blue uniform caused my aversion to my feelings.' If you had worn gray that night, I would have welcomed them, and the outcome of your stay would have been different. Somewhere during all my jumbled-up thoughts, l heard someone say that you cannot give orders to— " Sam's words stopped, and Morgan completed her sentence.

"Your heart. In other words, you cannot tell your heart whom to fall in love with."

"Am I in love with you, and are you in love with me, as you say?" Sam whispered softly.

"Sweetlin', you are my heart. My love for you is as sure as there is a God in heaven. You will have to know the truth of your love for me, but, from all the feelings and emotions we share, not to mention this last kiss, I would vote, yes."

Sam had no hands to grab the face of the cussed man, but he was near enough that she leaned across the space that separated them. Thoughts of blue or gray uniforms did not exist, as Sam placed Southern lips on the man she had fallen in love with the night of May fifth. However, in the days to come, Sam would face the most difficult mental battle and decision of her life.

Adapted from *The History of Hart County*
By John William Baker

EPILOGUE

As the author of *A Measure of Mercy*, I want readers to enjoy and fully understand my book and know the actual Hatcher family events that brought about my writings.

My grandfather, Willie Hatcher, great grandson of William and Martha Hatcher told my cousins and me the family events of 1862-1865, that his father Floyd Hatcher told him. I am passing on to you the actual Hatcher family events of that era, hoping to enlighten readers to why *A Measure of Mercy* was written and depicts a life I wish my great grandfather Floyd and his siblings could have lived rather than the one they were forced to endure.

Here is a summary of those family events, as told to us by my grandfather.

William had a small farm in Hart County, Georgia. He owned no slaves and was not an advent of the war between the North and South. Thinking the differences should be fought with words not bullets, he did not rush to join the fighting. In April of 1862, the Confederate government issued a consignment law making all able-bodied men become soldiers. This law also had a clause that enabled men of means to hire substitutes to fight in their place. William, realizing he was going to be made to join the army and leave his pregnant wife and three children, agreed to become a substitute for the heir of a man of means. William would not except money to shoot and kill his fellow Americans as his payment, so an agreement was reached for his payment to be the care and welfare of this wife and children. The Hatcher's minister was a witness to this agreement. William left Hart County in June of 1862, joining Dabney's Rifle Corp, fighting under the command of General Stonewall Jackson in General Robert E. Lee's Army of Northern Virginia. William was killed August 28, 1862, in the Second Battle of Manassas. Martha died October 2, 1862, in child birth, having overworked herself bringing in the harvest since the man of means did not send workers to help.

The Hatcher's minister loaded the children, along with Martha's body, in a wagon and carried them out to the home of the man of means. The children were not well-received. They were housed in a slave cabin. The three oldest were given daily chores and worked beside the children of slaves and took their meals with the slaves. After the war, sometime in 1865, the three oldest, Floyd, age fourteen, Ella, age eleven and David, age eight were sold (bonded) to three different homes and farms in two different counties in Georgia. Floyd, my great grandfather, saw his two brothers David and Lemuel for the last time at the age of fourteen.

The Hart County Census of 1870, listed Floyd as a mill hand in Hart County. Ella was listed as a domestic servant in a home in Hart County. I have not been able to find any record of Ella since the 1870 census. I could not find any marriage certificate, death certificate or in any further census. David was listed in the 1870 Hall County census as a farm hand. I learned from his family that David lost his eyesight as a child because his owner hit him in the head, knocking him unconscious. I have found no further record of Lemuel, age eight, since the Census of 1870, however, David's family thought David heard that Lemuel was finally adopted. But, I have found no record of that.

Thank you,
Margaret Hatcher House